An Unexpected Peril

A VERONICA SPEEDWELL MYSTERY

An Unexpected Peril

Deanna Raybourn

THORNDIKE PRESS
A part of Gale, a Cengage Company

Copyright © 2021 by Raybourn Creative LLC.
Thorndike Press, a part of Gale, a Cengage Company.

ALL RIGHTS RESERVED

Thorndike Press® Large Print Basic.
The text of this Large Print edition is unabridged.
Other aspects of the book may vary from the original edition.
Set in 16 pt. Plantin.

LIBRARY OF CONGRESS CIP DATA ON FILE.
CATALOGUING IN PUBLICATION FOR THIS BOOK
IS AVAILABLE FROM THE LIBRARY OF CONGRESS.

ISBN-13: 978-1-4328-8710-0 (hardcover alk. paper)

Published in 2021 by arrangement with Berkley, an imprint of Penguin Publishing Group, a division of Penguin Random House, LLC

Printed in Mexico
Print Number: 01   Print Year: 2021

For the readers, booksellers, reviewers, bloggers, librarians, and bookstagrammers who have taken Veronica to their hearts and made her their own. Excelsior!

CHAPTER 1

London, 1889

"Stoker, I cannot say that I care much for your goat. He is leering at me."

Stoker grunted by way of reply. The Honorable Revelstoke Templeton-Vane — Stoker to friends and enemies alike — was my professional collaborator in endeavors of natural history as well as murderous adventures. (The solving of them, I should note, not the committing of them.) He was also, as of the previous month, my bedmate. The fact that our relationship, once an elevated meeting of the minds, had evolved to include a rapturous commingling of our persons did not preclude him from taking umbrage when I criticized his work. He was nothing if not exacting in his practice of the taxidermical arts.

"Protest all you like," I told him with my usual firmness, "but that goat is most definitely looking at me, and with an expression I can only describe as unwholesome."

Stoker rose from where he had been brushing out the pelt of the animal in question and gave me a pointed stare of his own. "That goat, I will have you know, is an example of *Capra ibex,* the European mountain goat. Furthermore, this particular specimen is an extremely rare variety found only on the slopes of the Alpenwald. You will note that the development of the horn —"

It was at this point that I stopped listening, letting the gentle tirade flow over me like a burbling river. Stoker was never happier than when imparting information, whether one asked for it or not. This, I had observed frequently upon my travels, is common in the male of the species. Did I hold forth at length on the details of Alpenwalder lepidoptery? I did not, although, I reflected as I regarded the display case before me, I had rather better cause than Stoker and his smelly old goat. Alpenwalder butterflies — and one rather spectacular moth — were few in number but charming, with a subtlety of color and line that only a true connoisseur would appreciate. One in particular, *Papilio athena,* sported a delicate blue coloration, its hindwings touched lightly with a spot of white, like a tender

8

bloom against an Alpine sky. I gently adjusted the angle of a wing, showing it to best advantage against the dark cloth I had pinned for a backdrop with as much care as a theatrical impresario considering his leading lady.

"Are you listening, Veronica?" Stoker demanded.

"Not in the slightest," I assured him cheerfully.

"I was saying that it is no doubt the pupils which account for the expression," he informed me. "They are both square and horizontal, which is decidedly uncomfortable for human sensibilities to appreciate. I daresay another goat would find this fellow quite handsome."

I flicked the goat a sidelong glance. "Perhaps his mother."

Stoker went on as if I had not spoken. "Besides which, the horizontal pupil is, I suspect, a function of evolution. It may well provide a wider aspect for a grazing creature, which is naturally subject to predation, to be forewarned when a predator is about. If you consider the necessity of passing such a trait to one's offspring —"

"If you speak of Lamarck's theory one more time, I shall scream," I warned him.

His expression was cool. "I certainly do

think that Lamarck had some perfectly sound ideas," he began.

I opened my mouth to deliver the promised shriek when the door opened and Lady Cordelia Beauclerk entered. "Good morning to you both. Getting on with the exhibition, I see?" she greeted us. Her color was good and her step firm, both of which I observed with real pleasure. In addition to being the sister of our patron and employer, the Earl of Rosemorran, Lady Cordelia was friend to both of us. The previous year had been a trying one for her in every possible way, and she had consequently suffered considerable lowness of spirits. I had attempted to counter this malaise by the occasional evening spent in reading fashion papers and drinking copious amounts of aguardiente, a potent South American intoxicant — to mixed effect. But with a new project in hand, she seemed invigorated. She had been chosen to oversee the installation of an exhibition of mountaineering including Alpenwalder flora and fauna at the Hippolyta Club, an establishment devoted to the edification and fellowship of women of adventure.

To those of us who were members, it was affectionately known as the Curiosity Club, a private aerie where we might gather and discuss our exploits and pursuits with like-minded women. We ran the gamut from mathematical geniuses (Lady Cordelia) to world-traveled lepidopterists (myself), with everything from botanists to zoologists in between. We gathered for lectures and magic lantern shows, photographical exhibits, musical evenings, scientific demonstrations, and the presentation of academic papers.

And we gathered to mourn. Ours was an intrepid and fearless group of wanderers, and whilst some, like the academics, rarely traveled beyond the shores of the British Isles, there were always those scattered about the globe in pursuit of their passions. One such, a mountaineer by the name of Alice Baker-Greene, had perished a few months previously on the highest peak in the Alpenwald, a tiny country lodged precariously on the border between Germany and France. Located somewhere vaguely north of Switzerland, it boasted one impressive mountain, the Teufelstreppe, an alp whose position on the map gave the impression that it had wandered off from its brothers after a quarrel and taken up solitary residence a little distance away.

The Alpenwald as a country was aloof, seldom deigning to mix in the quarrels of its neighbors, counting postage stamps —

rful and highly collectible — and mounеering as the pillars of its economy. The tact that an English climber had lost her life on their alp had been a source of keen embarrassment to them. They had shipped over Miss Baker-Greene's effects, which her grandmother, a noted alpinist herself, had immediately forwarded to the club for an exhibition dedicated to her granddaughter's life and work. Lady C., who had known Miss Baker-Greene and admired her, immediately volunteered to undertake the arranging of the exhibition, recruiting Stoker's assistance in creating a diorama of mountain fauna as well as enlisting me to prepare the butterfly mounts and attend to the rest of the preparations.

Lady C. had taken a keen interest in every detail, supervising us with an attentiveness that bordered upon the oppressive, but I could not find it in my heart to begrudge her. It was the first real interest she had shown in any project since our voyage to Madeira the previous year, and I was delighted to observe her healthful appearance as she stepped close to the wall, peering intently at a detailed watercolor map of the Alpenwald that had been handsomely framed and hung at eye level. It depicted the thick black evergreen forests that fringed the tiny country, giving way here and there to fertile valleys that shimmered with the silvery green tributaries of the Rhine. In the center, the vertiginous peak of the Teufelstreppe hung above the tidy capital of Hochstadt. A series of photographs next to the map showed narrow streets little larger than alleyways, twisting beneath the overhanging upper stories of half-timbered houses whose balconies were laden with colorful blossoms and banners. All led eventually to a main square that fronted the royal castle, a faery-tale eminence of grey stone and peaked turrets that would have looked very much at home in any child's storybook.

Lady C. gave a cluck of approval. "Very good. The average person has never even heard of the place. This will provide a sort of context for the rest of the exhibit," she remarked, more to herself than to us. She turned to me. "Butterflies next, I think. We ought to build up to Stoker's rather more arresting goat," she added with a nod towards the alcove where Stoker continued to work on his mount. She tipped her head thoughtfully. "I cannot say that I like that drapery very much," she said.

Stoker poked at the thick folds of figured scarlet damask hung behind the alcove. "It does rather ruin the effect." He stepped back, stroking his chin, leaving a trail of sawdust along the whisker-roughened jaw. "What if I painted a mountain scene, something simple, just to set the stage, so to speak? I could position the canvas just behind the mount."

Lady C. nodded. "That could be quite effective indeed."

"But not with that carpet," I pointed out. The goat's cloven hooves balanced atop a gold-and-scarlet carpet woven with a running H pattern, much like a mayoral chain. It had been specially woven for the club's display hall, adding a touch of grandeur to an otherwise staid room.

Stoker shrugged. "I could sculpt a base and cover it with moss to give the effect of spring upon the mountain," he offered.

"Perfect," Lady C. pronounced. "I think that will make Her Serene Highness very happy indeed."

Stoker and I exchanged glances. "Her Serene Highness?" I ventured.

Lady C. nodded. "Her Serene Highness, Gisela Frederica Victoria Helena, the Hereditary Princess of the Alpenwald and ruler of that country. We have just received word that the princess herself wishes to open the exhibition."

"Why on earth would the Alpenwalder princess come here to open an exhibition honoring an English climber?" Stoker demanded.

It was Lady C.'s turn to shrug. "Miss Baker-Greene's greatest achievements as an alpinist came on the Teufelstreppe. The mountaineering community in the Alpenwald is very close and the princess is a casual climber herself. Perhaps she simply wishes to pay her compliments to one of the most accomplished mountaineers of the age. In any event, the princess wants to be present and we can hardly refuse a head of state."

"There might be a more cynical reason," I proposed. "The Alpenwalders derive a good deal of their national income from the money spent by mountaineers traveling to climb the Teufelstreppe. They must be desperately embarrassed that Miss Baker-Greene died on their alp."

"You may indeed be right," Lady C. said briskly. "Alpinists are a superstitious lot and one of their contingent has already let slip that the numbers of planned expeditions for the next season are decidedly low. A bit of good publicity will certainly not hurt, if that is what they are after. I only know that I have been instructed by Her Serene Highness's people to make certain the grand tradition of climbing in the Alpenwald is sufficiently reflected in this exhibition to further formal Anglo-Alpenwalder relations."

"I wasn't aware there *were* formal Anglo-Alpenwalder relations," I put in.

"God yes," Stoker replied. "Father used to do business with them. We do not have a proper embassy in Hochstadt, but he acted as a sort of de facto consul for a few years — well before I was born. He said it was the oddest little place he had ever been. One mountain, one small city, one castle, and seventy varieties of beer. He remembered it with great difficulty," he finished with a grin. I was not surprised the late Viscount Templeton-Vane had afforded himself of whatever libationary charms the Alpenwald offered. He had not been a particularly abstemious man, if his reputation was correct.

"And one of our own royal family married into theirs a few generations back," Lady C. put in. "A sister of George III? Or was it George IV? In any event, we have an entire exhibition to finish and less than a week in which to do it. Do you think we can manage?" A trace of worry touched her brow, creasing it.

"Certainly," Stoker soothed. "If I have to hold this blasted goat together with my bare hands while the princess walks by."

She smiled. "Thank you. And naturally, you will both be expected to be here for Her Serene Highness's official opening of the exhibition. You will be presented to the princess."

Stoker and I exchanged glances again. After a few of our more recent adventures, I had had quite enough of princesses, but Stoker's concern was more pragmatic.

"Surely you do not mean to present me," he said gently.

Stoker's status as a man whose marriage had ended in divorce put him socially beyond the pale. He could never be presented at Court, nor would any member of the royal family or the highest circles of society recognize him in public. This troubled him not at all; in fact, on more than one occasion he observed he would have divorced his mildly homicidal wife far earlier if he had known it would result in people leaving him in peace.

Lady C.'s expression was one she did not often adopt, but it was sternly effective. She could not bear hypocrisy, and the notion that Stoker should be ostracized for divorce when almost every member of refined society was cheerfully committing adultery was one she found enraging.

"I have spoken to the princess's entourage and made it quite clear that the dictates of the Hippolyta Club forbidding exclusion on the grounds of marital status are to be honored, regardless of royal custom."

I grinned at him. "You know the rules, Stoker. We do not discriminate against the divorced here, but the fact that you are a man means you are welcome only on sufferance."

I turned back to Lady C. "And I am to be presented as well?"

"As one of the official representatives of the club," she said, clearly expecting I would appreciate the honor.

I thought of what would most likely be endlessly boring rules on protocol and forced conversation with a princess who would most likely be dull in the extreme if not actively stupid. I bared my teeth in a smile. "What an unexpected delight," I told her. "I cannot wait."

CHAPTER 2

The next few days were ones of frantic activity, with more boxes being delivered from Alice Baker-Greene's grandmother. That imperious old lady sent each with lengthy instructions on how the memorabilia were to be displayed written in a firm, bold hand. There was a small crate filled with tiny belts and pickaxes — a child's collection of climbing gear. I brandished the murderous little things at Stoker.

"Can you imagine learning to climb as a child?" I asked.

Stoker looked up from where he was applying lavish amounts of glue to a sculpted base. "Did she?"

"She did indeed. Her grandmother taught her. Have you not read *Climbing in the Peaks: A Lady Mountaineer's Guide to the Pennines* by Mrs. Pompeia Baker-Greene?"

"I have not," he admitted.

I curled a lip. "She is a pioneer of the

alpinist movement, a founding fellow of the Hippolyta Club, and yet you haven't read her magnum opus. You are a dreadfully lax explorer."

He gave me a repressive look. "I have had *rather* a busy time of it lately," he reminded me. He was not entirely wrong. Between sleuthing out murderers, cataloging the Rosemorran Collection, and allowing ourselves to experience the rumbustious pleasures of the flesh, we had had little time to spare for hobbies.

"It is quite a good read, although she does spend rather a lot of time discussing rocks. Mountaineers do love their rocks," I added wistfully. "In any event, she chronicles her attempt first to teach her son to climb as a child still in skirts and later her granddaughter."

"Where is her son now? Alice Baker-Greene's father?" he asked as I plucked a jaunty little Tyrolean cap from the box.

"Dead," was my succinct reply. "A climbing accident in the Karakoram."

"Two climbing deaths in one family?" He gave a visible shudder. "How unspeakably tragic."

"Three, actually," I corrected. "Pompeia Baker-Greene's husband, Alice's grandfather, also perished on a mountainside.

Somewhere in the Andes, if memory serves."

"I wonder what on earth drives them to it?" he asked, almost more of himself than of me.

He returned to his diorama, gathering up a handful of fresh, springy moss to apply to the damp glue. "The same that keeps us at it," I surmised. "The thirst to net each new specimen or mount each new mammal. There is nothing in natural history that is not new again every time we encounter it, no greater mystery than things that exist apart from man and with no interest in us."

"How poetic," he murmured before favoring me with a few appropriate lines from Keats. There were *always* appropriate lines from Keats, I had learnt from my association with Stoker. He maintained that there was not a single occasion to which a few stanzas might not be applied. I had, during one rather notable interlude, challenged Stoker to produce a fitting quote, and I can only say that what followed was highly instructive although not wholly coherent, diverted as he was by my own distracting efforts at the time.

I rummaged in the drifts of excelsior in the box, finding a few unremarkable books — a selection of climbing memoirs and geological surveys with a decrepit and outdated collection of flora and fauna, all inscribed by various family members now perished on assorted mountainsides. At last there was nothing left to the box but bare boards and a single photograph.

I extracted it, wiping the last shreds of excelsior free. The photograph was framed in rosewood inlaid with a mountain motif of darker woods and mother-of-pearl. It depicted a woman posed against an outcropping of rock, a light dusting of snow on the ground. She was dressed in a lady's mountaineering garb, a coil of rope slung across her torso, ice axe poised at her side, a jaunty spotted handkerchief knotted at her throat. Her face was turned to the camera and her expression was serene, guarded almost. But there was no mistaking the faint lines of good humor at her eyes and mouth. She was just past the first flush of youth and had obviously never been a beauty, yet it would have been apparent to anyone unacquainted with her that this was a woman of great strength of character and irrepressible spirit.

And I was not unacquainted with her. "It is a very good likeness," I remarked to Stoker.

He came to look over my shoulder. "Good climbing hands," he said, nodding towards them, crossed as they were over the head of her ice axe. They were broad of palm and long of finger, surprisingly elegant. "You met her, then?"

"Once," I said. "Here at the club — it must have been more than a year ago. She gave a lecture on climbing in Bolivia. She was, quite simply, one of the most remarkable people I have ever met."

I paused and looked again at the photograph. As I had observed, it *was* a good likeness, but could any image capture the vivacity, the bright spark of courage and animation that drew one's attention like a moth to a candle flame in the darkness?

It had been a chill and wintry evening, I recalled, when I made my way to the Curiosity Club in the company of Lady C. I had attended other, smaller, events at the club, but this was my first "occasion" and I was conscious of a buzz of anticipation the moment I stepped over the threshold. As chair of the events committee, Lady C. bustled away to attend to a few last-minute details whilst I amused myself by inspecting the paintings hung in the main hall. Life-sized and rendered in oils, each depicted a different founding member of our organization. One in particular captured my imagination. The woman was sharp-eyed and sharp-chinned, and while most of the subjects had been painted looking off to far horizons, this explorer stared directly out of the canvas, as if to dare the viewer to take up the mantle of discovery for herself. She was clearly a mountain climber — holding an alpenstock, with one hand resting lightly upon a coil of rope — but she was dressed in the style of the early lady alpinists, with heavy skirts and thick plaits of hair bundled into a knitted snood. A boa of ostrich feathers softened the neckline of her tailored jacket, and I could detect the gleam of pearls in her ears. At the bottom of the frame, a small brass plaque identified her as the renowned climber Pompeia Baker-Greene.

"It is a dreadful painting," came a gruff voice at my side. I turned to see an imposing old woman in a Bath chair, her hands lightly gripping the wheels as she came to a halt.

"I like it," I said.

She jerked her chin at me. "Then your sight is defective or you are lacking in taste," she pronounced.

"Grandmama." A woman stepped forward, resting her own hand lightly on the older woman's shoulder. There was a touch of reproof in her voice, but she was smiling.

"You will have to forgive her. Grandmama's manners are not what they used to be."

"Feathers," said the old woman. "My manners were never very good to begin with. Most of what passes for politeness is simply a waste of time." She patted the hand at her shoulder fondly as she gave me a searching look. "What do you like about it?"

I tipped my head and considered the painting. "She is not a woman who would step back from a challenge," I said finally. "I suspect she is a kindred spirit."

The old woman nodded slowly. "A kindred spirit. I like that." Her gaze sharpened. "I am Pompeia Baker-Greene, alpinist," she told me, flicking her gaze to the small brass plate affixed to the frame of the painting. It was the custom at the club to introduce oneself with a mention of one's field of expertise. She turned her hawk's eyes back to me as she put out her hand. "What is your name?"

"Veronica Speedwell, lepidopterist," I told her, extending my hand. She shook it gravely and I could feel the strong sinews and slender bones even though the years had not been particularly kind. The knuckles were swollen and red, and her skin was heavily blotched with liverish spots.

"The indignities of age," she said, sketching a vague gesture. "And if you think those are regrettable, you ought to see what has become of my bosom."

"Grandmama," the younger woman said, but she was grinning outright and I smiled.

"Gravity comes for us all in the end," I remarked.

The older woman gave a bark of laughter as she eyed my own décolletage. "Mind you enjoy those whilst you can. Make the most of them before they make their descent."

"I will," I promised her. She gave me another nod and rolled herself away, but her granddaughter lingered.

"Thank you," she said quietly. "She is a little too revered sometimes, and people forget to speak to her as if she was a human being. It can be lonely on Olympus."

"I would have enjoyed speaking with her longer," I said truthfully. "I mean to be a tremendously outrageous old woman in due course and I might learn a thing or two from her."

She laughed, her grandmother's quick, sharp laugh. "Indeed, you would." She put out her hand. "Alice Baker-Greene, alpinist."

"And tonight's guest of honor," I finished. "I am very excited to hear your talk."

She pulled a rueful face. "I dread these sorts of occasions," she confided. She glanced around as if to make certain we were not overheard. "I would far rather sit in my study with a good glass of cognac and write up my climbing notes than stand up in front of a group of people and talk about myself. Still," she said, brightening, "at least I will not be asking you lot for money."

"Is that the normal course of affairs?" I inquired.

She rolled her eyes heavenwards. "My dear girl, I can only think that you must have been born to wealth or have a most generous benefactor if you have never resorted to pleading with strangers to open their pocketbooks and sponsor your expeditions."

"I am neither," I said mildly. "But lepidoptery is a singularly inexpensive proposition. I require only my net and a supply of killing jars. I lodge in tents or modest hostelries. I have neither porters nor dragomen and rarely do I require a guide."

"You are fortunate," she said fervently. "I spend more time begging for money to pay those wretched men to accompany me than I ever do on a mountainside." There was a note of real bitterness in her tone.

"That must be terribly frustrating when I imagine all you want to do is climb," I remarked.

"It is in my blood," she told me. "My grandparents were the first Europeans to climb in the Karakoram, and my father was the first to summit the South American peak of El Infierno." Her eyes gleamed with unmistakable pride. "I never had a dream but to follow in their footsteps. Quite literally," she added. "I climbed El Infierno myself last season and then made an ascent of its higher companion peak, El Cielo."

"The first woman to do so, were you not?"

"The first person," she corrected sharply. "Or at least I ought to have been." Her expression darkened and her complexion was suffused with anger. She pressed her lips together for a moment before continuing. "How familiar are you with mountain climbing, Miss Speedwell?"

"Vaguely. Butterflies are much more common in the tropics, so my travels seldom take me into the mountains."

"Well, I do not know how lepidopterists conduct themselves, but amongst climbers, there is a code of behavior."

"What are the terms?"

"That when one has been hired as a guide, one may choose the route and lead. One may even insist upon turning back if conditions are judged to be too dangerous. But what one may never, *ever* do is take the summit for oneself. That is the client's privilege."

"And someone took your summit of El Cielo?"

"He did indeed," she said, clipping off the words sharply. "Douglas Norton is the scoundrel's name. I engaged him at extortionate terms to accompany me and help manage the porters in Bolivia. They are not always inclined to take orders from a member of the gentler sex," she added with an expressive gesture. "But I made it quite clear to him from the very beginning that the expedition was mine. In the end, the porters proved perfectly amenable to my suggestions and Norton was an unnecessary extravagance."

I was not surprised to hear it. She was, to put it plainly, a force of nature, and I could well imagine most men bending before her. But then, any person who pitted themselves against mountains must be fashioned of something indomitable.

She went on. "The afternoon of the last day, we had climbed for eleven hours and paused to rest before the final push to the summit. I took a little refreshment, and when I had gathered myself and was ready to resume, Douglas was nowhere to be found. The porters dared not betray him by giving away his intentions when he slipped ahead, but I discovered his intentions soon enough. I climbed like a demon to reach him, but by the time I joined him, he was perched atop the summit having already written his name into a book for the purpose and left it atop. The glory was his."

"What an odious man!" I exclaimed. Lepidoptery was not without its scoundrels — let any collector get so much of a whisper of a Rajah Brooke's Birdwing in the vicinity and blows might easily be exchanged — but this was a completely different level of infamy. There could only ever be one first summit, after all.

"Yes, I think so. And I believe I might have forgiven him if he had stood up for himself and defended his actions. Boldness, arrogance, audacity — those are crimes of character that I can understand. I share them. But he whimpered and whined like a kicked dog all the way down the mountain, pleading for forgiveness and for me not to think too badly of him."

"I begin to hate him," I told her. "I hope you pushed him off the mountain."

She grinned. "Again, the code of climbing, Miss Speedwell. One never endangers anyone whilst on the mountain. No, I waited until we had descended to the village at the base, where everyone could see. I seized the first weapon to hand — a buggy whip if my memory is to be trusted — and I thrashed him."

"Well done!" I cried, wishing I had employed such tactics myself upon one or two occasions.

"Not my finest hour," she said with a shrug, "but he deserved it. Unfortunately for him, a reporter happened to be in the village to write the story of our attempt and witnessed the entire imbroglio. It caused the most enormous fuss in the mountaineering community. The British men, who are notoriously devoted to their own sex, seem to have sided with him, the Americans with me. And now we are both of us infamous."

"Surely his is the greater shame," I protested.

"I think," she said gently, "you must have enough experience of the world to know better than that. There will always be men who rally to the cause of another man in his moment of disgrace simply because they fear their own so deeply." She drew in a deep breath and her mien became instantly more cheerful. "But I have put this behind me. I mean to make a fresh start after tonight."

"What is tonight?"

"My farewell to the Hippolyta Club," she told me, even as I made a noise of protest. She raised a hand. "You would not attempt to dissuade me if you knew where I am bound — a veritable paradise on earth for a mountaineer. I am off to the Alpenwald. Do you know it?"

"Somewhere between France and Germany, is it not?"

She led me to a map of the world and pointed to a minuscule dot between the two great European powers. "Just there, that lovely tiny patch of green." Her expression softened and her eyes grew misty at the thought of the place. "Oh, Miss Speedwell, you cannot imagine the felicity! The whole of this small nation devoted to the climbing of mountains. It is in their blood, their very souls, I daresay. And what a mountain! It is a lonely alp, but a worthy one. I mean to learn every inch of it, in summer and winter, in meadowgrass and snowfall."

"It sounds ideal."

"It is. The Alpenwalder economy is largely driven by its mountaineering," she explained. "I found there such a worthy mountain and such stalwart friends, I could scarcely bring myself to leave! And then I was offered a house of my own to make the Alpenwald my base. How could I refuse?"

She gestured towards the jeweled badge pinned at her collar and motioned for me to make a closer examination. It was a small thing but exquisitely fashioned, a medallion struck with a tiny image of a snowy mountain peak, a sun rising behind it, the sky enameled in brilliant blue. The effect was modern and arresting, the work of a significantly gifted craftsman, I realized, and no inexpensive trinket. Around the perimeter were the words *ALPENWALDER KLETTERVEREIN GIPFELABZEICHEN.* The only flaw was a nick on one edge, no doubt the result of being much worn.

"The Alpenwalder Climbing Society. I was made a full member, an honor never before accorded to a foreigner," she related with obvious pride. She touched the nick with a rueful finger. "I managed to strike it upon a stone the last time I climbed, but I will not give it back to be repaired. I quite like the little scar."

"A badge of honor," I said lightly.

"Yes, but I should not like to damage it further. I will keep it properly tucked away when I climb in future. I am looking forward to many more days upon the Teufelstreppe," she said with shining eyes.

"Well, the Alpenwald's gain is our loss," I told her. I extended my hand again and she

33

shook it warmly.

"You must come and visit me there," she urged. "I have every hope of perfect happiness and it will be my joy to share it."

She was called away then to meet other members, and I had no chance to speak to her afterwards. But I thought often of her forceful, dynamic personality and her apparent pleasure in anticipating the future she planned in the Alpenwald.

"And yet here we are," I said as I finished recounting the meeting to Stoker. "A little more than a year later, preparing an exhibition to commemorate her death. Such a short time for her to know happiness!"

His expression was thoughtful. "If she had had a Scottish nanny, she would have known that sort of happiness would never last."

"What on earth are you talking about?" I demanded.

He shrugged. "It sounds as if that last night here, she was fey." My expression must have betrayed my bemusement for he went on. "It is an old Scots word, it means a sort of hectic happiness that cannot last. It usually presages a disaster."

I looked at the photograph in my hands, Alice's proudly raised chin, the bright glint of the jeweled climbing badge on her jacket.

And I thought of her, falling to her death on the mountain she had considered a worthy foe.

"Disaster indeed," I murmured as Stoker returned to his mosses.

I turned the photograph over and saw the notation penciled in her grandmother's hand. *Alice's Last Photograph. On the slopes of the Teufelstreppe.* It was dated the previous October. There was no hesitation in the handwriting, no weakness or sentimentality. Just the stark facts of her granddaughter's life and death in a few strokes of the pencil. I put the photograph aside, making a note to find an easel to display it near the map at the start of the exhibition.

"Teufelstreppe," I mused aloud. "Your German is better than mine. It means the devil's what?"

"Step or stair," Stoker called in a distracted voice.

I looked again at the photograph, the sharp ridge cut by a series of steep, unforgiving steps. The devil's staircase indeed, I decided with a shudder.

I moved on to the next box, a crate stamped with chalk marks in various languages. "This seems to have come directly from the Alpenwald," I told him, circling the crate. I tested the lid, but it was hammered firmly. "It does not appear to have been opened yet."

Stoker passed me the pry bar and I applied myself to levering off the lid. The crate was not large, a cube of perhaps three feet on each side. Excelsior had been packed inside, securing the contents, and this I deposited neatly in a pile. Underneath I found a hefty coil of ropes tied with various bits of climbing impedimenta. "Good God, these weigh a ton," I muttered.

Stoker left off his moss laying and came to lend me a hand. "Good ropes are quite dense," he explained, his eyes gleaming with interest. I ought to have known better than to mention the ropes. In his previous exploits as a circus performer and naval surgeon, he had had better cause to appreciate a good stout rope than anyone, and he often amused himself with the tying of various knots — excellent practice, he pointed out, for the times we were bound hand and foot by the occasional villain. His knowledge of hempcraft had been more than useful to us, so I said nothing as he occupied himself happily in examining Alice Baker-Greene's climbing equipment.

"I wonder if these are the ropes she was using when she died," he said, his brow furrowing as he tested their strength.

"They must be," I said, brandishing a sheet of thick, crested paper stamped with assorted seals of Alpenwalder officials. "This is the manifest for the crate and it specifically notes that the ropes are those she was using when making her ascent of the Teufelstreppe that day," I told him.

I dug deeper under the excelsior. "Here are her spare set of climbing clothes and a box of personal effects," I added. There was a brief note explaining that she had been buried in her favorite climbing clothes, an ensemble not unlike my own adventure costume, with a fitted shirtwaist and trousers under a tailored jacket and narrow skirt which could be buttoned up over the thighs to permit ease of movement. I scrutinized the cut of her spare skirt to see if there were variations I could make upon my own costume. The tweed was thicker than mine, no doubt due to her choice of occupation — the unforgiving rock and equally unforgiving climate would demand the strongest of cloth. When I turned it inside out, I detected an arrangement of loops threaded with a drawstring that, when pulled, would instantly lift the skirt, securing it out of the way.

"Ingenious," I murmured. It was a decided improvement on my own costume, but I noted with some satisfaction that Alice Baker-Greene's ensemble lacked one singular innovation that Stoker had added to mine — pockets.

Packed beneath the climbing costume was the little box of personal effects, trifles really. There was a small looking glass painted with roses and gilt initials, her mother's, I suspected. There was a jar of cold cream of roses, my own favorite for protecting my complexion on my travels, and a small assortment of personal items — a toothbrush and tin of tooth powder, a few books, a stack of plain handkerchiefs, each embroidered with her monogram in a simple design and plain white thread.

At the bottom of the small box, wrapped carefully in another handkerchief, was the enameled charm — the summit badge of the Alpenwald. I ran a finger over the edge, touching the nick where it had been damaged and remembering her obvious pride when she spoke of it. I understood her reluctance to part with it long enough to have a repair effected. Tucked into my own pocket at all times was a tiny grey velvet mouse called Chester, the constant companion of my adventures and the sole memento of my father. He had weathered many perils, including a drowning off the coast of Cornwall, but thanks to Stoker's excellent surgical efforts, he lived to fight another day.* Such talismans and trophies were not to be scorned at, I thought as I put the badge carefully aside.

With the badge was a notebook, clearly well used, for the green kid of its cover was watermarked and ink stained, the pages filled with notes written in a tiny, tidy hand. The markings were cryptic, many of them numerical notations of altitude and temperature, I discovered. There were longer passages, descriptions of flora and fauna accompanied by surprisingly detailed sketches. She had turned her artistic hand to mapping out the routes she had taken up the mountains she climbed as well, I realized, tracing one with a finger as it wound its way up the Teufelstreppe. Tucked in the back was a photograph, clearly taken the same day as the larger portrait, for the background was the Alpenwalder mountain. But in this version, Alice Baker-Greene was not alone. She stood beside a man of medium height with a strong, muscular build and a spectacular set of moustaches. There was something arrogant about the tilt of his mouth, barely visible under those lavish

* *A Dangerous Collaboration*

moustaches, and the set of his shoulders. I turned it over, but there was no inscription on this photograph, and the man would remain a mystery. I remembered Alice's ebullience on the subject of the Alpenwald, and I wondered if this man had anything to do with her enthusiasm for the place and her determination to make her home there.

I held up the photograph to show Stoker, but he was staring down at the rope in his hands, his expression grim.

"Whatever is the matter?" I teased. "Find a knot you cannot unravel?"

"Nothing like that," he said in a hollow voice. "What do you know about Alice Baker-Greene's death?"

I shrugged. "Only what I read in the newspapers in passing. She died early in October," I reminded him. "We were rather occupied with the investigation into Madame Aurore's doings." October had been fraught with peril for many reasons, not least an investigation that brought us into the highest circles of royalty and within the sphere of the malefactor known as Jack the Ripper.*

"I read the newspapers too," he told me. "Including the pieces about Miss Baker-Greene in the *Daily Harbinger*."

* *A Murderous Relation*

I pulled a face. The *Daily Harbinger* was the lowest sort of rag, trading in sensationalist news and lurid illustrations. The fact that our sometime nemesis and occasional friend, J. J. Butterworth, wrote for the *Harbinger* did not improve my opinion of it. I took great pleasure in watching Stoker use it for wrapping the nastier bits of the animals he preserved.

"And?" I prompted.

"And they were quite specific as to the details of her death," he said. "The Teufelstreppe is not called the devil's staircase by accident. The mountain was named for a challenging passage in the middle of the climb, a perilous series of granite steps just before the turn for the long final stages of the ascent. Alice Baker-Greene attempted the climb so late in the year because there had been an unseasonably late warm spell, clearing the snow from the steps. But the exposed ridge of the granite was sharp. It frayed her rope as she climbed and the rope failed her."

"A tragic accident," I began.

Stoker held up the end of the rope. Instead of a broken collection of frayed fibers, it was taut and neat, cut straight across.

"Stoker, you cannot think —"

"That someone deliberately cut her rope? That is exactly what I think."

CHAPTER 3

I put out my hand for the rope. "Show me." He did, bending near enough for me to smell the delectable scent of honey drops on his breath as he explained. "This rope, like all good climbing and rigging ropes, is —"

A sympathetic reader will understand that I regarded Stoker's subsequent explanation as so much background noise as I examined the rope. He held forth at some length about hempen fibers and tensile strength and spiral braiding and all manner of technical details whilst I raised the rope at eye level, noting the single strand of scarlet in the middle and inspecting the end with care. It was perfectly, brutally straight.

Stoker, detecting my lack of attention to his remarks, gave a sigh and retrieved a short length of rope from his pocket with his clasp knife. "Here. I will demonstrate."

He always carried a bit of narrow rope in

his pocket to amuse himself in idle moments with the tying of elaborate knots, a holdover from his days in Her Majesty's Navy. His nimble fingers made quick work of the knots he had tied, and he folded the rope over the blade of his knife. He sawed once or twice and the rope snapped in two. He held the cut ends against the larger sample from Alice Baker-Greene's climbing apparatus. "My rope is smaller in diameter, but the principle is the same. A cut rope will present a sharp, flat plain to the eye," he said. "A frayed rope will not."

I peered closely at the ropes but there was no arguing with his hypothesis. Still, I turned over all the possibilities in my mind. "Ropes are sold by the length. Perhaps this is the end that was cut when she purchased it."

He shook his head. "For mountaineers, the fresh-cut ends are whipped with twine to keep them from fraying. There is no twine in evidence and the cut is obviously new."

"Then perhaps Miss Baker-Greene cut it herself because it proved too long or there was a spot of weakness?" I suggested.

"Again, she would have secured the end immediately by whipping it with twine. No experienced climber would go out with a rope that has not been whipped. This is fresh," he added, pointing to the brighter color of the exposed rope compared to the weathered hue of the rest.

I nodded slowly. "Very well. The rope was deliberately cut. We must inform the Hereditary Princess that Alice Baker-Greene was murdered."

Stoker blinked slowly at me. "I beg your pardon?"

"It is the only logical conclusion," I began.

"It bloody well is not! I can think of a dozen other explanations," he countered.

"I will wait." I tipped my head to the side, adopting a patient expression.

After a long moment, Stoker exhaled gustily. "She might have cut the rope herself."

"I already suggested that," I reminded him. "And you said it was not possible because the rope has not been whipped."

"Perhaps it became tangled on the climb and she had to cut it free," he said, his eyes glinting with possible triumph.

"No, I think you were quite correct the first time," I said cheerfully. "This is a case of murder."

"I reject this," Stoker said in a tone that bordered on desperation.

"Stoker, as you well know, murders happen," I told him.

"But why must they happen to *us*?"

I patted his shoulder kindly. "Because Fate knows we will always rise to the occasion, for we are the servants of Justice."

"Even servants have the occasional month off," he said in some bitterness.

"Do not look so downcast," I chided. "We have once more the opportunity to test our mettle, to pit our wits against those of a killer. Do you not find it exhilarating? We will apply ourselves to this latest puzzle and emerge triumphant," I assured him. "But our first task must be to inform the authorities that Alice Baker-Greene was murdered."

A gasp cut through the silence that followed my pronouncement. So intent had we been upon our discussion, we had neither of us noticed the trio standing in the doorway. Lady C., accompanied by a pair of ladies I did not know. One was shorter, a little inclined to stoutness, although it was well concealed by her expensive walking suit of dark blue. She would never see forty again — and perhaps not fifty — and would have been an interesting-looking woman were it not for her companion, an arrestingly comely young woman near to my own age. Her hair, black as a raven's wing, was piled atop her head in an enormous and elaborate coiffure secured with jeweled pins. Her eyes, a peculiar dark violet, were bright

46

with interest as she stared from Stoker to me and back again. It was her companion who had gasped, the older woman's mouth still rounded with astonishment.

"Who is this person?" the older woman demanded of Lady C.

Lady C. stepped forward, turning to address the younger lady. "Your Serene Highness," she said, her demeanor unruffled despite the strangeness of the moment, "may I present the pair working most closely to assemble the exhibition, Miss Veronica Speedwell and Mr. Revelstoke Templeton-Vane. Miss Speedwell is a member of the club, a renowned lepidopterist, and Mr. Templeton-Vane is the younger brother of Viscount Templeton-Vane." She turned to us. "Veronica, Stoker. Her Serene Highness, the Princess Gisela of the Alpenwald and her lady-in-waiting, the Baroness von Wallenberg."

Stoker inclined his head to the princess, but I merely stood. I had long ago given up any form of genuflecting.

The princess came closer, leveling an assessing look at us. I had the oddest sensation that I had seen her somewhere before, but I could not place her amongst my acquaintance. I had not included the Alpenwald on my travels — the butterfly population, as previously noted, was pretty but hardly worthy of a special expedition — nor did I collect postage stamps or pungent cheeses, the other two principal attractions of the Alpenwald.

The princess spoke, her English fluent and only lightly touched with a very faint German accent. "You have shocked my companion, Miss Speedwell. You believe Miss Baker-Greene was murdered? This is a most distressing accusation."

"Observation, Your Serene Highness," I corrected quickly. "Not an accusation."

She lifted one fingertip in a gesture of dismissal. "Semantics, I think. In order to observe that a murder has been committed, there must be a murderer, must there not." It was phrased as a question, but without the upward inflection that would have invited a response. She put out her hand for the rope.

Wordlessly, Stoker gave it to her, and she spent a long moment studying it. "You believe this rope is proof of something nefarious?" she asked, frowning.

"Mr. Templeton-Vane has some experience with ropes," I said demurely.

Stoker shot me a look but stepped forward. "With your permission, Your Serene Highness." He took the rope back, pointing to the significant marks. "Here and here, you can clearly see the effect of a blade."

"I see the end of a rope," the princess said coolly. She turned to her companion. "Margareta, what do you see?"

The Baroness von Wallenberg lifted the monocle pinned to her collar and fitted it into place. She bent to peer through the lens, shaking her head after a long moment. "I suppose it is possible," she added with an apologetic little glance towards Stoker. "This gentleman is doubtless more learned than I on the subject of ropes."

The princess looked at Lady C., who hurried to supply Stoker's bona fides. "Mr. Templeton-Vane spent the years of his youth in a traveling circus, madame. He was responsible for rigging the tents as well as the lines for the tightrope walkers. He later served for several years in Her Majesty's Navy as a surgeon's mate."

The princess's ebony brows rose slightly. "A surgeon's mate. Not a sailor?"

"Not a sailor," Stoker admitted.

The princess pressed the matter. "And you worked in your youth in a circus." She surveyed him from tousled hair to scuffed boot tips. "I think it is perhaps a few years since your youth?"

"I am more than thirty," he agreed.

"And do you have experience with climbing ropes?" she asked in the same blankly conversational tone.

"I regret that I do not. I have done very little climbing in my travels, and never for sport."

"For what purpose, then?" she asked, her frown deepening.

"Mr. Templeton-Vane is a natural historian," Lady C. offered. "He has traveled extensively in Amazonia."

The princess flicked her a glance, then returned her gaze to Stoker. "Amazonia. There are not many mountains there, I believe."

"There are not," Stoker said, his mouth tightening a little. "But ropes are ropes."

"And mountains are mountains," the princess returned coolly. "It was very warm on the Teufelstreppe this year. The step from which Miss Baker-Greene fell had almost no snow, and the stone is quite sharp."

"Which would have frayed the rope," I put in. "And this rope was clearly cut through with a blade."

Lady C. gave a single pointed shake of the head, but I ignored her and pressed my point. "If Stoker says that Miss Baker-Greene's ropes were tampered with, you would do well to believe him."

The baroness gave a little gasp, which she covered with a cough. "We do not speak so directly in the Alpenwald," she murmured helpfully in my direction.

"Well, in England, we do," I replied with as much firmness as I could muster.

The princess gave me a long look. "You are forthright, Miss Speedwell. And a — what was it? Lepidopterist? This is a word I do not know in your language."

Her lady-in-waiting stepped forward and gave a quick explanation in the native dialect — a form of German mixed with French and what sounded like the odd Italianate phrase. The princess's expression turned from puzzled to mildly amused. "A butterfly hunter? You chase wingy insects for a living?"

"I do."

"You must travel widely," she observed.

"I have been round the globe four times," I said.

"Impressive. And have you ever visited my country?" she inquired pleasantly.

"I regret I have not, but the Alpine clime is not the most agreeable for butterflying. There are a few perfectly charming *Lassiomata* and *Erebia* at altitude, of course, and the *Papilio athena* is quite pretty, but in the main it is an unsatisfactory environment for such activities."

The princess bared her teeth in a smile. "I am sorry we disappoint you, Miss Speedwell. And I am sorry that I must disappoint you again. But I see no reason to believe in such sinister things as murder on the Teufelstreppe." She made a melodramatic little gesture of dismissal.

"Naturally we see no reason to trouble Your Serene Highness personally with such a matter," I began. "But surely there is someone to whom the matter can be referred —"

The princess paused, then flicked a glance to her lady-in-waiting. They exchanged a few quick, muted words in their language.

The princess gave me a long look. "I will speak with my chancellor of this matter. I do not believe he will be inclined to take action, but I will ensure he knows of it."

I opened my mouth to speak but Stoker stepped neatly upon my foot. "Certainly. And thank you for your time, Your Serene Highness. Would you care to see what has been assembled thus far? I am certain Lady Cordelia would be only too happy to show you."

The princess nodded graciously, permitting Stoker and Lady C. to guide her to where the sinister mountain goat was to be displayed. The baroness stayed behind, putting a hand to my sleeve.

"Miss Speedwell, your indulgence, please," she said softly. "The princess is quite correct. You do not understand us. Permit me to help you. We are a small country." She gestured towards the map hanging on the wall. "You see where we are situated? We are nestled just beyond the Swiss border, between France and Germany, a tiny jewel set in a remote and isolated place. But we are not so isolated anymore," she said, her expression darkening. "The world wishes to come to us, and it must be so. We cannot survive unless we throw open the gates of our city, invite the foreigner onto our mountain. We need the visitors who will come and fill our pockets, and we need the allies we have come to England to meet."

"Allies?"

She gave me a confused look. "Perhaps I chose the wrong word. English is my fourth language," she said apologetically.

"Friends?" I suggested.

"Friends, yes. Friends. We wish to make friends in England who will come to visit us and climb on our mountain. It is essential to our economics," she explained, rather more forthrightly than I would have expected.

"You must be very frightened with that behemoth on your doorstep," I observed, pointing towards the glowering bulk of the German Empire hovering just at the edge of the map.

Her mouth was a thin, sober line. "You have no idea, Miss Speedwell. I grew up in a different world — dozens of tiny German principalities and duchies, each vying with the others. And then this," she said, jerking her chin angrily towards the map. "All of them swallowed up by Bismarck in his mad dash to power. And now they are under the rule of your queen's grandson and the rest of us are afraid, desperately afraid."

I wanted to console her, but in good conscience I could not. Count von Bismarck, the German chancellor, had spent the better part of a few decades cobbling the small independent states into a German confederation that had eventually been consumed by the gaping maw of the German Empire. Reactionary, conservative, and deeply militaristic, the new German Empire looked back to the grandeur of the bygone Prussian days of glory, longing to rival the power of the Russian and British thrones that hemmed it in. The new emperor, Kaiser

Wilhelm, was the grandson of our own Queen Victoria and desperate to prove himself more than a match for his aging grandmother. His enthusiasm for violence was matched only by his ambition and neither by his intelligence. He was a brute, thirsting for glory but lacking the humanity or wisdom to govern well. Continental Europe was rapidly becoming a powder keg, and it was little wonder the Alpenwalders were afraid.

"I am sorry," I told the baroness truthfully.

She spread her hands. "It is as God wills it," she said, crossing herself. Like Bavarians, Alpenwalders were nominally Catholics, I remembered, often mingling religion with a hefty dose of fatalism and Germanic superstition. "But we will do all that we can," she added, her expression briefly fierce.

"In other words, you want no scandal," I finished for her.

She had the grace to look apologetic again as she touched my arm in an imploring gesture. "Please, do not think too badly of us. I will speak with the chancellor. If there is anything I can do to persuade him, you may rest assured that I will do so."

She glanced towards the coil of rope, her

expression thoughtful. "If it is possible that this is evidence of some misdeed, it would perhaps not be wise to display it."

"Perhaps not," I agreed. "What do you suggest we do with it?"

She lifted her hands as if to ward off any talk of authority. "You must not think me more elevated than I am!" she protested, a small smile touching her lips for the first time. "I am merely the lady-in-waiting. It is my task to attend Her Serene Highness, one I am failing at present," she added with a rueful look. She tipped her head, light glinting off her monocle as she studied my face. "The resemblance is most remarkable," she said at length.

"What resemblance?" I asked.

Her mouth rounded in astonishment. "Between you and my princess," she told me.

"Is there one? I had not noticed."

The baroness seemed inclined to press the matter, but the princess approached us then. "You have done very well indeed," she said, sweeping her gaze over the mountain tableau that Stoker was creating. "I can see how it will be when you have finished, and it conveys the magnificence of our Teufel-streppe," she told him, a note of unmistakable pride in her voice.

"Thank you, madame," Stoker replied.

She looked at her lady-in-waiting. "Why have you gone red in the face, Margareta?"

"Forgive me, madame," the older woman murmured. "I was surprised to find that Miss Speedwell does not notice the resemblance between you."

The princess studied me a long moment. "I confess, I do not see it," she said.

"I must be mistaken," the baroness told her smoothly. "Has Your Serene Highness seen this part of the exhibition?" she asked, guiding her mistress to the collection I had been unpacking when Stoker discovered the cut rope. The princess stood a long moment and stared, taking in the toilet articles and books and garments, her expression inscrutable.

"A very personal collection of Alice Baker-Greene's effects," Lady C. observed. "If Your Serene Highness does not think it appropriate, we do not have to make them available for viewing."

The princess said nothing a long moment, then shrugged. "It makes little difference to the dead," she said at last. She clasped her hands together. "Still, I would not like for this to become an exercise in the sentimental. She was a climber, an explorer. That is the story you must tell. That is what will bring other visitors to the Alpenwald."

I produced the badge I had unearthed from the box of Alice Baker-Greene's personal effects. "Like this?" I suggested. "A significant piece of Miss Baker-Greene's climbing memorabilia, I think."

"Memorabilia?" Her mouth twitched with suppressed amusement. "This is the badge of the Alpenwalder Climbing Society. The usual badge is plain silver, but for those who summit the peak of the Teufelstreppe this enameled version is presented. It is a very great honor." She turned it over and studied the reverse a long moment, frowning as she noticed the nick on the edge. No doubt the damage to such a prestigious badge of merit was a matter of some annoyance, but I suddenly felt quite protective of Alice Baker-Greene and could not bear the notion that the Alpenwalders might think she had been careless.

"She was, I believe, very proud of the achievement," I ventured.

The princess's expression was one of acute displeasure. "It is a source of much pain and embarrassment to our society that a climber as famous as Miss Baker-Greene should be lost on our mountain," she said, pushing the badge back into my hands as if to rid herself of it.

She glanced around at the boxes and piles of excelsior and unsorted oddments. "There are a few things I have brought from the Alpenwald that will perhaps make good additions to your display," she offered. "A native costume, a few stuffed birds, a horn which is unique to our music. It will give a little more flavor of our country."

And a little less emphasis on a dead mountaineer, I thought wryly.

"We can certainly find room for such a generous contribution," Lady C. assured her.

The princess nodded. "Very well. I have seen enough." She inclined her head towards us and swept from the room, the baroness gliding in her wake.

Stoker sighed. "Well, so much for your theory," he said, picking up the rope.

I took it from his hands. "Do not touch the evidence," I instructed. "I have a plan."

CHAPTER 4

As soon as the royal party left and we were alone with the exhibition, we embarked upon a spirited discussion on the advisability of presenting the rope to Scotland Yard. The fact that we were well acquainted with the head of Special Branch, Sir Hugo Montgomerie, was a point in our favor. The fact that I was the natural daughter of the Prince of Wales with a semi-legitimate claim to the throne was another. Sir Hugo knew my antecedents and knew exactly how much trouble I could make if I chose to make my parentage public. That I had not done so counted very much towards the quality of my character, I reminded Stoker. And our recent exploits in helping Sir Hugo during a particularly nasty case meant that, all things considered, he rather owed us a good turn.

"He bloody well won't see it that way," Stoker objected.

"Then we must make him see it," I replied, wrapping the rope in a parcel of brown paper.

"The baroness told you she would speak to the chancellor," he reminded me.

"And I have precious little confidence he will act if his princess is against it. Alice Baker-Greene was a British citizen. If she was murdered, she deserves justice from the British authorities."

"The British cannot simply go and investigate a possible crime in an autonomous nation," he protested.

"No, but *we* can. We simply need to make quite certain that Sir Hugo knows what we are about so that —"

"So that when we provoke an international incident, he will be ready with the cavalry to ride to our rescue?"

"Something like that."

Stoker snorted. "You are the most maddeningly delusional woman I have ever known." He took the rope parcel from my hands and looped his arms about my waist. "Can we, for just the next few hours, put this aside?"

I slipped neatly from his grasp. "Murder? You wish to put murder aside?"

He slanted me a curious look. "You seem rather more certain than when I suggested it was murder," he said.

I shrugged. "You caught me unawares."

"And now that you have had time to think on it —"

"I agree with you."

His mouth twitched. "Do not make a habit of it. It is upsetting to see you so quiescent."

"I will always agree with you when your arguments are based upon sound common sense and scientific fact," I said smoothly.

"Leave it," he urged. He picked up the parcel and slipped it behind the draperies of the diorama. "There. No one will disturb it, and if the chancellor decides to take up the matter, we can hand it over."

"And if he doesn't?" I inquired hopefully.

"Then we will revisit the subject of Sir Hugo," he said with a heavy sigh.

I grinned and he tipped up my chin, kissing me, quickly and firmly. "Do not gloat, Veronica. No one loves a boorish winner."

That evening, Stoker amused himself with the earl's latest purchase for the Rosemorran Collection — an enormous walrus that had required the combined strength of numerous porters to wheel into the Belvedere, the freestanding ballroom that had been given over to the various artifacts and works of art hoarded by seven generations of earls. It was, in due course, to serve as a museum once the contents were properly sorted and arranged for the edification of the general public. The fact that Stoker and I were the only two people working to organize the thousands of items meant that the museum was projected to open sometime in the middle of the next century. The Belvedere was a place of unending magic and mystery, crammed to the rafters with every variety of trophy — jewels, statues, fossils, paintings, coins, suits of armor, one or two moldering mummies, and natural history specimens of all descriptions. The acquisition of the walrus had long been a pet dream of Stoker's and its arrival had kindled in him an enthusiasm akin to that of a child on Christmas morn. He had fallen upon the massive crate with a pry bar and single-minded determination. The fact that it smelt strongly of rotting fish had done little to dampen his ardor.

"It wants cleaning out," he explained happily, anticipating with real pleasure many hours spent raking bits of decaying filler from its imperfectly preserved insides.

"Your tastes will ever surprise me," I remarked dryly. I expected some vigorous rejoinder, but he was already peering intently into the creature's mouth, neatly eluding the long, menacing ivory tusks.

"Amazing!" he exclaimed. "Do you realize that this is the largest single specimen of *Odobenus rosmarus* ever to be seen on English shores? Two thousand two hundred and forty-five pounds. And a half," he added with all the pride of a new father observing his offspring for the first time.

"You don't say," I murmured. Stoker's dogs, Huxley and Nut, and his lordship's enormous Caucasian sheepdog, Betony, sat patiently at his heels, waiting for the destruction of the trophy to begin. Stoker had — upon several occasions and in *exhaustive* detail — explained that the fashion for stuffing specimens had been discarded for the more aesthetically pleasing and accurate method of mounting them. Older examples of the taxidermical arts had been stuffed with sawdust, newspapers, old book pages, rags, whatever was to hand when the job was in progress. Stoker had even unearthed a foul nest of dead kittens in one particularly vile specimen. It was his practice to take such trophies and deftly unstuff them, if one may be permitted to use such a word, removing the putrefying fillers and cleaning the various hides and skins to restore them to lustrous life. He fashioned his own eyeballs after intensive research into the

64

proper shape and color and pupillary details, and he sculpted his own armature to hold the refurbished exteriors. It was a gift, of that there could be little doubt, to bring these creatures back to life, resurrecting them so perfectly that one could easily imagine they had been alive only a moment before — indeed might still be alive, only arrested in mid-breath. More than once I had glanced quickly back at one of his trophies, certain I had caught movement in the tail of my eye. I was not surprised the walrus had diverted him. I had met him when he was engaged in assembling an elephant of dramatic proportions, and with Stoker size was always a consideration.

I took myself up the narrow twisting stair of the Belvedere into the gallery that provided a snuggery of sorts. It was furnished with low bookshelves and a campaign bed once belonging to Wellington as well as a few other cozy comforts. My own dog, Vespertine, trotted obediently behind, coming to rest lightly at my feet with a hopeful glance. The poor fellow had lost his mistress a few months previously and had taken to following me about with persistent devotion. He was a Scottish deerhound, tall and elegant, and had a habit of looking down his aristocratic nose at Huxley the bulldog and Nut the pharaoh hound. Huxley had belonged to Stoker when I met him, but Nut — like Vespertine — was the souvenir of an investigation, and it occurred to me, not for the first time, that Stoker and I were going to have to be a little more judicious in our acquisitions of animals unless we meant to start a dog circus.

I rootled through the stacks of newspapers until I found the ones I wanted: issues of the *Daily Harbinger* from the previous October. The front pages were covered in lurid illustrations from the murder scenes of that fiend popularly known as Jack the Ripper, but in the latter pages of one edition, I saw a mention of Alice Baker-Greene. It was the merest snippet, a paragraph only, stating that the renowned climber had died upon the slopes of the Teufelstreppe in an attempt to summit the mountain out of season. There was no byline on the piece, and I flapped it aside in irritation. I rummaged through a few more issues until I found a proper tribute. This one was more informative, detailing Miss Baker-Greene's history as part of the noteworthy Baker-Greene climbing family. Her grandparents had begun the tradition, using the Pennines as their training ground. They took along their son, who soon distinguished himself as one of the youngest men ever to summit the Matterhorn. He was an ambitious youth, determined to gain access to peaks previously unchallenged by Englishmen — notably the Himalayas. There was a brief mention of his demise in the Karakoram and his father's later death in an avalanche in the Andes. The only surviving member of the family was the elder Mrs. Baker-Greene, who had taken charge of her orphaned young granddaughter. She had curtailed her climbing in order to raise the child, but when she discovered the girl perched atop a substantial deposit of talus, she realized that it would be futile to think she could keep young Alice from mountaineering. The elder Mrs. Baker-Greene had resumed her travels, taking the girl with her when school terms permitted, teaching her everything she knew about the pursuit.

By the time she was twenty, Alice Baker-Greene had surpassed her family's achievements, becoming the first woman to summit Coropuna. She gained fame for never shying from a challenge, setting herself impossible tasks and working doggedly at them until she achieved them. She was the first to climb without male porters or guides on the grounds that her accomplishments would never be recognized if there was the slightest possibility that a man might be credited with the work. She led teams of amateur lady climbers around the world in order to finance her solo climbs upon the more demanding peaks. She was outspoken, arguing forcefully for admission to the various mountaineering clubs that refused her entry on the grounds of her sex.

The piece went on to describe the contretemps that arose on the fateful expedition to South America with Douglas Norton, adding rather more colorful detail than the lady herself had included when she had related the tale to me. According to the *Daily Harbinger,* upon the descent of El Cielo, she had publicly horsewhipped Douglas Norton, challenging him to a duel and claiming that he had stolen her summit. In return, he had laughed at her and claimed that El Cielo was no longer fit to climb since a woman had touched its summit. It was the last time she climbed with a man. From then on, she climbed alone or with her ladies, proving her achievements by planting a small green banner blazoned with her name at each peak. When guides removed her banners to call her accomplishments into question, she had begun to climb with photographic equipment, hauling the heavy camera to the summit in order to prove her success. I thought of the collection of photographs hung along the stairs of the Curiosity Club, silent testimony to one woman's determination to prove her worth.

"I wish we had met again, Alice," I murmured as I paged through the newspaper to find the conclusion of the piece. "I think we would have got on rather well."

The rest of the article discussed her political leanings. Rebelling against the cult of True Womanhood with its insistence upon domestic virtue and bodily delicacy, Alice Baker-Greene had been a vehement advocate of fresh air and robust exercise, putting forth the notion not only that were women strong enough physically to endure the arduous requirements of mountaineering, but that they were *better* suited to the challenges of solitude or cooperation that different expeditions required. She claimed women were, by nature and nurture, more adaptable and easygoing than men, better able to govern their tempers and work in harmony with circumstances rather than against them. She detailed the numerous examples of men who had perished on mountaintops from their stubborn refusal to accept that conditions had turned murderous. She did not have to cite her father and grandfather as examples. It was well-known that on her grandfather's fatal climb, her grandmother had protested against the prevailing wind, pointing out that the damp warmth of it was likely to spawn avalanches. The men had pushed on, and only Alice's grandmother, with the wisdom born of long experience, had turned back, and she alone survived.

Doubtless that event had shaped young Alice's perspective and her determination to listen to her own instincts and experience rather than those of others. She gave speeches crediting her grandmother with the courage to resist even those who loved her when she knew they were wrong. And she pushed for women to do so in their own lives. She spoke at rallies for women's suffrage and posed for a photograph of herself in climbing gear for a pamphlet on the subject. She wrote letters in support of Irish Home Rule and liberal immigration policies and comprehensive education for women. Her lectures on mountaineering were often picketed and protested, but she did not censor herself. Some of her articles took on a hectoring tone, lecturing against the evils of keeping women on pedestals that too often served as cages and advocating for rational dress. She had spent a night in jail in America for publicly burning a corset before climbing Pikes Peak. She was, in short, a firebrand who lived life on her own terms, and I felt oddly mournful as I read the conclusion of the article.

"But who would have wanted you dead?" I wondered as I put it aside. Again, there had been no byline, but I suspected J. J. Butterworth might have known a thing or two about it. I made a mental note to run her to ground and see if I could pry a little information free.

The last article was decidedly more salacious in tone, detailing her frequent visits to the Alpenwald in the last years of her life and the fact that she had often been seen in the company of an Alpenwalder aristocrat, the Duke of Lokendorf. There was an accompanying photograph of the duke, an official portrait of a handsome young man dressed in a dashing uniform lavishly covered in medals. The author of the piece hinted that Alice might well have found herself a duchess if she had lived, a minor member of the Alpenwalder royal family. I peered more closely at the photograph, reaching automatically for my magnifying glass. The photograph was poorly reproduced — the *Daily Harbinger* was not known for the quality of its prose or of its paper — but I could just make out the fine features of the duke, features that were enhanced by the presence of a lavish set of dark moustaches.

"Goodness me, you were a dark horse, weren't you, Alice?" I murmured. So, the gentleman who had posed with her for a photograph on the Teufelstreppe was the Duke of Lokendorf. It had been apparent from the picture in Alice's possessions that they had enjoyed a certain closeness. Had there been an understanding between them? I steepled my fingers together as I studied the newspaper cutting, wondering exactly how well such a connection might have suited a formal European court, no matter how small.

Just then Stoker appeared, hair disordered and hands streaked with unspeakable substances. I gave him a close-lipped smile. "You will want a bath," I remarked, wrinkling my nose against the odor that clung to his clothes. It was a furious bouquet of mouse, sawdust, and fish heads, heightened by the pungent note of formalin.

He grinned. "His lordship informed me this morning that the Roman baths have been repaired. I thought you might care to join me."

The Roman baths were one of a series of small follies situated on the estate. Room and board were included with our wages, and both of us had been given a choice of folly to serve as our private quarters. Stoker had selected a Chinese pagoda near the Roman baths whilst I had contented myself with an enchanting Gothic chapel, a miniature of Sainte-Chapelle, complete with star-flung skies and gilded tracery. These were, ostensibly, our private domains and not to be entered into by members of family or staff without our permission. The reality was somewhat less absolute. It was not uncommon to find one or another Beauclerk child lurking somewhere about, getting up to mischief.

Our affair, though not entirely secret, was conducted with due discretion thanks to the presence of the Beauclerk offspring. There were some half a dozen of them, ranging in age from eight to twenty, of varying degrees of intelligence and comeliness. The youngest of them, Lady Rose, had formed a firm dislike of me on the grounds that she adored Stoker and would not countenance a rival for his regard. I had won her over by giving her the perfect recipe for dosing her despised brother with a rhubarb concoction that would see him heaving up his guts, but the ensuing punishment from her father had swiftly put an end to our accord. Given her slightly alarming tendency towards physical violence, Lady Rose was not an enemy I cared to provoke.

"Lady Rose returned home this afternoon," I informed him. "She has already told his lordship that she intends for you to take her stargazing this evening. Something about a meteor shower."

Stoker swore under his breath. "What the devil is the little menace doing home? She is supposed to be at school." Stoker was smiling in spite of himself. He had a real fondness for the child and her obstreperous ways, no matter how much he railed against her.

"Sent down," I said briskly.

"Again? Did she try to burn this school down as well?"

"No," I told him. "The headmistress."

Stoker blinked. "She tried to burn down her headmistress?"

I shrugged. "She meant to light a firework off to stop them having to go to chapel, but the thing shot the wrong direction and ended up in the headmistress's wig, according to Lady C." Her niece's waywardness was a frequent source of vexation to Lady Cordelia, who was often left to the practicalities of caring for her brother's motherless children. The rest of them had their challenges, legacies of seven hundred years of Beauclerk eccentricity, I had little doubt, but Lady Rose took the peculiarities to new heights.

I tipped my head. "I was just reading about Alice Baker-Greene. She advocated for strong physical education for high-spirited girls."

"Perhaps Lady Rose needs to be taken to a mountain," Stoker suggested.

"And shoved off it," I finished.

"I am sorry about our evening," he said, a faint note of hesitation in his voice.

I waved a hand. "Never mind. I have a great deal of reading to do in any event. And with Lady C. busy finding another school for Lady Rose, more of the work of the opening of the Baker-Greene exhibition will fall to us."

"Besides," I added, resting a fond hand on Vespertine's broad head, "I have a companion for tonight."

His mouth curved into a smile. "Replaced by a hound," he said lightly. But the smile did not reach his eyes, and when he turned to go, I did not stop him.

CHAPTER 5

I slept, as is my custom, quite well that
night, waking to a chilly, fogbound morning
and the weight of Vespertine draped over
my legs and pinning me to the bed.

I shoved him off and made my ablutions,
reaching for a comfortable work ensemble
of dark blue tweed piped narrowly in velvet.
It reminded me a little of the princess's
costume although nothing near as fashion-
able. But the cut was serviceable and the
color flattering, and I made my way to the
Belvedere with a brisk step. Stoker and I
habitually took breakfast there, the food
brought down from the main house by
George, the hallboy, and laid out in a sort
of buffet atop a Greco-Roman sarcophagus.
I had just finished my repast when Stoker
appeared, looking a little the worse for wear.
He had not shaved and the dark growth
always in evidence after a day's passing was
a heavy shadow. He wore his eye patch, a

sure sign that his old injury — the one responsible for damaging his eye and leaving the narrow scar running from brow to jaw — was troubling him.

I gave him an inquiring look. "How was your meteor shower?"

"Nonexistent," he growled. "The bloody fog rolled in and we could not see two feet. Lady Rose was so mightily put out I had to teach her sea chanties until two in the morning to get her to go to bed like a nice child."

"Sea chanties?"

"I was rather hoping that a little forthright naval language might persuade Lord Rosemorran he should forbid her from associating with me," he said, his expression hopeful.

"She will find a way," I warned him.

His face fell and he helped himself to a plate of eggs and sausages. He ate in silence for several minutes, then began to toss scraps to the dogs. "Was it a jealous rival in mountaineering? A thwarted lover? A failed climbing student?"

I roused myself from my reverie. "I beg your pardon?"

"Alice Baker-Greene's murderer," he said. "I presume you have spent the last few hours inventing theories."

"I do not invent theories," I retorted in my chilliest tone. "I look at the facts and make deductions. There is such a thing as proper scientific method, you know."

He shrugged. "I presumed you couldn't resist the urge to fling yourself headlong into another investigation, regardless of my objections."

I folded my arms over my chest. The fact that he had so neatly deduced my state of mind was maddening. "I do not *fling* myself anywhere. I have, upon occasion, been called upon to use my talents in the pursuit of justice. If I am called upon in the future, I shall of course do so again, but I have no need to go looking for such a thing." The fact that this statement was not entirely a truthful reflection of my intentions was not, I decided, relevant to the conversation.

"Good," he said flatly.

I opened my mouth, but the expression upon his face stopped me. The resentment at being told what to do ebbed and I almost reached for his hand. Instead, I sipped the last of my tea, taking a moment to meditate upon the conclusion of our last adventure and how easily it might have ended in tragedy.

"We have been fortunate," I began.

"We have been damned lucky," he corrected, his expression somber. "Veronica, either of us might have been killed through these ridiculous endeavors. I admit, I ought not to have said anything about the rope. That was akin to running a hare in front of a hound. But we decided yesterday to leave this with the chancellor to see what he decides. And the more I think on it, the more I believe we should, just this once, let things lie as they are. Alice Baker-Greene's grandmother is her only family, and she is satisfied. So should we be."

"How?" I demanded. "How can we let such an injustice pass without making at least an attempt to see it rectified?"

"We did," he reminded me. "We presented the evidence, scant as it was, to the princess. She promised to pass the matter along to the chancellor."

"And what if he is not inclined to pursue it?"

"Then it is at an end," he said with a shrug.

"And you are content with that?" My tone betrayed my astonishment.

"Why does it surprise you?" He helped himself to another piece of toast, lavishing this one with honey.

"Because the Revelstoke Templeton-Vane I have known flings himself headlong into adventure," I jibed. "He does not shrink from a challenge."

His gaze was level and perhaps even slightly amused. "That is what you think I am doing? Shrinking from a challenge?"

I felt instantly the unfairness of the charge. Stoker, more than any person I had ever known, had shown himself not just willing to hurl himself into danger, but *happy* to do so. I could never consider without a shudder the glint of unholy excitement I had detected in his gaze when he prepared to do battle with an enormous combatant armed only with a *rebenque,* a narrow leather whip that might have flayed the flesh from his bones.* Coupled with that the numerous near drownings, stabbings, shootings, and broken bones he had acquired in my company, I had done him a gross disservice in needling him on such a point.

"Perhaps not," I conceded, muttering the words into a sausage.

"Let us finish the exhibition to the best of our ability," he suggested. "That will honor Alice Baker-Greene's memory and improve the cause of mountaineering, especially for women. Surely that is a worthy tribute to her?"

* *A Curious Beginning*

"Indeed," I said, my expression brightening. "And then we will devote ourselves anew to the work here. My case of *Ornithoptera priamus poseidon* chrysalides are very nearly ready to emerge." This was no fabrication. I had been sent a case of the rare creatures as a Christmas present from Stoker's elder brother, Lord Templeton-Vane — Tiberius to his friends. His lordship had embarked upon a series of travels with an eye to mending his grieving heart, and I had taken the opportunity to suggest a few stops of arresting natural beauty that might contribute to restoring his peace of mind. The fact that the locations were all host to the most elusive and coveted specimens of lepidoptera was the merest coincidence. The first parcel from Tiberius included a collection of *O. p. poseidon,* Common Green Birdwings, with a considerable supply of their favorite host plant, the Indian birthwort, or Dutchman's pipe.

"Interesting how Tiberius' travels are taking him to the most fertile hunting grounds for butterflies," Stoker observed mildly. "The merest happenstance, I presume."

His mouth twitched, and I knew he was close to laughing.

"I might have sent him a letter or two with suggestions on beauty spots he would appreciate," I allowed. "But I suspect you know that, as you no doubt sent him a few hints of your own."

He colored slightly. "There is a pretty little sloth I have been coveting," he admitted. "If he happened to find one, I should not be entirely displeased."

"I shall tell him to make you a birthday present of one," I promised.

With that rare sympathy we shared, he fell silent then, holding my gaze, and I knew what he wanted.

I sighed. "I give you my word that I will not seek out any further involvement in the matter of Alice Baker-Greene's death."

"Then why," he asked gravely, "do I suspect you of crossing your fingers?"

Before I could form an indignant response, young George appeared, waving a note overhead. "Delivered by messenger," he said in breathless excitement as he thrust it into my hands. My name and Stoker's were scrawled on the envelope. The missive inside contained only a few hasty words — *Come at once. Curiosity Club. C.*

I snatched up my hat and cloak and urged Stoker to haste. "Something is amiss," I told him as he thrust his arms into his greatcoat, the tails flapping behind him as we strode along Marylebone Street. "Lady C. has the tidiest penmanship I have ever seen, but this looks as if it were written by an inebriated moose."

I stood on tiptoe on the edge of the pavement, straining to see an empty cab.

Stoker cupped his hands to his mouth and made a sound of such eldritch horror that half the horses in the street started in surprise. But a cab came trotting smartly around the corner and we sprang inside, urging the driver to make haste. Still, the streets were thick with traffic, wagons and carriages and carts all jostling for place with the monstrous bulk of omnibuses while pedestrians picked their way as best they could through the throng. There were a few hours of short, sharp daylight that time of year, and the city never seemed more alive to me than in the brief bright hours in which so much business was conducted. Amidst the odors of horse and burning coal I could smell roasting chestnuts and the occasional whiff of woodsmoke. The air was damp and heavy, the clouds gathering to draw a grey veil over the sun.

"The weather is turning," Stoker remarked as he cast a practiced eye upon the line of rooftops. "It will be icy by morning."

I shivered in my seat. Like all butterfly hunters, I was most at home in tropical lands where the most flamboyant species of lepidoptera flourished. Give me a jungle, a forest lush with green and thick with flower-scented air that steamed gently, pulsing with life and promise, and I was a happy woman. This sooty, smirched chill that penetrated one's clothes and settled into the bones was most difficult to bear in January. The calendar had turned, the days were lengthening, spring was a promise, but it was a long and shiversome season until May blossoms would ripen.

It took longer than I might have preferred to reach the club, but we arrived at last to find Lady C.'s anxious white face peering from one of the upstairs windows. She dropped the curtain when she saw us alight from the hansom, hurrying downstairs to meet us as we entered.

"Whatever is the problem —" Stoker began but she hissed him to silence.

"Hush! Not here. Upstairs," she said, bustling us up to the exhibition room. She drew a key from her pocket and unlocked the door, making it fast behind us once she had peered down the corridors to make certain we were not observed.

Stoker did not have to repeat his question. There was a gentle crunch underfoot as we trod on broken glass, powdering it into the carpet. The display cabinet had been broken.

"An unfortunate accident," I began. But Lady C. shook her head.

"There are scratches on the lock," she told us, her expression grim. "Someone had a go at forcing it but couldn't manage it. They might have feared to take too long or simply lacked the strength to break it. In any event, they found it easier to break the glass."

"What is missing?" Stoker asked, peering in the cabinet.

"Only one thing, as far as I know," she said. "Alice Baker-Greene's summit badge from the Alpenwalder Climbing Society."

Stoker and I surveyed the contents of the case. Everything I had placed there was accounted for, albeit several things had been jostled in the miscreant's theft and bits of glass sparkled like diamonds on the velvet display cloth.

"Have you looked through the rest of the exhibition?" Stoker asked.

Lady C. shook her head. "That is why I asked you to come. I thought you might notice more than I would if anything else had been taken."

We made a quick appraisal of the various shelves and cabinets, looked through the photographs and mementoes. Stoker quietly moved behind the draperies where we had stowed the parcel with the climbing rope as I turned to Lady C. "Nothing else appears to be missing."

Her shoulders relaxed. "Well, that is a mercy, although how I am to explain to Mrs. Baker-Greene that her granddaughter's summit badge is missing is anyone's guess. I am not looking forward to telling her we have managed to lose one of her most treasured mementoes."

"You hardly lost it," I pointed out. "It was stolen."

"Because we were lax with security," she returned in some bitterness. "Perhaps we ought to engage some sort of security, although we have never had need of it before. There has always been an atmosphere of trust in this place, a trust that has now been grossly violated."

"Who was here yesterday evening?" I asked.

She spread her hands. "The members come and go, as you well know. The ledger is supposed to be used to sign in whenever one visits, but that is not always practiced," she added with a slightly reproachful glance at me. It was not undeserving. I myself occasionally failed to sign the ledger and had even earned a stern rebuke from the club authorities for omitting to declare Stoker as a guest one evening. The club had strict rules about the admission of gentlemen, permitting them only by prior arrangement or during events which were open to the public.

Lady C. went on, furrowing her brow. "I suppose I ought to go and inspect the ledger and see what I can learn from that."

"I cannot imagine any member of the club doing such a thing," I began.

"They didn't," Stoker said soberly as he came to join us.

Lady C. brightened. "What makes you say that?"

"Because it is not just the badge that has vanished," he said, giving me a level look. "The cut climbing rope is missing. Veronica and I put it behind the draperies for safe-keeping and it is gone."

Lady C. stared at him a long moment. "I do not understand. The badge at least was metal. Why on earth would someone wish to take an old rope?"

"Because it was very likely a murder weapon," I told her.

She took a deep, shuddering breath. "I must go to Hestia," she said, invoking the name of the portress and directress of the club. "She has been deciding upon a course of action and wishes to meet at once."

"We will clear it up," I told her. "I know where the brooms are."

She hurried off and I bent to tidying away the broken glass, no easy task when much of it had been ground to slivers in the carpet.

"You can leave off smiling anytime, you know," Stoker said as he plucked splinters of glass from the velvet display shelves.

"I am not smiling."

"Veronica, I can see your face. I know precisely what your mouth is doing."

I sat back on my haunches. "Very well. I am smiling. Do you know why?"

"Because you think this will change something," he said, calmly dropping the splinters into a dustpan.

"It changes *everything*! We know now that our hypothesis was correct. Alice Baker-Greene was murdered."

"That is not *our* hypothesis," he pointed out. "It is yours and it demonstrates a woeful failure of logic."

I made a scoffing noise. "You were the one who first introduced the possibility of murder," I reminded him.

"For which I am immensely sorrowful," he replied. "One cut rope does not a murder make."

"It does if that cut rope meant a woman plunged to her death. Ow!" I swore as a bit of glass jammed into my finger.

"Let me see," he ordered. "Here in the light."

I went to stand next to him, extending my finger where a bright bead of ruddy blood stood. He peered at it, then took a slender knife from his pocket. Stoker's pockets were invariably a repository for all manner of oddments — coins, vestas, paper twists of sweets, great crimson handkerchiefs, assorted glass eyeballs, lockpicks. One never knew what lurked in there, but Stoker always managed to produce the proper tool for any occasion. He bent his head to the task, plying the knifepoint so quickly and deftly that I never felt the splinter move. He dropped it into the dustpan with a delicate clink and the blood welled afresh. I expected him to wrap it in one of his enormous scarlet handkerchiefs.

Instead, he took the fingertip in his mouth, giving it a gentle suck. A jolt of a most arresting sensation coursed through me, so much so that I was entirely incapable of speech.

After a moment, he removed my finger from his lips, examining it in satisfaction. "The suction and the saliva help with clotting," he told me. "Of course, it is not a technique one would care to employ on anyone to whom one was not intimately connected."

I said nothing. I stepped closer, lifting my face to his as I applied a caress to a specific and wholly enthralling portion of his anatomy to assess its readiness.

"Veronica!" He grasped my wrists, putting me firmly away. "This is hardly the time or place," he began.

I moved forward again, pressing my hips to his. "That is rather the point," I murmured.

"We will be discovered," he protested.

"Will we?" I breathed, trailing a kiss from his earlobe down his neck. "How very dangerous."

"Veronica." This time it was a groan and he did not push me aside. Instead he buried his hands in my hair, kissing me as thoroughly as he did everything, which is to say, expertly and with exquisite attention to detail. I was just reaching for the hem of my petticoat when he gave a maidenly gasp and thrust me away. "Veronica, what has got into you? That is quite enough," he said, straightening his disordered garments. He buttoned his shirt, finishing just as Lady C. appeared. I dropped the last splinter of glass into the dustpan.

"Hestia has spoken with the Alpenwalders. It has been decided the less said about this the better," she told us, her expression grim.

"The Alpenwalders! What business is it of theirs?" I demanded.

Lady C.'s tone was even, but it seemed an effort. "They are underwriting the expenses of the exhibition and Hestia felt obliged to inform them of this development. They were most insistent upon discretion. They have a horror of any sort of bad publicity."

"Reasonable enough," Stoker put in. "If the mountaineering business is already suffering thanks to Alice Baker-Greene's death, then any news story which revives the whole sordid business must be unwelcome."

"Exactly that," Lady C. said. "And Hestia agrees with them. She will have a joiner come tomorrow to fit a new panel of glass to the cabinet. In the meanwhile, the room is to be kept locked at all times and I will keep the key."

"What of the thefts?" Stoker inquired.

"At Hestia's encouragement, I will of course write to Mrs. Baker-Greene to inform her of the loss of the summit badge," she said evasively.

"And the rope?" I challenged.

She smoothed her skirts. "There is no

need to mention it further."

"You cannot possibly mean to condone theft," I began.

"I am not condoning anything because I do not know who has perpetrated this deed and it will profit no one to pursue it," she pointed out in a too-reasonable voice. "It is out of my hands, Veronica, and the decision has been made. The matter goes no further." She looked around. "Very tidy," she said, giving an approving nod. "Your hard work is much appreciated. Now, if you do not mind, I have to leave and I am under orders to permit no one to remain without either myself or Hestia in attendance."

"You do not trust us alone in the exhibit we are helping to mount?" I asked, my voice dangerously calm.

"It is not a matter of trust," she said, moving towards the door. "It is a matter of knowing when to let things be for the greater good."

She escorted us from the room and locked it firmly behind us, pocketing the key. "Thank you for your assistance today. You have been most helpful."

"Not as helpful as we might," I protested, sotto voce. It occurred to me to storm Hestia in her aerie and demand she take the matter seriously, but I did no such thing. To begin with, I had Stoker in tow, and gentlemen were not received in the offices except by prior appointment. And, if I am to be honest, I was distracted and unhappy at the turn of events.

"I am rather put out with Lady C.," I quibbled as Stoker and I journeyed back to Bishop's Folly. "I thought she had more spirit than to simply accept a directive from on high. She seems to forget that we are highly experienced in these matters and brushes us aside as if we were kitchen maids! Come to think of it, she might as well have summoned maids to tidy up that mess and I wonder she did not."

"She needed people she could trust," he pointed out as he stared at the passing scenery.

"She did *not* trust us," I reminded him. "She set us to clearing up and then ordered us out."

"She trusted us with the truth of the burglary."

"Until she decided to take orders from Hestia and sweep the whole matter under the carpet," I said darkly. It was the first time Lady C. and I had even approached a falling-out. We had traveled together the previous year and she had shared confidences with me that I knew she had enjoyed with no other soul on earth. It rankled then that she would not trust me now with something so much less personal.

"I thought we were friends," I muttered when Stoker did not reply.

He continued to stare out the window, distracted.

I poked experimentally at his ribs, and he jumped a mile. "What in the name of seven hells was that for?" he asked, rubbing at his torso.

"I was abusing Lady C. Your response to that ought to be one of undiluted support for my position."

"I was friends with Lady C. before you and I were ever acquainted," he reminded me. "And I happen to think she is right in this case. The Alpenwalders are a notoriously touchy lot. It would no doubt sour relations between our countries to pursue this incident."

"It is not an incident," I corrected sharply. "A woman has been murdered and I am apparently the only person who cares."

He sighed. "We have no proof —"

"Because it was stolen."

He gave a growl of frustration and reached for me, but I slid to the far end of the seat. "Do not put a hand on me or I will demonstrate for you the Corsican stranglehold taught me by a very nice bandit chief of my acquaintance."

He gave me a wary look as if he doubted my purpose, but he remained where he was, clearly reluctant to risk my willingness to inflict bodily harm.

"You seemed eager enough for me to put a hand on you at the club," he said mildly.

"That was different." My cheeks were hot, beating with blood. "That was when I thought you cared about innocent victims and righting injustices."

"Or," he said slowly, "was it when there was a possibility we might be discovered and you found yourself excited by the danger of it?"

I said nothing, keeping my gaze pinned to the seat opposite. He gave a little laugh and settled back in the seat. His hand crept near mine and I slapped it away. He laughed again and when the cab drew to a stop outside the little side gate at Bishop's Folly, I sprang from my seat, leaving him to pay. By the time he had sorted out the fare and bade the driver farewell, I was halfway to my vivarium. I did not look back.

CHAPTER 6

For the remainder of the day, I busied myself in the vivarium in contemplation of my chrysalides. The butterflies were proving decidedly reluctant to emerge, but I attended the Indian birthwort faithfully, watering it and pruning the odd dead leaf, to ensure a proper food supply when they chose to make their appearance.

When I had finished, I moved on to a special corner where I was nurturing the last of my Malachites. I had secured a very small population of *Siproeta stelenes* caterpillars from the Iguazu Falls of the Argentine and had guarded them fiercely through their pupation. They had rewarded my care with a brilliant display of color and size, the largest growing to an astonishing four and three-quarters inches, well beyond the average for that particular lepidopteron. They were, as their common name suggests, a pretty shade of green, albeit without the emerald flamboyance of the Rajah Brooke's Birdwing, one of my personal favorites.

But the viridian of my Malachites was enchanting in its own right, and I watched them with tremendous satisfaction as they flapped and fluttered their way around the vivarium. Like most other butterflies, they suckled nectar from flowers, but their favorite food was rotting fruit, lavishly supplemented with bat dung and the occasional mammalian corpse. His lordship's coachman provided a steady supply of mice from the carriage house, which my greedy Malachites devoured with gusto. It was a curious thing to observe butterflies feeding eagerly on dead flesh — a sight that caused more than one lady visitor to recoil and reach for her smelling salts. I never begrudged them their curious diet. They offered too much joy in return to quibble over a few bloated mice here and there.

It was in the nature of butterflies to live transitory lives, fleeting as they were lovely, and it was with resignation that I watched as they lived out their brief existence, bursting into jeweled magnificence and then, after a few short months of activity, fading into oblivion. It was no easy feat to keep them alive throughout the deepening chill of a British autumn. The coal fires were kept stoked and the steam heat pushed through the pipes of the vivarium with the warmth of Hades, but still it was a struggle to drive the temperature above eighty degrees Fahrenheit, the necessary threshold for Malachites to fly. They drooped lower and lower upon their leaves, sulking amidst the bushes until, one by one, they perished, fluttering gracefully to the stone floor like drifts of paper born on an ill wind. I had collected them as they died, removing them gently to the Belvedere, where I mounted each upon a piece of card penned with the name of the species and its place of origin and date and place of death.

There was one last holdout against the intemperate frosts, the largest and most theatrical of the males, an enormous fellow who winged slowly about the females, dazzling them with his size rather than his speed. The smaller males darted furiously about, displaying their wings in lavishly acrobatic maneuvers, but my big, slow, steady favorite — whom I nicknamed Hercules — outdid them all, securing the favors of even the most timid of maiden butterflies. The vast majority of the dainty green eggs that had been laid amidst the shrubs were the product of his bridal flights, and in the end, he was the only one left, moving like a sad shadow through the limbs of the little jungle I had created, as if searching for the friends and wives he had lost.

I was not entirely surprised to find that his time had come at last. He lay on the floor of the vivarium in the shadow of a bush, his wings still trembling with the effort of flight. I lifted him onto my palm, bringing my hand up to my face so that I might see him clearly. He raised one forewing in what a fanciful person might have called a salute.

"Good-bye, my dear little friend," I murmured. "Rest now."

He flapped again a time or two but remained nestled in my palm. I sat in the fragrant steamy air of the vivarium, perspiration pearling my temples, and marveled at this exquisite creature with his viridian wings, so delicate they seemed hardly capable of holding his weight aloft. And yet they had, bearing him throughout his adventures until at long last his voyaging was finished. They were miracles of architecture, the lepidoptera, and I felt, along with a pang of loss, a fervent gratitude that I had discovered them as my life's work. There was nothing so fragile as a butterfly wing, nor anything as lovely.

When at last he lay still, I rose to my feet

and carried him out of the shocking warmth of the only home he had known, through the bone-snapping cold of the gardens and into the Belvedere. I worked for some time, pinning him gently whilst his wings were still pliable and unlikely to break. I wrote a description of this most extraordinary avatar of *Siproeta stelenes.* After a moment's consideration, I took up my pen again.

Known to his friends as Hercules. It was a curious thing to write an epitaph for a butterfly, but it seemed wrong not to honor the dead when we have known them, no matter how small.

As wrong as leaving Alice Baker-Greene's murderer unpunished, I thought in some agitation. Dropping the matter was not a choice I made with any great enthusiasm, and I knew it was one Stoker and I would revisit at another time. But I stood a better chance of persuading him if I could marshal a little proof, some tiny indication that a villain had been at work, snatching the life of an innocent woman before her time. And somehow, I promised myself, I would find it.

Whilst I brooded, Stoker was busily engaged in wrestling with his walrus, an occupation that kept him occupied through the dinner hour. In the end, I ordered a tray from the kitchen, choosing to take my meal in solitude, opening the last post of the day as I ate in my little chapel. Cook had sent a fine breast of duck with a potato and apple galette, but the food gave scant satisfaction when I read my letters. There was one from Lady Wellingtonia Beauclerk, the earl's elderly aunt and my unexpected friend. Born on the eve of Waterloo, she had served as the power behind the throne for decades, clearing up the untidy messes of the royal family and protecting them from their worst impulses to self-destruction. Given her loyalty to them, she might well have destroyed me for the danger I presented with my secret and semi-legitimate status.

Instead, she had befriended me as she had Stoker, offering wisdom and an unsentimental affection that meant more to me than most attachments I had ever known. Her usually robust health had taken a turn for the worse during the Ripper's reign of terror, and after much reflection on her own mishandling of the affair, she had taken herself off to Scotland to her shooting box to recuperate. Given the inclement nature of Scottish weather, I rather suspected she had gone to sulk instead, and she had missed the yuletide, usually spent in the bosom of her rumbustious family. I surveyed the scrawled note as I picked at my duck. She had scribbled a few lines, indicating that she was recovering her health, albeit more slowly than either of us would have wished. I missed her dreadfully, and I was not entirely comfortable with that emotion. Between her departure and that of Tiberius, I felt abandoned by my friends, a state of affairs I would not have credited only a year before. I was accustomed to living my life as unfettered as one of my beloved butterflies, and these new bonds of attachment brought with them not only connection and warmth but a dreadful sensation of loss when my companions were not present.

I shoved her letter aside and picked up another, this written on heavy paper embellished with the heading of the Sudbury Hotel. It was short and equally unsatisfying.

My dear Miss Speedwell,
I hope this note finds you well. I am writing to inform you that His Excellency, Chancellor von Rechstein, declines to address the matter you brought to our attention. With kind regards, Baroness Margareta von Wallenberg.

I shook the envelope, but there was nothing more. Only a single line of dismissal to indicate that nothing would be done to investigate the murder of Alice Baker-Greene. My chance to persuade Stoker to undertake this new adventure was at an end and I was, quite plainly, bereft.

But why? I had not known the woman well, I reminded myself. And countless miscarriages of justice were done every day. Why did this particular lack of conclusion feel so brutal?

I put this letter aside, shoving away the plate of duck. It was congealing now, and I had no appetite for it. I was conscious only of a keen, sharp-edged sense of loss. I had, by any measure, all that I could wish for. I was healthy and not uncomely. I had work I loved, friends I treasured, and a man for whom I would walk through fire — and, in fact, had upon occasion and in the most literal sense. I could find no reason for the overwhelming sense of agitation I felt, but I rebelled against it.

I had experienced such emotions once or twice before. The remedy, I had found, was movement. To hurl one's few possessions into a carpetbag and embark for a new adventure was the only solace. To leave behind one's woes in a damp and fogbound land, awaking in brilliant sunshine, the air heavy with spices and the promise of fresh endeavors, this was true happiness. A train bound for anywhere, a ship unfurling its sails for some new shore. Steam whistle and snapping canvas, those were the lullabies that soothed a savage soul. And I had no recourse to them, I reflected bitterly. For now that I had joined myself in affection to Stoker, I could no longer run from myself as I had once so blithely done. I must, instead, sit and face my demons.

For a long while — too long — I sat sulking in the gloom as the candles guttered out and the fire burned low. Unlike the Roman baths and the vivarium with their lavish steam heat, the follies had not been fitted with modern conveniences. It was left to me to tend my own modest hearth. After the clock had struck ten, I noticed a growing chill, something more insistent than the usual January cold. I opened the door of the folly, gazing up at the moon. It was waxing, very nearly full, a lopsided baroque pearl of a moon. But it was shrouded in grey shadows, rimmed with cold blue light, and I saw splinters of ice dancing in the glow of the doorway. I shut the door quickly against the brutal cold, stirring up the fire until it crackled merrily. I whistled to Vespertine, curling myself against his wiry, woolly warmth as I watched the flames. I could pretend to myself for just a little while that they were not plain London flames, kindled on a hearth of simple stone. They were the flames of a bonfire scented with herbs on a Corsican hillside, of a funeral pyre lavish with incense on a riverbank in India, of a cook fire in South America, smelling of roasting meats.

I smiled to myself, thinking of my adventures, and in due course, warmed by my memories and my dog, I slept.

I woke to bitter cold, the windows rimed with a narrow tracery of ice. I washed, gritting my teeth against the frigid water, and dressed in my warmest ensemble, a costume of heavy violet wool tweed with lapels of black velvet. I had had a little coat made of black velvet for Vespertine, but he gave me a reproachful look from under his heavy brows as I tried to fit it, preferring instead to bound out into the frosted gardens as soon as I opened the door. Betony, whose thick coat was meant for the wind-ravished steppes of the Caucasus, was romping happily in the brittle, frost-blackened grass whilst Huxley and Nut were nowhere to be seen. I found them, curled one on either side of Stoker as he finished his breakfast, his attention fixed upon the newspaper propped against the teapot.

I hastened upstairs to examine once more the file of cuttings on Alice Baker-Greene. There was no new information to be found. I had read every piece thoroughly the day before. I tossed them aside in exasperation. A single new snippet of information would be enough, I told myself. Just one small wisp to dangle in front of Stoker to coax him into action. I had no notion of what I required, only that there must be *something* to intrigue him, goading him to undertake the investigation of his own volition.

It took me less than a quarter of an hour to find it. An issue of the *Daily Harbinger* from the end of November. The Ripper news had settled into something less than hysteria, and one or two measured voices suggested his reign of terror might have come to an end. Without fresh victims to exploit, the *Harbinger* had been forced to revive other stories, raking them afresh to blaze back into the white-hot heat of scandal. And they had done their best with the meager details of Alice Baker-Greene's death, revisiting the story of her fatal fall, this time with eyewitness accounts in lurid detail and assorted photographs. One picture I had seen before, the posed portrait of Alice on the Alpenwald, but it was bracketed with an earlier photograph of her standing atop a peak in the United States, suffragette banner in hand. The last was a particularly unappetizing funeral portrait of Alice lying in her coffin after her funeral.

My eyes flicked swiftly from the photograph to the byline and I found no surprises there. J. J. Butterworth from Hochstadt, the Alpenwald. Our old friend had taken herself off to the tiny principality to interview witnesses, no doubt embellishing their stories with a few enhancements of her own invention. She had included a summary of the coroner's report — verdict: accidental death — as well as the formal testimony of Captain Durand, the commander of the princess's personal guard and a frequent climber himself. He testified to witnessing Alice climb that day, explaining that it was a common pastime of the Alpenwalders to observe the tiny black dots of mountaineers through telescopes fixed to the castle balconies. He explained that her climb had begun much in the usual way and that he had watched her until she rounded the breast of the mountain, heading upwards to the unseen challenge of the devil's staircase. Some minutes later, he revealed, he had heard a scream and then she had hurtled into view, falling from a terrible height to her instant death. Naturally, he rushed to the scene, as did many others who had witnessed her fall. The most usual route up the mountain, as sketched by the intrepid Miss Butterworth, began in a little wood just beyond the central square of Hochstadt, lying in a verdant green forest that nestled against the walls of the castle courtyard. To sit in one of the many biergartens with a warm glass of spiced wine or a cold stein of beer and watch the climbers toil up the mountain was one of the Alpenwalders' favorite pastimes, it appeared. And dozens of people had watched Alice Baker-Greene fall to her death. There was nothing unusual in the circumstances, Captain Durand had insisted. A tragic accident and no more.

It was not until I read through J. J.'s interviews with Alice's landlady, the local priest, and the cheesemonger that I spotted it. The cheesemonger had seen Alice Baker-Greene that morning. It was her custom to carry a small cheese and a loaf in her knapsack when she climbed. She often departed shortly after dawn, preferring to watch the sun rise on the slope of the mountain and take her breakfast on the devil's staircase as she rested and sketched the routes. That morning, she had been in high spirits, he said, planning to test a new variation on the devil's staircase that might prove useful when the snows set in before her winter climb. He had waved her off and watched her begin her climb. One other climber appeared that morning, a slender mustachioed man who began to climb a little while before Alice, but whose appearance was nothing near as thrilling as a sighting of the famous mountaineer. J. J. slipped into sticky sentimentality when she concluded that the climber might well have been the last person to see Alice alive on the mountain and ended the piece with a plea to the young man to come forward so she might tell his version of events to the public. She dangled the promise of a reward, but though I scoured the later numbers of the newspaper, I could find no further mention of Alice Baker-Greene. No doubt J. J.'s publisher refused to sanction any further Continental adventures and had ordered her home before she could track down the elusive young man.

I suppressed a sigh. This was precious little bait to use to entice Stoker into an investigation, I reflected darkly as I tucked the newspaper under my arm, but I would make a manful attempt nonetheless. I went downstairs to the sarcophagus we used as a buffet — Greco-Roman and scarcely worth the cartonnage — and peeked under the lidded dishes dispatched from the main house's kitchens. Cook had outdone herself. In addition to the usual eggs and bacon, she had sent down a heaping portion of kedgeree and a plate of deviled kidneys.

"How bad is the storm?" I asked Stoker as I filled my plate.

"Snow in Kent," he told me in a tone of bemusement. "And west of the Tamar into the north of Cornwall, if you can believe it. It has snowed so heavily in the Midlands that the trains have stopped and nothing moves. Wales is completely cut off. What is the world coming to?"

"What of Scotland?" I asked in some concern. I worried for Lady Wellie, marooned as she was in her Highland aerie.

Stoker intuited my thoughts, but his expression was unconcerned. "She took Baring-Ponsonby with her. I daresay she will be warm enough." His mouth twitched with a suppressed smile as he spoke.

Cecil Baring-Ponsonby was a gentleman of even more advanced years than Lady Wellie, but they had been lovers for decades. "Poor old Cecil is nearly ninety," I reminded him. "He has no more business in such a climate than she does. They ought to have gone to Egypt or a nice remote island in the

South Pacific. His lordship owns property all over the world. Surely he might have made her the loan of a handy archipelago."

Stoker snorted but said nothing and I returned to the copy of the *Daily Harbinger,* scouring J. J.'s piece again. I focused this time on the photographs, feeling a sudden spear thrust of irritation that so robust and engaging a woman should have had her life cut short so brutally, so tragically. I peered at the funeral photograph, putting down my toast and reaching slowly for my magnifying glass. After a long moment, I sat back, smiling.

"I can hear you thinking, Veronica," Stoker said from behind his newspaper. "What is it?"

Wordlessly, I produced the cutting and handed it over, using the magnifying glass to point out the detail in the photograph that had captured my attention.

After a long moment, Stoker slumped in his chair. "Bloody bollocking hell," he managed. I smiled, a purely feline expression of contentment, and he immediately bristled.

"See here, Veronica —"

I held up a hand to forestall his objections. "No. Let us have it plainly with no brangling. Alice Baker-Greene was laid to her eternal rest wearing a climbing costume and the enameled badge of the Alpenwalder Kletterverein Gipfelabzeichen."

"Your German pronunciation is execrable," he put in.

"Do not sulk. It is unbecoming in a man of your age," I replied calmly. "Now, this badge is not the plain badge worn by every mountaineer who climbs on the Teufelstreppe. It is the particular and very special badge awarded to those who achieve the summit. So, Miss Baker-Greene is buried in her mountaineering garb with an accolade from the society, a very special society marking her accomplishment. Why, then, I am forced to ask, did we find that exact badge amongst her personal possessions at the club? And furthermore, why was Alice Baker-Greene's climbing badge stolen from the exhibition on the night before last?"

Stoker's response was pointed. "You cannot possibly know the answers to those questions."

"I am a scientist," I told him ruthlessly. "I do not require perfect knowledge in order to form a working hypothesis, only possibilities. Alice Baker-Greene was buried with an Alpenwalder summit badge. This we know from the photograph," I said, jabbing a finger towards the newspaper in his hand. "Yet an identical — or *nearly* identical —

badge was sent with her personal possessions from Hochstadt. Since an item cannot occupy two places at once, we may safely deduce that there are two badges." I paused and he gave a grudging nod.

"I suppose so."

"Now, the badge we saw at the Curiosity Club was packed with Alice's personal possessions from her lodgings and conveyed directly here. It is, I happen to know, Alice's own badge."

"How can you know that?" he demanded.

I described the nick at the edge of the medal. "Alice showed me herself. She said it got bashed about when she wore it climbing once and she intended never to wear it climbing again."

I paused again and he made a restless gesture. "Get on with it," he growled.

"The badge at the club is undoubtedly Alice's own," I repeated. "But the badge she was buried with was not pinned to her clothing because *it was not hers.*"

Stoker waved the newspaper at me. "It is most definitely pinned to her clothing in this photograph."

"But that is not where it was found," I pointed out. "Read the article carefully, and you will be struck by one curious fact — the badge was found with her lifeless body

113

on the Teufelstreppe, but clutched in her hand. This is the badge, the undamaged badge, that was pinned to her garments as she lay in her coffin. And I propose that this badge belonged to her murderer," I finished triumphantly. "And was wrenched from his shirt as Alice Baker-Greene reached out for the last time whilst she struggled for her life on that mountain."

He gave a deep groan. "Veronica, of all the melodramatic codswallop —"

"It is not codswallop. What is more logical than that Alice, whose rope was clearly cut in an act of sabotage, might have struggled with her attacker and ripped a badge from his clothing, carrying down the mountain a clue to his identity? Furthermore, you thought the same yourself, otherwise you would not have had so strenuous a reaction to the realization. 'Bloody bollocking hell' were your words, I believe."

"I admit, I may have thought something along those lines at first, but almost at once I saw that there might be a dozen other perfectly logical explanations for the presence of a second badge amongst her things."

"I would settle for one," I told him sweetly.

"It might be a memento," he said, shoving the newspaper back at me. "Surely she had a love affair or a friendship of some sort —

one she mightn't have wanted made public. So the badge was a sentimental keepsake."

"Possible, but weak," I told him. "Two marks out of ten."

"That suggestion is at least a seven," he countered.

I flapped a hand. "Two and I am being generous. First, she did have a possible relationship in the Alpenwald with a minor member of the royal family — Duke Maximilian of Lokendorf —"

Stoker's crow of triumph broke into my narrative. Naturally, I ignored him and carried on, raising my voice only slightly.

"Say what you like but it fits the facts," I protested. "The badge discovered in Alice's hand was that of her murderer — and I know who he was."

Stoker blinked in astonishment. "The devil you do."

I gave a little sigh of pleasure. "The moustachioed man." I nodded towards the newspaper. "Read on. Miss Butterworth was most thorough, but even she failed to deduce the likeliest explanation — that the mysterious man on the mountain was there for one purpose that morning: murder."

"More likely her editors were afraid of drawing a costly lawsuit," Stoker replied.

Stoker read through the piece, his brows

drawing further and lower with every line. When he had finished, he prowled through the rest of the cuttings, laying them side by side in a sort of timeline as he came to the end of each. "All right, let us suppose, for just a moment, that what you have said is possible — that Alice was murdered and that the summit badge was stolen because it provides a clue. That gets us no closer to discovering who this person might have been."

"Of course it does!" I enumerated the points on my fingers. "First, someone else's badge in Alice's dead hand means that the murderer must have been a climber, a proposition that is further confirmed by the presence of the moustachioed man on the mountain that day, our possible murderer. Second, only an experienced climber would have known how to tamper with the ropes at just the correct spot to ensure she fell to her death. Third, why else steal the rope and badge from the club if not to conceal the fact that it was murder and that the killer was a mountaineer? Altogether, this means that our villain must have been someone who not only climbs but knew of the existence of the badge and rope in Alice's effects. In short, my dear Stoker, it was an Alpenwalder."

"Not necessarily," he said slowly.

"You are determined to be difficult."

"It is a poor scientist who is so attached to her theory that she cannot entertain criticism of it," he countered.

"Very well. Go on."

"If it were an alpinist who killed her — and I do concede that only a skilled climber could have ascended to the devil's staircase in order to dispatch her — then yes, the badge and rope might offer clues as to the murderer's identity. But it does not necessarily follow that the murderer was an Alpenwalder."

"The description fits Duke Maximilian," I protested.

"The description of a man of mystery and moustaches also fits Douglas Norton."

"Perhaps," I admitted.

He gave a snort and produced the cutting with Norton's photograph. "Moustaches. And slender."

I pulled a face.

"Don't pout, Veronica. It does not suit a woman of your age." He grinned.

I thought a moment, then gave him a triumphant look. "Douglas Norton could not have known the badge and rope would be in the effects sent to the club. Only someone in the Alpenwald would have known that."

He rolled his eyes. "The exhibition is a celebration of Alice Baker-Greene's lifetime as an alpinist. It is a reasonable expectation it would include artifacts from her last climb."

"Possibly."

He grinned again. "So, we are in agreement insofar as we believe it is possible that Alice was the victim of a calculated and deliberate murder, carried out by a man with moustaches and climbing experience."

"Correct."

"But how does that fit with the theft of the items from the club?" he asked, stroking his chin thoughtfully. He had shaved, imperfectly as usual, and there was a blue-black shadow at his jaw. With his long, tumbled ebony locks and the glint of gold hoops in his ears, he bore a striking resemblance to an Elizabethan buccaneer, even more so when he donned the eye patch he occasionally wore to rest the eye that had been injured in a dispute with a jaguar. (Stoker, I should mention, emerged wounded and scarred from the fight but very much alive, which is more than one can say for the jaguar.)

In any event, surveying his physical charms was a distraction I could not afford,

I told myself sternly. I had a murderer to catch.

I clipped the last article I had unearthed and placed it with the other cuttings, bundling them neatly into a file while Stoker continued to muse.

"It might have been anyone," he said finally.

"How can you possibly think so?" I demanded. "The only people in the room were the Alpenwalder delegation of the princess and her lady-in-waiting, Lady C., and the pair of us. In case it has escaped your notice, none of us is a moustachioed man of superlative climbing ability."

"No, but we were not the only ones to see those particular items," he pointed out. "Someone recovered Alice's things. Someone packed and shipped them."

"Surely if the murderer was involved in conveying her things, they would have removed them," I protested.

"Perhaps they could not," he theorized. "Perhaps they were never alone with her possessions. They might have bided their time until now when they were relatively easy to retrieve from the club."

"It would take an audacious murderer to do such a thing," I said slowly.

"More audacious than attacking a world-class climber on a mountain? If this is indeed how she was murdered, then the killer is a man of tremendous nerve and excellent timing — both skills that a mountaineer must possess, in any event. And if it was," he went on, "there is always the possibility that the killer never intended to retrieve the rope and badge at all. Think of it, if some of Alice's things go missing, it draws attention to them. But a bit of rope and a badge that everyone already knew she owned? By themselves they are unremarkable. Far safer to leave them be and let everyone get on with burying the dead."

"But then you discovered that the rope had been cut," I said, "suggesting murder had been done and leaving the killer open to exposure for the first time. Which leads us back to the people in that room at the club."

"Except that we were not the only ones who would have known about it," he countered. "You and I have mentioned it to no one, but Lady C. has told Hestia and the board. The Alpenwalders have most likely discussed it amongst themselves."

"They have," I said heavily. "I had a letter last night from the baroness." I told him what the note had said and he gave a nod of satisfaction.

"Well, there it is. Nothing more to be done."

"Nothing more to be done! You just agreed there is most likely a murderer walking free."

"And we can do nothing without the co-operation of the Alpenwalders except provoke an international incident, which I, for one, do not intend to do. We can do nothing," he repeated firmly as he poured a fresh cup of tea for himself.

I thought of the last flutter of Hercules' wing as it brushed against my skin. I had given Stoker my word we would not pursue the matter of Alice Baker-Greene's death. But in the cold light of morning, I regretted it.

I regarded him over the breakfast table as he stirred in his sugar and considered my options carefully. We were in the throes of a relationship that was perilously new. Neither of us was accomplished at such things, and I found myself suddenly resisting the compromise and cooperation that were the obvious cornerstones of such endeavors. Was I always to be biting my tongue, squelching my most intrepid impulses in the name of keeping the peace? Was he?

It was a chilling thought and one I rebelled against instantly.

I raised my chin and gave him my most

defiant look. "Can't we?"

"Veronica," he said in a dangerously low voice, "you promised."

"A promise made under duress is not binding," I said with cool detachment.

"Duress! What duress?" he demanded. "I did not exactly hold you at swordpoint."

"No, but our relationship is one of an intimate nature. Such things can be coercive upon the weaker sex," I said demurely.

"Weaker?" He choked and only recovered himself when he had drunk half a cup of tea. "My dear Veronica, any person who would consider you an exemplar of any variety of weakness wants his head examined."

"That is very kind of you to say, I am sure," I replied, "but the fact remains that I am not entirely comfortable with the promise I made to leave this investigation alone."

"There is no investigation," he reminded me.

"All the more reason to begin one. Perhaps a quick word with Sir Hugo," I suggested.

He pushed aside his teacup with a sigh. "I repeat, what you propose has the potential to create an international incident. The crime, if there was one, occurred in another country, a *sovereign* country. We have no right, nor does Sir Hugo or any other member of Her Majesty's government, to interfere in their system of justice."

"Justice!" I rejoined in real bitterness. "Where is the justice in refusing to look into the murder at all?"

"I know this is a matter of frustration for you," he said gently, "but you agreed enough with my arguments yesterday to give me your word. Unless you *were* crossing your fingers," he added with a small smile — the smile one might give to a recalcitrant child.

Sudden rage boiled up within me, but I smothered it, determined to keep our conversation civil and not, as I was inclined to do, hurl the toast rack at his head.

Striving for patience, I attempted a different tack. "It is not for my own sake or even the sake of justice that I suggest such a thing," I said, adopting a wistful tone. "It is only for that poor old granny."

He furrowed his brow. "What granny?"

"Mrs. Baker-Greene, of course. Alice's grandmother. She has lost so many people dear to her," I said sadly. "Her husband. Her son. Now her granddaughter. All taken from her by the mountains she loves so desperately. I cannot imagine bearing up under that kind of loss."

"All the more reason to leave her in peace," he said sternly.

"She is very old, you know. Nearly seventy-five. And confined to a Bath chair," I added.

"Poor old dear. All those decades of hauling herself up mountains in the coldest and most unforgiving of climates have left her victim to the most devilish rheumatism. I can imagine her now," I went on, painting a picture of maudlin isolation, "sitting by the hearthside, praying just a little of the warmth of the fire will sink into her bones and ease her aching joints. And the long lonely hours with nothing but the wind for company as it blows in the lonely casement."

Stoker looked baffled. "For all you know she lives in a modern building with steam heat and gaslights."

"Of course she doesn't," I retorted. "She is a woman of advanced years. Women of advanced years always live in cottages. Usually with cats of malodorous appearance."

"That is the most absurd statement," he began.

"Your old nanny," I hazarded, "probably lives in a cottage." It was always a winning strategy to prod his overweening sense of chivalry.

He snorted. "My old nanny has a boardinghouse in Brighton that is fitted with an electric generator because she blackmailed my father into giving her half of my mother's jewels."

I blinked at him. "She what?"

He picked up his teacup again. "That is a tale for another time."

I returned to the subject at hand only with great difficulty as I made a mental note to revisit the subject of his nanny at a more opportune moment. "But surely Mrs. Baker-Greene would want justice to be done," I pointed out. "I know it."

"You do not know anything of the sort," he retorted. "Furthermore —"

He did not have the chance to finish that sentence because just then George the hall-boy appeared, trotting quickly with a note that he waved like a crusader's banner. "Miss!" he exclaimed, thrusting the missive into my hands. It was thick, creamy paper, sealed with blue wax marked with a complicated cipher and only slightly begrimed by his grubby hands. I cracked open the seal and noticed at once the elaborate crest at the top.

"What new intrigues?" Stoker asked, lazily breaking up the last of the oatcakes to fling to the dogs.

I skimmed the few lines. The hand was firm, the language formal. I brandished the page with a smile. "It is a summons. From a fellow called von Rechstein. Chancellor of the Alpenwald."

He read over the note in obvious astonishment. "You cannot be serious."

I shrugged. "It appears we are wanted. And I have kept my promise — I did not pursue this."

Stoker swore then, an entirely new phrase I had not heard before.

"Some new addition to your vocabulary? Or did they teach you that in naval college?"

He repeated it as I folded the note. "Come along and don't be sulky," I instructed. "We are needed."

CHAPTER 7

The note directed us to come with all haste to the Sudbury Hotel, a luxurious establishment located in the heart of London. It was new and furnished in the height of discreet good taste. Here were no gilded embellishments such as may be found in the more opulent hotels of New York, none of the silken debaucheries of Parisian enclaves. There was only a quiet richness of décor that whispered of excellent service and perfect comfort. I sighed as we crossed into the lobby, trading the sooty, befogged streets of the city for the glowing warmth of the hotel's interior. Our journey had been lengthy and cold, traversing the frost-slicked streets in an imperfectly heated hackney with a driver who swore the air blue with his imprecations against the weather and the congested traffic.

But within the doors of the Sudbury all was calm and inviting. It was the newest and most luxurious of London accommodations, fitted with lifts and steam heat and modern plumbing in every room. A battalion of porters dressed in bottle green plush livery trimmed in gold braid moved swiftly and quietly through their appointed tasks as a harpist played softly in the corner of the hotel's lobby — a selection of Brahms pieces, I realized, which only added to the atmosphere of gentle and satisfied wealth. Nothing ever truly dreadful could happen in this bastion of warmth and security. Everything, from the thick pile of the dark gold carpet to the heavy draperies of green silk and enormous green marble vases filled with hothouse blooms, had been designed to provide pleasure and serenity. I enjoyed the Sudbury for many reasons, not least that it was the site of employment for Julien d'Orlande, Stoker's longtime friend and a pastry chef of immense talent and creativity. No matter the purpose of the chancellor's summons, at the conclusion of our interview I had every intention of visiting the kitchens and sampling the latest of Julien's creations.

As we entered the Sudbury, I was aware of a new atmosphere, a heightened sort of buzzing, like that of an agitated beehive. Porters moved more quickly, doors were closed with a decisive snap, and everywhere was a sense of purpose and watchfulness.

I had expected to give our names to a porter, but it was the manager himself who approached the moment we entered. "Miss Speedwell, Mr. Templeton-Vane," he said, bowing from the neck. "I am Gerald Lovell, general manager of the Sudbury. Permit me to escort you to the princess's suite." He ushered us through the lobby, where I spied a number of what could only be policemen in plain clothes, unconvincingly pretending to read newspapers or hold conversations as they surveyed each new arrival in the hotel with a gimlet eye. I did not recognize any of them, but still I was grateful for the instinct that had caused me to pin a heavy veil to my hat, obscuring my features slightly. Stoker, I noticed, averted his face as we passed them. Whether any of our acquaintance at Scotland Yard had been assigned to the princess's security detail, we had no desire to call attention to our presence. That was a complication we could ill afford.

Mr. Lovell led us up the stairs and around a wide gallery to a set of double doors closed firmly against the hushed noises of the public areas. From here we entered a small private lift which carried us up a number of floors. Unlike the older hotels, where a grand suite would be located on a lower level for convenience, the Sudbury's modern lifts ensured that their most august guests could be accommodated on the higher floors in rooms with more light and less noise from the bustling streets. Instead of a series of tiny, cramped rooms for maids tucked under the eaves, the Sudbury had given over the upper levels to their most exclusive and expensive suites, with enormous French windows and balconies installed to give the guests the impression they were on a vast sailing ship, gliding above the city below. The maids, I had been told, were stashed in a stark dormitory belowstairs.

The lift arrived with a gentle pause, and the operator, a young man garbed in more of the bottle green plush and a lofty sense of his own importance, opened the gilded gates, bowing stiffly as we exited. A guard in what I could only imagine was Alpenwalder livery stood outside another set of double doors, eyeing us with suspicion. He was well over six feet tall, perhaps nearly six and a half, with a set of wide blond moustaches that curled at the ends like the horns of a ram. He saluted smartly at the manager's approach, clicking his boot heels together. But his gaze took careful note of us and his hand fell to the sword at his side as we passed. He might be a showy sort of protection, but he was clearly determined to defend the Alpenwald delegation from intruders. As we passed, I noticed the glint of an Alpenwalder summit badge on his uniform, polished as proudly as his military orders and insignia of rank.

"The princess's private bodyguard, Captain Durand," Mr. Lovell informed us as he escorted us through the doors. Durand! I resisted the urge to turn and study him, but I recognized the name at once from the *Daily Harbinger.* Durand was one of the eyewitnesses to Alice's fatal climb. There had been no description of him in the newspaper, but I made a careful note to discuss his significant moustaches with Stoker upon the first opportunity.

Mr. Lovell went on, waving an airy hand as we walked. "Our most illustrious guests stay in a completely private wing." The carpets were even thicker here, muffling our footsteps. The walls were hung with green silk brocade, gaslights flickering shadows onto the pattern. There was something watchful about the place, a sense of breath being held, waiting. I was not much given to fancies, but I felt a trifle uneasy as we made our way down the corridor.

He bore us to the end of the hall, where yet another set of double doors stood closed. A small brass plaque proclaimed it to be the Queen Victoria suite. "Our most elegant suite, always assigned to visiting royalty," the manager informed us. He made a tiny tap against the door, the merest scratch, and instantly it opened. A maid, dressed in deepest black bombazine with a stiffly starched apron, stepped sharply aside, scuttling into the shadows, not even daring to glance up from under the edge of her enormous ruffled muslin cap. Mr. Lovell left us then and the maid hurried after him, leaving us standing just inside the doorway.

The Baroness von Wallenberg came forward, making a gesture of welcome. She was dressed in a fine day gown of mulberry velvet, her monocle attached to a black velvet ribbon at her collar. An enameled watch was pinned to her lapel, and a wide belt held a chatelaine of finely wrought silver at her waist. It jingled with various implements — a tiny metal purse, a thimble, miniature scissors, and assorted other tools as well as a ring of keys. The baroness was clearly attired for whatever task might fall to her as a lady-in-waiting. "Miss Speedwell. Mr. Templeton-Vane. This way."

She led us into the sitting room, a luxurious chamber furnished in various shades of mossy green velvets and petal pink silks. A fire leapt merrily on the hearth, but there was no friendliness in the welcome. A gentleman stood stiffly at attention, his posture distinctly Teutonic, his uniform covered in medals from various honors. Like the guard captain's, his moustaches were lavish and curled elaborately, but his head was bald as a new egg, shiny as the decorations on his chest. A second look told me that one of those decorations was a summit badge of the Alpenwalder Kletterverein Gipfelabzeichen, and I repressed a sigh of mild irritation. If every man from the Alpenwald sported moustaches and a summit badge, we should be overwhelmed by possible villains.

If I had to choose a likelier of the two men to prove the murderer, I should have selected this fellow without hesitation. A pair of long, narrow scars puckered his left cheek, and I was instantly reminded of my old friend the Baron von Stauffenbach, who sported identical marks as the relics of Bavarian duels fought in his youth. They lent dash and a certain devil-may-care air to a man, I always thought. But there was nothing of the baron's warmth in this Alpenwalder, only a wary watchfulness as he clicked his heels and bowed from the neck. He fixed us with an icy blue stare, the hungry stare of a bird of prey assessing a small movement in the grass.

"Miss Speedwell. Mr. Templeton-Vane."

Mindful of my manners, I raised my veil, then went forward, hand extended. "Chancellor von Rechstein, I presume?"

He regarded my hand with an expression akin to distaste, then took it, shaking only the fingertips. "Forgive me," he said, inclining his head once more. "The shaking of hands is not a custom of our country."

He overcame his disinclination to shake Stoker's hand and waved us to a sofa that had been neatly placed in the center of the room, taking a chair opposite. The arrangement felt artificial until I realized it had been done quite deliberately to keep his face slightly shadowed while the light fell full upon ours. If I considered such a thought to be far-fetched, I had only to wait for his next remark to know it was not. He flicked a glance at Stoker but riveted his attention upon me, studying my features at some length before Stoker finally coughed, recalling the chancellor's attention.

"Again, I must beg your forgiveness," he said. He turned to the baroness. "You were quite right, Baroness. The resemblance is remarkable." His expression was thoughtful. "But she would have to be intelligent for it to work. Uncommonly intelligent. The risks are too great otherwise."

"I can vouch for Miss Speedwell's gifts," the lady murmured. "I have made inquiries."

"Inquiries?" I asked. "What does this have to do with Alice Baker-Greene's death?"

The chancellor's pale blue eyes turned again to me. "Nothing whatsoever."

"But isn't that why you have asked us to come?" Stoker asked.

The chancellor pursed his lips. "The baroness related to me your observations about the rope, Mr. Templeton-Vane. It is my opinion that the rope was frayed on the climb and that Miss Baker-Greene's death was an accident — a tragic and deplorable accident as was the verdict of our official inquest." The note of finality in his voice made it clear he would brook no further discussion on the subject.

But I would not be discouraged by a little Teutonic forcefulness. I sat forward on the sofa. "Surely, Chancellor, you will agree —"

The baron turned to the baroness. "She is stubborn. Do you think it will present a problem?"

The baroness tipped her head, studying

me like a zoological specimen. "I do not believe so."

I exchanged glances with Stoker. "Do you know what they are talking about?" I murmured.

He shook his head. "Not in the slightest, but I have a very bad feeling I shan't like it."

I smiled at the pair of Alpenwalders. "Chancellor. Baroness. Perhaps we should begin again. If you did not summon us to discuss the death of Miss Baker-Greene, then why are we here?"

The chancellor said nothing but made a low, guttural noise of dismissal. He circled the sofa, surveying me slowly from all angles, as if inspecting a purchase. "She is shorter than Her Serene Highness," he pronounced. "I noticed it at once when she entered."

"High-heeled shoes will remedy that," the baroness assured him. "And a high coiffure like the one the princess wears. The difference will not be detectable once I have finished with her."

"Finished with what?" I demanded.

The chancellor scowled at the baroness. "You did not tell them?"

She dropped her eyes. "I thought it best coming from you, Excellency. I merely sent along your summons."

He threw his hands heavenwards and muttered something in the Alpenwalder dialect. The baroness flushed a little, not unbecomingly, and I wondered how many decades they had been having these sorts of misunderstandings. He heaved a final sigh at the baroness and turned to address us. "Miss Speedwell. Mr. Templeton-Vane. My countrywoman has not done her duty by you," he said with a faint note of reproof. The baroness flushed again but said nothing. He went on. "I have asked you here today on a matter completely unrelated to the death of Miss Baker-Greene. Two days ago, you made the acquaintance of Her Serene Highness, the Hereditary Princess. Today, I am distressed to relate to you that the princess cannot be found."

I blinked at him. "I beg your pardon, Excellency?"

He looked at the baroness. "Is my English that poor? I thought I was perfectly clear."

"You were," she soothed. "The princess," she repeated slowly, enunciating each syllable with care, "cannot be found."

Stoker and I continued to stare blankly at the Alpenwalders. "Perhaps if we said it louder," the baroness suggested.

The chancellor grunted in agreement.

"THE PRINCESS," he thundered, "CAN-NOT BE FOUND."

My ears ringing, I held up a hand. "We heard you, Excellency. I am afraid we do not comprehend you. Do you mean your princess is missing?"

"Not missing," the baroness said unhappily. "Just not here."

"Do you know where she is?" Stoker asked.

"No," was the reluctant answer.

"Then she is missing," he replied flatly.

"And you want us to find her," I finished, the familiar thrill of a quest thrumming in my veins.

"Not quite," the chancellor corrected.

"You see," the baroness interjected smoothly, "this is not the first time we have misplaced Her Serene Highness."

"You mean she runs away?" Stoker suggested.

"The princess cannot run away," the chancellor bellowed. "Wherever she is, that is where she is supposed to be. The sun does not run away."

I resisted the urge to roll my eyes at his overwrought language. He was clearly distressed, and I was eager to get to the bottom of the matter.

"Very well. You have simply misplaced

your princess," I said in a consoling tone. "If she has done this before, I presume she must always have returned in due course."

"Always," the baroness said promptly. "Only we never know quite when to expect her." Her face puckered a little. She was a court lady, schooled in concealing her emotions, but I noted that her hands twisted around her handkerchief, pleating and unpleating the scrap of embroidered lawn.

"I can see how that must be difficult —" I began.

"Difficult! It is impossible," interjected the chancellor. "Today of all days."

"Why, particularly, today?" Stoker asked.

"Tonight the princess has an engagement. There is an entertainment in her honor at the Royal Opera, a gala performance featuring Mademoiselle Sophie Fribourg."

"The soprano? I heard her sing once in Paris," Stoker offered.

I raised a brow at him, but he merely shrugged. "I am not entirely unsophisticated, you know," he murmured.

" 'Mademoiselle' Fribourg?" I asked.

The baroness hastened to explain. "Society in the Alpenwald is rather more stratified than in your country. Artists and performers, like tradesmen, are always referred to by French titles, whilst the nobility is addressed in German."

Stoker twitched at that, no doubt longing to make a comment that would have done Robespierre proud. I laid a quelling hand upon his sleeve and smiled at the baroness. "You were saying, Baroness? The opera?"

"Mademoiselle Fribourg is singing the title role in a new work tonight — *Atalanta* by Edouard Berton," the baroness confirmed, the furrow in her brow easing. "To have an opera written by an Alpenwalder composer sung at such a venue, and by an Alpenwalder soprano . . ." She trailed off.

"It is the pinnacle of Alpenwalder cultural achievement," the chancellor finished.

"It will secure the place of our music in the pantheon of achievement," the baroness added. "And it will be the making of Mademoiselle Fribourg's career. Already she has booked a concert tour of America on the strength of this one performance."

"I am sure it will be a very great evening for all of you," I said.

"Not if the princess fails to appear!" the chancellor cried, striking his open palm with his fist.

"You see," the baroness explained, "if the princess is not in the royal box to put her imprimatur on the performance, as it were, it will all be for naught. There would be a presumption that somehow she disapproved of the opera or Mademoiselle Fribourg. The young lady's career would be ruined, but far more importantly, it would be said that Alpenwalder culture is inferior," she finished on a horrified whisper.

I moved to question her priorities in the matter, but Stoker spoke up first. "But surely you can simply issue a statement saying the princess is indisposed."

The Alpenwalders exchanged meaningful glances. "Unfortunately, that is not possible."

"But why not?" he persisted.

The chancellor looked at the baroness and gave a sharp shake of his head, sending his moustaches trembling. The baroness's expression was grave. "We are devoted to our princess. Unfortunately, not everyone in the Alpenwald shares our regard. She has, upon occasion, failed to fulfill her duties in a manner that will satisfy all of her subjects."

"Failed how?" Stoker pressed.

The chancellor pursed his lips. "She has not made appearances that were scheduled and announced in the Court Circular. She has permitted some of the royal patronages to lapse."

"She has put off her wedding," added the baroness, her mouth thinning a little in obvious disapproval. I glanced to her hand and saw a heavy set of rings on her left hand, the gold wedding band and ruby engagement ring held in place by an extravagant ring of black enamel. A widow then, I realized. But she had clearly prized her status as a married woman and wanted the same for her princess.

"Is she betrothed?" I asked.

"Net yet," the chancellor replied mildly. "There is a suitable match, the most suitable, but she va— va—" He tipped his head, clearly searching for the proper word.

"Vacillates?" Stoker suggested.

"Just so, vacillates," the chancellor said in obvious satisfaction. "She will not make up her mind to a formal announcement of the engagement."

"If she would only permit the betrothal contracts to be signed and a date to be set," the baroness lamented. "She would be happy then, I think. But she is frightened of marriage and so she resists, every day putting off the inevitable and causing the gossips." The baroness sighed. "She can be very whimsical," she added.

This view of the princess did not conform to the serious, imperious young woman I had met. But it was little surprise she did not wish to commit herself quite yet to the rigid formality of marriage and court life.

"The princess is young," I began.

"She is your age," the baroness said.

I gave her an oblique look. "You have indeed made inquiries."

Her smile was faint and apologetic. "You must forgive the impertinence, Miss Speedwell. But I had to be certain."

"Certain of what?"

"That you would be an acceptable candidate," the chancellor answered.

"You still haven't told us — a candidate for what?" Stoker asked.

"To impersonate the princess, of course," the chancellor replied, his moustaches looking very satisfied indeed.

CHAPTER 8

I ought to have stared in astonishment or protested or demanded further explanation. Instead, I sat forward, gripping my hands together in excitement. "I will do it."

Beside me, Stoker gave a start. "You must be joking."

"Indeed, I am not," I said.

The chancellor's austere features relaxed in obvious satisfaction, and the baroness nodded gravely. "You are courageous, Miss Speedwell."

"Courageous?" I asked.

She looked to the chancellor, but he merely waved a dismissive hand. "A head of state will always receive threats most unsavory. We shall not discuss them."

"I think we bloody well shall," Stoker stated, his innate courtesy deserting him for once.

"You dare to swear in my presence?" The chancellor's moustaches were quivering in indignation.

"I will do a damned sight more than swear if you think you can simply dismiss dangers to Miss Speedwell with a flap of the hand," Stoker told him in a tone of ringing finality.

"Now, see here," the chancellor began.

I held up a hand. "Gentlemen, please. No brangling. Stoker, you have been decidedly rude to the chancellor but your concern is understandable. Excellency, what sort of dangers do you anticipate?"

"One cannot anticipate every danger," Stoker said icily. "That is why they are dangerous."

"I am aware," I told him, maintaining my composure. "But forewarned is forearmed, is it not, Excellency? Now, what form have these threats taken?"

The chancellor was clearly not pleased to have his feet held to this particular fire. He turned to the baroness and she hastened to reassure me. "A few letters, nothing more. The usual sort of thing one encounters when traveling. And even at home. A ruler is never universally popular."

"What sort of letters?" Stoker asked.

She shrugged. "The odd complaint about a matter of policy. The occasional anarchist."

Stoker and I exchanged glances. Our

previous encounters with anarchists had been decidedly less than pleasurable. The baroness went on. "Those who wish to see the Alpenwald annexed to France. Those who wish to see her annexed to Germany. Those who want the princess to marry, those who want her to remain unwed. The sentiments are predictable."

"But you suggested there were real dangers," Stoker reminded her.

"I spoke out of turn," she replied with a submissive look at the chancellor.

I turned to Stoker. "You see? Nothing to be concerned about. Just the usual madmen and fanatics."

"*Nothing to be concerned about.* Veronica, have you entirely taken leave of your senses? Have all of you?" he demanded, looking from each of us to the others. "Your princess is missing. Have you not considered the possibility that one of these threats has at last materialized? Have you not considered the possibility that she may have been abducted?"

The chancellor shifted in his chair. "Her Serene Highness left a note."

"A note! I should like to see it," I told him.

His gaze slid from mine. "It was destroyed. We cannot risk the story being made public that the princess is not at hand."

"What did it say?" Stoker demanded.

The baroness sat forward, perhaps eager to make amends for raising the specter of violence in the first place. "That she was leaving on a personal matter and did not wish us to worry."

"What does that indicate to you?" I inquired.

"That she meant to return before tonight when her presence is required," she said promptly.

"Then why worry now? She may yet turn up," Stoker pointed out.

"And if she does not?" the chancellor countered gruffly. I did not think it was possible for his posture to be any more erect, but he stiffened noticeably. "My dear fellow, my position in the Alpenwald is the pinnacle of all possible appointments. I did not achieve this by failing to anticipate every difficulty. We cannot risk the princess failing to appear tonight." He turned to me, his tone gentle. In another man, I might have called it coaxing. "If the princess does not show herself in the royal box, she will gravely offend her hosts as well as the other dignitaries. Do you think the English will forgive such a slap in the eye? No, they will not! Help us, *Fraulein.*"

"Of course, Excellency." I turned to

Stoker. "You see what is at stake here. It must be done."

"I do not like it," he replied.

"I am rather afraid you have no choice," the chancellor said, his moustaches almost concealing a triumphant smile. "Fraulein Speedwell has consented."

"But I have not," Stoker returned, baring his teeth. "And I have only to alert the authorities or the newspapers to the fact that the princess is being impersonated to bring the entire house of cards down around your ears."

The chancellor's hands curled into fists at his sides. "You would not dare!"

"Wouldn't I?" Stoker crossed one leg lazily over the other and regarded the chancellor with the icy hauteur of four hundred years' worth of English noble blood.

The chancellor drew a handkerchief out of his pocket and dropped it to the floor. "Then I challenge you to a duel as you are a man of honor!"

I looked at the baroness. "Is there any way to stop this nonsense?"

She gave me a helpless shrug. "The chancellor likes to duel. It is a very common sport in our country. Almost as popular as mountain climbing. It gives the people something to do when the peaks are too dangerous to climb."

"What about the women?" I asked.

"Oh, the women duel as well," she assured me. "We use wooden swords, but it is very exciting all the same."

Stoker had picked up the handkerchief and risen to his feet, a slow smile of acceptance spreading over his features. Recognizing the look, I plucked the handkerchief from his grasp and returned it to the chancellor. "Mr. Templeton-Vane will not duel you."

"I rather like the idea," Stoker protested.

"I know you do, and you really ought to examine that, but now is not the time," I said. "Excellency, you and Mr. Templeton-Vane will not duel because if you do, I will not impersonate your princess."

"That sounds like a win on both counts for me," Stoker began.

I held up a hand. "I will take on the role of the princess on the condition that you be permitted to accompany me," I told Stoker. He rocked back on his heels, thinking.

"Why would I agree to that when I can put an end to the whole bloody mess?"

"We both know you will not do that. You are too fine a gentleman to ruin a young woman's career because of trifling matters. Mademoiselle Fribourg is depending upon

149

this performance, and I daresay the composer is as well. Your concern is for my safety. Very well. You will come along and see to it personally. This meets with your approval, I take it, Excellency?" The chancellor gave a grudging nod as he returned his handkerchief to his pocket.

"But do not forget, the challenge has been issued and may be accepted at any time," he told Stoker darkly.

"I will remember that," Stoker promised.

"We are in agreement," the baroness said in obvious relief.

"Excellent," the chancellor said, rubbing his hands together. "There is much preparation to be done. I suggest you return here no later than teatime —"

"I think," Stoker broke in, "that Miss Speedwell and I may be permitted a few moments to discuss the matter. In private."

The chancellor looked as though he would like to protest, but the baroness gave him a long look and he nodded. "We will withdraw and you may have until the mantel clock chimes," he told us. He pointed to the clock, a hideous affair of folksy wooden carving that could only have been crafted from some Bavarian nightmare. It was a sort of cottage or chalet, lavishly embellished with fruits and animals and great flowers picked out in garish paints. The door of the cottage was a particularly lurid shade of scarlet.

"How very unusual," I said, attempting a polite smile.

"It is an example of our native Alpenwalder work," the chancellor said with unmistakable pride. "I shall make you a present of one. But only if you are successful in this endeavor," he added firmly.

He nodded brusquely to the baroness as he withdrew, and she darted us an apologetic glance. "Take whatever time you need," she urged. "We will not trouble you until you call."

She closed the door softly behind them and I turned to face Stoker.

"I will not point out the peril of this undertaking," he said slowly. "I know you too well to believe that is any sort of deterrent to you."

"You raised the subject with the chancellor," I reminded him.

"Because I rather hoped he had more sense." The words might have stung but for the gentle mournfulness of the tone. My insistence upon this rash scheme had obviously struck a stretched nerve.

"It is the best opportunity to discover more about Alice Baker-Greene's death," I told him. "We believe someone in the Alpenwald wanted her dead, and someone in the royal entourage might know something."

" 'Someone,' 'something,' " he mimicked. "I think the connection is tenuous at best."

"Did you not mark the name of the guard captain? Durand. It is he who witnessed Alice's fall. *And* he has a rather impressive set of moustaches — as does the chancellor, who, I would like to point out, also sports a summit badge of the Teufelstreppe. We have been here a quarter of an hour and already discovered two potential suspects."

"Suspects! You really believe one of them pushed an Englishwoman off a mountain?"

"Not necessarily," I countered smoothly. "But at the very least, Captain Durand has knowledge of Alice's final climb — knowledge we will have the opportunity to extract if we spend time amongst these Alpenwalders. We might even be able to persuade them to reconsider opening a proper investigation, for I believe in my bones one of them is guilty of her murder."

"I highly doubt that," he said.

"Would you care to wager upon the fact?" I challenged. "We used to do so. I believe the stakes were a pound."

He drew his watch chain from his pocket. From it dangled a single sovereign coin, pierced to make a sort of charm of it. That coin had passed between us and back again as we had exchanged winnings on the wagers of our investigations. As a joke, Stoker had had the thing adapted to hang from his watch chain, a gesture of arrogance, I decided, as it meant he never intended I should win again. It was only in a moment of tender intimacy that he had admitted to wearing it because it was the one possession he had that I had also owned, and in the darkest days, when he dared not hope I would return his love, it was his consolation.

Now he gently removed it from the chain and pressed it into my palm. "Take it. You believe you are correct and I have lost the will to argue the point."

The metal was warm still from where it had nestled in his pocket, near his body. My fingers reached nearly closed around it, but I pushed it back into his hand. I would win it fairly or not at all. After a moment, he returned it to the chain.

"It is not like you to be so acquiescent," I said mildly. "Are you ill?"

"Not ill, but neither am I naïve. I understand why you are driven to do this thing and I will not fight you."

"I am driven by the need to see justice done for Alice Baker-Greene," I began, my

153

blood warming with indignation.

He put out his hand to touch mine, but seemed to think better of it. "If that is what you believe, then who am I to argue?"

"Stoker, if you have something to say, then be plain about it," I told him in a sharp tone. "I have no wish to play games with you."

"I am not the one you are attempting to deceive," he said.

"Deceive!" I squared my shoulders, preparing to defend myself with vigor, but just then the clock on the mantel began to chime. The little scarlet door opened and instead of the expected cuckoo, a small mountain goat toddled out. Whilst we watched, both horrified and entranced, it opened its mouth and noisily bleated the hour, sticking out its ruddy tongue for good measure.

"That is the ugliest thing I have ever seen," Stoker said at last.

"And possibly the loudest," I agreed. We exchanged a look of understanding, a sort of conspiratorial comprehension that had marked our relationship almost from the start, even when we were at our most adversarial.

"Stoker," I began, reaching for his hand.

But as quickly as the moment had come,

it fled again. Stoker slipped just out of reach and moved towards the door where the baroness and chancellor had disappeared. He knocked on it and the chancellor opened it at once. Clearly the Alpenwalder had been waiting, possibly with his ear to the door.

"Yes?" he asked eagerly.

"You have your princess," Stoker told him. "For tonight."

The chancellor did not bother to conceal his delight. "I am pleased to hear it. Naturally, there shall be a generous remuneration —"

Stoker bridled so hard I thought he might do a modest violence upon the chancellor.

"We do not require payment of any sort," he said through gritted teeth. The very notion of money changing hands was anathema to the British nobility, and Stoker still retained enough of his upbringing to have an uneasy relationship with wages of any variety. His accounts, I need not mention, swung wildly between lavish overdraft and equally impressive prosperity. As an aristocrat himself, the chancellor would have realized that offering payment was tantamount to insulting Stoker.

"That is very generous of you, Chancellor," I put in smoothly. "You should put any funds in the hands of the Royal Society for the Prevention of Cruelty to Animals on his behalf. Now, if you will excuse us, we have a few matters to attend to before returning this afternoon. I believe you said teatime?"

We took our leave of the Alpenwalders, and as Captain Durand closed and bolted the door of the suite behind us, I turned to Stoker.

"Is it absolutely necessary to let him put your back up like a feral cat?" I asked mildly as he rang for the lift.

"I do not like that man," he told me, his jaw set in a stern line. "I hope he ends up being the murderer. I can well imagine him pushing someone off a mountain."

"Perhaps he did," I soothed. "And we will be the ones to bring him to justice. In the meantime, I know precisely how to restore your good humor."

The doors of the lift opened and the operator gave us an inquisitive look. "Lobby," Stoker ordered.

"Not yet," I said, pressing a small coin into the operator's hand. "The kitchens, please. We have a call to make."

CHAPTER 9

One floor below the street level lay the true heart of the Sudbury, the various kitchens and workrooms and offices where the magic of the hotel's luxurious majesty was conjured.

The door dividing the public areas from the private was thickly lined with green baize to muffle the noises and odors from belowstairs, and it was heavy. Stoker put his shoulder to it and heaved it open, leading us immediately into a service corridor painted a sober workaday grey, a far cry from the lavish velvets of the levels above. We had been here before, guests of the pastry chef, Julien d'Orlande, and it was to his particular workroom that we made our way. Julien was hard at work, dressed in his usual elegant white coat, his head covered by a velvet cap of deep crimson. He held a bowl of gleaming silken chocolate in his hands, spooning it delicately over tiny choux buns, and his precision never wavered, not even when we burst in upon him.

"My friends!" His smile was, as ever, broad and genial. "This is a pleasure."

Yet something in the twitch of his lips told me this might be a pleasure but it was no surprise. "You knew we were here," I accused.

He dipped his spoon into the chocolate and dripped it slowly over another bun. "I know everything that happens in the Sudbury Hotel," he informed us.

"Useful if true," Stoker told him.

Julien looked affronted. "You doubt me? Everyone finds their way to my workroom sooner or later."

He put the bowl aside and reached for one of the buns he had enrobed earlier, the chocolate just set. "Try this," he urged. "It is a new confection, a choux bun stuffed with a *crème pâtissière* flavored with *myrtille* to make them a royal purple. I mean to top them with a little sugar crown as a *cadeau* for the Princess of the Alpenwald," he added, gesturing towards a tray of dainty golden crowns fashioned from spun sugar.

"*Cadeau?*" Stoker asked, rolling the word in an imperfect imitation. "Why not just say 'gift'?"

Julien shrugged. "Because French is so

much more elegant on the tongue, and it reminds Veronica that I am, unlike you, a cultured and sophisticated man. Now, do you want one or not?" he asked, pointing to the tray of crowns.

Stoker required no further invitation. He popped one of the buns into his mouth, his eyes rolling heavenwards as he chewed. Julien smiled again. "You like, my friend?"

The question was very nearly rhetorical. It was impossible to sample any of Julien's confections and not be enchanted. But like all geniuses, he lapped up praise as a kitten laps cream.

"Heavenly," Stoker assured him.

I opened my mouth to speak, but Julien stuffed one of the little buns in. "Taste," he commanded.

I did as he ordered, savoring for just a moment the lush extravagance of the berry-flavored cream, the crisp pastry, the darkly seductive chocolate. "Divine," I managed through a mouthful of choux.

Julien gave a nod of satisfaction, an emperor receiving his due.

Stoker began to speak but Julien raised a hand in mock horror. "My friend, we do not talk of unsavory things before the stomach has been prepared. It is almost time for luncheon, and you will eat with me. We will have good food and some excellent wine I have liberated from the hotel cellars as part of my wages, and then we will talk of other matters."

Stoker did not have the fortitude to resist Julien's offer. In a trice, one of Julien's minions had whisked away the trays of pastries and bowls of chocolate and cream, laying the worktable with a fine linen cloth and bringing chairs. An array of delectable dishes appeared — a simple soup, a game pie flavored with herbs, juicy cutlets, delicately roasted vegetables, a savory custard of leeks and cream. All was piping hot and served with a quiet deference that demonstrated the respect Julien commanded in the kitchens. With the food came the promised wine, soft as velvet on the palate, and I watched Stoker visibly relax, as contented as a jungle cat after bringing down a tender gazelle.

When the last bit of custard had been scraped up and the last crumb consumed, Julien spread his arms expansively.

"Now, why do you burst into my workroom without notice? You might have caused my masterpiece to collapse," he said with a gesture towards the marble table behind him. It was covered with tray after tray of dainties, each lovelier than the last —

rosewater puffs, fruits-of-the-forest tartlets, violet and blackberry gâteaux — but in the center sat an enormous meringue mountain, carefully sculpted to resemble the Teufel-streppe. Rivers of glacier-pale blue sugar flowed down the sides, and the top was heavily dusted with icing sugar. A soft drift of white sugary threads had been fashioned into a cloud and was, through some confectionary sorcery, attached to the peak, as if captured just at the moment it had drifted past the summit. Halfway down the mountain, an edible escarpment had been crafted, an outcropping to support a castle fashioned of golden pastry. It was very like the castle I had seen in the engravings at the Curiosity Club, complete with turrets and machicolations and a tiny silken banner attached to the flagpole.

"It is the most spectacular thing I have ever seen," I told Julien.

A lesser genius would have preened a little, but Julien merely accepted it as his due. "Of course it is because it is the best thing I have ever done."

"What is it for?" Stoker asked, putting out a tentative finger.

Julien slapped his hand away. "Do not touch it! Have another choux, have twenty, but do not even breathe upon my darling."

He stood protectively between his pastry sculpture and Stoker, who happily picked up the tray of choux buns and set to work. Mollified, Julien explained.

"It is to be displayed in the grand foyer of the hotel and then taken to the Curiosity Club for the opening of the exhibition. It was commissioned by the princess herself," he said proudly. I did not begrudge him his pleasure in his accomplishment. Julien had been born in the Caribbean to enslaved parents. His journey to France and to culinary excellence had required talent and sacrifice as well as an ironclad belief in his own abilities. His friendship with Stoker had been born in an instant when they recognized in one another the same character of bone-deep determination to do what they believed right, no matter the cost. My own relationship with Julien was grounded in flirtation and a keen appreciation for the talent behind his work as well as the sheer pleasure in looking at a handsome face.

"Wait here."

He disappeared into another room and returned bearing a tray which he presented to me with a flourish. *"Pâte de guimauve,"* he said. "In honor of the cat of the princess which is called by that name." The tray was laden with tiny delicacies molded in the shape of dainty cats.

"How charming! What are they?" I asked as I selected one.

"Rosewater meringues. They will melt upon the tongue. Try one," he urged. I did as he bade me. The confections had been tinted the palest shade of pink, the outside glossy and ever so slightly crisp. It dissolved almost instantly to a mouthful of rose-scented sweetness, not soapy, as one might expect, but tasting of sunshine and summer and a garden bursting into bloom.

"Exquisite," I told him.

He preened. "You say such delightful things to me, *ma chère* Veronique."

I fluttered my lashes a little and he puffed out his chest before plying me with dark chocolate bonbons topped with sugar-dusted violets. I ate two, emitting a tiny moan of pleasure as I did so.

Julien beamed at me in satisfaction. "For you it is a pleasure to create. You have the Gallic appreciation of the senses."

Stoker snorted at him, but Julien waved him away. "All Englishmen are philistines," he pronounced sternly before turning back to me. "You would do better with a French-man who would appreciate your subtleties."

He waggled his eyebrows at me in a sort of invitation, and I plucked another *gui-*

163

mauve from the tray, licking the marshmallow from my fingers when I finished.

"You are very good to me, Julien," I said. "And perhaps you would be better still and tell us if the manager of the Sudbury, Mr. Lovell, has recently taken on a new chambermaid. Tall, slender, clever eyes?"

Stoker darted me a look, and I mouthed a name at him. He suppressed a groan and stuffed another choux bun into his mouth.

"Ah! What Frenchman could resist those eyes?" Julien asked, rolling his own heavenwards. "So knowing, so full of promise."

"I thought you were attached to another maid, Birdie or Billie or some such," Stoker pointed out.

Julien's expression was pained. "Attached? 'Attached' is not a word that I like. It means to be tied, restricted, imprisoned. No, my friend. I prefer to think of my dalliances as larks, as light and dainty as the pastry in your mouth."

Stoker snorted and I sighed. "Julien, I do hope you are not seducing chambermaids and then leaving them unprotected in the world."

"I am shocked that you would suggest such a thing," he told me in an aggrieved tone. "Julien d'Orlande is a gentleman. Besides, I take always the precautions."

I held up my hands. "I have no wish to hear more. Now, what name did the chambermaid give you?"

"Jane," he said promptly. "I call her Jeanne, the French is nicer, no?"

"Did she give you a surname? Did she give you any hint as to her purpose in coming here?"

His brows drew together. "Surnames are so impersonal! Why would I wish to know such a thing when I could be discussing the shape of her lips instead? And her purpose in coming to the hotel is to work. I presume she is in need of wages."

"Has she given you any indication that she has another purpose?" Stoker inquired, taking up the thread of interrogation. "Asked any indiscreet questions? Particularly about the princess?"

"Now that you mention it," Julien said slowly, "she does ask quite a lot about the princess's tastes and habits, but this is because she wishes to do her job well. She must serve the princess, and perhaps she will receive a gratuity if she is quick and capable."

"Or because she wishes to write about her," I told him.

His mouth rounded in astonishment. "To write? She is a journalist, this Jane?"

"She is. Her name is J. J. Butterworth," Stoker supplied. "She writes for a filthy little rag called the *Daily Harbinger.*"

"I know this newspaper," Julien said, his mouth curving in disgust. "It is an abomination. Always with the ugly pictures and the sensational headlines. But they do have a very nice little column on the basic cooking," he added. "I did save a receipt for a perfectly adequate roast of the pork. It calls for a sauce made of apples which might be easily improved with a little freshly ground cardamom —"

"Julien," I said sternly. "To the matter at hand. Where might we find this Jane?"

"There is a sort of sitting room for the chambermaids when they are not about their business," he told us with a shrug.

"It will be full of other maids," Stoker said. "We need privacy in order to speak with her."

"Julien," I said, sweetening my voice. "We could use your assistance."

Julien quickly summoned one of the hotel pages to deliver a message, and within a very few minutes there was a low knock at the door of the workroom. Julien called a greeting and the door opened and closed swiftly. A slim figure, wrapped in a long white apron, and topped with a mobcap, had entered. The maid took one look at us and whirled, her hand on the knob, until Stoker clamped his firmly over the top and propelled her back to where Julien and I stood. He pushed her down onto a stool and folded his arms, looming just a little.

"Stay there," he ordered.

J. J. Butterworth looked up at him with sullen eyes. "I have work to do, you know. Those beds will not make themselves."

"It is lovely to see you as well, J. J.," I said politely.

"What do you want?" she asked, folding her arms over her chest.

"You wrote a piece on the death of Alice Baker-Greene," I began. "I presume you actually conducted interviews with the witnesses in question?"

"Of course," she said, tipping her nose into the air. "I would never write such a piece without a proper source."

"Why did you take on employment as a maid in this hotel? Surely it was a risk, given that you have spoken to Captain Durand. Were you not afraid he would recognize you?"

She snorted. "He has eyes only for the princess's little Slav maid, Yelena. They are betrothed but there has been trouble."

"What sort of trouble?" Stoker asked.

She shrugged. "A member of the guard doesn't earn much — not even the commander. And Yelena works for pennies. The Alpenwalders do not pay well on the grounds that it is an honor to serve them which is a heaping pile of *rot.* I mean, they dirty their sheets and fill their wastepaper baskets same as the rest of us."

"Careful, now. You begin to sound like a revolutionary," Stoker teased.

"If it could eliminate all the arrogant ne'er-do-wells I have seen in my time, I would build the guillotine with my bare hands," she said darkly. "But as to your question, the guards are bachelors and live in a sort of dormitory within the palace walls. In order to marry Yelena, Durand needs a house and they don't come cheaply in Hochstadt. It is a very small place and when it is crowded with mountaineers, the prices are steep as their blasted mountain. Well, Durand has served the Crown, loyal and true, since the princess was scarcely out of pinafores. He was promised a sort of grace-and-favor house on the castle grounds."

Julien looked puzzled, so I hastened to explain. "Grace-and-favor lodgings are given at the behest of the monarch in most countries, a sort of perquisite for faithful service. They are provided free of charge or for a peppercorn rent."

He nodded and J. J. resumed her tale. "But just as he was set to make an honest woman of Yelena and carry her over the threshold, the house was taken back again."

"For what purpose?" Stoker inquired.

She paused, holding the moment to heighten the drama with all the practiced theatricality of a Duse. "So that the house could be given to Alice Baker-Greene."

"Alice!" Stoker exclaimed. "Why on earth should the Alpenwalder Crown give her a house at the expense of the loyal Captain Durand?"

"Because of Duke Maximilian," I guessed.

J. J. slanted me a curious glance. "What do you know of Duke Maximilian?"

"I know he was friends with Alice Baker-Greene. *Close* friends," I added, waggling my brows in imitation of Julien.

"Ah," he said. "They were lovers."

J. J. shrugged. "I do not know what they were. I only know that Duke Maximilian was very keen to befriend her when she arrived in the Alpenwald, and after her death he has all but disappeared."

"Disappeared?" My voice sharpened with interest. "He is a member of a Continental royal family. How can he simply disappear?"

"A minor member of a minor family," J. J. corrected. "And he has not disappeared in the proper sense of the word. He has been spotted at his usual haunts — casinos and theatres and the odd house party. But he has kept a very low profile since Alice's death."

"That sounds rather suspicious," Stoker mused aloud. I was pleased to see he was taking a proper interest in the investigation, but I hoped he was not going to change his choice of murderer from the chancellor to the duke. I rather liked the duke as the villain and hoped it would earn me a sovereign.

J. J. prickled like a hedgehog. "Rubbish," she said succinctly. "He has nothing whatsoever to do with Alice's death. *Nothing*," she repeated with emphasis.

"How do you know?" I asked.

"Because I spoke with him and he was standing with Captain Durand during Alice's fall," she replied with a swiftness that seemed almost rehearsed. "Both of them swore to it in the inquest testimony as well."

"A good enough alibi," I said thoughtfully. "Of course, I do not imagine there is a guardsman alive in any country who would swear a member of his royal family was a liar," I added.

Her expression did not change, but her hands curled into fists, twisting her skirts. "Duke Maximilian had nothing to do with Alice's death. I would stake my life on it."

"Then who do you think did?" I asked. She hesitated and I went on. "I know you believe her death was not accidental and neither do we — no matter what the inquest verdict said. Stoker and I have come to the conclusion that Alice was murdered."

She choked a little and Julien hastened to bring her a glass of water. She drank it down, giving him a puzzled look. "It tastes odd."

"Mint," he said. "It adds a little something special."

"Water ought to taste like water." She thrust the glass back into his hands. She patted her lips with her apron. "It is a shock to hear it said aloud. I half thought I was going mad after that inquest. There were just so many things, peculiar things, and nobody in the Alpenwald seemed to care." She enumerated them on her fingers. "Why was Alice given Durand's house? Who was the moustachioed man on the mountain the day she died? Why was she climbing alone? Why was the inquest held so hastily?"

"Is that why you came here?" Stoker asked in a gentle tone.

She nodded. "My father was a writer, you know. He wrote for the *London Eagle*," she said with unmistakable pride. Although not as prestigious as the *Times,* the *Eagle* was a solidly respectable newspaper that prided itself on impeccable standards. Liberal politicians subscribed to it; Radicals adored it; Conservatives gave it to their servants for the wrapping of fish and use in the privy. "Forty years he wrote, chasing stories like a lurcher after a hare. And he always said the best journalists have a sense for it, nose as keen as a hound's for game. I had to keep after this because I smelt a story."

"And you thought you could discover something from the princess's entourage?" Stoker encouraged.

She shrugged and her entire demeanor seemed evasive. "My editor would not pay for another trip to the Alpenwald. There was no other way to pursue the story."

"What have you discovered?" I demanded.

Her gaze shifted only slightly. "Nothing of note," she said, studying her fingernails. "It is a private visit, not a state occasion, so there are no grand official events involving our royal family or politicians. A good deal of shopping and some private dinners is as exciting as it gets," she added.

"And have you been in the princess's suite

every day?" I asked.

She pulled a face. "As much as I dare. The work rota is jealously guarded, especially when there is royalty about. I have managed to slip into her suite twice, once yesterday and once this morning when you lot arrived." She narrowed her eyes. "And what exactly is your business with foreign royalty?" she inquired.

"We are assembling the exhibition at the Hippolyta Club meant to honor Alice Baker-Greene's life and achievements," I said quickly. "The Alpenwalders have taken a keen interest, naturally, and they sent for us to discuss a few details of the event."

She seemed contented with that, and I only hoped Stoker would not take it in his head to confide in her our real purpose in coming to the Sudbury.

To my immense relief, he steered her back to the subject of murder.

"Who do you think the moustachioed man was? The one on the mountain the day of Alice's death?"

J. J. gave him a narrow look. "Why should I tell you?"

"Because if you do, we might have something to share in return," he said.

"Stoker," I hissed by way of warning. He did not so much as look at me.

"J. J.?" he coaxed.

She stared at him a long, level minute. "Very well. I think it was Douglas Norton. I believe he was in the Alpenwald at the time of Alice's death, but I cannot prove it."

"This is nothing new," I protested. "You suggested as much in your last piece."

"For which I was let go from the *Harbinger*," she burst out. "Norton threatened the newspaper with a slander suit and they told me my services were no longer required. I have not been able to find proper work since then."

I looked at her work-roughened hands and the marks of fatigue under her eyes. And I thought of the story she knew — a story so explosive it might have detonated a revolution all on its own — and she had not sold it in spite of her necessity. She knew exactly who I was and only her promise kept her from exposing me to the world. She had given her word and would not go back on it, but only then did I realize how much it might cost her and how much she might resent me for it. I thought of my own circumstances as a lepidopterist and what choices I might make if I learnt of the choicest hunting grounds for the rarest of species and could never visit. What a poisonous secret that would be!

She must have intuited my thoughts, for she gave me a sharp look. "I have kept my word, you know. I haven't printed anything I oughtn't."

In spite of myself, I softened a little. I gave Stoker an almost imperceptible nod.

"J. J., we are not here on behalf of the exhibition. You will have gathered that we, too, believe there was foul play in Alice's death." He stopped just short of sharing with her the clues we had discovered — the duplicate climbing badge and the cut rope.

"We came here hoping to persuade the Alpenwalders to embark upon an investigation into Alice's death, but we have been unsuccessful," I temporized. J. J. Butterworth might have proved herself an able ally — and even a possible friend — in the past, but ours was an uneasy partnership, and I still hesitated to trust her fully.

"Is there anything else you can tell us that might help bring her murderer to justice?" I asked.

J. J. thought a moment, then shook her head. "I am afraid I cannot help you." She rose, smoothing her apron as she gave us a brittle smile. "I must take my leave of you now. The bathtubs will not scrub themselves, you know."

She left then without a backwards glance.

Julien sighed softly. "Such a waste of those hypnotic eyes," he said.

"How so?" Stoker reached for another choux bun.

"I have never met a woman so inflexible, so incapable of succumbing to pleasure," Julien lamented.

"You mean you were unsuccessful in luring her to your bed?" I asked.

"One of my few failures," he said with a mournful expression. "She thinks I am too fancy, too French. She likes plain words and plain deeds and I am not a plain man. She would be just the woman for you, my friend," he added with a laugh at Stoker.

I did not join in his amusement. Instead, I thought of her parting words.

Stoker looked at me. "She did not say she did not know. She said she cannot help."

"She knows something," I agreed. "But never mind J. J. Butterworth. We have no need of her," I added, collecting another bun to slip into my pocket for the next time Stoker felt peckish. "The devil helps those who help themselves."

CHAPTER 10

We spent the early afternoon at the Natural History Museum, bickering happily over the quality and position of the specimens, before presenting ourselves back at the Sudbury, where the baroness whisked me immediately into the princess's private rooms. The next few hours were deeply instructive. As the semi-legitimate daughter of the Prince of Wales, I might have had my own claim to a throne — at least in Ireland, where my father's marriage to my mother according to Catholic rites might have been recognized. But if this was what it meant to wear the purple, I had no inclination for the life. The baroness set to work as if she were planning a military operation and I was her objective. She hurried me into the bedchamber, where a young woman dressed in a simple blue gown with an enormous lawn apron waited at attention.

"This is Yelena, the princess's personal

maid," the baroness told me. "She is Russian. Her Alpenwalder German is passable but the accent grates upon the ear and her English is nonexistent. You might try a little French if you must speak with her but I do not encourage it."

I said a polite hello but the girl merely looked at me with enormous, slightly blank eyes. Her face had the broad, high-boned look of the Slav, and her blond hair was neatly plaited and coiled at the nape of her neck. I recalled what J. J. had said about Captain Durand's interest in the girl and I was not surprised. She was quietly pretty with the watchful look of all good servants. The baroness rattled off a series of instructions at her in the peculiar Alpenwalder dialect, and the girl bobbed a curtsy to show she understood.

I glanced about the room, taking in my surroundings. Furnished in the same quiet luxury as the rest of the suite, the bed-chamber was a study in tastefulness. Yelena might not have been the most articulate of servants, but she kept the room neat as a pin. No stray articles of clothing, no traces of face powder or trimmed threads, were to be seen. The books on the bedside table had been stacked in order of size, squared off at a precise angle. The pillows on the bed were plumped to an exact sameness, and the chairs tucked in the embrasure of the French windows were as rigidly correct as the sentry outside. Even the recamier of dark raspberry velvet had been positioned exactly in the center of a *faux bois* screen stretched across one corner of the room. The only unexpected note came from the plump Persian cat sitting majestically upon the dressing table. It regarded me with a long, unblinking stare.

"How do you do," I said politely, for I have always believed that while one may be familiar immediately upon making a dog's acquaintance, a cat will stand for no such informality.

The cat gave me a slow blink of its jeweled eyes.

"That is Guimauve," the baroness told me. "He is spoilt beyond redemption."

"Guimauve," I repeated. "What an apt name!" It was the French word for the marshmallow flower, *Althaea officinalis,* a most useful herb with a broad white bloom that bore a striking resemblance to the creature before me.

The baroness issued another order to Yelena, who immediately collected the animal from the top of the dressing table and placed it on an azure silken cushion. It

179

meowed by way of complaint, but it seemed to be a token protest only, for it instantly fell to grooming its snowy fur and ignoring us entirely.

As the cat attended to his ablutions, I was stripped of my own clothing down to the bare skin, my nakedness swiftly covered with a silk chemise of such delicacy it felt like a fall of rose petals whispering over my flesh. I would rather enjoy playing at being a princess if all the garments were going to be so lavish, I decided.

But no sooner had the chemise settled on my skin than I was trussed within an inch of my life into a strangulating corset of merciless dimensions. Unlike my own light-weight athletic corset, which permitted great ease of movement with only modest support, this monstrosity was clearly fashioned of steel with stays that might uphold a battleship if necessity demanded.

"I . . . cannot . . . breathe," I protested through gasps.

"Her Serene Highness has a very small waist," the baroness replied pitilessly. "You will not fit into her clothes if yours is not as narrow." She and Yelena together bore down with ruthless purpose on the laces again, drawing them tighter still until the stays creaked in protest and the baroness pronounced herself satisfied.

Once I was trussed like a pheasant fit for roasting, she sat me down — with difficulty — at a dressing table, where she gave Yelena detailed instructions about my hair. I watched the girl's reflection in the looking glass as she worked, pins held in her lips, hands moving quickly, deftly, as she first tonged my hair into long, smooth ringlets, then plaited the loose curls into a series of coils at the base of my neck and around my ears. Once this was done, a box of false hair was opened, and the baroness and the maid took a long time selecting the appropriate pieces, the baroness peering through her monocle as she chose.

"Does the princess wear false hair?" I asked in some astonishment.

The baroness shrugged. "Sometimes. Her own hair is much longer than yours — past her knees, in fact. But even she will augment her coiffure if the occasion demands."

"But why?" I asked. "Exactly how much hair does an Alpenwalder woman require?"

"Quite a lot," the baroness told me as she began to weave in the false pieces herself. Mercifully they were a match for my own, as the princess and I had nearly identical coloring.

The baroness explained as she worked.

181

"The Alpenwald played host to a very august visitor some years ago — the Empress Elisabeth of Austria. She was traveling incognita, you understand, but she is very fond of walking and our lakes offer excellent vistas for such sport. She is a distant cousin of the late Hereditary Prince and it was a very great honor to welcome her to the Alpenwald. As a gesture of respect, the court ladies dressed their hair like hers."

"The Austrian empress has hair like this?" I asked, gesturing towards the lavish construction taking shape upon my head. I had seen photographs of the empress, of course. She had been one of the great beauties of Europe in her youth. But I had not realized the effect was quite so painstakingly won.

The baroness gave a little laugh. "To her ankles! The loveliest hair you have ever seen. Chestnut brown and shining like silk. Of course, now she is an old woman like me and her hair has probably fallen out, but still we keep to the custom at our little court," she added pragmatically. I darted her a look to see if she was fishing for compliments, but none seemed expected. The baroness was past her youth, but in spite of the monocle and walking stick, she did not seem worn down by her years. Her eyes were still bright with vitality, and her skin was firm and supple.

She deftly wove in another false plait, securing it with a jewel-tipped pin handed her by Yelena.

"Do you always dress the princess's hair?" I asked. "It seems rather mundane work for a noblewoman."

She reconsidered the pin, removing it and thrusting it into place at a more becoming angle. "It is my honor. For everyday wear, Yelena's talents are sufficient, but when Her Serene Highness is making a public appearance, she prefers the traditional hairstyles of the Alpenwald, for which Yelena has not yet been trained."

Yelena went to the wardrobe and extracted a series of boxes with labels from the most exclusive couturiers in Paris. From the largest, she removed a gown covered in a muslin shroud, laying it as tenderly as she would a babe upon the bed, unwrapping it inch by inch. I stared in awe when it was at last revealed in all its glory. Cut in the most recent fashion, it was narrow of skirt with an elegantly draped train sweeping to the back in elaborate folds like those of a butterfly's wing. The neckline was low and rounded and the bodice had been fashioned without sleeves, designed to bare a considerable expanse of flesh. Yelena busied herself laying out the various outer garments and accessories, leaving it to the baroness to apply the various layers of cosmetics, which she did with a heavy hand, further enhancing my resemblance to the princess.

"Luckily, Her Serene Highness has thick brows," the baroness told me, lighting a match. She burned it a moment, then blew it out, waving it for a few seconds to let the glowing end subside to a sooty tip. "Just a bit of embellishment and they will be very similar." She dotted the soot into my brows, blending it carefully and deepening the black hue. She stepped back to regard her handiwork. "The princess is a little paler than you. She is very mindful of the delicacy of her complexion." The baroness's tone carried a light reproof as she pounced my face thickly with rice powder scented with orchid. "That is better."

She glanced at my hands. "These have the marks of a woman who works." I was surprised. My hands were scrupulously clean, but pens leaked, specimen pins scratched. I held them out for her and she coated them with cream scented with a fragrance that was almost but not entirely familiar.

"It smells floral, nearly of rose, but something else," I said, trying to place it. "Something like mint."

"It is St. Otthild's wort," she told me. "It is the only thing that grows above the tree line of the Teufelstreppe. It has medicinal properties as well as being fragrant. It will soften your hands, but it will take many applications. You will not remove your gloves tonight," she told me sternly.

"Your Teufelstreppe must be an interesting place," I mused. "Named for the devil and yet hospitable to such a plant."

The baroness smiled. "Do you know the history of our mountain?"

"Only that it is named for the devil's staircase, a difficult part of the climb."

She rolled her eyes heavenwards. "That is the talk of men. Every Alpenwalder climbs the mountain to prove his manhood and many of them reach the summit — it is practically a rite of passage for them. They speak of the danger and the difficulty, but it is the women who know the real story of the Teufelstreppe."

Her hands moved deftly, almost automatically, as she went about her tasks. Her voice pitched low and soothing, as if telling a bedtime story. "Long ago, when the mountain had no name, the prince who ruled our land was a pagan with a beautiful daughter called Otthild."

"Like your saint," I put in.

"The very same. Now, this prince was eager for riches and honors, so he pledged his beautiful daughter to a great king who was also a pagan. But the Princess Otthild had become a Christian and she refused to marry her father's chosen bridegroom. Her father beat her for her willfulness and threatened other tortures and so she ran away, climbing up the mountain. Her father and her bridegroom brought search parties up the peak, but no one could find her, for the maiden princess had prayed and a mist descended from heaven, cloaking her from view. She remained there, safe in her aerie where no one could find her. But someone did," she added, pausing for dramatic effect.

"Who?" I demanded.

"The great tempter himself — Lucifer! He came to the princess and offered her riches to repudiate God and take a pagan husband."

"Why should the devil care?" I asked.

The baroness clucked her tongue. "Do not ask questions! You look for logic with a scientist's mind and this is a story about magic."

I fell silent and she went on.

"The devil tempted her for three days, and each day the princess refused, growing

186

colder and fainter from hunger. But she would not give in, and at last the devil, too cold himself to stay upon the mountain, ran away. Now the princess was too weak to move. The cold and the hunger had stolen her strength and she lay near death, but she had held fast to her principles. So God called upon the creatures of the forest to help her. 'Not I,' said the mountain goat," the baroness said in a deep basso profundo voice. " 'Nor I,' said the fox," she continued, raising her voice to the sharp edge of a fox's bark. " 'Nor I,' said the squirrel. And so it continued with all the creatures of the forest. Except the otter. He climbed from his river, sleek and quick, and he stole a loaf of bread to carry up the mountain to the dying princess. And when she had eaten, he curled himself around her, giving her warmth until her strength was restored. She came down the mountain with the otter at her side, and lived long enough to tell her story to the priest who found her. She died in the priest's arms, but her story became legend, and she was made a saint. And that is how the devil's staircase, the Teufel-streppe, earned its name."

"An unfortunate young woman," I remarked.

"Unfortunate! She was called to sainthood," the baroness corrected. "She was one of the great virgin martyrs and the only one from the Alpenwald."

She carried on with her grooming tasks, and in between she schooled me on matters of etiquette and deportment. "You must carry your head at all times as if you were wearing a crown," she instructed. "Of course, tonight you will be."

"I have to wear a crown?" The assorted false pieces of hair and jeweled hairpins were constricting enough. I was not entirely certain my head would bear more weight.

"Not a crown precisely," she assured me. "But a very fine tiara. It *is* a gala performance, you will recall. The princess must represent her country as a monarch."

She hefted the ring of keys from her belt and went to a portable cabinet in the corner. It was a beautiful affair of inlaid wood depicting mountain scenes with forests and lakes and dancing bears and lissome maidens. "It is a lovely piece," I told her.

She lifted out a casket and locked the cabinet carefully up again. "The princess never travels without it. It is an example of our artisans' works." It might have been another example of Alpenwalder craftsmanship, but it was much more charming than the dreadful goat clock. The casket was also made of wood, but as the baroness opened it, she showed me the steel panels inside, cushioned with velvet. "A strongbox, but made to be pretty. All things that may be made beautiful ought to be," she explained. She drew out a velvet case and with a flourish flung back the lid. I gasped aloud. The jewels inside were shimmering, catching at the light and tossing it back again, a thousand times over in an endless parade of brilliance. It was a parure, a matched set of enormous sapphires and amethysts shading from the wine-dark hues of midnight seas to the pale blues and purples of an Alpine evening. Larger stones had been set in the frame of the tiara whilst high loops of jewels circled around smaller gems hung *en tremblant* to swing gently as the wearer moved. Diamonds twinkled like stars throughout, leading the eye from the tiara to the girandole earrings and on to the high, collared necklace. A pair of bracelets and a wide stomacher completed the suite.

I stared at them, mesmerized, hardly daring to breathe upon their magnificence.

The baroness's stern expression softened. "They are exquisite, are they not? A collection that once belonged to Marie Louise, the second empress of Napoléon. One of her nieces married into the Alpenwalder royal family and brought the parure with her. Our princess prefers it to the state jewels because it is lighter."

She signaled to Yelena, who fastened the earrings to my ears the old-fashioned way, by means of narrow silk ribbons tied around the ear to hold the weight of sapphires the size of cherries. They swung heavily against my neck, almost touching the necklace she clasped about my throat. The last piece to go on was the tiara, nestled into the arrangement of plaits. I poked it idly with a finger, watching in concern as it wobbled a little.

"How on earth am I to keep it steady?" I asked.

The baroness reached for her chatelaine, extracting a threaded needle. She advanced upon me, and without a word, she stitched the tiara into my hair, whipping the needle around the base of the coronet and through one of the false plaits. When she was finished, she gave the tiara a hearty, painful tug. "There," she pronounced in satisfaction. "It will sit as it should."

I could scarcely turn my head for the combined weight of the wigs and jewels. "You will soon accustom yourself to it," she assured me. "The more you wear it, the less you will notice it."

"Luckily it is only for tonight," I replied. The baroness said nothing but turned to Yelena, signaling to her to pack away the various cosmetics as the baroness herself locked away the jewel cases.

"It *is* only for tonight," I pressed.

The baroness gave me a thin smile. "We have a saying in the Alpenwald, *Fraulein.* Plans are jokes written by men for God's amusement."

"That is hardly reassuring," I told her.

"It sounds better in German."

CHAPTER 11

The baroness carried on with her preparations by going to the bed, smoothing over the folds of the gown that Yelena had laid out, straightening the various ribbons and laces. She handled the princess's things respectfully, reverently almost.

My eyes fell to a large gilded box on the dressing table, the wares of one of our most exclusive chocolatiers, I realized. The baroness's attention never left the clothing she was inspecting, but nothing escaped her.

"You must help yourself, Miss Speedwell — but do so now if you wish a chocolate. It will not be possible once you have begun to dress."

I lifted the lid of the box to find a selection of violet and rose creams — Stoker's favorites.

"These are rather too rich for me," I said politely, thinking of the delicacies Julien had pressed upon me during luncheon. "Would you care for one, Baroness?"

The baroness's nostrils flared in an expression akin to outraged horror, but she managed a polite refusal. "This is not possible, *Fraulein.* It is not my place to eat with my princess unless I am invited."

"But I am not your princess," I pointed out. "And I have invited you."

She drew herself up, her posture impeccably straight. "I think it best if I treat you as I would Her Serene Highness in order to preserve this masquerade."

The baroness bent again to her task.

"You are very fond of your princess," I ventured.

She carefully plucked a bit of fluff from the skirt of the gown before replying. "I have been in the service of the Crown all my life. It is my honor to serve."

"How is it that all of you speak such good English?"

"The princess's great-grandmother was English, one of your own princesses — Sophia Amelia, a sister of your King George III, the poor mad one," the baroness said as she moved a pair of evening slippers exactly perpendicular to the end of the bed.

I had known that one of King George's sisters had married the Danish king and had a very bad time of it — husband run insane, lover beheaded, early death from fever, that sort of thing — but I had not realized any other of his relations had married onto the Continent. He was my great-great-grandfather, but I had scarcely given him a thought other than as the sad old man who had lost the colonies and himself gone mad, ending his life stone deaf and blind to boot, wandering around Windsor Great Park in his nightgown and talking to the oaks. It gave one pause to realize such possibilities were lurking in the family tree.

"Was your English princess happy in the Alpenwald?" I asked.

The baroness blinked. "Happy? What do you mean?"

"Simply that," I said. "Was she content to live so far from home? Did she love her husband? Her children?"

The questions seemed to put her at a loss and she struggled to answer. "I do not know how to reply to this, *Fraulein.* It is not for princesses to be happy. Their duty is to rule, to set an example."

It sounded ghastly, I decided. "Did she have a say in the marriage or was she simply shipped off?"

"Shipped off?" The idiom seemed to puzzle her.

"Yes, carted to the Alpenwald like so

much fruit for sale," I said, a trifle tartly. "It is a barbaric custom, the exchanging of royal daughters in the manner of livestock trading for the purpose of sealing treaties. Was that her lot?"

"There was a friendship established between our two nations," the baroness admitted. "But this was a good thing. Your kings named George brought German values to England. We understand that."

"And did the princess bring English values to the Alpenwald?" I asked.

She primmed her mouth. "It is not, you will forgive me, the place of the English to teach the Alpenwalders anything. We were good to your princess."

She turned away, obviously offended. I hastened to make amends. "I did not intend any insult," I assured her. "I merely wondered if she did a good job of things, if she ruled well."

The baroness said nothing for a long moment, continuing to straighten and tidy, her chin high in her wounded dignity. I ought to have remembered, with countries — like men — the more diminutive the stature, the more overweening the pride.

Finally, she unbent a little. "She was only a consort," she told me. "It was not her destiny to rule, but she was popular. She was a pious woman and conducted herself with dignity at all times. There was a grandeur to her that was deeply respected by her people."

Dignity and piety, I thought ruefully. If those were the qualities respected most by the Alpenwalders, it was a devilishly good thing I was only pretending at being their princess. I gave her a winsome smile. "And is her granddaughter much like her, the Princess Gisela, I mean?"

To my surprise, the baroness did not parry. She threw up her hands in exasperation. "I wish she were! To run away like this, so indiscreet, so irresponsible!"

She collapsed onto the recamier, head in her hands. I rose and went to her, putting a hand to her shoulder. "You are obviously very fond of your princess. Have you been her lady-in-waiting long?"

"Since her accession," she said with obvious pride as she dropped her hands. "But I was her governess before that. I came to her when she was fourteen after I finished my duties as governess to her cousin, Duke Maximilian. I have always served the Alpenwalder royal family. And now —" She broke off, clearly overcome.

"Do not worry so, Baroness. I am sure it will all be quite all right in the end."

She lifted her head, moisture gathering in the corners of her eyes. "You are an optimist, *Fraulein.* You are very young."

I shrugged. "It has been my experience that things generally work out for the best."

"For the best!" She gave a hollow laugh. "How can that be? If she does not return —"

I tightened my grip on her shoulder in what I hoped was a reassuring gesture. "She will. We can have no doubt."

She smiled in spite of herself. " 'We,' *Fraulein*? Already you speak like a royal."

"I have a very good tutor, Baroness," I told her seriously. "Now, come and teach me how to wave."

She surged up, horror blanching her cheeks. "One does not *wave* at the theatre," she said sternly. With that she launched into a lengthy explanation of the correct way to acknowledge the public in a theatre — "a slow inclination of the head from the neck beginning with the most august personages —"

When she finished, she led me to the bed, where the gown lay waiting. The fabric shimmered, the heavy silk woven with some starry silver bits that punctuated the extraordinary blue of the background.

"It is such a glorious color." I breathed at

last, putting out a fingertip to touch the folds of the skirt. I trailed down to a silver sequin. A rope of these had been stitched around the base of the skirt, edging the train as well as the neckline.

"It is Alpenwalder blue," she told me. "The color reserved for our royalty as it most closely mimics that of the heavens above our country."

Her face shone with pride as she helped me into the gown, drawing it carefully over my undergarments and lacing it tightly into place.

As she finished knotting the ribbons, she paused, peering intently at my upper arm. "What is this?" she demanded.

She put a fingertip to my flesh, pointing out the small gathering of fresh scars scattered over my arm like a constellation.

"Battle scars, I am afraid," I told her. "I was shot."

She reared back in astonishment. "Shot? With a firearm? By whom?"

"My uncle," I replied truthfully.

The baroness stifled a gasp of horror. "Tell me no more. But this is a noticeable flaw, *Fraulein,* and it will mark you as different to the princess to anyone with sharp eyes. We must have a remedy . . ." She trailed off as she went to the dressing table, rummaging through the drawers until she emerged, triumphant. She held a wide ribbon of silver satin, which she tied firmly about my upper arm, securing the ends in a bow.

She stepped back to survey the effort, frowning. "What do you think?"

"Rather dashing," I assured her. "And who knows? If anyone does remark upon it, I may find myself in the fashion papers as an innovator."

She did not return my smile. She merely gave a grunt and stooped to help me into my shoes, court shoes of velvet in the same shade as the gown, and presented a long velvet mantle furred with a curious silver pelt.

"The *Geistenfuch*," she explained. "The ghost fox — a small silver fox that lives in the mountains. Very rare and very beautiful."

I wondered how many of the poor little beasts had been sacrificed for the robe, but it would be the rankest hypocrisy not to acknowledge that I was glad of the warmth. She draped and pinned a wide riband of white watered taffeta across my chest, securing it with a remarkably ugly brooch of considerable age. It was set with heavy, old-fashioned stones depicting a jeweled otter rampant.

"The order of St. Otthild," she informed me. "The otter is her badge, and this order is one of great antiquity. The lesser degrees feature the flower of St. Otthild's wort, but of course the princess is a member of the first degree," she said proudly.

Then she pulled on my kid gloves, thin and tight as a second-skin, buttoning them past my elbows. She clasped the bracelets of the parure over them, then positioned the mantle atop everything, handing me a matching muff of silver fox before stepping back to view her efforts.

"Will I pass muster?" I asked lightly. But I was conscious even as I uttered the words of a rather desperate desire for her approval. It suddenly seemed quite important to me that I do this well, for reasons I dared not even contemplate.

She regarded me a long time, sweeping her gaze from the tips of my evening slippers — embroidered with sequins and silver thread — to the tiara atop my crown of false hair. After an agonizing wait, she gave a slow nod. "You will do."

And I knew that faint praise held a wealth of emotion for her. She swallowed hard as she looked at me, no doubt missing her vanished princess. It was clear the baroness had great affection for her mistress, no matter how wayward she could be. Before I could offer some comfort, she turned away, briskly.

"I must go and make my own toilette," she told me. "You must not crease."

"I should not dream of it," I promised her. "I will sit here until you return."

"Sit!" The word was nearly a shriek. "You cannot sit! You must stand. Right there. Do not move. Pretend you are a waxwork from that Madame Tussaud until I return," she instructed.

She left me then, earrings quivering in indignation that I might be foolish enough to do anything as abjectly stupid as sit. I shifted my weight from foot to foot, suddenly acutely conscious of how very awkward it was to simply stand. I listened to the mantel clock — mercifully *not* an Alpenwalder goat clock — tick over the minutes, and just as the quarter hour chimed, the door from the sitting room eased open.

Stoker darted in, closing the door softly behind him. I gasped and instantly regretted it; the corset permitted no deep breaths, and I whooped with laughter as I attempted to catch my breath.

"You needn't be rude about it," Stoker reproached me in an injured tone.

"Forgive me," I managed. "I did not mean

to wound your pride. But . . . *moustaches.*"

Stoker had been scrubbed and polished to within an inch of his life, his chin freshly barbered, his nails cleaner than I had ever seen them, every trace of ink and glue removed. His hair had been clubbed back into an old-fashioned queue, and perched atop his head was a shako of dark blue trimmed with silver braid. They had found him a spare uniform, dark blue and silver, each button struck with an image of the Alpenwalder otter of St. Otthild, but it was his face that had undergone the greatest transformation. Between his nose and his lip burgeoned the most extravagant set of moustaches I had ever seen. Like those of the chancellor and Captain Durand, his had been waxed into the shape of a ram's horns, extending out from the edge of the mouth and then curling back in a grand flourish as black as his hair, thick and dense as a shrubbery. I went to him and poked with an experimental finger.

"It looks like a hedgerow. Have you got wildlife in there? I think I spy a badger," I said.

He grimaced, or at least I think he did. It was rather difficult to tell with the concealing layer of facial hair. "How on earth did they happen to come by such a monstrosity?" I asked him.

"Apparently they travel with contingencies," he explained. "The moustaches are part of the uniform and in case any of the officers meet with an accident, there is always a spare to hand."

"But why are you even in uniform?" I demanded. "Surely plain clothes would have been more discreet."

"That is what I thought," he told me in an aggrieved tone. "But then the chancellor happened to mention that a certain Inspector Mornaday has been tasked with the role of liaison with Special Branch."

"Hell and damnation," I muttered.

"I said a good deal worse when I discovered it," he told me. Mornaday was a complication we could ill afford. Our sometime ally and occasional champion, Mornaday was unpredictable as quicksilver. He longed for promotion within the confines of Special Branch — something he had recently achieved. But there was no telling how long his goodwill might last. The fact that he harbored a tendresse for J. J. Butterworth complicated the situation. He had, once or twice to my knowledge, fed her titbits that would give her an exclusive story for the *Daily Harbinger.* As keen for her advancement as his own, he made certain to paint his involvement in a good light. In payment for his indiscretion, she always mentioned him in laudatory tones. It was a symbiotic relationship, that of parasite and host, I thought bitterly. It was Mornaday's deficiencies of imagination that led him to think he was the host. I knew perfectly well he was often steered towards a story by the impetuous and deeply ambitious Miss Butterworth.

"What of Sir Hugo?" I asked suddenly. "If Mornaday is there, his superior cannot be far behind."

"Sir Hugo is abed," he told me. "With gout."

"Poor fellow," I said with real sympathy. "We must send him a nice calf's-foot jelly."

"Or perhaps just a calf's foot," Stoker suggested, a gleam in his eye. He and Sir Hugo enjoyed a state of armed neutrality at the best of times.

I sighed as best as I could in my confining garb. "I suppose we will simply have to make the best of it. Keep your moustaches primped and your shako pulled low."

Stoker gave me an appraising glance, from extravagant jewels to exuberant décolletage. "I do not think I will be the one they are looking at." He nodded to the impossible slimness of my waist. "How can you eat in that?"

"I cannot eat," I told him coldly. "I cannot bend. I cannot breathe. In short, I cannot do anything for which the human body is fashioned. I am an automaton for the evening, a doll, dressed and polished for your amusement."

I might have carried on in the same vein, but his attention was drawn to the large gilded box on the dressing table. I sighed. "Rose and violet creams. Help yourself."

He required no further urging. With a soft moan of pleasure, he reached into the box and took one of each, mingling the heavy floral creams in a single mouthful. His eyes rolled backwards. "Heaven," he managed through the chocolate and cream. He reached in to take another, but suddenly his gaze sharpened and he plucked out a piece of card.

"What is this?"

I shrugged — a mistake, I realized at once, for it sent my earrings swinging painfully against my neck. "A note from the sender, I presume."

He shook his head. "I doubt it. It was hid beneath the top layer of chocolates. And it is not precisely friendly." He handed over the bit of card, a little grubby thanks to its proximity to the chocolates and printed simply. It smelt of sugar, but the message was none too sweet. *PREPARE FOR YOUR END.*

"A threat to the princess," I breathed. I inspected the note for clues, but it had been hastily scrawled in an obvious attempt to disguise the handwriting, each letter printed in a harsh block capital on a torn bit of paper. I turned horrified eyes to Stoker. "Poison," I said succinctly.

He heaved a sigh and went into the washroom. I do not know exactly what precautions he took to rid himself of the chocolates, but there was the distinct sound of retching and then the running of water. When he returned, his moustaches were a fraction less exuberant than they had been before, but he appeared well enough. I gripped his face and peered into his eyes.

"Your pupils seem normal. Stick out your tongue," I ordered.

He pushed my hands aside, but gently, as he stuck out his tongue. His breath smelt of peppermint drops. "I am perfectly fine," he insisted.

"You may have been poisoned," I pointed out.

"Hardly likely," he said. "The chocolates smelt and tasted fine."

"Some tasteless substance," I began.

"Much more common in fiction than in reality," he assured me. "And I have rid myself of anything possibly noxious, which was a dreadful waste of good chocolate."

I gave him a narrow look. "You will tell me if you feel at all unwell?"

"Well, I am hungry now," he told me, stroking his chin thoughtfully. He rummaged in his pockets, unearthing a slab of shortbread wrapped in paper.

"You have the digestive capabilities of a gannet," I told him. I turned my attention to the box. "When was this delivered?"

He examined it closely, shrugging. "There is nothing to indicate when it arrived or from whom."

"Do you think she saw it?"

He considered a moment. "I should think not. If she saw it, she would have surely shown it to Durand or the chancellor."

"She mightn't have liked to," I pointed out. "It is rather unpleasant."

"All the more reason to pass it to the men responsible for her security," Stoker countered. "And if she chose not to do so, why replace it in the box?"

"Out of sight, out of mind?" I suggested. "A stalwart soul might have faced the thing directly, but we have heard from those nearest to her that she has been known to be elusive. Perhaps this is the sort of thing she runs away from."

His gaze sharpened. "You think she saw this and left of her own accord rather than being abducted?"

"I think we cannot rule anything out at present."

I thrust the note back into the box, carefully concealing it with the remaining bonbons. "There is no time to deal with this at present, but it is evidence of something. I only wish I knew what."

Stoker reached for my arm. "Veronica, I do not like this —" he began.

Before he could finish, the air was rent with a shriek. "Unhand her, sir! You will mark the velvet!"

The baroness entered, as stately as a ship in full sail. She had dressed her own hair in a more modest approximation of my own coiffure, piled high and embellished with plaits and jeweled pins. A tiara of garnets and enormous pearls sat atop, the *tremblant* pearls quivering in outrage. Her gown was the same hue as her gemstones, dark velvety red and edged in sables, the colors warming her pale cheeks almost as effectively as her rouge. A sash of the Order of St. Otthild crossed her bodice, pinned neatly with a jeweled otter badge. She wore no other decorations, but it was enough. She looked every inch the regal court lady.

She flicked a closed fan at Stoker, rapping him sharply upon the knuckles. "Know your place, sir."

He gave her a deferential bow and tried to catch my eye, but I let my gaze slide just to the side, never quite meeting his. It would have been an excellent joke to share if I had permitted it. But I felt unlike myself in the princess's clothes, armored almost, in satin and diamonds, aloof and untouchable. And when the baroness beckoned for me to walk ahead of her, I stepped forward on feet that scarcely seemed to touch the ground.

Just then, the sound of raised voices came from the sitting room. The chancellor made an exclamation — of some strong emotion, although whether it was pleasure or rage, I could not say. The baroness raised an imperious hand to me and to Stoker.

"Wait here," she instructed. She slipped through the door, and after a moment her voice was added to the muffled conversation. I could hear a man's laugh — distinctly not the chancellor's — and then the voices carried on for a few minutes, low tones occasionally punctuated by a quick question or exclamation from the visitor. At length the baroness flung open the door, her color high.

"*Fraulein,* you will come," she said. Stoker followed in my wake and I could feel the warmth of him standing just behind me when I stopped. The chancellor had been joined by a gentleman slightly taller than average height. He wore the customary Alpenwalder moustaches, but his were of a rich chestnut hue, only a little darker than the burnished waves of his hair. His eyes were very dark and bright with interest as he regarded me. He was wearing a uniform similar to the chancellor's, but with a dozen more medals and a riband of the princely order. Everything about him was just a shade more — where the chancellor and the baroness were limned in watercolors, this fellow was cast in brilliant oils.

His mouth, pink and plump lipped, curved into a smile as I approached. He surveyed me up and down, quickly at first, then a second time more slowly and not as respectfully as he would have done his princess, I was certain. He did not scrutinize; he ravished.

"Enchanting," he said in a low, melodious voice. He swept into a sudden low bow, his half cape touching the carpet. "I am Your

Serene Highness's most humble servant," he said.

I froze. Was I meant to play the part of the princess already? I had not been prepared for this meeting.

Before I could respond, he looked up at me through his lashes, grasping my hand. "Your *most* humble servant," he repeated, brushing his whiskers over my fingers. But his thumb was doing something decidedly uncourtly to my palm and I withdrew my hand as he laughed, showing a good deal of his straight white teeth.

He turned to the chancellor. "She is the very image of Gisela. Well done."

"You have the advantage of me, sir," I told him, but I already knew. I had known the moment I laid eyes upon him, although the photographs had not done him half justice.

He grinned. "Permit me to introduce myself, mademoiselle. I am His Grace, Maximilian, Duke of Lokendorf and the Alpenwald and your fiancé."

CHAPTER 12

From behind me, Stoker gave a muffled growl, which I stifled by stepping carefully backwards onto his foot. I turned to the baroness for an explanation.

"We did not expect His Grace until tomorrow," she said tightly. "This is an unexpected honor."

"What are the pleasures of Monte Carlo against the incomparable joy of spending time with my betrothed?" he asked, his mouth twitching.

"Are you not in the least concerned that she is missing?" Stoker put in.

The duke gave him a dismissive glance. "Who is this man? He is not one of us."

"No," the chancellor hastened to explain. "He is a friend of the *Fraulein*'s and insisted upon accompanying her for her own safety. I am to duel him later. Perhaps," he added swiftly as the baroness shot him a look of displeasure.

The duke smiled again. "How very interesting. Perhaps we will duel as well," he said, touching two fingers to his brow and saluting Stoker in a manner that was clearly calculated to annoy.

But Stoker refused to rise to the bait. "I have no objection," he said mildly.

The duke turned back to me. "They have made a good job of you, mademoiselle. But you stand a much better chance of passing as Gisela with my help."

"What sort of help?"

He raised his brows in mock reproof. "How forbidding you look! Not easy with such a lovely face. I mean, mademoiselle, that I shall accompany you to the opera tonight."

"Out of the question," the baroness stated in her best governess voice.

The teasing expression turned serious. "I think," the duke said in a dangerously soft voice, "that you do not mean to be impertinent, Baroness."

She flushed a little. "I meant no disrespect, Your Grace."

The duke gave her a hearty kiss upon the cheek, smacking his lips loudly. "I am jesting with you, Margareta! You know your little Max better than that."

Her smile was indulgent. "I spoilt you as a

child, I fear."

"Impossible!" he cried. "For I am perfect, just as I am." The baroness's distress had fled and I wondered how strange it must be to rule the nursery — no doubt with an iron fist — only to have one's charge grow into manhood, poised to take the reins of power.

The duke turned his smiles to me, but there was something a little aloof in his manner, and I realized he was forcing himself to cordiality. "The baroness worries when she should not. Her princess is in very good hands with me, and so should you be," he assured me.

"You are not betrothed to our princess yet," the chancellor said, lifting his chin.

The duke's eyes rested on him a moment too long for comfort. Then he nodded. "It is truth, what you say, Chancellor. I have asked and she has not yet accepted me. But I think we know that she will. In time."

"Are you not concerned about her whereabouts?" Stoker asked bluntly. "Surely that is of greater importance than helping Miss Speedwell sustain this ludicrous masquerade."

The duke gave a thoughtful nod. "You make an excellent point, sir. But this 'ludicrous masquerade' is more important than you perhaps understand. I have no doubt that Gisela is perfectly fine. She is always slipping away to avoid engagements she would rather not attend. She will turn up in a day or so, looking quite pleased with herself, I promise you. Besides," he added smoothly, fluffing the plume on his shako, "if it were made public that I had arrived in London and was not permitted to escort my intended wife to the opera, what a scandal this would make!"

The baroness gave a little cry of distress. "You would speak to the newspapers — Max, no!"

The duke shuddered. "You wound me, Baroness. I, highest-ranking duke of the Alpenwald, lower myself to speak to a journalist? You insult me," he said, shaking his head with a mournful downward pull of the lips. "But naturally as I am in London and it is Sophie Fribourg making her debut in the role of Atalanta, it is my duty to attend and to witness her triumph. I would not let it be said that I am slow to uphold the glory of my country," he finished with a little bow.

The baroness made no further objections, giving her former charge another of her exasperated smiles. It was left to the chancellor to agree. "Of course, Your Grace," he said quietly.

The duke, having got his way, rubbed his

hands together and beamed a smile around the room. He put out his arm and I laid my hand on top of it. He leaned close enough so that I could smell his toilet water — something with sandalwood and herbs. "What fun we shall have together, my pretty," he murmured.

Behind me, Stoker growled again.

"There is another person you ought to meet," the chancellor said. He signaled to the baroness, who opened the outer door and beckoned to the guard outside. Captain Durand stood at attention, snapping his heels together as he reached the chancellor and giving a sharp bow.

No doubt for my benefit and Stoker's, the chancellor spoke English. "Captain, you have been informed of the circumstances and what is at stake. This is Miss Speedwell, who is assuming the role of the princess for the evening. Miss Speedwell, the commander of the princess's guard, Captain Durand."

The etiquette of the little court in the Alpenwald was clearly one of formality, but there seemed no obvious protocol for greeting an ersatz princess. I nodded to him and he clicked his heels together, giving me not the deep bow that royalty would have demanded, but a cursory nod in return.

"The captain will naturally escort us this evening, but arrangements for the princess's security have been made by the Special Branch of the Metropolitan Police," the chancellor informed us. I resisted the urge to exchange glances with Stoker. There was an excellent chance that someone of our acquaintance would be amongst the policemen assigned to the princess, but I was not worried that my own masquerade would be revealed. I had long ago learnt in my field experiences as a lepidopterist that invariably one sees what one expects to see. Many species of butterfly are gifted with protective coloration lending them the appearance of a predator's eye or a dried leaf in order to discourage those who would feed upon them. Would-be marauders give such species a wide berth because they do not see them as they are, but as what they present themselves to be. With my formal gown and jewels and royal entourage, I would appear a princess to all who looked, so long as I made no obvious missteps. Stoker, however, was another matter altogether. He was entirely too remarkable. He had pocketed his gold earrings, but the eye patch and uncommonly intelligent expression were impossible to disguise. I could only hope that with most eyes upon me, those likeliest to expose him would pass by him, oblivious to the cuckoo in the nest.

The chancellor looked at the hideous mantel clock and clucked his tongue. "Come now, it is time," he urged, taking up his own befeathered hat and swirling cloak. We assembled, and as we made our way downstairs, the captain took the opportunity to speak with me.

"The resemblance is most remarkable, *Fraulein*," he said at last, his English heavily accented.

"Thank you, Captain. I presume you have met Mr. Templeton-Vane?" I gestured towards Stoker and the captain's mouth pursed beneath his moustaches.

"I have. That is my uniform," he said with a lowering look. "It has been altered because you are a very small man."

Stoker, whose inches just topped a perfectly respectable six feet, raised a brow. "Not where it matters," he said just loudly enough for me to hear.

"What is that you say?" the captain demanded.

"Nothing at all, Captain," Stoker said, smiling broadly at him. "Nothing at all."

I received the first of many surprises that evening when we emerged from the hotel to

218

the sight of crowds assembled on the pavement. Several constables were holding them back as they surged forward, eager for a glimpse of a princess. I cut my eyes to the baroness — the tiara was far too heavy to permit quick movement — and she gave an almost imperceptible nod.

"Wave," she murmured as she bent near to fuss with my mantle. "Just hold your hand up in the air — not like that! You are not a bank clerk hailing a hackney." I tried again, simply lifting my gloved hand in a small salute. The crowd responded with a muted roar and pushed forward. The constables linked arms to push them further back, but by the time they had managed it, the baroness had bundled me into a waiting carriage. It was a handsome affair, lavishly polished and marked with the hotel's crest.

"The Sudbury has made their equipage available for the duration of our stay," the chancellor said as he climbed in after the baroness and I had settled ourselves. The captain swung himself up into a seat next to the driver, his hand resting loosely upon his sword. Duke Maximilian vaulted in next, leaving Stoker standing upon the pavement.

The duke favored Stoker with a grin. "The help rides on the outside," the duke told him as the hotel's doorman stepped smartly up to slam the door. The carriage gave a lurch as it sprang from the curb, leaving the crowds behind.

Stoker must have secured a seat for himself somewhere — or perhaps he hung on the back like one of the larger brachiating primates — for he was the one who opened the carriage door as soon as we arrived at the opera house. I was familiar with the venue, having attended the opera on the arm of Stoker's eldest brother, Tiberius, upon occasion. Tiberius and I were enthusiasts whilst Stoker maintained that, apart from sea chanties, no decent music had been written since Handel.

With his witty urbanity and love of luxury, Tiberius was a delightful escort for an evening's entertainment, and I had thoroughly enjoyed the hours spent in his velvet-draped box. But we had attended for love of the music, largely ignoring the crowds of society peepers gathered to gossip and survey with sharp-eyed interest all the goings-on — a far cry from being the guest of honor at a royal gala. My anonymous pleasure was at an end.

Stoker gave a smart bow as he handed us from the carriage, and I left my hand in his a moment longer than necessary, squeezing his fingers as I let go. An even larger crowd awaited us here, intent upon seeing the elusive Princess of the Alpenwald as well as the other dignitaries making an appearance. A long line of them stood on an azure carpet — the distinct Alpenwalder blue, I noted, laid no doubt as a compliment to the delegation. I walked towards them, inclining my head just enough to make the jewels swing a little. Any harder and they clattered against the frame, the baroness had warned me. The officials were a collection of diplomats, opera patrons, society beauties, and assorted hangers-on. The baroness prodded me discreetly in the ribs to stop in front of the most heavily decorated one, a tiny little man with the usual lavish Alpenwalder facial hair.

"Your ambassador," the baroness said, concealing her mouth with a subtle flick of her fan. She had explained in the carriage that the ambassador had been an appointment of the princess's grandfather and had not met the princess since she was a child. He would not recognize an imposter, she had assured me, and seeing his thick-lensed spectacles, I was inclined to agree with her.

I put out my hand, leaving it hanging in the air between us. "Excellency," I began.

He seized it with real vigor and touched it to his forehead. "Your Serene Highness," he pronounced, clicking his heels together as he bowed. "It is a very great honor to welcome you to our host nation's most illustrious cultural institution for an event which will bind our two countries together even further in harmony."

He bowed again at the conclusion of this pompous little speech and snapped his fingers. A child dressed in traditional Alpenwalder costume of embroidered dirndl and apron came forward, staggering under the weight of an enormous bouquet of white roses. The ambassador presented them to me with a flourish, and I took one deep, heady inhalation of the blooms. They were so wildly out of season, they must surely have come straight from the hothouse. I smiled my thanks and passed them to the baroness. She took them with a practiced gesture and I moved on. Duke Maximilian stepped up to escort me up the grand staircase, turning this way and that to nod to the assembled crowds as we ascended.

He shot me an amused glance. "You are a natural at this," he whispered, taking care that his moustaches should brush my cheek.

"It is hardly difficult," I said. I was aware of the baroness and chancellor hard behind us with the captain and Stoker bringing up the rear. The duke and I were presenting a picture of an intimate conversation, I had little doubt.

His smile deepened. "You would be surprised. Our late Queen Adelaide was not at all personable. She used to scowl at people. Of course, it might have just looked that way because of her moustaches," he said with mock seriousness.

"Do not make me laugh," I told him severely. "I am meant to be regal."

He squeezed my hand where it lay upon his sleeve. "You are delectable and delicious and all things delightful, my dear. Do not wish to be anything other than you are."

I opened my mouth to reprove him, but we had arrived at our box. A few minutes later we were seated, the baroness and myself in the front in a pair of little gilt chairs, with the duke and the chancellor behind us. I was glad of the baroness's company — if for no other reason than she could continue to instruct me on points of etiquette — but I wondered at the wisdom of the arrangement as the duke leant forward and put his hands upon my shoulders.

"Do not look so startled, Princess," he murmured. "I am to help you off with your cloak. You will be much too warm with it on."

He exposed my bare shoulders, drawing

the velvet and fur slowly away, teasingly. From behind him, I heard Stoker growl again and gave a sigh. It was going to be a very long evening.

No sooner had we settled into the box than the concertmaster and conductor appeared, accepting the enthusiastic applause from the audience. The conductor turned, bowed to me, and lifted his baton, signaling the orchestra to strike up a thunderous tune with a martial melody. Immediately, the Alpenwalders leapt to their feet, but the baroness put a slipper firmly upon my dress, forcing me to stay seated.

"The anthem," she muttered. I realized then that the tune they were lustily singing was their national song, "Verlorene Seelen," a rather macabre invocation to the spirits of dead comrades-in-arms. The melody concluded with a martial crash of cymbals and I inclined my head to the conductor to acknowledge the compliment.

The duke leant forward, his moustaches tickling my neck. "Do you like our national anthem, Princess?" he inquired. I did not have to look round to know he was smiling.

"My German is imperfect, but from what I could translate, it is a trifle bloodthirsty," I whispered back.

He gave a short laugh, his breath ruffling my hair. "We made the mistake of trying to stop Napoléon on his way to Russia. Every Alpenwalder who fought was slain — except one."

"Lucky fellow," I replied.

"He was my great-grandfather," the duke told me. "And the luck did not end with him."

I wondered what he meant by that, but the orchestra was beginning the overture and I settled back to listen. It was a very modern opera, with a good deal of strident posturing and aggressive passages for the brasses, but all of this was nothing compared to the verve of the leading lady. Mademoiselle Fribourg threw herself into the role with tremendous passion. The first act saw the intrepid Atalanta besting every suitor at the sporting games hosted by her father, a lively scene full of color and movement with Mademoiselle Fribourg's legs shown to excellent advantage in a short tunic. But immediately after the athleticism of the competition, the mournful heroine stepped behind a convenient bush to lament her loneliness, pouring out her pain in a piercing aria of such sweetness, such pain, I was forced to blink back tears as the curtain came down upon the first act.

"Well, what do you think of our Atalanta?" the duke asked, moving his chair nearer to mine and edging the baroness aside a little.

"I think she is immensely talented," I told him.

"You do not find her figure a trifle generous for a loose-limbed athlete?" he teased. There was something I did not quite like in the challenge of his gaze. It was as if he knew a secret joke at my expense, and I wondered at the nature of his relationship with the princess.

"On the contrary. It would require a robust physique to excel at such activities," I told him firmly. "She puts me in mind of the Rubens painting of the same lady."

He leaned closer then, his medals clinking together. I glanced at them. "You seem to have distinguished yourself in the service of your country, Your Grace."

He gave a shrug that seemed to convey both modesty and pride in his accomplishments.

"I trained at Woolwich, at your Royal Military Academy," he told me. "And then I spent some time with your queen's army in Afghanistan as an attaché to your general Sir Samuel Browne. They like to give out medals for such things."

He spoke casually, but any man who had

served under the commander of the British Army during the Second Anglo-Afghan War had seen some sharpish things. He gestured towards one of the medals, a medallion struck with Queen Victoria's image hanging from a bar of crimson and green ribbon. I peered closely at the medal, noting the inscription circling the queen's face.

"Victoria Regina et Imperatrix," I read aloud. I sat back, scrutinizing him. "You were content to risk your life in the service of another country?"

His smile was enigmatic. "One does foolish things in one's youth and in the service of love."

I started to ask him what he meant, but my gaze fell upon the decoration hanging just below the Afghanistan Medal.

"The climbing badge of the Teufel-streppe!" I exclaimed.

"Not just a climbing badge," he corrected proudly. "A summit badge." He indicated the edge of tiny diamonds set in blue enamel. "This indicates the bearer has successfully climbed the mountain."

Excitement surged through me, like that of a lioness catching the scent of a gazelle. "I remember reading that you climbed," I began.

His laugh was quick, displaying excellent

white teeth. "My dear, everyone in the Alpenwald climbs. There are even special leading reins of leather to attach to small children to help them with their first ascents on the lower slopes. That mountain is our birthright." He canted his head, his eyes bright with amusement. "You have been reading about me? What sorts of things?"

I paused a moment, letting a smile ripen between us. "About your relationship with Alice Baker-Greene," I said softly. I watched carefully for his reaction, and there it was — a quick bob of the Adam's apple, a brief hesitation before he spoke.

"She was a gifted climber," he said casually. "And the alpinist community is a small one. Everyone meets everyone else sooner or later."

"So you were just friends?" I asked, widening my eyes at him.

"What a minx you are!" he exclaimed. "You think to bewitch me into indiscretions with those beautiful violet eyes, do you not? Shall I be your devoted slave?"

His tone was arch, but there was a distinct lack of humor in his eyes.

I ignored his question and decided to thrust once more, as I seemed to have knocked him a little off his balance.

"What do you remember about the day

she died? I hear you were an eyewitness."

"You seem to have heard quite a lot," he said, his gaze sharply watchful.

I shrugged. "I am by profession a lady explorer, traveling the world in order to study butterflies. Naturally, I take an interest in other such women. We were both members of the same club, you understand."

He blinked. "A woman's place is at the hearth and in the bed," he remarked, giving me a fathomless smile. He gazed warmly at my face, then deliberately dropped his gaze to my décolletage and back again.

"Careful, Your Grace. You are verging on boorishness," I murmured. I waited, and after a moment he sighed.

"Very well. Yes, I saw her depart that day. It was very much as usual."

"Was it usual for her to climb alone? That seems dangerous."

He shrugged. "Yes, but she was highly experienced and it was a climb she had done many times before and she was not planning to attempt the summit."

I lifted a brow in inquiry and he rolled his eyes at me. "We did not discuss her climb, so you have not discovered some great secret. If she had meant to summit, she would have gone out better equipped and with a guide. She often climbed sections of the mountain in order to try different routes. She kept notes, you know."

"Notes?"

"In a notebook." He sketched a size with his hands. "About so large. Green kidskin. She always carried it with her to record conditions, to make little maps and notes on her experiences. There are those who say it was the key to her success as a climber. She was meticulous in her research and she was often able to offer suggestions and tips to other mountaineers."

"Such as Douglas Norton?" I suggested.

He made a brusque gesture of dismissal. "A disgruntled, odious little man. He was not worth half of Alice's merit as a climber."

"What would you say if I told you that he was in the Alpenwald when Alice made her fatal climb?"

All his theatrical postures and poses fell away at that moment and his mouth rounded in genuine astonishment. "Was he indeed?" He sat back a little, suddenly pre-occupied. After a moment, he shook himself a little and gave me a faint smile. "You are a very knowledgeable woman, my dear."

"I know very little, but I am curious about a good deal," I corrected.

"You know, I am sure, what they say about

curiosity and cats?" The comment was well pitched. It might have been a threat or merely a warning. He had resumed his attitude of lazy good humor, but he watched me closely and I wondered which of us might really be playing at being the cat.

"I suppose I ought to congratulate you on your forthcoming betrothal," I said softly. "Tell me, was the princess at all vexed by your attentions to Alice Baker-Greene?"

At this he let out a sharp bark of laughter, drawing the attention of several people seated in the boxes nearest ours.

"Why do you laugh?"

"Because you are ridiculous and beautiful."

"You mean she was not at all distressed that you developed a friendship with another woman? A friendship so important that you secured a permanent home for Alice in Hochstadt?"

His brows shot skywards in astonishment. "Who told you that?"

"Alice. I met her once and she spoke most enthusiastically of your country."

"What else did she tell you? Did she speak of me?"

"No. She talked of her eagerness to settle in the Alpenwald and how happy she was. I only learnt later that the house given to her was taken from Captain Durand at the behest of the chancellor — no doubt acting upon the orders of someone very highly placed," I finished.

He gave me a long, appreciative nod. "Well, I can only say again that you are a most surprising young woman."

"I shall take that as a compliment."

He smiled thinly and I fell to thinking that this sophisticated nobleman with his weathercock moods might well have had an excellent motive for murdering Alice himself. He was a royal of the old, Continental variety; it was not difficult to imagine that he would find nothing untoward in settling a woman who might well have been his mistress in proximity to the castle he hoped to share with his future wife. But what if Princess Gisela had taken a different view of the matter? There was gossip about Duke Maximilian and Alice Baker-Greene, that much I knew, and it was likely that some of it reached the ears of the princess. In previous generations, a nobleman could expect to establish a cozy situation for himself — his wife comfortably settled in his official residence whilst his paramour feathered their love nest. But these were modern days. Not every royal marriage included genteel adultery on the part of the husband. Our own Prince Albert had been a paragon of marital virtue, I reflected. And Gisela, as the reigning hereditary princess, held all of the cards. She could easily refuse to accept his proposal except on her own terms, and the most logical demand would be for him to remove his ladylove from Hochstadt. All of this was quite reasonable enough and no motive for murdering the woman.

Unless she refused to go quietly. I thought of Alice Baker-Greene, standing flushed with delight in the Curiosity Club as she related her future plans to me. I remembered the photographs of her posed on a mountaintop with her suffragist banners and the stories of her whipping Douglas Norton down a Bolivian street to assuage her honor. Oh no. Alice Baker-Greene was most definitely *not* the sort of woman to meekly accept being cast off by a lover who found her presence burdensome, I decided. She would have staked her claim to him as stalwartly as she did a mountain summit.

These thoughts chased and tangled in far less time than it takes to describe them, and as I considered them, the duke continued to smile his oblique smile at me until the baroness rapped him sharply with her fan. She said something in the Alpenwalder dialect too rapid for me to understand and he moved his chair back again and fell into conversation with the chancellor.

"I hope he does not trouble you too much," she began in a low voice.

I shrugged. "I have encountered many such men in my travels, Baroness," I assured her. "If he chooses to make trouble with me, he will find me a worthy adversary."

Her expressions were carefully schooled, but I could tell she was distressed. "I beg you, do not make an enemy of him. He might take it in his head to create mischief, and when he does, no one can be naughtier than our Maximilian."

There was something modestly revolting at the notion of a grown man being described as mischievous, but the baroness was obviously troubled and I had no wish to add to her burdens. I put a fingertip to her arm, startling her a little.

"You are clearly distressed," I said. "Be of good heart, Baroness. I am certain your princess will return unharmed and soon."

She said nothing, biting her lip before she darted me a grateful glance. She cleared her throat and opened her program. "Ah, act two is the love duet. That should be a most excellent scene," she began. She carried on talking about the opera whilst a steady stream of visitors appeared at the door of the box, offering flowers, confections, and other little tributes from admirers whilst being carefully discouraged from entering by the lowering Teutonic presence of Captain Durand. The gifts were heaped on a small table in the corner — armfuls of carefully arranged blooms, boxes full of sugared almonds and tiny jeweled fruits, and an assortment of envelopes.

"Correspondence?" I asked the baroness.

"Petitions," she explained. "Whenever the princess appears in public, there are those who present her with their needs. If it is in her power to assist them, she will do so."

I watched the chancellor carefully bundle the envelopes before tucking them into his pocket. "It is my responsibility to assess the worthiness of each claim before passing it along to Her Serene Highness," he told me smoothly. I realized then how very isolated the princess must be. She seldom traveled outside her own country, and even when she went in public, there was little opportunity for anyone to speak to her without the interference of her entourage.

Before I could ask, Duke Maximilian spied a bottle of costly champagne amidst the offerings and pounced upon it like a house cat upon a mouse. "Now we have the makings of a party," he proclaimed. He snapped his fingers at Stoker to find glasses. I held my breath, waiting for Stoker's response, but I need not have worried. He was finding the entire affair amusing, I realized. He signaled to an usher passing by the open door of the box for coupes as the duke popped the cork with a lavish gesture, sending it flying into the crowd below. They laughed and dove for it, a little memento of their night at the opera with a foreign princess.

"Madness," I murmured as Duke Maximilian handed me a frothing glass of the golden wine.

"That they leap for rubbish? It is indeed. But such is the lot of royalty, my dear," he said, touching his glass to mine. "Blue blood carries magic in it."

"You cannot really believe that," I protested.

He shrugged. "I am a pragmatist. I believe what serves me."

"You are an opportunist," I corrected and he laughed, loudly enough that half the theatre turned to look.

"Ah, they see now how well we get on! I must thank you for that," he said, raising his glass. "It is because we make such a beautiful couple. Just think how handsome our children will be."

"You are impossible," I told him.

"I am adorable," he corrected. "I am a charming rogue and you are perplexed because you find that you like me more than you want to."

"Did someone tell you that confidence is attractive in a gentleman?" I asked sweetly. "Because if they did, you have taken it entirely too far."

"A gentleman can never be too confident. He must believe in his abilities even when no one else does," he said. "I have always believed that I possess the qualities necessary to make a worthy consort." His gaze dropped to his glass, where bubbles were still rising through the champagne. It was excellent stuff, the color of pale straw and tasting of toast with a hint of jam. I finished my first glass and the duke hastened to refill my coupe.

"But there is doubt in some quarters?" I guessed.

"I enjoy life very much — too much, some would say. They think me not serious enough to play such an important role in my country's future." He seemed sincere then, and I liked him better than I had up to that point.

"What would you like that role to be?"

He considered this a moment. "I should

like to be the sort of man who could make Gisela proud. This surprises you? Do not deny it, I can see the astonishment on your face, my dear. But it is true."

"You really care for her then?"

"How can you doubt it?" His expression softened. "I have known her since childhood. We are cousins, after all, though distantly so. I was always the disgraceful boy with the untidy hair and the pockets full of frogs or French cigarettes."

I widened my eyes and he smiled. "I was a very mature boy. But I cared much for her, and I still do. She was so serious, so lovely and always restricted!"

His gaze fell to the tight lacing of my waist and rose slowly to the heavy jewels at my wrists and head. "You feel a little of that, do you not? How one must suffocate? I always tried to relieve her of that."

"You encouraged her to misbehave," I guessed.

"She needed little enough encouragement," he told me. "There was always a rebel beneath the royal. But whenever we got ourselves into trouble, I took the blame. It was easy enough. Everyone knew who we were — Gisela the good girl and Maximilian the scoundrel." His tone was mocking, but his lips took a wistful turn. "More than once I was whipped for some plot of her making. Still, I do not regret it."

"I imagine there is little you do regret," I said.

"Why don't we do something scandalous and find out?" With that, he settled back into his chair and sipped his champagne, never breaking eye contact with me.

"Enjoying yourself?" came a voice at my ear. I turned to see Stoker kneeling just behind me in a posture of supplication.

"What are you doing on the floor?" I demanded. "Get up at once."

"I cannot sit in your presence," he told me in mock seriousness. "It is a violation of royal etiquette. But I can kneel in devotion to my princess."

"You are an ass," I hissed.

"I am also about to save you a good deal of trouble," he told me. He turned his head away from the theatre. "Do not look now. In the stalls. Second row on the end."

"Who is it?"

"Who is the very last person you would want to see in your current guise?" he asked.

"Mornaday." It was a name, but I said it like an expletive.

Stoker nodded. "Mercifully, his duties demand he pay closer attention to the audience than the royal box and he has not looked often this way. If he suspects for a moment —" He broke off. There was no need for him to finish the sentence. Mornaday had occasionally played the ally; one might even consider him a friend. But an ambitious second-in-command at Scotland Yard was not the person to conspire with to impersonate a foreign royal. If he got as much as a sniff of something amiss with the Alpenwalder delegation, he would be after it like a hungry dog with a juicy bone.

Stoker spoke again. "Try drawing a little less attention to yourself," he suggested.

I edged my chair back a little, casting my face deeper into the shadows. "That is the best I can do. I *am* supposed to be the guest of honor at this event," I reminded him.

"Imperious as a princess already," he returned lightly. "I think I shall make you clean my walrus when we go home just to put you in your proper place." He dared a quick wink before resuming his post in the rear of the box. I drank deeply of my champagne.

Home. The word was jarring in this context. I had never had a home, not a real one. My aunts and I had moved frequently for reasons I had come to understand only too late. My travels had taken me around the world, drawing me across the globe and

back again in pursuit of my beloved butterflies. I never tarried long in any spot for
the fear that I would become too rooted,
too settled. But with our employment at the
Belvedere and the eccentric lodgings of
which we had both become fond — to say
nothing of our personal attachment — I
found myself for the first time perched on
the edge of domesticity.

It was a terrifying thought. Hearthsides
and cradles held no charms for me. I was
unfettered as the east wind, I reminded
myself. And the sooner Stoker realized I had
no interest in darning shirts and stirring
cook pots, the better off we would both be.

I turned in my chair to meet Duke Maximilian's delighted gaze as I held out my
glass again. "I would like more champagne,"
I announced.

"With pleasure, Princess," he said, obliging me.

I caught the baroness's glance of reproof
as I started on my third glass. The coupes
were small, scarcely bigger than thimbles,
and I was well capable of handling my
intoxicants, I thought in some irritation.
Besides, the combination of the handsome
duke, the jewels, and the danger of what I
was doing was heady enough. I had spent
too long cocooned in the security of the

Belvedere, pinning mounts and answering correspondence. For just these few hours, I was on the tightrope again, balanced precariously between glory and disaster, and the thrill of it coursed through me with far more effect than the glittering wine.

I raised my glass to Duke Maximilian. "To your very good health, Your Grace."

He grinned and touched his glass to mine.

CHAPTER 13

The rest of the performance passed in a golden haze from the faery-tale circumstances — heightened no doubt by the excellence of the champagne as well as the liminal magic of the opera itself. The librettist had clearly been inspired by Handel's work of the same name, but his handling of the myth of Atalanta was altogether darker. The first act saw the princess thwart her father's attempts to see her matched with a man who could best the fleet-footed heroine in a race. In this version, a suitor dropped enchanted golden apples to distract her, but Atalanta was guarded by Artemis, protectress of chaste maidens, and the goddess gave her heightened speed so she might win in spite of the conspiracy of men to cheat her into marriage. The act had finished with the princess singing of her triumph but also of her loneliness, her longing for someone of her own choosing to share her victories as well as her woes.

The second act had been set upon an enormous ship, the *Argo,* as Atalanta and a crew of heroes sailed for the Golden Fleece, a quest in which the princess distinguished herself by her daring although the men around her plotted to take her share of the spoils. Enraged, she took her revenge upon them before running away to hide out as a shepherdess. Her disguise was penetrated when the hunt for the Calydonian Boar passed and she must join or die. Reaching for her spear, she embraced her true destiny at last, spitting the beast and saving the kingdom from his ravaging. When the other hunters disparaged her, a young huntsman named Meleager stood alone in her defense. The tenor cast in the role was heartbreakingly young, bewailing the fact that he would never be worthy of her love, but vowing he would take her side against his own uncles, who plotted to kill her. Finding at last a man whose honor was as great as hers, Atalanta bestowed her hand upon him, and a tremendous wedding chorus was sung as the lovers were joined in marriage. But the goddess Artemis, petitioned by Meleager's uncles and angered at losing her devoted handmaiden, cast the bridegroom into a pyre, causing Atalanta to deliver a widow's aria, shivering the rafters with its eldritch lament. It was a thing of fire and rage, her grief smelted in the crucible of loss into purest anger and a vow of revenge against those who plotted against her. The opera ended with Atalanta, silhouetted by fire, spear raised against a dying sun, triumphant even in the knowledge that she will go to her death, destroyed by the goddess she once served for her blasphemies.

"We do not much care for happy endings," Duke Maximilian murmured in my ear. "We are too pragmatic for that. But I think it disturbs you British," he added with a nod towards the audience below.

The English crowd, rather uncomfortable with equivocal endings, applauded politely. Suddenly, I realized all eyes were fixed upon the royal box. My reaction, for good or ill, would determine whether the work was a success or a dismal failure. In that moment, I held the fate of Mademoiselle Fribourg, of the entire cast, of the composer Berton, of the world's opinion of Alpenwalder culture, in my gloved hands.

Slowly, deliberately, I rose to my feet and began to clap. The kidskin muffled the sound, but still it echoed throughout the opera house. The applause began haltingly, like drops of rain pattering on a roof. I fancied I could hear each pair of hands, clapping alone in the darkness. Then more, and still more, the sound rising to a storm, then a deluge of approbation as the curtain rose and the cast took their bows, the chorus and lesser performers first. Then the goddess and the suitors, and finally Mademoiselle Fribourg herself. Bouquets were hurled along with cries of "Brava!" and the lady curtsied deeply, gesturing towards the orchestra pit. The conductor, Monsieur Berton, who had also composed the work, leapt onto the stage at her invitation. They joined hands and faced the royal box. As one, the entire cast and orchestra bowed deeply to me, Mademoiselle Fribourg's nose nearly touching the stage. When she rose, I saw tears glittering on her cheeks, and Berton seized her hand, kissing it ardently. Whatever else happened that night, I told myself, I had done some good for these people.

When the ovations were ended, the chancellor shepherded us out of the royal box just as the ambassador appeared, his moustaches quivering in delight.

"A triumph! An absolute triumph!" he exclaimed. "And all due to Your Serene Highness's enthusiastic response."

"I think it is rather more to do with the

quality of the music and the performance," I told him.

"So gracious!" he murmured. "Naturally, you will wish to pay your compliments directly to the performers and the composer, madame, so I have arranged for a private audience backstage. If you would step this way —"

He bowed low, extending his arm. I looked to the chancellor for help, but he merely lifted one shoulder in a tiny shrug. I should have to make the best of it, I decided. I followed the ambassador, the rest of the Alpenwalder entourage trailing behind. The cast and orchestra and stagehands were arranged in a long line in the wings. The proprietors naturally took pride of place, beaming and bowing, and obviously enormously relieved, as their gamble on a new production would pay handsomely now that they had a bona fide success on their hands.

I accepted their fervent thanks with a solemn inclination of the head and a few words murmured in the faint Germanic accent the baroness had made me practice. They pressed bouquets of roses upon me — heaps of blooms, all tied with Alpenwalder blue. The baroness fairly staggered under the weight as she tottered behind me. The proprietors presented the various singers and musicians and I felt my face would crack with the effort of smiling at them all.

At last, the presentation was finished and I moved to leave, Mademoiselle Fribourg doing her best to hold back tears of joy as Edouard Berton clasped her hand and the others crowded around, staring avidly at what must have been their closest sighting of royalty. It was astonishing to see the effect it had upon them. I was still myself, as much plain Veronica Speedwell as I had ever been, but since I had been presented to them as a princess, they believed it. The jewels and the gown and the fact that people called me "Highness" had somehow rendered me almost sacred, and there was a touch of worshipfulness I did not entirely like. Strip away the costly trappings and I was no more or less than any of them, I thought angrily. And yet they could not see past the dazzling display of wealth and power.

The atmosphere of the theatre suddenly seemed oppressive. So many pairs of staring eyes, gleaming in the darkened wings, so many hands reaching out to touch just a fingertip to the hem of my gown. I remembered then that it had once been the custom for the common people to be given the carpets walked upon by medieval royalty, how the cloth laid for a coronation had been cut to bits by the flashing knives of a joyous, terrifying mob. How quickly they might turn, I realized in horror. How suddenly the mood of a group of people might shift from adulation to anger. And what might they do if sufficiently provoked?

Something of what I felt must have shown on my face, for the baroness whispered urgently to the chancellor, and he stepped forward. "Her Serene Highness must take her leave of you now," he pronounced in a tone that brooked no argument. I nodded to them all one last time and followed the chancellor gratefully as he forged a path for us through the opera house and out onto the pavement. The carriage was waiting, I saw with a sigh of relief. I suddenly could not bear the weight of it all a moment more. The jewels and corset and heavy gown conspired to make me feel like a draft horse, and I was exhausted from carting them about. I could scamper up and down hillsides from dawn 'til dusk in pursuit of my favorite butterflies, but the notion of keeping myself trussed up for another minute was utterly unthinkable.

The Alpenwalder entourage and I moved towards the carriage, the operagoers gathered on two sides and penned by the Metropolitan Police in an orderly fashion to shout and wave their good-byes. I raised my hand to acknowledge them, turning to look behind me, and just as I did so there was a pop, a flash of light, and a vibration that nearly knocked me off of my feet. The events of the next few moments were so swift, they seemed to happen simultaneously. There was a scream — I later learnt it was from the baroness — and a roar of outrage — this from Stoker. A scuffle ensued and I saw Stoker flying through the air and into the crowd in front of me and to the left. The captain rushed from my right side to hoist me into his arms. He did not bother to put me on my feet to enter the carriage but rather hurtled himself through the open door, still clutching me to his chest. We landed on the seat, my body crushed beneath him, knocking the wind from my lungs as he shouted for the driver to whip the horses.

Behind us came the chancellor and the baroness, thrown through the door of the carriage by Duke Maximilian, who was still standing with one foot on the steps when the driver sprang the horses and they leapt from the curb. The duke turned, extended a hand, and Stoker emerged from the crowd just in time to grasp it. The pair of them fell into the carriage at our feet and the door swung madly on its hinges as we raced through the streets. Sounds were oddly muffled, but I could make out screams as I struggled to push the captain off of me.

"What is happening?" I demanded. My voice sounded strange to my ears, distant and small.

The captain sat back and helped me up, settling me gently into my seat. It took some time for us to disentangle ourselves and take stock, but apart from a burnt patch on Stoker's uniform and medals torn from the duke's and the baroness's badly dented tiara, we were fine if badly shaken.

"What happened?" I repeated.

Stoker's expression was grim and I had to watch his mouth move to understand his words. "You have just survived your first bomb attack, Princess."

CHAPTER 14

We traveled in stupefied silence — or at least I think it was silence. The bomb had set my ears to ringing, and I doubt I could have heard anything short of a foghorn. We were a dazed group, horror and disbelief mingling with a profound sense of relief that there had been no injuries to speak of, at least amongst our party. I thought of the crowds gathered on the pavement and wondered what had become of them.

When we arrived back at the hotel, the onlookers had mercifully dispersed. A bitterly cold wind had whipped off of the river, and tiny splinters of ice once more danced in the nimbus of the streetlamps.

I shivered and Maximilian wrapped his hand around my arm. "You must pretend to like the cold, *Liebchen*," he told me. "Ice runs in our veins, you know." I knew he was not speaking of only the weather. The fact that a bomb had been hurled mere inches from us had been upsetting, but the Alpen-walders were making every effort to behave normally. I suspected his little speech was as much for his own benefit as mine. His fingers trembled where they gripped my arm, and his expression was grim, but it seemed quite in keeping with his character to make a jest in order to lighten the mood.

We hurried into the hotel, the chancellor leading the way as the captain brought up the rear. Stoker had given his arm to the baroness, and she leant upon it with a grate-ful look. The suite seemed a haven when we at last reached its security and bolted the doors behind us. I thought of medieval criminals who hurled themselves into churches to claim sanctuary, secure that they were safe within those walls.

The chambermaid — not J. J., I noted with some relief — was just kindling a fire upon the hearth in the sitting room to aug-ment the steam heat of the suite, and she scuttled out as we arrived, curtsying clum-sily to each of us, even Stoker, as she hur-ried away. The captain locked the door and went to assure himself that the remaining rooms were secure as the rest of us col-lapsed into chairs near the fire. The baron-ess and I shared the sofa, sitting as comfortably as possible given the constraints of our corsets.

"Drinks," the duke said succinctly. He did not ring for the maid to return but went himself to a cabinet in the corner and fetched a tray of glasses and a bottle with a label I did not recognize. The liquid inside was clear as ice and he poured a stiff measure for each of us.

"Drink it quickly," he instructed me. "In one go."

I tossed my head back and swallowed. It tasted of nothing, just a sensation of cold and then a ripe blooming heat took hold of my chest.

"Better?" he asked.

I nodded. He turned to the baroness. Her complexion was ashen, and I wondered if she was about to faint.

"Drink, Baroness," he urged. She took the glass he held out to her with an unsteady hand. She looked doubtfully at her glass, then took a deep, shuddering breath to steel herself before drinking. She gasped, and the color finally returned to her cheeks.

"I am sorry about your tiara," I told her as the duke moved on to offer restorative libations to the chancellor and Stoker. The baroness looked down at the badly damaged coronet still clutched in her gloved hands.

"It is nothing, a bagatelle," she said. It was clearly a valuable piece, but she was right; compared to the cost of human life, it was nothing.

She looked at Stoker. "Mr. Templeton-Vane, I must thank you. If not for your swift action —" She broke off, pressing her lips together to control her emotion.

Stoker flushed, the tips of his ears reddening adorably. "Do not speak of it," he said softly.

"Well," I said, "we shall have to agree upon a story for the police. No doubt they will be here in short order to question us."

"We cannot afford scrutiny from the Metropolitan Police," the baroness said, her lips compressed. "Miss Speedwell's masquerade, as effective as it is, will not stand up to lengthy questioning by the authorities."

The chancellor's expression was grim and Duke Maximilian sat slumped in an armchair in the corner, his face pale. He was clearly still shaken, and I was a little surprised at his lack of spirit. For all the courage he had displayed at the time, the experience seemed to have left him oddly cowed.

"I do not think we need worry about

that," Stoker said slowly. "In fact, the Metropolitan Police can easily be put off on the grounds that this was not an assassination attempt at all."

"What do you mean?" the chancellor demanded.

The baroness bristled. "My good man, we were there. We saw the explosion. Someone tried to harm our princess with a bomb."

"That is precisely the point, Baroness," Stoker explained patiently. "They did no such thing. The bomb was a squib." He looked around at our collective confusion and began to elaborate. "I spent a good deal of time near munitions in the navy. The bomb hurled at us tonight was nothing but sound and fury. There was a mighty noise and a flash, but no destruction. If we had really been standing so near a proper explosive, there would have been injuries, deaths even. The bomb that went off under the tsar of Russia's carriage blew his legs entirely off, and we have sustained nothing worse than a little soot and some ringing in the ears. Someone wanted to sow a little panic without doing real harm. This was nothing more than a vicious prank."

"My God," Maximilian said faintly. He dropped his head into his hands.

"But who on earth would do such a

thing?" the chancellor asked. "People might have been trampled to death trying to get away. It is a monstrosity."

I furrowed my brow and thought a moment. "Anarchists?"

"Anarchists do not play at murder," Stoker reminded me soberly. "Their intention is to kill, always. No, this was something entirely different, designed to frighten but nothing worse." He turned his attention to the chancellor. "What will you say when the police come calling?"

The duke gave a start, dropping his hands. "The police? The *English* police? We are not subjects of your Crown." His bearing, always proud, took on a new hauteur.

"No," Stoker agreed, "but you are guests in our country and your princess is a head of state. This event occurred under the noses of the Metropolitan Police. I recognized one of their inspectors at the opera. Surely you do not believe they will simply let this go and not investigate?"

The duke flushed angrily. "It is an outrage! To suggest we cannot protect our own —"

The chancellor waved his hands. "Be calm, Your Grace. Naturally the English police will have questions, but we will simply give them a statement saying we believe it to be a silly prank and tell them the princess does not wish to pursue the matter. They will have no choice but to leave it there. And regardless of who was responsible, the fact remains that they did not succeed. We must move forward. And, as Mr. Templeton-Vane says, we must proceed with our objectives as if nothing untoward has happened."

"I do not believe I said anything of the sort," Stoker began, but the chancellor carried on as if he had not spoken, turning to me. "*Fraulein,* you performed very well, although I am certain the baroness will have notes for you."

That august lady drew herself up stiffly. "Naturally, all performances may be improved upon. But I think the *Fraulein* has had enough for one day."

Stoker stared from one to the other in frank astonishment. "For one day? This was the arrangement, Your Excellency. Miss Speedwell impersonated your princess for the gala and it is finished. We will naturally be returning to our own lodgings now."

The Alpenwalders exchanged glances, and by some unspoken agreement, it was the baroness who appealed to him. She came towards him, her expression pleading.

"Mr. Templeton-Vane, you are right. We have asked a tremendous thing of you and your friend. And she has been a triumph. But our princess is still missing and what we must accomplish here is not at an end."

He opened his mouth to speak, but she put her hand on his arm. "Please. I beseech you. Not for myself, but for my princess. Stay here tonight. The princess may return by tomorrow morning and then we will send you on your way with gratitude, such fervent gratitude!"

"And if she has not?" Stoker asked.

"That is the bridge yet to be crossed," she said.

He looked to me, but we both realized it was a formality. Stoker could never refuse a woman in distress of any variety. To have the baroness, a noble and handsome woman, pleading with him for so small a favor was far beyond his ability to rebuff.

"Baroness," he began, his tone doubtful.

She must have known she had won as soon as he failed to reject the proposal outright, but she pressed anyway. "Our suite is very comfortable," she urged. "And it is late and you both have had a terrible shock. The explosive might have been a nasty prank, but it was still a dreadful experience and we feel responsible. We have prevailed upon you both so far beyond the bounds of good manners, I shudder to think what opinion you must hold of us. To host you here, in luxury, with the most comfortable beds and the most delicious food, to send you home well rested and well fed, it is the least we can do. But perhaps you do not want to allow us the chance to repay your kindness and to make amends for what you have already endured?"

Stoker looked helplessly at me. He always was far too malleable where women were concerned. I gave the baroness my most gracious smile. "You are very kind, Baroness, but I think we should sleep better in our own beds. As you say, it has been a most exhausting day. We will, of course, be at your disposal should you wish us to call again," I told her.

She inclined her head. "Very well. Come, *Fraulein*. I will help you change into your own clothes."

The chancellor turned to Stoker.

"Thank you for your efforts tonight, sir. You may change in the room you used earlier."

Stoker allowed the chancellor to lead him to the room put aside for his use while the baroness took me to the princess's bedchamber, careful to lock the door once we were inside. The business with the bomb seemed to have unnerved her even more than I had first realized.

"The chancellor may be quite right and you may wake up tomorrow to find her here, wondering like the Three Bears who has been sleeping in her bed," I added with a nod towards the vast silken four-poster.

"Just so," she replied, but the frown did not leave her brow, and she moved mechanically through the lengthy process of disrobing and dismantling the royal creation she had made of me. Jewels were replaced in their boxes, hairpieces were combed out, garments were folded away. After some delay, Yelena appeared carrying a tray with a small teapot and earning a scolding from the countess for her tardiness. She gave the noblewoman a sullen look as she carried the gown off for sponging, banging the door behind her.

"That girl," the baroness fretted as she lifted the lid on the teapot, releasing a cloud of fragrant steam. "She has been harboring thoughts above her station ever since she took up with Captain Durand."

"I understand they mean to marry," I ventured.

The baroness gave me a knowing look as she poured a thin stream of liquid from the pot into a fragile china cup marked with the Alpenwalder otters. "In our country we

261

would say you have long ears, like a hare, *Fraulein,* the better to hear gossip. But yes, Yelena is little better than a peasant, you understand. For her to marry a man of the captain's station is a very great thing for her. It gives her ideas."

"What is wrong with ideas?" I asked gently.

"La! You Englishwomen are all the same," she clucked as she handed me the cup. "So modern with your bicycling machines and pamphlets on voting. Some woman shouted at me on the pavement the other day because she wanted money to stop vivisection. I told her, I do not even know what this is, but whatever it may be, ladies should not be shouting on pavements to stop it."

"Vivisection is the performing of operations on live animals for research," I told her as I peered into the cup. The liquid was green in color and bits of dried petals floated on the surface.

She pulled a face. "That does not sound very nice. Perhaps I should give her a few coins if I see her again." She nodded towards the cup. "This is a tea made of St. Otthild's wort," she explained. "We drink it in the mountains for all things — to ease us when we are wakeful, to soothe us when we are sad. It is even good for women's troubles," she confided. "I thought it might calm your nerves after that dreadful incident at the opera. And perhaps give you a little energy as well."

I sipped it and felt myself beginning to relax at once. As a cream for the skin, it had smelt of roses, but the aroma of the tea was similar to our own elderflower, subtle and elusive. It was a gentle concoction, and I thanked her.

"There is no need to drink it if you do not like the flavor," she told me. "It is an acquired taste to some."

"I do like it," I assured her.

"Do you require anything else? Biscuits? Honey?" she asked. But I could see the signs of worry and fatigue stamped upon her features.

"Nothing at all. I am quite revived, Baroness," I said.

My eyes fell then to the chocolate box containing the threat against Gisela. I took a few more sips of the tea. "On second thought, a chocolate might be nice," I ventured.

The baroness looked at me in surprise. "Of course, *Fraulein.*"

She pressed the box upon me. "You must take it."

"I could not possibly," I protested. "It is

the princess's."

The baroness shook her head firmly. "I insist. You have done a tremendous service for us this night. It is the least of what my princess would want you to have. You must take it or you will offer a grave insult."

Her expression was mulish, and I knew we had already caused them unease by refusing to accept their hospitality for the night. Besides, it was easier to take the whole box than to steal the threat.

"That is very kind of you."

She helped me into my own things, which Yelena had sponged and pressed in spite of their being perfectly clean, then put out her hand.

I regarded it with some astonishment. "You do not shake hands in the Alpenwald," I said.

"But you are an Englishwoman, and I must thank you the English way," she said. I shook her hand gravely and she inclined her head, a gesture of profound respect from this proud aristocrat. I felt a quickening of some emotion — regret, perhaps? — that my time with her had been so short. She was interesting in spite of her hedgehog prickles, and I should have enjoyed getting to know her better, not least because she might have been able to shed some light on

Alice Baker-Greene's death or Gisela's disappearance. It had been my experience that people often knew far more than they realized, and sometimes extensive conversation was required to winkle the information out of them.

She walked me to the door of the suite, where Stoker stood ready, divested of his moustaches, gold earrings glinting from his ears. More handshakes all around, and the chancellor favored me with a formal kiss to the hand. They were subdued, as a group, no doubt because of the attack on their princess and the fact that her whereabouts were still unknown.

Duke Maximilian was still dreadfully pale as he bowed and kissed my hand, all trace of the flirtatious seducer quite absent as he pressed my hand. *"Gute Nacht, Fraulein.* I hope our paths will cross again." He gave me a tiny smile at the sight of the gold box in my hands. "I see you have a souvenir of your time with us."

"I do. Would you care for a rose cream before I go? A violet cream perhaps?"

Stoker lifted the box out of my hands. "I am certain the duke's tastes do not run to English sweets," he said blandly.

The duke's smile turned wintry. "As you say. I have the Continental inclinations. I will wish you both farewell."

He stepped sharply back and we took our leave of the Alpenwalders. It had been an evening none of us would soon forget.

CHAPTER 15

The doorman of the Sudbury was still on duty despite the lateness of the hour and, at the sight of a copper from Stoker, summoned the hotel's comfortable brougham for us. I settled in against the velvet squabs, and when the door was closed upon us with the curtains drawn, we were cocooned in a dark and comfortable little nest against the frigid, frosty midnight. I ought to have been exhausted, but I found myself instead exhilarated, in an exaltation of spirits I had seldom enjoyed whilst in England. Upon my travels, I was often in the grip of strong emotion, hot upon the trail of an elusive butterfly or brought up to my highest mettle by the demands of arduous travel. Those experiences sharpened the senses and tested the resolve, resulting in a sense of vitality and purpose difficult to explain to those who choose a more sedate existence.

But on my home soil, there were precious

few occasions for such keen endeavors. The odd abduction or attempt on my life and the bouts of physical congress I enjoyed with Stoker were the only times I had felt that knife-edge of authentic experience and I reveled in the sudden thrum in my blood.

I turned to Stoker, whose eyes gleamed catlike in the dark. He said nothing, but the growl he emitted was eloquent as any love poem. What followed has no bearing on this narrative, but I will note that the rhythmic movement of a carriage at a brisk trot is most conducive to certain pleasures, so much so that at a particularly sharp moment, Stoker was forced to cover my mouth with his hand to muffle my most forceful exclamations. The fact that in my enthusiasm I unwittingly bit his finger was something I did not discover until I had removed myself from the most suitable position — sitting astride him and using the velvet hanging straps to great effect to secure my balance — and smoothed my skirts back into place.

Stoker had tidied his own clothing and sat with his hand wrapped in one of his enormous scarlet handkerchiefs, glowering a little.

"Did you not enjoy yourself?" I asked in some surprise. Whilst Stoker's preference was for a lengthy and languorous coupling accompanied by comfortable beds and extensive recitations of poetry, he could always be relied upon for applying himself with diligence and dexterity to a more vigorous interlude.

"I did," he ground out between gritted teeth. "Until you bit me."

He brandished the injured limb and I apologized prettily. "I thought you heard my groans of pain," he went on, still sulking.

"I did," I explained. "But I fear I mistook them for the culmination of your pleasure. Your groans all rather sound the same."

"Yes, it did seem to spur you on," he added a trifle nastily.

"It is hardly my fault if you are inarticulate," I pointed out. "Do attempt to clot faster, Stoker. We have arrived."

The carriage drew up at Bishop's Folly, Lord Rosemorran's estate, and we alighted. Stoker clutched the box of chocolates to his chest with his good hand and it was left to me to pay the coachman. He caught the coin I flipped with a nod. "Much obliged, madame. I do hope you enjoyed the ride," he added with a wink as he sprang the horses from the curb.

"Of all the cheek," I muttered. "Did you

hear the fellow?"

But Stoker was in no mood for my imprecations against the coachman. He sulked and stormed until I settled him at my little Gothic folly, building a fire and handing over my best velvet cushion for his head before passing him a bottle of my favorite aguardiente. I left him to clean his wound himself on the grounds that I thought he was making rather a tremendous mountain of this particularly small molehill, but once I saw the depth and detail of the bite, I was assailed by guilt. His left index finger was marked by the perfect imprint of my teeth, the flesh scored nearly to the bone and still bleeding freely.

"I *am* sorry," I told him in true contrition as I bound the finger in a clean handkerchief. "I do not know what came over me."

"I do," he said, sipping thoughtfully at the liqueur. "You are bored."

"With you!" I cried. "You cannot think so. You must not."

"I don't, as it happens," he said dryly. "Your enthusiasm for my person is both comprehensive and much appreciated. But there is something in this fog-shrouded island that dulls the senses."

"You feel it also?"

He gave me a searching look. "Why do

you think I rejected everything about the life to which I was bred? I ran away from my father's home when I was little more than a child in search of — I do not know what. Adventure, I suppose. That part of myself that I chased but could never seem to find. I was suffocated in that house, listening to my parents' quarrels and wondering if the whole of my life was meant to be nothing but a repetition of theirs. It was as though they never really lived. That house was merely a stage set and their lives were theatrical parts played upon it. The angry aristocrat, the long-suffering wife. The servants looking on. And every day the same thing — tea with scones and silences. Hatred for dinner, resentment at luncheon. I wanted nothing more than to breathe, to feel something other than that oppression."

I said nothing and he went on, his voice a little dreamy from the aftereffects of our vigorous activities and the aguardiente.

"And so I left, searching out experiences, both good and bad. And God knows I have found them. The bad were the bombardment in Alexandria, the Amazonian expedition. Marrying Caroline. And the good were the friends I found, the kindred spirits I have met along my travels and who have known me as one of them."

A sudden dart of fear lanced my heart. It thudded awkwardly in my chest. "I would hope that I am counted among the good that has happened to you," I said, summoning a smile.

He did not return it. He leant forward a little and cupped my chin in the breadth of his palm. "You are not."

The thud in my chest became a hammering, slow and painful on the ribs. "Oh."

He went on. "You are not among the good that has happened to me. You are the best of all that I have known. You are what I searched for when I left that house and wandered this earth, boy and man. You are the part of myself I never thought to find because I did not even dare to dream you existed. You are all that I want and more than I deserve, and I will go to my grave thanking a god in whom I do not believe for bringing me to you."

I was silent a long moment, but the tears upon my cheeks said everything I could not.

"Well," I said finally, wiping my cheeks upon my sleeve, "it was not Keats, but I suppose as declarations go, it is sufficient."

He smiled, a smile of such infinite tenderness that my throat tightened to speechlessness.

"I understand you, Veronica, because I am

you. I know that England is too small and too safe to contain you because it confines me as well. Do you think a day does not pass that I do not long to be aboard a ship, salt spray in my face and sails snapping in the wind, bound for the other side of the world? We have known such liberty, such wideness of experience that most can only imagine. And we will know such things again," he promised. "But I should reconcile myself to the fact that whilst we are here, we must take our adventures where we can."

"What do you mean?" I asked.

His hand still gripped my chin and he bent his head to press his brow to my own.

"I mean that you ought to change out of your skirts and into a pair of trousers. Because we are going to break into the Curiosity Club. Tonight."

I blinked in astonishment. "You cannot be serious."

"Serious as a parson in a pulpit." He kissed me soundly upon the mouth and sat back, draining the last of his aguardiente. "Go on, then. It grows late and we have work to do."

I hurried to the corner where a chest of drawers and series of pegs had been arranged to hold my wardrobe. A modest screen shielded the corner and, although I had few secrets from Stoker, I stepped behind it, stripping off garments in haste.

"Explain," I ordered as I shook out the suit of clothes I had ordered for butterflying. At first glance, it seemed much like an ordinary town suit — a narrow skirt and fitted jacket of becoming and serviceable cut. But upon closer inspection, it was easy to see the fabric was costly and durable thin tweed and the skirt was layered over a pair of very slim matching trousers which tucked into flat boots that laced to the knee. I buttoned and laced and tucked whilst Stoker talked.

"Amongst Alice Baker-Greene's possessions is a notebook, her climbing journal," he said. "I think we need to steal it."

I poked my head around the screen. "How did you learn about the journal?" I demanded. "I know I showed it to you the day we met the princess, but how do you know its significance?"

"Captain Durand," he said in obvious satisfaction. "We had a most illuminating discussion whilst he was helping me with my moustaches. Apparently, Alice kept detailed records of her expeditions — including companions. If she meant to climb with someone that morning, she might have made note of it and it may well lead us to the moustachioed man on the mountain. Besides which, it is a notable co-incidence that the princess has disappeared just after we discovered that Alice Baker-Greene was likely murdered and I do not like coincidences. Alice apparently wrote at length about the people where she traveled. She may well have recorded something which could lead us to the princess as well."

I emerged from the screen, pulling on a heavy cloak. "That was my discovery," I told him in some irritation. "I was meant to persuade *you* that we needed to see the ledger."

He shrugged a shoulder. "Perhaps I am better at this investigative business than you are," he said lightly.

"How dare you —" I began, but then I noted the unholy light in his eyes. "You are enjoying this. I think you have *always* enjoyed this. Being shot and stabbed and nearly drowned, you complain about all of it, yet here you are, haring off in the dead of night to commit some sort of illegal entry into a private club to secure a possible clue after we have nearly been bombed to bits. Do not argue with me, Revelstoke Templeton-Vane. I see you for the seeker of thrills that you really are."

He rose and picked up his hat, grinning. "Excelsior!"

It took a little time to hail a cab in the Marylebone Road, no surprise given the lateness of the hour. Stoker took the precaution of giving an address a street before the Curiosity Club. We wanted no witness to our presence in the vicinity once the theft was inevitably discovered.

On the way, we discussed what we knew of the case so far and my theory that Alice Baker-Greene might have been eliminated as an obstacle to the duke's marriage to the princess.

"A sound enough idea in theory," Stoker agreed. "If she was the duke's mistress —"

"And why else give her the house intended for Captain Durand?" I interjected.

"It is certainly a possibility," he said. "But how could he go so quickly from providing Alice a love nest right under the princess's nose to wanting to kill her?"

"To ensure his marriage to Gisela," I said promptly.

He shook his head. "I do not believe it. If he loved Alice enough to set her up in a house of her own in Hochstadt, in the very shadow of the castle, we are told, then he would not murder her within a few months."

"I think you, above all people, would understand the possibility of a relationship going badly awry in a short period of time," I said gently.

"Touché. I did myself change from husbandly devotion to incandescent rage within a few months," he acknowledged. "But between those times were months of abject sorrow. I had first to recognize that the woman I thought I had married did not exist. I could not hate her until I had learnt to mourn her. You are suggesting something quite different — that Maximilian murdered Alice in cold blood to secure his marriage."

"To a princess," I corrected. "There is a throne in the equation. You cannot discount the lengths to which a man will go for a crown."

"A consort's crown of a tiny, insignificant country," he said. "Would any man kill for that? Least of all the woman he loved?"

I considered this. "It took a betrayal for you to move from love to hatred," I reminded him. "Perhaps Maximilian experienced the same."

"You mean Alice had a lover besides Maximilian?"

"Why not? She was a woman of keen independence. She embraced many modern ideas — votes for women, rights for workers. Why not free love as well? Or perhaps she simply fell out of love with him and found someone else. If Maximilian had already gone to the trouble of arranging for her establishment in the Alpenwald, he would be enraged to find himself a laughing-stock."

"So he killed the woman he loved either to sacrifice her to his own ambitions or to punish her for failing to return his fidelity?"

"Both of those are understandable actions if a man is proud — and Duke Maximilian is excessively proud," I pointed out.

"As I said, in theory, either explanation makes perfect sense."

"However?"

"However, I think there is something more we have not yet discovered. And perhaps the answers lie between the covers of Alice's notebook."

I harkened back to something he had said at Bishop's Folly. "Do you really believe there is a connection between Alice's death and Gisela's disappearance?"

"I cannot imagine what, but it is entirely possible the two events are unrelated."

"They had Maximilian in common," I mused. "What if he did not remove Alice from the picture, but Gisela herself did?"

"She had only to order Alice from the Alpenwald," he reminded me. "She is the hereditary princess. If she wanted Alice banished, then Alice would go."

"But Maximilian, if he was still in love with Alice, might make a good deal of trouble. Would you want to start a marriage on such a footing?"

"Better than killing my mistress, if that is what you mean."

I lapsed into irritated silence. "Their motives are so oblique. I find these people vastly annoying."

"Annoying, but interesting," he said with a smile. "It is a tangled skein to be sure. Now let us set to raveling."

Naturally there ensued a rather spirited discussion on which of us ought to break into the Curiosity Club. We stood on the pavement, tucked into the leafy shadows of the square across the street. The club had once been a private residence, deeded to the organization by one of the founding members. It stood in a quiet street not so very far from a royal palace. The houses that stood like sentinels around the square were tastefully embellished and uncompromisingly white — austere wedding cakes, I always thought of them. During the day, the square would hum with discreet activity, nannies pushing their charges in perambulators buffed to a perfect gloss, maidservants moving on silent feet, starched aprons and cap ribbons snapping behind them. There were a hundred such streets in London, each of them pristine and tidy and secure in their own respectable prosperity. It seemed nothing scandalous or criminal could ever happen in such a place. Except that we were currently bent upon thievery.

We argued in hushed tones as we surveyed the building that housed the Curiosity Club. Stoker pointed out his greater skills in the art of lockpicking — to say nothing of shinning up a drainpipe like a monkey, a product of years spent in circus tents and on naval ships. But I replied that his skills were entirely immaterial in this case.

"I have a key," I told him, brandishing the article in question.

"Veronica, you cannot just bloody well walk inside and steal Alice's notebook," he protested.

"Of course I can. I am a member of the club and you are not even the proper gender to be allowed inside its hallowed walls. I shall enter and slip upstairs to the exhibition room. If I am detected, I will simply say that I have come at Lady C.'s behest to attend to a detail regarding the exhibition and that the hour may be unconventional but was the only time I could spare."

"And what if Lady C. is the one who apprehends you?" he demanded.

"That is a river I will ford when I come to it," I told him. I lifted up on tiptoe and kissed his cheek. "Stay in the shadows and try not to look quite so menacing or someone will report you to the police as a lurker."

He grumbled something entirely unprintable in a polite memoir and I hurried off, drawing in great lungfuls of cold, crisp London air. The door of the Curiosity Club sat in a tiny pool of warm light from the gas lantern hung next to it. Around me were silent shadows. In this quiet and largely residential part of the city, there were only houses and private clubs barred to outsiders. Even the garden in the center of the square was locked and barred against those who did not belong. Stoker had moved backwards to conceal himself still further against the high iron gate of the garden in the square, and I could not see him as I moved on careful feet to the top of the stone steps and fitted my key to the lock.

I gave a soft call — the cry of the hoopoe and our arranged signal. One call for success and two for danger. I waited for Stoker's answering call and slipped into the club, closing the door silently behind me and thanking providence for Hestia. As portress, she was a ferocious guardian at the gate and took exquisite care of the property as well as the organization itself. Her exacting standards meant that there were no creaking hinges, no groaning floorboards to betray my presence. Inside the hall, a nightlight burned, a single gas jet illuminating the interior. I groped my way up the stairs, keeping one hand lightly on the stair rail as I moved, fingertips skimming the freshly polished wood. It smelt strongly of beeswax and lavender. I forced myself to move slowly, advancing a step with each new breath, willing my heartbeat to calmness. The walls were thickly hung with paintings and photographs, framed maps and expedition gear. The last thing I needed was to upset one of them and send something crashing down to rouse the household. Hestia slept on the premises, I recalled, and there were a few rooms always reserved for members who did not live in London but wished to use the club as a sort of base camp whilst in the city. Heaven only knew how many women might be sleeping under that roof while I crept about, but my plan was to leave them to their slumbers.

The door to the exhibition room was

unlocked. As I turned the knob, I heard a soft noise — a footfall? a snore? — and instantly stopped, standing as still as one of Stoker's stuffed specimens. I waited an eternity, but there was no further noise, only the occasional gentle creak of an old house settling its bones against the icy weather. After a thousand heartbeats, I slipped inside the room, shutting the door gently behind me. I took the precaution of turning the key in the lock and slipping it into my pocket. Without it, there would be a delay of several hours at least before anyone was able to gain access to the room and discover the theft of the notebook.

I was conscious at once of how cold it was in the room, far colder than the rooms downstairs, and I shivered as I crossed the carpet to the display case where the note-book had been locked. It was darker here as well. No night-light softened the darkness, and the heavy draperies had been drawn across the window. It was a large French window giving on to a small, balustraded parapet that overhung the ground floor, making the house far more attractive than the buildings with flat façades, I thought, but desperately drafty in winter, it seemed. The draperies even stirred a little in the chill of the night air, and I realized I could, quite possibly, leave that way, eliminating the need for a return trip through the club. All it required was a convenient bit of ivy or even a few architectural embellishments upon which to place my weight. I was no climber in the fashion of Alice Baker-Greene — or even as skilled as Stoker in such matters — but butterflying required considerable scrambling over rocks, hauling oneself up and down steeply scrubby hillsides and modest mountains. I had more than once launched myself into ravines or over a precipice, and the thought of doing so under these conditions caused my pulse to quicken with excitement.

So distracted was I by such thoughts that once I struck a vesta, the burst of light blooming into the darkness and dazzling my eyes, I did not realize at first that the door of the case stood open, a twisted wire lodged in the lock. On the shelf, where the notebook had been left, there was only an empty place. I like to think that my wits might have functioned more quickly had my eyes not taken a moment to adjust to the change in the light, but the truth was, I had approached the endeavor far too complacently. When I am coursing along the trail of a most elusive butterfly, I must still be watchful, vigilant against poisonous vipers, assorted venomous spiders, rock falls and sinking sands, and the occasional brigand. In the cushioned security of the Curiosity Club, those lessons deserted me, and I did not scent danger until it was upon me.

The drapery at the window bellied out with a sudden frosty gust, and I realized too late that the window was not poorly fitted and drafty — it was open. The gust caused my vesta to gutter and die just as a figure launched itself at me from behind the drapery. I had but a fragment of a second's warning. I dodged to my right, eluding the heaviest part of the blow, but still a solid strike from a closed fist landed upon my jaw, hurtling me to the ground and causing stars to sparkle across my vision.

Without thought or hesitation, I forced myself up onto my hands and knees in time to see the intruder flee through the open window, pausing only briefly, entangled in the thick curtain before vanishing out the window and onto the parapet. Our collision had cost me a second or two at most, and by the time I reached the parapet, the villain had only just swung a leg over the side of the balustrade. The figure was male, with a cap pulled low over the brow, concealing the features. The head turned, the shadowed eyes seeming to bore into me, and then he was gone, as silent and weightless as if he had dropped from the parapet.

I vaulted to where he had disappeared to find he had not, in fact, fallen, but was climbing swiftly and quietly, with an economy of motion that would have done credit to an orangutan. I swung my leg over the parapet, giving a double-barreled cry of the hoopoe, two quick calls to alert Stoker to danger. The figure looked up as I secured my hold on the drainpipe. The apparatus swung alarmingly under our combined weight but it held, the bolts biting into the masonry of the building as we descended. He hit the ground at a dead run, his boots making a peculiar metallic noise as he moved. There was no sign of Stoker and I cursed him roundly under my breath as I undertook the pursuit myself. The stranger ran across the street towards the square, hauling himself hand over hand up the iron bars and into the garden, disappearing into the thick foliage.

"What in the name of the oozing wounds of Christ is happening?" Stoker demanded as I pounded on the bars in frustration.

"The devil has gone in there!" I exclaimed. "He has the notebook!" Stoker, to his eternal credit, required no further urging.

He dropped at once to his knee, forming a stirrup with his hands. He rested these on his thigh and as I set my foot into his cupped palms, he surged upwards, vaulting me up and over the top of the fence. He followed hard upon my heels, both of us landing rather gracelessly in a particularly nasty evergreen shrub.

We helped one another to our feet, stopping to listen. There was no noise save the sigh of the wind and the click of the bare branches of the plane trees overhead as they rubbed together.

"He cannot be far," I whispered. "His boots make noise. Metallic."

"Climbing boots," Stoker said grimly. "Nails in the soles, no doubt."

I nodded and peered into the darkness. Only a sliver of a waning crescent moon illuminated the sky, giving nothing but a cold, faraway glow to the rooftops beyond the garden. Of the square itself, it showed nothing, and there were no friendly lanterns to light the way. It seemed impossible that one could be in the heart of London and yet so completely silent, but we were as remote as that silvery, slivery moon, I thought.

But then I knew, although I could not

have said why. Our miscreant was close at hand.

I turned to Stoker. "We have lost him," I said in audible dejection. "And I cannot stand any longer in this freezing cold. We might as well go home."

Stoker opened his mouth to protest, but I pressed his hand. "Oh — er, yes. Quite right. It is devilishly cold and I think I am taking a chill."

He gave a racking cough that was as false as it was loud, and I tugged on his hand, pulling him towards the gate. "Have you your lockpicks handy? I've no liking for going over that fence again and it would be far more comfortable to leave by the gate."

"Yes, of course." We dared not light a vesta, so he worked by touch, taking a little longer than he might otherwise have done. I was conscious the whole time of a presence, nothing more than a feeling. Not by footstep or rustling branch did he betray his presence. But I knew he was there.

When the gate was at last open, I motioned for Stoker to go through first. He eased himself out onto the pavement, looking for any passersby, but he shook his head, indicating the streets were quiet. I tested the gate on its hinges, finding it silent and smooth, and opened it widely.

"Thank God this night is over," I said with a yawn, and I gestured for Stoker to walk a little ways down the pavement, his footfalls echoing around the silent square. I stood in the shadow for a long minute, so long I began to think our quarry would never emerge. But at last I heard the peculiar metallic scrape of his boots on the gravel, coming closer and closer still as my hand gripped the gate.

He stepped onto the pavement and I flung the gate forward with all my might, the end post catching him squarely upon the chin and knocking him flat onto his back as his feet soared over his head.

Stoker was at my side in an instant. "I presume you had an excellent reason for doing that?" he asked mildly.

"He hit me in the jaw," I said, tapping the spot on my face that I was quite certain would bloom with a bruise by morning.

"Well then," Stoker replied, "you ought to have hit him harder."

"He is unconscious," I pointed out. "I was not trying to kill him." Stoker lit a series of vestas to illuminate the scene as I bent swiftly to the villain's recumbent form and searched his pockets. The notebook was in the second and I handed it to Stoker for safekeeping. I might have proved myself a match for the fellow, but I had little doubt he would think twice before attacking Stoker.

"Who do you think it is?" Stoker asked as he buttoned the notebook securely into his pocket. His vesta struggled against the chill wind, giving only a small pool of light, and the miscreant's face was still concealed by his scarf and cap.

I shrugged. "It has all been too confusing to venture a guess. Maximilian perhaps?"

Just then the villain groaned and moved his head. "What in the name of Sam Hill did you do that for?" he demanded.

He sat up, his scarf falling away, but even if I had not glimpsed the features, I would have known him from the American idiom. "Douglas Norton!" I cried.

CHAPTER 16

Douglas Norton gave another groan and dropped his head into his hands. "It feels like my head is about to fall off," he complained as he raised his face to Stoker. "What did you hit me with?"

"I did not hit you at all, my good fellow," Stoker replied. "That is the lady's handiwork."

Norton gave a soundless whistle. "That was as hard a hit as any I've taken," he said with something that might have been respect.

"Well, you did hit me first," I pointed out.

He had the grace to look embarrassed. "You surprised me. And I am not exactly experienced at breaking and entering."

"Good," Stoker said, hauling him to his feet. "Then you will not mind coming with us for a little conversation on the matter." With one hand on Norton's collar and the other on his belt, he propelled the fellow forward and around the corner — in the direction whence he had come as I had been busily flinging myself down a drainpipe. Stoker stopped next to a green cabman's shelter, one of the tidy little chalets that had been built for the comfort and security of the city's drivers to keep them from cold and wind and the lure of drink whilst they waited for fares. The chimney smoked gently and there was a convivial sound of scraping cutlery and manly conversation within. Gas lanterns hung outside over window boxes that must have bloomed with good cheer in warmer months. Now they were empty and forlorn, but the shelter provided a little respite from the wind and the lanterns illuminated our strange party.

"We cannot take him in there," I protested. "The shelters are for cabmen only. They are quite strict upon the matter."

"I know," Stoker said, pushing Norton up against the wall of the shelter. The thump of Norton's body hitting the wall must have echoed inside, for the door opened and a round, ruddy face wreathed in ginger whiskers peered out.

"Back again, are you, Mr. Stoker?"

"I am, Tom. I need a few minutes' private conversation with the gentleman, you don't mind?"

The fellow flapped a meaty hand. "Lord love you, no. If you need a hand, I'll bring the lads, I will. Otherwise I shall leave you to get on with it." He gave a nod and withdrew into the snug warmth of the cab shelter, taking with him the aroma of bacon and new bread and horse.

Stoker turned to Norton, who had been furtively examining his pockets.

"You took it, didn't you?" Norton's expression was a mask of fury.

"Of course we did," I told him. "And there is no purpose in trying to get it back. We will only strike you again."

He held up his hands as if to ward us off. "I think we've had enough fisticuffs for one night. But what do you want with Alice's journal?"

"What do *you* want with it?" I countered.

"If you know who I am, you will know what I want with it," he said flatly.

"Her professional notes," Stoker guessed. "Her routes up and down the most challenging climbs in the world. All the secrets of one of the most accomplished alpinists ever to set foot on a mountain."

Norton's expression struggled between anger and misery. "You've no idea what it's like, trying to make a name for yourself as a climber these days. You've either got to have family money or a rich sponsor to pay the way, and those are scarce as hen's teeth."

"Alice Baker-Greene managed to secure a few," I reminded him.

"She did," he said with real bitterness. "She had only to smile at a camera and they came flocking to her. It took me two years to find a sponsor of my own — a Colorado miner who had struck it rich and liked to spread his money around. He gave me a partial share for a season and said he would give me enough for the Karakorum if I distinguished myself. Distinguished! That's a laugh."

"What happened?" Stoker asked.

"I went climbing with Alice Baker-Greene and lost my sponsor because she kicked up a fuss and said I beat her to the summit in violation of our agreement." He rubbed at his jaw, drawing his fingers away to look at the blood streaming from his chin.

"Did you? Or did she lie?" I demanded.

His gaze met mine and then shifted. "I hardly like to say. It was a difficult and dangerous time on that mountain. A storm had risen. We were out of provisions and Alice was faltering. She wanted to rest and I thought she meant to turn back afterwards. She said later that she made it plain she intended to try for the summit, but I never heard that. It was screaming blue murder with wind on that mountain," he added. "Impossible to hear anything, really."

"So your climbing partner was, you believed, in difficulty and without provisions, in dangerous conditions, and your solution was to abandon her in order to secure your own glory?" I made my tone as pleasant as possible, but he bristled.

"When you put it like that, it sounds bad."

"It is bad," I assured him. "And your reputation suffered accordingly. So much so that you have scarcely been on a mountain since. Unless you count the Alpenwald."

He flinched as if I had hit him again. "I was never in the Alpenwald."

"Really?" Stoker said. "I seem to recall a newspaper piece suggesting you were."

"That is slander," he said stoutly. "Or libel. Whichever. It is a filthy lie."

In spite of the cold, tiny beads of perspiration beaded his hairline. "Attempting to summit the Teufelstreppe in order to prove your merit as a climber seems a perfectly reasonable and worthwhile thing to do," I suggested. "And nothing worth flinging accusations of libel and slander about. Unless you were really in the Alpenwald for a more nefarious purpose."

"Like cutting Alice Baker-Greene's rope

and pushing her to her death," Stoker finished.

Douglas Norton's eyes rounded and his mouth fell slack. "What are you talking about?"

"We are talking about the murder of Alice Baker-Greene," I said.

"Murder! It was an accident," he said, thrusting his hands through his hair. His cap fell off and he left it on the pavement. "Oh no." His voice fell to a series of soft, desperate murmurs. "No, it cannot be."

"I assure you it is," Stoker told him.

"I cannot believe it was murder," Norton said. "The inquest —"

"The inquest was not privy to certain evidence we have uncovered," I replied. "Evidence that makes it quite clear Alice was murdered. And most likely by a slender man with moustaches," I added, flicking the end of his with a finger. "Moustaches just like these."

He drew back sharply. "I had nothing to do with her death," he said. "I didn't even know she had been murdered until just this minute."

"And I suppose you also had nothing to do with another burglary of the club," Stoker said, nodding towards the direction of the club.

Norton blinked. "What burglary?"

"Two nights ago," I said. "Someone broke in and stole the rope which Alice was using the day she died — a rope that had been deliberately cut." I did not mention the badge. It seemed best to hold back at least a little of the story.

"And a rope which was the single best indicator that she was murdered," Stoker added.

"I had nothing to do with that either," Norton said, his eyes darting desperately.

"And yet here you are," I told him in a pleasant tone. "Playing the thief, and stealing something that belonged to Alice Baker-Greene. What else have you stolen, Mr. Norton?"

It was a mistake, I reflected, as he thrust himself suddenly away from the wall of the shelter and took off as if the hounds of hell were after him, his nailed climbing boots striking sparks on the pavement as he ran.

Stoker heaved a sigh. "Shall I fetch him back?"

I shook my head. "We have the notebook and that is all that matters." I bent to the pavement and retrieved Norton's cap. Inside the band, there was a small card bearing the name of a rather unsavory lodging house in Clerkenwell. "Besides, we know where to find him if we want him," I added.

"Just as well," Stoker said with a broad yawn. "I doubt he is our miscreant of two nights' past."

I whirled on him. "How on earth can you think him innocent?"

"Because I had a delightful little chat with Ginger Tom."

"Ginger Tom?"

"The cabman. He used to be a draftsman, driving wagons for the circus. He took his brother's hackney when he died and moved his family to London. Our paths occasionally cross," he told me. "I knew this was his favorite shelter, so I thought I would look in on the chance he might be here."

"You were supposed to be keeping watch outside the club," I reminded him coldly.

"Empires have fallen in the time it took you," he replied. "I meant only to ask him a question or two about the night Alice's rope and badge were stolen from the club."

"And?"

He shook his head. "I know you would dearly love for him to have driven the guilty party to their breaking and entering and provide us with a solid description, but I am afraid he was not here that night."

I swore fluently, bringing a smile to Stoker's lips.

"However," he said, holding up a hand, "no chambermaid ever gossiped as much as a cabman. One of his mates was bringing a fare back late that night and saw two people on the pavement. There is nothing to indicate they had anything to do with the theft of Alice's things, but they were behaving quite furtively, the fellow said."

"Two people?" I considered this. "I suppose it might have been Norton working with someone. Maximilian? Captain Durand?"

Stoker shook his head. "I am afraid not. The man was wearing his collar turned up to his cheekbones, he told me. Impossible to describe him at all. But the second . . ." He paused to heighten my interest. "The second was a woman."

We discussed this development at length as we made our way back to Bishop's Folly courtesy of Ginger Tom. He dropped us at the gate, neatly catching the coin Stoker flipped and saluting us with his whip as he whistled softly to the horse to walk on. We entered the grounds just as the clock above the stables was chiming the hour.

I gave a broad yawn. "Heavens, that's half the night gone," I murmured.

Stoker's reply was a few words of Keats nuzzled into my temple as he walked me to the door of my chapel. He left me there, saluting with the hand still wrapped in his handkerchief, and I stared after him, conscious of a rush of emotion the likes of which I could never remember feeling before.

You are all that I want and more than I deserve, and I will go to my grave thanking a god in whom I do not believe for bringing me to you.

I was still smiling when I fell asleep.

The next day I slept rather later than was my custom — not unusual given our nocturnal adventures. The morning was well advanced and bitterly cold by the time I had washed and dressed and applied an ointment of arnica to my bruised chin. Stoker was already in the Belvedere surrounded by the bevy of dogs looking hopefully at the heap of bacon on his plate. He was reading the *Daily Harbinger* and breaking off bits of rind to throw to them. His finger was neatly bandaged and only a little swollen, I saw with relief.

"Good morning," I said brightly. "Anything of interest?"

Amusement twitched the corners of his mouth. "Only this." He lifted the newspaper to show me the front page — PRINCESS AT-

TACKED BY PRANKSTER OUTSIDE OPERA HOUSE, trumpeted the headline. It was accompanied by a few lurid sketches of the pandemonium outside the opera house and an official portrait of Gisela complete with crown and royal orders.

"Prankster!" I exclaimed as I leant forward to read the article. It was a breathless account of the entire evening from the triumph of Mademoiselle Fribourg in her début as Atalanta to the enthusiastic reception of the Princess of the Alpenwald. After a full page of this, the story turned to the drama that had played out upon the pavement.

It went on at great length describing the event and quoting Inspector Mornaday of Special Branch of the Metropolitan Police, who characterized the event as nothing more than an ill-timed and nasty joke perpetrated by a japester who had vanished into the crowd. It concluded with a statement from the Alpenwalder delegation that they were perfectly content that this had been a prank and not a serious attempt upon the princess's life.

"It seems Mornaday has come to the same conclusion you did," I said, tossing the newspaper back to Stoker.

"There were no injuries and little damage

apart from a few torn garments and broken feathers in the jostling from the panic," he replied. "It was the obvious conclusion — even Mornaday could not fail to draw it. And the chancellor's statement would prevent him from investigating further, even if he were so inclined."

"He will not like that," I mused. I produced the card from the chocolate box and examined it again. " 'Prepare for your end.' Ominous."

"And timely," Stoker added, forking up a kidney for Huxley. "A threat like that appearing around the same time as her disappearance and the bomb at the opera house? Not a coincidence, I think."

"A squib," I reminded him. "As you so cleverly deduced. It would have no doubt made a powerful effect, receiving a threat like that coupled with the fright of the explosion."

"Did she bolt because she received it?" he wondered aloud as Huxley nibbled daintily at the fork.

I shook my head. "I had a good think and remembered something I ought to have recalled earlier. The seal on the chocolates was unbroken when the baroness offered the box to me. Gisela never saw the threat."

"So, she did not disappear because it unnerved her," he said, offering a titbit to Betony. Under his elbow, Nut sidled up to his plate and lifted off a poached egg. "Why then did she leave? And why is the chancellor so certain there is no cause to worry about her?"

"Perhaps he knows where she is," I ventured. "He does seem the least anxious of the lot of them." I helped myself to a piece of toast from the rack and spread it liberally with quince preserves. "So what can we infer?"

"That Gisela is being threatened but not harmed. The chocolates carry only a paper threat, but no real danger, it seems," Stoker said, scratching Vespertine gently behind the ears. "Of course, the chocolates I ate seemed fine, but I suppose we ought to investigate the rest in case any have been tampered with."

I shook my head. "I examined them carefully first thing this morning. There is no sign they have been adulterated — no discoloration, no peculiar odors. No marks of hypodermic syringes or seams where the chocolates may have been opened and put back together."

"Very well, we will assume the chocolates and the squib were meant to frighten, but nothing more. To what end?"

303

"To force her to leave?" I guessed.

"Which she has."

"But she never saw them," I pointed out.

"Perhaps they were not the first." He shook his head. "It's a damnable puzzle. The only thing we can be certain of is that they are being perpetrated by someone who does not know Gisela has vanished."

"Because otherwise, why carry them out?" I agreed. "So, someone outside the Alpenwalder entourage. And that might be anyone — including our favorite investigative journalist."

He grunted his agreement and pushed his chair back, slapping his thighs for Nut to jump onto his lap before giving me a searching look. "You do not really believe J. J. would do such a thing?"

"I do not know what to believe," I said evenly.

"Veronica, I know she is a difficult person to like at times, but I find it hard to believe she would stoop to such depths."

"Do you? I wonder. She is ambitious and intelligent and her career has been thwarted by the mediocrity of lesser men. What if she felt pressed to produce a story so gripping that her editors were forced to take her back? It mightn't feel like much of a crime to introduce a small card with a few words into a box of chocolates. She must know any number of miscreants willing to hurl a small explosive, particularly if she stressed that the thing was to be harmless. And she is on hand."

He sighed, rubbing Nut's ears gently until the dog gave a little sigh of contentment. "You are correct in that it is a good theory, but I cannot believe it."

I rose and dropped a kiss to his head. "Your trouble, Revelstoke Templeton-Vane, is that you are too sweetly naïve where women are concerned."

His laughter was still ringing in my ears when I left him.

As soon as I had finished my toast and dealt with the most pressing of our correspondence, I turned my attention to Alice Baker-Greene's notebook. I might have had to fight Stoker for the privilege, but he had been the delighted recipient of a gift. His brother Tiberius, taking his leisure in Paris, had paid a visit to Deyrolle, the temple of natural history on the Left Bank, where he encountered a rare trophy of a roseate spoonbill — *"Platalea ajaja,"* Stoker happily informed me. "I have not seen one of these beauties since I was in South America." He fell at once to studying the quality of the mount and would likely not have noticed had I divested myself of all my garments and done a dance to shame Salome. So I quietly collected the notebook and retired to my desk with a good reading lamp and a quantity of paper for taking notes.

The notebook was far denser than I had realized, the leaves being the thinnest vellum imaginable, and each page written in a tiny hand quite unlike Alice's usual bold style. She had devised a sort of shorthand for herself that took many pages to decipher, and even then much of it was unintelligible to anyone not familiar with the intricacies of alpinism. There were coordinates and materials lists, sketches of routes and notes on traverses and conditions. It was as thorough a record as I had ever seen, both scientific and personal, and I vowed to see it returned to the Curiosity Club in perfect condition so that others might benefit from its contents. (I also roundly cursed the hide of Douglas Norton for very nearly making off with it, no doubt ensuring it would be lost to mountaineering history if he had been successful.)

Most of this material I skimmed past, recognizing my own limitations in interpreting the data she had recorded. But I paused to read more closely her paragraphs on the people she encountered on her travels. She was unflinching in her assessments, detailing flaws and foibles as fluently as she did favors and virtues. From the dates inside the cover I deduced this was not the notebook she had carried during the expedition in which she made such an enemy of Douglas Norton — much to my irritation. I should have thoroughly enjoyed reading her acerbic comments about *him.* But it began some year and a half before, just about the time she had decided to settle in the Alpenwald. There were frequent mentions of trips from Hochstadt to various mountain towns in the vicinity in Switzerland and Italy, short climbing expeditions in small, out-of-the-way villages, often accompanied by the notation *Climbing with D.* or *Lazy day with D.* These mentions were always finished with a tiny sketch of a flower. I peered through my magnifying glass at the distinctive little petals and realized they were meant to be St. Otthild's wort.

"D. is an Alpenwalder," I murmured to Vespertine. My hound had taken up his post next to my chair, laying the broad weight of his head upon my feet as I worked. Whenever I spoke to him, he raised his shaggy brows before subsiding again into a deep slumber.

"But who?" I wondered. "Durand? Possible, but he is meant to marry Yelena. Unless he found his attentions wandering. And surely she does not mean Douglas Norton," I said with a snort. Vespertine snuffled in his sleep as if to agree. I reached for the Rosemorran copy of *Twistleton's Continental,* a compendium of European nobility that ran to some forty volumes. The Alpenwald was in the first, and it took only a moment to find the entry for Duke Maximilian.

" 'Maximilian Detlef Reinhardt Luitpold von Hochstadt, Duke of Lokendorf,' " I read aloud to Vespertine. Detlef. Or duke. Either began with a "d." On a whim, I turned a few pages to the entry for the chancellor, running my finger down the page until I came to his paragraph. "Dagobert," I said, snapping the book closed decisively. "It appears every man who knew Alice is a candidate." I replaced the volume and returned to the notebook with a sigh of irritation. As I reached for it, the book slipped a little and my fingernail caught on the endpaper, tearing the corner. It was marbled stuff, Florentine and heavy, and I swore under my breath for damaging it. But when I inspected it more closely, I could see that I had not torn it at all. Rather, my nail had slid beneath the edge of the endpaper where it had been pasted down, cracking it free of the spine of the book.

I took it nearer the lamp to assess how easily I might glue the endpaper back again, but as I held it to the light, I noticed the endpaper stood very slightly proud of the cover in the center. Something had been pasted inside it, I realized. I took up my paper knife, a dagger I had liberated from the Rosemorran Collection. It had once stabbed a Venetian nobleman, but I employed it for a far more quotidian purpose. I slipped the blade beneath the edge of the endpaper, levering it gently, ever so gently. The paper resisted, then came away, bit by bit, until I laid it back, revealing a single page, folded carefully. I extracted it and opened it cautiously.

I had expected a letter, perhaps. Something romantic, maybe a bit of poetry or a few sentences of passionate declaration. Instead it was a sketch, detailed and done with skill and exquisite care. Noted at the bottom was the word "Dolcezza," and I laughed aloud. The word meant "sweetness" in Italian, and suddenly I understood the reason for all the climbs in Italy and Switzerland. *D.*

I studied the sketch for several minutes, realizing I was doubtless the first person to have seen this since Alice had pasted it into her notebook — the notebook she had carried with her everywhere, the notebook that had been with her when she died. "I am glad," I said quietly. "I am glad you had a little happiness."

I was still looking at the sketch when Stoker left off playing with his spoonbill and came to look over my shoulder. He glanced, then peered closely with astonished eyes. "Veronica, why is there a nude sketch of you in Alice Baker-Greene's notebook?"

"Because that is not me," I told him. "It is Princess Gisela."

CHAPTER 17

Stoker brewed us a strong pot of tea whilst we considered the implications of the sketch. I retrieved a stack of newspapers from the Germanic section of the Belvedere and pointed him to the relevant dates whilst I took over the chore of making the tea. His German was rough but much better than mine, and with the assistance of a German-English dictionary — not quite as good as an Alpenwalder-English dictionary but such a volume has yet to be written — he managed to decipher the broad strokes of the Hochstadt Court Circular for the dates in question.

By the time the last of the tea had been drunk and the better part of an entire tin of Cook's candied ginger shortbread consumed, he was finished. "I have compared the dates of Gisela's absences from the Alpenwald to Alice's expeditions when she climbed with 'D.' You are correct. They tally in every particular."

"That is why she was making her home in the Alpenwald," I said, still not entirely believing how blind we had been to the possibility of Alice's affections being fixed upon Gisela.

"How devastated she must have been!" I added.

"What do you mean?" Stoker's brow furrowed.

"They clearly spent much time together, cared deeply for one another — Gisela must have been distraught when Alice died. And yet, as princess, she could never publicly reveal her grief. Imagine her, forced to conceal her emotions all this time." I fell silent as a growing horror dawned swiftly upon me.

Stoker was quick to intuit my thoughts. "And then we told her that the woman she loved was murdered. Worst of all, she overheard it! It was not put to her gently or kindly. It was a passing piece of gossip and we discussed it as if it were an academic matter rather than a tragedy of the most intimate variety."

And then a new horror introduced itself, a crawling, wriggling, nasty little doubt. "Unless . . ." I let my voice trail off uncertainly.

"Unless?" he prompted.

"Unless Gisela is the one who murdered her," I finished grimly.

"You cannot be serious," Stoker said in a tone which did not invite argument.

But I would not be deterred. "We are investigating this matter. As logical thinkers, we cannot ignore the possibility of Gisela's guilt."

He folded his arms over the breadth of his chest. "I am listening. Lay out the argument."

"Very well. Most murders are committed within the confines of a domestic relationship. For all its unorthodoxy, this attachment falls within that frame. In fact, I would argue that it does so even more than a conventional relationship."

"How so?"

"Those whose love is not sanctioned by society are forced to hide their affections. Such a situation can draw people closer together, heightening both passions and tensions. There may be no one in whom they can confide if there are troubles, no one who might advise or give them wise counsel on how to manage such a situation. It is easy then for matters to simply move beyond their control."

"Are you speaking from personal experience?" he asked, one corner of his mouth quirking up.

"Some might say I am engaging in such an experience now," I returned tartly. "Our liaison is not sanctioned by society. Neither the law nor the church will give us a veneer of respectability. If we were to find ourselves frustrated by one another, there are precious few to whom either of us might turn for succor."

"Are you?"

"Am I what?"

"Frustrated with me?"

"At the moment, yes. Wildly so. We are speaking of a murder investigation and you have turned the tables to make this conversation about us."

He seemed about to offer a rejoinder, then shrugged instead. "All right. Carry on."

I resumed the thread of my argument. "Without the possibility of loving openly, Gisela and Alice would be forced to conduct their affair in secret, stealing time together." I gestured towards the list of dates and scribbled names of villages. "A handful of expeditions together, no doubt with Gisela incognita, and each time she leaves the Alpenwald, she must . . ." I foundered. "She must what? How did she leave? I know they said she slipped away from her royal duties, but she is the head of state. She has guards, ladies-in-waiting. Someone must have helped her. Someone must have known about Alice."

"Not necessarily." Stoker crossed one booted ankle over the other. "She might have made some sort of excuse — taking the waters at a spa town or needing a rest. She might have pleaded ill health or nerves, neither of which the Alpenwalder court would want to publicize. It is always bad for business when a head of state is in ill health, a holdover from the mediaeval belief that the body of the king was connected to the welfare of the country itself. Healthy king, healthy land."

"And you think the Alpenwalders would have been content to let their princess fob them off with such stories?"

"It is one possibility. They are her subjects, Veronica. They would not pry too deeply even if they suspected she was off on an as-signation — and if they did suspect it, they would never tell us," he pointed out. "Every one of the Alpenwalders we have spoken to has been evasive on the subject of Gisela's absences. Whatever story she spun them, they trust that she can manage her own af-fairs and will always return. Except that this time, she has not. She left, no doubt of her own accord, after learning that Alice was most likely murdered. Perhaps she simply needed time to come to terms with the possibility."

"Or she realized she was about to be unmasked as a murderess," I said.

He rolled his eyes heavenwards. "And what was her motive to kill the woman she loved?"

"Exposure," I told him quickly. "If Alice decided to reveal the affair, it would be catastrophic for Gisela. People are intolerant enough of Sapphic practices amongst private citizens. What would the conservative Alpenwalders have to say about their princess loving another woman? It could spark a revolution."

"And why would Alice do that?"

I spread my hands. "A quarrel, perhaps. People do strike out against the ones they love when they are disappointed and hurt. What if Alice threatened her in a moment of anger? Gisela would have been frightened out of her wits."

"You almost sound sorry for her," Stoker said coldly.

"Pity and empathy are not the same," I replied. "I can understand her actions if that is what happened. She would have been terrified of the affair coming to light, the scandal it would have caused. So she could have determined that Alice would have to die."

"Why not simply send her away with a sum of money?" Stoker suggested.

"Alice would never be bought," I told him. "She had a peculiar sort of integrity. No, she would never have taken a penny of Gisela's money if the princess tried to purchase her silence."

Stoker thought a moment. "There are two rather gaping holes in the fabric of your theory. First, Gisela was not in the Alpenwald when Alice died. I seem to remember you saying she was abroad at the time. And second, the only one seen on the mountain that day was a moustachioed man, so even if you are about to suggest that Gisela made a pretense of leaving and came back, she does not fit the description of the possible murderer."

I gave him a withering stare. "She was disguised, of course."

"As a man with moustaches," he finished in a voice dripping with scorn. "It sounds like a penny dreadful, Veronica. I refuse to believe that Her Serene Highness, the Hereditary Princess of the Alpenwald, pasted on false moustaches and climbed a mountain to murder her lover."

"She would not have to," I said slowly. "She would not have to be there at all. The princess could have had an accomplice. And who better than the man who intends to marry her? Duke Maximilian of Lokendorf," I finished in triumph.

Stoker stared at me a long moment. "Bloody bollocks," he muttered.

My smile was one of purely feline satisfaction. "It is a very good theory," I told him.

"It is not the worst you might have fashioned," he said with a grudging nod. "It does at least tick every box."

"Indeed it does," I said, smoothing my skirts. "Now we have only to find proof."

"Proof? How in the name of seven hells do you intend to do that?"

"We must gain access to the Alpenwalder suite," I told him.

"Absolutely out of the question," he replied.

I blinked at him. "Whyever not?"

"Whyever not? Let me enumerate the reasons," he said, holding up each finger in turn. "First, a possibly homicidal princess who has gone missing. Second, her possible accomplice, a potentially murderous aristocrat who is a little too free with his admiration of your person. Third, courtiers who may or may not have knowledge of the princess's liaison with a murder victim and who could have easily conspired with her to commit the crime. Did it never occur to you, Veronica, that they might *all* have done it? What if they plotted together, all of those bloody Alpenwalders, to remove Alice from the scene? The chancellor and the baroness would do anything for Gisela, they adore her. And Durand is captain of her guard. I do not know if he would draw the line at murder, but there is every chance he would not. And Yelena's entire world is bound up in her employer. There is not one member of that retinue that would balk at killing for her or covering it up if she ordered someone killed, of this I have absolutely no doubt."

As he finished his impassioned speech, a lock of long black hair fell over his brow. His nostrils were flaring like a stag's, and I realized we had taken positions in opposition to one another, squared off like combatants, our hands curled into fists.

"You are, of course, correct," I told him. My humble reply caught him off guard and he dropped his arms, unclenching his fists.

"I am?"

"Naturally," I said in the same soothing tone. "But I am afraid your opposition, while well considered, is not enough to keep us from continuing this investigation."

"What makes you say that?" he demanded.

"Because George has just come in behind you, and from the envelope in his hand, I believe we have been summoned once more to the Sudbury."

CHAPTER 18

Stoker sulked all the way to the hotel whilst I tried very hard not to gloat. And failed.

"Smugness does not become you, Veronica," he told me in icy tones as we alighted at the curb. I said nothing. I merely favored him with my most dazzling smile and swept inside the hotel, careful to keep my veiled face averted from any of the reporters or detectives who were no doubt loitering in the lobby.

The Alpenwalders received us warmly. The baroness answered the door herself, and as we moved into the drawing room of the suite, I could see the chancellor sitting behind the desk, but of Duke Maximilian there was no sign. "Thank you so much for coming," the baroness said in a fervent tone as she pressed my hands.

"Your note only asked us to call," I told her. "Have there been any developments? Has the princess returned?"

"Not yet," she replied, her mouth set in a serious line. "But I know she will come soon. She must."

The chancellor rose from the desk, gesturing towards a stack of newspapers. "There have been many reports about the bomb, naturally," he told us. "And we had a call very early this morning from an Inspector Mornaday."

At the mention of Mornaday's name, my heart skipped an uncomfortable beat. I exchanged a quick glance with Stoker. "Oh?"

"He came to tell us that it was as Mr. Templeton-Vane surmised — the bomb was no bomb at all, really only a glorified firecracker," he said. "He wished to pay his respects and apologize personally to the princess, but the baroness and I were able to prevent this by saying Her Serene Highness was in need of rest after the upset of last evening. We also made a statement canceling all official engagements today, which will work quite well, I think, since we are still without a princess," he added with a moue of regret. He turned to me. "You have done well, *Fraulein.* So well, in fact, that I am afraid I must prevail upon you once more."

Beside me, I felt Stoker stiffen like a pointer.

"I think Miss Speedwell has accommodated your schemes quite enough," Stoker began.

The chancellor held up a hand. "Please," he said, nearly choking on the word. So startled were we by his pleading that we fell silent and let him continue. He did so with obvious difficulty, speaking slowly, as if extracting each word cost him pain.

"How much do you know of the situation on the Continent?" he asked, but it was apparent the question was rhetorical as he launched into a discussion that echoed the one I had enjoyed with the baroness on our first meeting. "If I told you it was a powder keg, it would not be an exaggeration. Matters are so delicate that all it wants is the slightest spark and —" He spread his fingers upwards, making the gesture of an explosion. "Loyalties are so conflicted and convoluted that if Germany went to war, it would plunge the rest of Europe into chaos." He paused and went to rummage in a folio of papers, extracting a large map of the Continent. "Look here," he urged, pointing towards the middle of the map. "The German Empire is colored in blue. You see the change from only a few decades ago?" He laid another map beside it. "With the unification of the German states, the empire has become powerful. Too powerful," he added under his breath. I surveyed the maps. The earlier one looked like a broken plate, colorful bits strewn across the breadth of Europe, each representing a different tiny German-speaking principality or duchy. The current one was a single terrifying monolith collected under one banner and ruled by the Hohenzollerns from Berlin.

"This was the work of Bismarck," he said. "But he is a fool. He argued that knitting the German states together under the rule of the empire would make them more powerful, but the only one who has gained from it is the emperor himself."

"Kaiser Wilhelm," I finished.

"The second of that name," the chancellor said with a grave nod. "Those of us outside of the empire had hopes for his father, a great and progressive man. When he ascended to the throne last spring, we believed it was a new beginning for all of us. We did not realize he was doomed," he added, crossing himself. I had been in Madeira at the time, but I vaguely remembered reading about the three-month reign of Kaiser Frederick. He had been a gentle soul, progressive and forward thinking, unlike his warlike and reactionary son.

The chancellor went on. "For thirty years, Kaiser Frederick bided his time, waiting for his turn to remake Germany, to bring her into the light with the help of his empress." His empress was of special interest to me. She was the eldest child of our queen, Victoria, and had been named for her august mother. As Princess Royal, she had been the apple of her father's eye, schooled by Prince Albert in the English principles of liberality and fairness. Throughout her long marriage to Frederick, she had remained steadfast in her beliefs, in spite of the damage this caused to her popularity with the Germans. They clung to the glory of their warlike past, and her eldest son, now the kaiser, had followed in those traditions.

"The empress was unpopular," I began, but the chancellor made a noise of derision.

"Unpopular! She was reviled, treated with the greatest of contempt by her own son. All those years, waiting to put her mark upon Germany, and her husband's reign lasts no more than three months. A single season for them to rule, and even that was thwarted. Everyone knew Kaiser Frederick was ill when he ascended. The court and the army looked beyond him, as if he were already a ghost. They did not even bother to bend a knee to his will. They did as his son bade them, and as soon as Wilhelm became emperor, they turned on Empress Frederick with all the savagery of which they are capable."

"She was not mistreated?" Stoker asked in horror.

"She was," the chancellor confirmed. "Actually shoved about by her son's men. They came to her palace to remove her papers — her personal and private papers — because her son believed her a traitor to Germany. She, who did nothing but work for the peace of Europe," he added bitterly. His color was high, the dueling scars on his cheeks standing out white against his scarlet skin.

He took a few deep breaths. "But they found nothing. She is as cautious as she is clever," he added with a sly smile. "She sent her papers to England and she thwarted her son. For all his cruelty, he is not intelligent. He could never anticipate how far she would go to secure peace in Europe."

"How far would she go?" Stoker asked.

The chancellor paused, assessing us carefully. "I will tell you something that you must vow never to reveal outside of this room. I require your word of honor, both of you. On pain of death." The words were startling, but his manner was grave. Stoker and I did not look at one another as we swore. The chancellor reached into his portfolio and drew forth a document.

"The Alpenwald is one of the few German-speaking states to resist Bismarck's aggression. She remains independent in spite of the danger."

"The danger?" I asked.

He pointed to the map, sketching out a movement. "Should Germany decide to go to war, she will attack France first. The Alpenwald lies in the clearest and most direct route. We would be destroyed if we oppose the German Empire. But oppose her we will," he finished fiercely. He went to the desk and unlocked a drawer, drawing out a leather portfolio stamped with the crest of the Alpenwald. "This is a treaty between the Alpenwald and France. It is a binding pact of mutual defense against the German Empire."

Stoker gave a soundless whistle as we bent to read the text. It was in English and brief, bereft of the usual flowery diplomatic language that characterized such things. It was a promise, to be signed by both governments, to protect one another and come to each other's aid in the event of German aggression.

"How on earth did you manage to get the French to agree to this?" Stoker asked.

"I did not," the chancellor told him. "It was the work of the Empress Frederick."

"Our Princess Royal Victoria?" I goggled at him. "Our British princess has brokered a treaty against her own son's interests?"

"Because his interests are not those of good and peaceful men," the chancellor said sternly. "She has tried the whole of her life to instill in him the principles of democracy upon which she was weaned, but his upbringing was taken out of her hands by his grandfather. He was schooled to admire all things military and warlike, to love aggression and fighting and the glory of Germany." His moustaches quivered in disgust. "He was never taught to cherish peace, to work for the good of his people. His mother is deeply afraid, you see. She has seen a change in him since he ascended the throne. For decades, Bismarck counted upon being able to control Wilhelm when he came to power. But the chancellor grows old and he cannot keep Wilhelm under his thumb. The kaiser does as he pleases, and he sees himself as a new Frederick the Great, bestriding Europe and the rest of the world. He cares nothing for peace and freedom, and in the great battle, his mother will be on the side of the angels. She does what she can for the cause that is just, and we are grateful to her," he finished with fervor. He took out a handkerchief and mopped his bald head, dabbing at his eyes. The subject was clearly an emotional one for him, and Stoker and I looked at the maps until he had regained control of himself.

The chancellor grasped my hands suddenly. "Miss Speedwell. I would not ask if it were not of the greatest importance, my dear. But the future of Europe depends upon thwarting the ambitions of the kaiser. If we do not stand together, he will do everything in his power to set us against one another."

"What do you need of me?" I asked gently.

"The treaty is to be signed tonight," he began. "Miss Speedwell, you cannot conceive of what this treaty will mean for us. The protection of France! Of the whole of the British Empire! We will sleep easily in our beds at night."

"But surely there are other ways —" I began.

His hands tightened on mine. "There are none," he insisted. "Do you know how long it took to arrange this treaty? It has been accomplished with great difficulty and in perfect secrecy. The rest of the world believes that the princess is in London simply to honor the English mountaineer and to go to the opera. They have no idea why she is here, and that is how it must remain. A social visit, an occasion for beautiful clothes and pretty music. But it is so much more." His tone softened, and a pleading note crept in. "It is the very destiny of Europe. We want peace for our children, *Fraulein.*"

"I understand," I said slowly. "But if you put out a statement saying your princess has fallen ill —"

His grip grew painful. "We have talked of this!" he said, his brows snapping together sharply. "The French would take it as a grave insult. They would believe that the Alpenwald does not negotiate in good faith. They would look at your German queen here in England and think that because we too have German ties, we have persuaded her to deal more generously with us. They would become suspicious, the French. They would refuse to sign the treaty because they would fear we strike deals behind their backs. They believe everyone is as cunning as they are," he finished, his mouth tightening in disapproval.

Stoker stepped forward. "Even if Veronica does this for you, it will not be legal because the princess herself has not signed the treaty."

"I have thought of that," the chancellor replied happily. He dropped my hands and dove into another portfolio on the table. He drew out a lengthy piece of parchment also embellished with the Alpenwalder crest. "This document gives Miss Speedwell the authority to sign the treaty on behalf of the Alpenwalder delegation as a proxy of the princess. Naturally, it must remain secret," he added, "but if there were ever a need, it would stand up in court. Miss Speedwell would be acting with all of the authority of the Alpenwalder government."

I took the parchment and studied it, Stoker reading over my shoulder. "It seems legal enough," I murmured. "Do you not think so?"

He shrugged. "What I do not know about international diplomatic law would fill the libraries at Oxford," he said. He passed the page back to the chancellor. "The greater difficulty is not in Miss Speedwell performing this masquerade again. It is that this must end, sir. Surely you see that? She cannot continue the charade until you are ready to leave for home."

"Can she not?" the chancellor asked, patting his lips. He stroked his moustaches into shape. "The signing of the treaty is tonight. Then there is only the opening of the exhibition at your club of lady explorers. After that, we return to our own country and Miss Speedwell is free to resume her own life."

"And if Her Serene Highness is still missing?" Stoker demanded. "What then?"

The chancellor held up a hand. "There is no need to fear this," he said. "Our princess has always come back to us. She will do so again."

Silence held the room for a long moment.

"What must I do?" I asked at last.

The chancellor, realizing the battle had been won, did not revel in the moment, but his eyes gleamed in satisfaction. "There is a simple ceremony to sign the treaty. A representative of Her Majesty's government to witness the affair, a French delegate, and yourself. These are the only three people who will be signatories to the document. It will be a very short meeting. The treaty itself has already been agreed and copies sent to each party. Everyone brings his own and each of the three will be signed and countersigned. Once the signatures have been placed, that is all."

"That is not all!" the baroness put in sharply. "Have you forgot *where* the meeting is to take place?"

I turned to the chancellor, dread gripping my heart. "Excellency, where are you sending me this evening?"

"It is nothing, child," he said, raising his hands in protest. "An entertainment, a party."

"A formal dinner," the baroness interjected.

"Excellency?" I asked, narrowing my gaze.

He looked from one of us to the other, then surrendered. "Very well. It is a formal dinner. At Windsor Castle."

CHAPTER 19

I dared not look at Stoker; I dared not speak. With that perfect unspoken communication we sometimes shared, he intuited my disordered thoughts and gave voice to them.

"And who will be in attendance at this dinner?" he asked smoothly. "The queen? Members of the royal family?"

"Oh no," the chancellor hastened to explain. "Her Majesty is at Osborne House, as is her custom this time of year, I am told."

"And the rest of the royal family?" Stoker pressed.

The chancellor shrugged. "The Prince of Wales is also away. At his country house, somewhere in the east," he said, waving a vague hand.

"Sandringham House," Stoker supplied. "In Norfolk."

"Yes, that is it. I hear there is very fine shooting to be had," the chancellor said in a wistful tone. "He gathered there for the holidays with his children and he also plays host to his sister the Empress Frederick and her daughters."

"So there will be no member of the royal family at Windsor tonight?" Stoker said.

The chancellor's complexion turned ruddy again. "You are thinking it is an insult to my princess? To the honor of the Alpenwalders that there is no member of your royal family to receive her?"

"Nothing could be further from the truth," Stoker assured him. "I merely find the choice of venue curious if the family are not meant to attend."

The chancellor shrugged again. "It was the request of the Empress Frederick. She wishes to make it clear that although none of the British royalties will sign the treaty, it meets with their approval. A gracious gesture," he added.

"Indeed," Stoker murmured.

The tight band around my chest eased. I breathed a little easier. "Do you know who will be in attendance?" I managed.

"A French delegation and assorted English representatives from within your government. From our side, naturally I will escort the princess and she will be attended by the baroness."

"And by me." Maximilian appeared in the doorway looking like a man whose conscience had kept him awake. His eyes were a trifle puffed and his moustaches drooped a little.

The chancellor looked pained. "As you are not yet formally affianced to Her Serene Highness —" he began.

"All the more reason to include him," the baroness put in. "It will demonstrate to the French that the treaty has the support of the entire Alpenwalder aristocracy and not merely the princely family."

Maximilian smiled at the baroness. "Just so."

The chancellor huffed into his moustaches. "Very well. I will send word that there will be two additional members of our party," he assured the duke, as casually as if he were bringing an extra guest to tea.

Stoker turned to me. "You cannot attend a formal dinner at the queen's castle and pretend to be foreign royalty." The baroness began to speak, but Stoker raised a hand. "I think Miss Speedwell and I will require a few minutes' privacy to discuss the matter," he said in a tone that brooked no argument. The chancellor and baroness withdrew, Maximilian trailing after them. He closed the door behind him, but it would not have surprised me to find him spying through a keyhole.

I folded my arms over my chest and regarded Stoker.

"I managed it well enough last night," I reminded him.

"Because no one was near you! You were surrounded by Alpenwalders and by me," he pointed out. "You spoke to almost no one, and you had nothing to do but sit quietly and occasionally wave. A clockwork mannequin could have done as much."

"Thank you," I said, my tone acid. "It was actually a trifle more complicated than that."

"Yes, I quite forgot. You also had to hold up a tiara. However did you manage it?"

"There is no call for sarcasm," I said.

"What approach is called for?" he inquired. "Should I simply fling you over my shoulder and stalk out of here until you come to your senses?"

"Certainly not. Do not think I will play the Sabine," I warned him. "I mean to do this. Besides, we needed a pretext to spend time with the Alpenwalders to investigate Alice's relationship with Gisela. We could hardly do better."

"Than a semi–state occasion in a royal residence?" His tone softened. "You have

337

not considered the complications. Veronica, it is a formal dinner at Windsor Castle. It will be full of British dignitaries and officials, people who could easily unmask you for the imposter you would be."

"I am not acquainted with any members of the government," I protested.

"Just because they are not known to you does not mean you are not known to them!" He thrust his hands through his hair, disordering it violently. "Veronica, be reasonable. You simply cannot swan through the gates of Windsor Castle as if you have a right to be there."

"Don't I?" I asked softly.

I said nothing more, but I did not have to. He came forward and simply enfolded me in his arms. "I thought you wanted nothing from them."

"I didn't! At least until I met Eddy," I corrected. Our latest foray into murder had seen us making the acquaintance of my half brother, Prince Albert Victor of Wales, Eddy to his intimates. I had found myself growing quite fond of the young man during our short time together. He was silly and frustrating to an impossible degree, but I could not deny the attraction of spending time with those of my own blood. Growing up without family, I had never really placed much importance upon the connections of genetics. I had consoled myself with those whom I met upon my travels whose tastes and values aligned with mine, with those who had proven themselves loyal and trust-worthy out of true affection, not the obliga-tions of blood.

Eddy had been different. We were nothing alike, my half brother and I, but I had been conscious of a deep pull to watch over him, a protectiveness I had seldom experienced before. And I wondered if it were unique to that young man or if I would feel the same towards others of my family, towards the home I had never known but to which I was tied by blood. For eight hundred years, my ancestors had lived and died in that castle. Would I feel any sort of recognition? Any variety of belonging? This was perhaps the best opportunity I would have to find out.

"Well, I suppose it is only a mercy that she will not be there," Stoker said finally, resting his chin on the top of my head. He did not have to specify. I knew precisely whom he meant. "You can at least say hello to her portrait, I suppose."

"Something like that."

"You will be disappointed," he warned me. "She looks very much like a turnip."

I stifled a laugh and he drew back, his gaze

intent. "I am deadly serious. She looks like a turnip in a black bonnet. Or I suppose since they have state portraits there you might see one where she is a turnip in a tiny crown."

I poked him firmly in the ribs. "Behave. You forget I have seen her once before." I had watched her Golden Jubilee procession from a distance, scarcely able to see the small, rotund figure that had been smothered in ruffles and lace and tucked into a royal carriage. I looked up at him. "You understand, do you not?"

"Better than you think. For all my bluster about my family, I still find myself running to them in spite of my best efforts." He dropped a kiss to the top of my head. "I know you well enough to understand that you are going to do this with or without my blessing so I may as well accept it."

"Besides," I told him, "we still do not know anything about who might have been aware of Gisela's connection to Alice and who might therefore have wanted Alice dead."

He slanted me an odd look. "Tell me that is why you want to do this, and I will accept the lie. But at least be honest with yourself. There is nothing about Alice Baker-Greene's death that is drawing you into this particular scheme. You have ghosts of your own to exorcise that have nothing to do with her."

It was an unkind observation, but it was not wrong, I reflected as he went to open the door. As expected, Maximilian was hovering just outside and he tumbled into the room, followed hard by the baroness and the chancellor.

The chancellor's expression was watchful while the baroness's was one of naked hope.

"Very well," I told them. "I will do it. But the same terms as last night — I must be accompanied by Mr. Templeton-Vane, and not merely as my guard," I stipulated. "He must be acknowledged as a member of the delegation and seated at the formal supper."

To my surprise, they agreed at once, and I felt a rush of emotion. I was going to a banquet at Windsor Castle — home of my grandmother, the queen. And whether that emotion was fear or exhilaration, I could not tell.

After a lengthy lesson on royal etiquette from the baroness, Stoker and I were given a brief respite. Stoker complained of hunger and went to the room put aside for his use with the packet of honeycomb he kept in his coat whilst I rubbed my aching temples and picked up a discarded copy of the *Weekly Portent* that someone had stuffed beneath the sofa cushion. I could not imagine any member of the entourage taking an interest in such a periodical; it was a lurid little publication even more outrageous than the *Daily Harbinger*. I wondered if one of the maids had been reading it and hidden it away lest she be discovered shirking her duties.

EXCLUSIVE INTERVIEW WITH PRINCESS'S POTENTIAL BETROTHED, ROYAL MAN OF ACTION, shouted the headline. I read the article with mounting disbelief. It was a lengthy piece on Duke Maximilian, describing the events of the previous night at the opera house and detailing how his courage and perspicacity had saved Princess Gisela from harm when a bomb had exploded near her. The piece was stickily sentimental and flattering in the extreme, cataloging his virtues as a man of the people, accomplished and yet never lacking the common touch. There was a formal photograph of him in uniform and two more in hunting garb and evening dress. He presented a perfect image of a man of the world, destined for greatness. He was quoted as saying that he was a devoted lover of his country with no greater wish than to serve the Alpenwald by supporting the princess. He had many flattering things to say about England and the continued bonds between our countries, and the article ended with an encomium of praise so extreme I blushed for the author. The last lines were a direct appeal to the princess to accept the duke's hand in marriage and give the Alpenwald the prince it so richly deserved.

I nearly tossed the newspaper aside in disgust. The duke had not "flung himself on the perpetrator with complete disregard for his own personal safety" while "shielding the princess from harm with his own muscular form." And he had certainly not "apprehended the villain single-handedly before turning him over to the Metropolitan Police." Every other newspaper in the country reported the fact that the bomb thrower had not been identified much less apprehended, and a dozen different descriptions had been circulated — everything from a nut seller to a dowager duchess had allegedly hurled the explosive.

Just then my gaze went to the byline and I caught my breath, blinking hard. *J. J. Butterworth.*

I took the newspaper and hurried to find Stoker, running him to ground in the small bedchamber put at his disposal. He was reading a French novel and contentedly consuming the better part of the entire packet of honeycomb, happy as the proverbial clam. I thrust the newspaper into his sticky grasp.

"J. J. has lied to us," I proclaimed in a state of high dudgeon. "She indicated she was here in order to write a story about the princess, and yet she must have already seen Maximilian and interviewed him for this piece to run in today's newspaper."

He considered this a moment. "More to the point, how did she happen to find him when the chancellor and the baroness did not even realize he was in London?"

"Read the last paragraph," I instructed.

He skimmed it, his brows rising heavenwards as he did so. "Christ and his sleeping saints, do you realize what this means?"

"It means," I said grimly, "that J. J. Butterworth has a very great deal to answer for."

CHAPTER 20

We made our way to Julien's workrooms, appearing just as he was mournfully studying a bowl of curdled custard in the hands of a tearful assistant.

"Archie, this is not a custard. This is a crime," he said gently. "You must always handle a custard as you would a woman. Have you ever been with a woman?"

The youth shook his head, his face flaming.

Julien clapped a hand to his shoulder. "Let me tell you about my first love, Angelique. What a beauty she was! Martiniquais, like me, and a sheen to her skin as if it were polished by the hand of God. She was plump like a ripe piece of fruit, and when she undressed, her thigh, just above her stocking, it moved. What is the English word? Wibble?"

"Wobble?" the young man guessed.

"Wobble, yes. Her thigh would wobble.

You must find such a woman, Archie. And when she undresses for you, watch her thigh. Worship it," he instructed. "And when you return, you will know how a custard should move. It should look like the round and silken thigh of a woman." He flapped a hand at the bowl. "Now, take this away and feed it to a sad cat in the alleyway. It pains me to see it."

The boy fled, custard bowl in hand, and Julien sighed. "My work, it is very taxing."

"Clearly," Stoker said with a grin. "How is Angelique?"

Julien's expression turned mournful. "Married. With nine children. And skinny now like the handle of a rake. It is enough to break the heart. What do you want, my friends?"

We told him and he dispatched an errand boy to find J. J. I expected her to prove elusive, but she strode in, her chin lifted defiantly.

Julien made some tactful French noises and withdrew, no doubt sensing the interview would be an unpleasant one. He gestured towards a tray of *guimauves* as he went, and Stoker collected a handful as J. J. seated herself with ill grace.

"What? I have work to do, you know."

I held up the newspaper and she went

pink to the tips of her ears. "I do not apologize for writing for the *Portent.*"

"It is a rag," I told her.

"It pays," she said flatly. "And that is my first byline on a front page. One more story — the right story — and it will be enough to persuade the *Harbinger* to take me back."

"What kind of story?" Stoker asked. She twitched a little but said nothing.

"Very well," I put in pleasantly. "We have asked you nicely. Now we will be rather less than nice. It is entirely apparent from this article that you must have written it *before* the explosive was thrown last night. Didn't you?"

She shifted in her chair and set her mouth in a mulish line before bursting out, "Oh, very well. Yes! I knew. I interviewed Maximilian early yesterday. Before he went up to the suite."

"How did you know he was here in London?" Stoker asked. "The other Alpenwalders were surprised by his appearance."

"I saw him the night before. He used the service stairs to slip up to the royal suite. I was curious as to what was afoot and he had eluded the hotel's security. I thought if an intruder was up to no good and I could foil some sort of attack, the princess might be grateful enough to grant me an interview

347

— a nice exclusive I could sell to one of the larger newspapers. I crept up the stairs behind him, ready to catch him red-handed, as it were. Only he did not have to break into the suite."

"Someone let him in?" I guessed.

"Durand," she said. "He opened the door and called him by name, that is how I deduced his identity. I hid in one of the alcoves on the stairs and after a very few minutes he returned, only this time he was not alone. He was with someone in a cloak."

She paused for effect, but Stoker merely shook his head. "I do not see the significance."

"A cloak," she repeated. "A *maid's* cloak. It was a plain, rather ugly thing that belonged to Yelena."

"Why shouldn't Yelena go out? Presumably she has the occasional night off."

"Because it was not Yelena in the cloak," she said, her voice dropping to a thrilled whisper. "It was the princess."

"How do you know?" I put in.

"Because it was miles too short," she replied. "The princess has half a foot on her maid, and I could clearly see the hem of her frock hanging below the hem of the cloak. It was a dark blue velvet gown I had taken away to be sponged only that morning. It was edged with Mechlin lace. I was not likely to forget it."

Stoker did not bother to glance at me, but he heaved a sigh. "Veronica, I can feel the emanations from your person just now. 'Smug' does not begin to describe them."

J. J. looked from one of us to the other and back again. "What is all that about?"

"Never mind," Stoker and I chorused. He picked up the thread of the interrogation. "What next?"

"They walked around the corner and hailed a cab. I heard the address, so I followed in one of my own. I had the cabman drop me a street away and I kept to the shadows so they would not see me. They told the cabman to wait, and a short time later they got back in and went directly to St. Pancras station. The duke walked her in and when he came out, he was alone and I was waiting for him. I invited him to share my cab, and he got in."

"No doubt thinking you were offering him something rather different than a mere ride in a cab," I mused.

She smoothed her apron. "Well, he might have misunderstood me at first, but I corrected his thinking quite quickly. I simply told him what I had witnessed and that I thought we could help one another."

"And on the strength of that, Maximilian gave you an interview?" I asked.

She shrugged again. Stoker looked at me. "Well, at least we know that Gisela did leave of her own accord. Whatever happened that night, it does not appear that Maximilian harmed her."

"Max would never harm her," J. J. said succinctly. "He adores her."

"He has flirted outrageously with me and was prepared to avail himself of your services when he thought you were a prostitute," I told her.

"That is because he has very old-fashioned ideas about women, bless him," she said with some fondness. "He thinks all women are either saints or whores. He does not know what to make of the rest of us."

"That is positively archaic," I muttered.

"He is an Alpenwalder aristocrat," she pointed out. "They are not precisely known for their progressive thinking. The whole bloody country is mired in the Dark Ages."

"And you still wrote this," I said, brandishing the newspaper, "to help him secure the post of consort?"

"He is no worse than the rest of them," she said in a weary voice. "I am most heartily tired of men."

Stoker looked a little wounded. "Not

you," I soothed.

"Especially him," she corrected darkly. "He ruined my story."

He bristled. "What on earth did I do?"

"You threw yourself between the 'princess' " — she jabbed a finger in my direction — "and the explosive. And after I had written a beautiful piece detailing Maximilian playing the hero. Anyone standing on that pavement knows what really happened."

"It was chaos," I told her. "But your account was detailed — to a suspicious degree. In order for you to know how things were meant to play out, you must have had advance knowledge."

To her credit, she flushed again. "I *am* sorry. I ought to have told you, but Maximilian swore me to secrecy and said there was no danger whatsoever."

"Maximilian." This time I did not bother to conceal my triumph. "He knew."

"He arranged it," she said dully. "It was only a large firework. It was meant to make a good deal of noise and smoke and nothing more."

"Then what was the point of it?" Stoker asked.

"To let Max play the hero with Gisela," J. J. explained. "She has been dragging her feet over accepting his proposal and he is growing desperate. It was put to him that if she felt vulnerable, it might nudge her towards marriage. A situation where she was threatened — even if only for a moment — and he acted decisively and courageously might be just enough to tip her into his arms."

"Suggested?" Stoker pounced upon the word. "By whom?"

"By an unlovely gentleman to whom he owes money. Maximilian is a bit of a gambler. He likes betting on horse races, dog races, turtle races."

"Turtle races?" Stoker asked. "How the bloody hell does one race a turtle?"

"Slowly," she said with a ghost of her old smile. "He went to Deauville after a quarrel with Gisela and found himself overextended. The fellow to whom he owes the money has rather nasty schemes for getting his debts repaid. The French lads in his employ are not above using a few persuasions — a club applied to a kneecap, an explosive tossed through a window. Whatever the situation requires. One of them threw the squib last night at a signal from Max. He blended into the crowd and was back in France on the first Channel steamer. You can despise him all you like, but I can assure you, the alternative would have been worse. The duke has fallen in with a particularly nasty crowd who will not take it well if he fails to pay his debts of honor." She paused, drawing in a breath. "See here, I know what I did was very wrong, but no harm was actually done. I have spent my entire life taking risks like that — I haven't had any other way to get ahead. And I have my first front-page byline out of it, so if you are expecting an apology, I'm afraid you will be sitting in the anteroom of hell before you hear one out of me."

She lifted her chin, and in spite of her defiance, I was rather glad to see something of her old spirit in evidence. I did not like a defeated J. J.

"What about the chocolate box?" Stoker asked. "There was a threat left inside a box of rose and violet creams on the princess's dressing table."

"Another suggestion from Max's unsavory companion from Deauville. He wanted to put Gisela on edge a bit so the 'bomb' would feel even more frightening when it went off, make her feel like she was surrounded by enemies, that sort of thing."

"That is diabolical," I said. "How on earth can she possibly marry such a man?"

J. J. waved a dismissive hand. "He is no

worse than most and better than many. The duke is treading water just now, you know. He owes a great deal of money and he is frightened. I think we all know how stupid frightened people can be."

We all fell silent for a moment, and then Stoker spoke. "When Maximilian and Gisela stopped on the way to the station, where did they go?" I asked.

J. J. studied her nails. "I do not think I should say."

"What?" I asked, resisting the urge to shake her.

J. J. shook her head and smiled. "I have told you quite enough and got nothing in return. Now, if you want anything else, you will have to make it worth my while."

"Stoker, your notecase," I said quickly. "How much have you got?"

"I do not want money!" she protested, clearly offended. "I want something far more valuable than that." She sat back with an air of triumph.

"What on earth could we have that is more valuable than banknotes?" Stoker asked.

Her smile was rapacious. "It is very simple and will cost you absolutely nothing. I simply want to go to the dinner at Windsor Castle. As the attendant of Her Serene

Highness, the Princess Gisela of the Alpen-wald."

A long moment of horrified silence followed her pronouncement.

Stoker spoke first. "Out of the question."

"How do you even know about the dinner?" I asked.

"It is all the Alpenwalders talk about," she said. "They are very excited. Apparently, it is one of the grandest things to happen to them since the Holy Roman Emperor came to tea in 1225."

"No one in Europe was drinking tea in 1225," I informed her acidly.

She gave a shrug. "Details. Now, may I come?"

"Absolutely not," I told her, relishing the moment.

She sat back and folded her arms over her chest. "Make it happen or I will publish a story in tomorrow's newspaper about my time in the Sudbury Hotel working as a chambermaid where I uncovered the fact that an Englishwoman of dubious reputation has been masquerading as a missing princess," she said coolly.

"You would not dare," Stoker began, but his tone was doubtful. She absolutely *would* dare.

"My reputation is not dubious," I protested.

"It is not exactly lily white," she countered. "And, of course, I will make certain to mention your *innamorato*, the black sheep of a distinguished aristocratic family. And naturally, if his name is mentioned, it will revive all those nasty stories about his divorce," she added.

"You absolute —" The word I used was not relevant to this narrative, but it was entirely appropriate, causing Stoker to blush furiously.

"Sticks and stones," J. J. said calmly. "Do we have a bargain? I will tell you everything I know about the princess's departure, and I will promise not to write about your origins for publication if you take me with you to Windsor."

"Why?" I asked. "I find it highly suspicious that you would willingly relinquish as explosive a story as that simply for the chance to see Windsor Castle. It is open to the public, you know. You could visit some Sunday with a nice group of tourists. Take a hamper for a picnic luncheon."

She bared her teeth in what a foolish person might have thought was a smile. "I have bigger fish to fry, my dear. The scandalous peccadilloes of minor royalty are nothing compared to the story I want to write — something that will establish once and for all that I ought to be taken seriously by the editors."

"Something political," Stoker guessed.

"Full marks to Templeton-Vane," she said.

"You are a demon in a petticoat," I told her. "How can we be certain you will keep your bargain?"

She had the nerve to look offended. "I have never broken my word to you and I do not intend to begin now. I thought we were friends, Veronica. Or if not friends, at least that we understood one another."

In spite of myself, I felt my rage ebbing. The trouble was, I *did* understand her. The challenges of being an intelligent woman working in a world limited by the whims of narrow-minded and unimaginative men were legion. J. J. had struggled for years to secure respect for herself as an investigative journalist, one who wrote important stories about the people shaping events. She longed to influence discourse, to raise topics worthy of discussion, of international importance. Her ambitions were limitless, but her scope was small. She was, very, *very* occasionally, permitted to write a piece that touched upon something of real merit. But far more often, she was relegated to writing knitting patterns or describing teething remedies for children. It was an endless trial for her, and while I deplored her methods, I understood her motivation.

"Very well," I said.

Stoker spluttered, but I stood my ground. "She has us over the proverbial barrel," I reminded him. "The *Daily Harbinger* is no friend to you. I will not have the business of your divorce raked up again. The mud has only just dried."

He curled a lip in disgust, and J. J. had the grace to look a little embarrassed. But she did not back down and I put out my hand. "Very well. If the chancellor does not object, you may come as my maid, but you will conduct yourself at all times like a proper servant," I warned her. "It is absolutely essential that you make no trouble. I will not bother to explain the consequences to you if you fail me tonight," I added in a low voice. "I think your own imagination will suffice."

She blanched a little, but rallied. "I will not fail," she promised.

"See that you don't."

Stoker and I rose to leave, but just as we reached the door, he turned back, almost as an afterthought. "When Maximilian and Gisela stopped on the way to St. Pancras, where did they go?"

J. J. helped herself to a handful of sugared almonds, crunching them soundly before replying. "It is rather odd, I thought. They went to that club of yours, Veronica — the Curiosity Club."

"How long did they stay?" I asked.

She munched another almond, shrugging. "Ten minutes? I cannot imagine what they wanted there, but Gisela left with a parcel about so big," she added, holding her hands a foot and a half apart.

"What sort of parcel?" Stoker inquired.

"Something a little unwieldy. Max carried it into St. Pancras for her, but when he came back out, it was gone. Gisela must have taken it with her, wherever she went."

CHAPTER 21

As we left the kitchens, Stoker helped himself to the last of the *guimauves,* chewing thoughtfully as I vented my spleen.

"That monstrous, outrageous —" I broke off as Stoker held up a hand.

"Yes, J. J. is difficult," he began, stuffing in another *guimauve.*

"I was not talking about J. J.," I said as we made our way back upstairs to the suite. "I meant Maximilian. Imagine playing such dreadful games with the woman you claim to want to marry!"

"Well, they did break into the Curiosity Club together," he pointed out. "Clearly there is some trust if they are committing casual crimes with one another in a foreign country."

I snorted by way of reply. Once we made our way back to the suite, we seized the opportunity to beard the duke in his den. We found him in his room in a languorous pose, legs propped on a hassock, brandy snifter dangling from his fingertips. He was staring into the fire, his expression inscrutable.

He acknowledged our presence with a flick of his gaze. "I ought, out of politeness, to rise, but considering the fact that you did not trouble to knock, I will consider us equally bad-mannered."

I took the chair opposite him and Stoker stood behind me, arms folded over his chest. A small smile played about the duke's mouth, but his eyes were watchful and frightened. "I am, as you can see, quite busy. Please state your business and then be off."

"Very well," Stoker said in a pleasant tone. "Perhaps you would care to explain your arrangement with J. J. Butterworth."

The hesitation was so slight, anyone watching him less intently would have missed it. But a trained butterfly hunter's eye is acute, and I saw the brief, tiny inhalation, the almost imperceptible flare of the handsome nostrils.

The denial, when it came, was a shade too casual. "I am certain I do not know what you mean."

I looked over my shoulder to Stoker. "Perhaps we ought to go directly to the chancellor," I proposed. "No doubt he would be vastly interested in the duke's intentions with regard to his princess."

"Oh, very well," Maximilian said, quaffing the last of his brandy and letting the glass drop to the carpeting. His expression was distinctly unhappy. He had intended to play the game by bluffing and he had lost badly. He wiped a drop of brandy from his mouth and made an effort to focus his eyes. "If you must know, I gave the girl an interview. I thought to sway public opinion in my favor. If the English, our nearest ally, finds me a worthy partner to Gisela, it might influence her to finally accept my hand in marriage."

"You were looking to raise your prestige on an international level?" Stoker asked.

"Something like that," Maximilian replied with a tinge of real bitterness. "I have not always been a paragon of virtue. My reputation is a trifle soiled, and there are those in the Alpenwald and abroad who have wondered if Gisela could do a little better for herself."

"Hence seizing upon the chance to get J. J. Butterworth to write something laudatory about you," Stoker remarked.

"Just so." Maximilian's grin was broad and no doubt lubricated by the brandy he had drunk. "A nice, pretty profile of a prince-to-be." He refilled his glass and took a deep swallow.

"Indeed it was," I agreed. "And I am very glad to hear the article was your idea. I was afraid she had extorted it from you after discovering you in the act of doing something disreputable — such as breaking and entering the Curiosity Club?"

The fact that he choked on his brandy bothered me not at all except that he managed to spit a quantity of it on the hem of my skirt. "That will leave a stain," I informed him when he had recovered himself.

His face changed colors from puce to white and back again. "Miss Butterworth, I presume? She is the only one who could have told you. One ought never to trust the press," he added hoarsely.

Stoker poured him a fresh drink and Maximilian sipped at it, more gingerly than he had before. But his color seemed somewhat more natural after a few minutes.

"So you admit you broke into the club?" I pressed.

"I admit nothing," he said, his self-possession returning. "It would be my word against that of a rubbish-peddling guttersnipe."

"A rubbish-peddling guttersnipe who also knows you arranged for the explosion last night," Stoker put in mildly.

"And left a threatening note in Gisela's chocolate box," I added for good measure.

Maximilian dropped his glass and gave a deep moan, thrusting his hands into his hair as he bent double. "Mfffmmmfffmffff," he said.

"I am afraid that was not entirely audible," Stoker told him.

The duke raised his head; the fight had clearly gone out of him. "I did not mean to harm her — I would *never* harm her, you must believe that. I love Gisela." His protests echoed J. J.'s, but that proved nothing. She might well have been parroting what he had told her, falling for his persuasions in spite of her journalistic instincts.

"Tell us," I urged. I was conscious of Stoker fairly vibrating with satisfaction at what we had learnt so far.

The duke began to speak in a small, halting voice, very unlike his usual assured tones. "You must understand what it is like. I was born to a very minor branch of the family. I have a title, yes, but precious else. The lesser von Hochstadts have never been wealthy. We hang on the fringes of the senior branch of the family, hoping for crumbs. My parents always pushed the idea that Gisela and I should marry, and her father liked the notion of keeping everything within the family. We were thrown together constantly as children. We quarreled and made up, as children do, but we were friends, always," he insisted. "I was sent away to school here in England and then into the army. I scarcely saw her, but whenever I did, we picked up where we had left off. We understood one another very well. We got on. It seemed logical that we should marry." He paused, heaving a bone-weary sigh. "I am not permitted to propose to Gisela. Her rank is too far above my own. It must come from her, but the years have passed and still she does not speak. I am left on tenterhooks, never knowing when I will marry, when I will assume my responsibilities as consort." He smiled, a small and rueful thing. "I must amuse myself as best I can, which sounds as if it ought to be a very enjoyable life, but it is not. I have no purpose, no money, and no way of earning any. I gamble because that is the only way to afford decent tailoring," he said, plucking at the cuff of his sleeve. "I keep company with disreputable ladies because it is a way of passing the time, and I drink too much in order to forget that the woman I am meant to spend the rest of my life with does not think me worthy of her hand."

He retrieved his glass and examined the contents, draining a few remaining drops.

"Has the princess told you as much?" I asked.

He shook his head. "No. But I know she believes I am not serious enough, that I lack responsibility and proper feeling."

I rolled my eyes heavenwards. "And your idea of how to change that is to gamble and disport yourself with disreputable people?"

He turned to Stoker. "Does she always speak so plainly?"

Stoker shrugged. "No. In fact, she is being rather polite just now. You are quite fortunate she has not told you what she really thinks."

The duke put down his glass and laced his fingers across his flat stomach. "Very well. What do you really think?"

"I think you are entirely pathetic," I told him serenely. "You are gifted by nature with intelligence and ability and remarkable good looks and yet you cannot be bothered to lift a finger for anyone besides yourself. You have allowed indolence and bad company to influence you to do nothing more interesting than play baccarat and wager on horses, which makes you dull in the extreme. Not only do I not blame the princess for hesitating to betroth herself to you, I applaud her for her lucky escape."

He gaped at me, his complexion purpling once more. "No one has ever dared speak to me in such a fashion."

"You did ask," I reminded him. "And I am not finished. I have not even begun to express my feelings on the abject weakness of character that would cause a man to play vicious pranks upon the woman he professes to love."

"That was not my fault!" he exclaimed, thumping his thighs with his fists. "It was the devil to whom I owe money. He owns a casino in Deauville and I made promises to him — promises I would have been able to keep if Gisela had announced our betrothal."

"But she has not and so this blackguard instructed you to bring terror to bear upon the princess in order to shock her into marriage."

He covered his face with his hands for a long moment, and when he dropped them, the rage seemed to fall away. "I was drunk, very, very drunk. And I had lost a great deal of money. And I had quarreled with Gisela yet again about making our engagement official. I had done a favor for her — a very large favor. And she had given her word she would make the announcement. But when the time came, she did not. The reasons are not important, but I felt she had failed me. I took myself off to Deauville to have a good carouse to exorcise my feelings. I lost, heavily. They took me into the office of the owner of the casino and we had a little discussion," he said, his lips twisting in distaste. "I cannot tell you how much I hated myself in that moment. A Duke of Lokendorf reduced to sitting with such a fellow, asking him for his forbearance! Supplicating, like a beggar. It was his idea to play these pranks upon Gisela, but I agreed and that fault is mine," he said. There was sorrow in his eyes, and for the first time, I felt I saw the real character of the man.

"The favor you did for Gisela," I said gently. "Was it to conceal her relationship with Alice Baker-Greene?"

Astonishment flickered in his eyes before he dropped his gaze. "I do not know what you mean, *Fraulein.* Gisela barely knew the woman."

"They were lovers," Stoker said. "We have seen evidence. A sketch in Alice's own hand."

Maximilian groaned. "I beg you, do not share this information. Whatever you think of me, and I understand it is very little, believe me when I tell you that Gisela does not deserve to be ruined for this."

"We have no intention of ruining your princess," I told him firmly. "Her private affections are none of our concern. But her whereabouts and Alice Baker-Greene's murder are."

He leveled his gaze at me. "Alice Baker-Greene fell off the Teufelstreppe."

"After her rope was cut," Stoker put in. "Furthermore, you know that is what happened because why else go to the Curiosity Club and steal the rope if not to remove evidence of the crime?"

He was silent a long moment. "I think I am tired now," he said. "And this interview is at an end."

"Did you cut that rope?" I demanded. "Did you kill Alice to eliminate your rival for Gisela's affections? She was the obstacle to your marriage, was she not? Murdering her would have opened the way for you. Did you take it?"

"I did not," he said, clipping the words sharply. "She was my friend. And whatever you think of me, I am no murderer."

"But you might be an accomplice," Stoker suggested.

The duke shied in his chair. "What do you mean?"

"He means that you and Gisela stole the

rope from the club — rope that proves Alice was murdered. You helped her do it and you helped her get out of London," I said.

He gaped at me. "You think Gisela killed her? For what reason?"

"I met Alice several months before her death," I told him. "She was incandescently happy. She told me about moving to the Alpenwald, how she meant to make her permanent home there. And she was a very strong woman. If Gisela had wanted to break things off with her, turn her out of the Alpenwald, Alice would not have gone quietly. She would have stood her ground and made it impossible for you and Gisela to have married and begun a life together. Would that have been a happy life, do you think? Hochstadt is a very small city. You would have constantly seen Alice — a ghost of Gisela's former life — and a liability if she ever chose to share her damnable story. You would never have been secure, not until she died."

He listened in rapt attention, then burst out laughing until he wiped his eyes. "Oh, *Fraulein*. Whatever becomes of us all, I do hope you will take to writing stories. You have a prodigious imagination."

He poured another glass of brandy and it was clear he intended to say no more.

Before we left, I tried one final tack.

"Where did Gisela go that night?" I asked.

For a long minute, I thought he would refuse to answer, but at last he replied. "She did not tell me, I swear it."

"I almost believe you," Stoker told him.

Duke Maximilian hesitated, then reached into his pocket.

"Here, this is all that I know of her intentions — a railway timetable."

Stoker took the timetable from the duke. It was a little grubby and marked with a pencil.

He traced the penciled line with a finger. It highlighted a train leaving late that evening from St. Pancras.

"Nothing more specific?" I asked.

The duke shook his head. "No. Make of that what you will."

Stoker scoured the rest of the timetable. "We know from this that she must have been heading north, so that lets out Bristol or Southampton or the Continent, unless she meant to double back. If she were traveling directly, then she might have gone to Liverpool or Edinburgh."

"From Edinburgh she might have traveled back to the Continent," I surmised. "And from Liverpool, Ireland or even America."

I turned to the duke.

"Why not show this to the chancellor or the baroness?" I asked. "It at least confirms that she was not abducted, and you might have saved them some worry."

"I gave Gisela my word, *Fraulein*," he said, picking up the empty glass and staring into it. "She wanted no one to know where she went, and that is why she would not even tell me where she was bound. Take that to the chancellor and the baroness if you must, but it will accomplish nothing except anger them because I did not convey it myself. That is in no one's best interests."

Stoker tucked the timetable into his pocket. "There is no reason they need to know just yet. In fact, not having to worry about such an occurrence will free you to see to it that Miss Speedwell has all the support she requires this evening and makes a success of it."

The threat was unmistakable. Stoker was holding on to the timetable as insurance that Duke Maximilian would render me whatever aid he could during the course of the banquet and signing ceremony.

The duke gave him a grudging nod and smiled, a flicker of his usual insouciance playing about his mouth. "A worthy adversary, Templeton-Vane. I might duel you yet."

"I look forward to it," Stoker said, holding

his gaze for a long moment. "Did the princess give you any indication of how long she meant to be away?"

The duke shrugged. "She said only that she had something she must do and that I would have to trust her. And she promised to announce the betrothal upon her return."

"A carrot to secure the donkey's co-operation," I said blandly.

The duke raised his glass and made a braying noise. He was noticeably more intoxicated than he had been, and I wondered if inebriation might loosen his tongue.

"Did it ever occur to you," I put it to him pleasantly, "that your villainous little friend from Deauville might have followed you and seized the opportunity to abduct Gisela to hold her for ransom?"

A look of horror came over him and he drank off the last drops of his brandy in a single swallow. "No, that cannot be."

"Unlikely, I grant you. But possible. Miss Butterworth followed you that night. Why not this fellow? He must have kept rather a close eye upon you during your time in London?"

He licked his lips, his tongue brushing the hairs of his moustaches, which had gone limp from the dousings of brandy. "He owns a flat in Belgravia. I stayed there when I first arrived. He likes to know where I am, at least until the money is paid back. He might, that is to say, I don't know, but I suppose he might have followed us. Oh, Gisela," he said, falling to muttering something in impenetrable German.

Stoker elaborated on my theory. "Or Gisela mayn't have left of her own volition at all. We know she entered the station in your company. What if you delivered her to this man on his instructions?"

"I would never!" the duke cried in outrage.

"But you might have," Stoker persisted. "You could have taken her to the club on the pretext of retrieving the rope, pretending to help her, only to hand her over to this fellow. He may be preparing a ransom note as we speak, ready to take his money from the Alpenwalder treasury if he cannot get it from your pocket."

"That is monstrous," Maximilian said.

"Not as monstrous as the fact that if anything were to happen to her, you would be the Hereditary Prince of the Alpenwald, in your own right," I suggested. "In fact, what if that was your plan all along? Hand Gisela over and let this miscreant demand money for her, then kill her, eliminating all of your problems at one stroke. Excellent thinking, Stoker."

The duke surged out of his chair. "Enough!" he said, flinging his glass into the mantel looking glass and shattering both. "Gisela is not a problem for me to solve. I am in love with her!" Brandy dripped from the shards on the mantelpiece, dropping softly to the carpet. For a long moment, it was the only sound in the room apart from the duke's heavy breathing.

As quickly as the rage had come, it left him. His shoulders sagged and his face crumpled as he sank to his knees and buried his face in the chair cushion. He let out a low, mournful noise, rather like a very sad bull elephant, and I looked at Stoker. "What is he doing?"

Stoker bent to peer at the duke. "I think he is weeping."

"Well, that is awkward," I murmured. I knelt next to the duke and patted his back.

"There, there," I said in my best soothing voice. "We do not really think you want Gisela dead."

Stoker mouthed over the duke's head at me. "Yes, we do."

I pulled a face at him as the duke continued to weep loudly. He turned to me and lay his head on my shoulder, clutching me as his shoulders heaved and his tears soaked my gown. "Now, Maximilian, pull yourself together. Do try," I urged.

"Let him cry," Stoker suggested. "He might feel a good deal better if he gives vent to his emotions."

I put out my tongue at him. It was very well for him to encourage such a thing. He did not have the duke's not inconsiderable weight bearing down on him. My arms were beginning to cramp, but Maximilian was undeterred. He wept on, great heaving sobs, and in between he talked, or at least tried, the words choked out in gulps. There was a good deal of remorse and far too much self-pity for my taste, but he did seem genuinely sorrowful for the poor decisions he had made.

After a good quarter of an hour's sobbing, he began to subside to sniffles and moans, and eventually he pulled away, mopping his face on the large scarlet handkerchief Stoker provided for him.

"Thank you," he said, blowing his nose lavishly into the handkerchief.

Stoker turned to me as the clock chimed. "You might as well go and let the baroness get you into harness."

"What will you do?"

"I am going to help His Grace get sober," he said, baring his teeth in a smile.

"Good." I did not envy Maximilian. Stoker's ministrations, while highly skilled, were occasionally none too gentle. I turned to the duke. "A word of wisdom, Maximilian? Do not fight whatever Stoker does to you. It will go easier on you if you do not."

He groaned as I closed the door behind me.

CHAPTER 22

Before I was dressed, the baroness sent down to the kitchens for food and I recognized the handiwork of Julien d'Orlande as soon as it appeared. Not content with his usual elegance, he had truly outdone himself for the repast of a princess. There was a selection of tiny sandwiches and cakes, each decorated more lavishly than the last. Tarts filled with frangipane and hothouse fruits were glazed to glistening perfection while icing sugar dusted the snowy peaks of miniature mountain-shaped cakes of vanilla sponge. I gazed at the vast assortment of food, from the shimmering spun-sugar nest with its clutch of gilded chocolate eggs topped with a marzipan peacock to the pile of narrowly cut roast beef sandwiches cunningly stacked to look like a mountain. Little sprigs of watercress had been tucked in between to give the impression of alpine plants clinging to the mountainside. In pride of place, an enormous wheel of fragrant, almost pungent cheese rested in a nest of grape leaves and tiny savory biscuits.

"Our famous Alpenwalder cheese," the baroness told me. "It is most delicious with a glass of wine or toasted onto bread."

I surveyed the groaning trays as Guimauve, stretched on the bed, lifted his head to sniff at the various enticing aromas.

"Is it always like this?" I asked the baroness as Yelena presented me with a delicate china cup filled with clear chicken consommé. I sniffed appreciatively at the steam.

The baroness smiled. "Of course. People like to demonstrate their gifts and it is natural to do so for royalty."

"Quite a way to live," I mused, sipping at the soup. A single dumpling floated on the surface. I scooped it up and took a bite. It was full of minced chicken and some flavorsome herb — tarragon, perhaps? It was one of the most delectable things I had ever eaten, but I could scarcely force it past the corset.

"You eat like a small bird," the baroness said in disapproval. "Now, I must go and retrieve the jewels for tonight from the lumber room. Eat," she ordered. She rattled off a series of instructions to Yelena in the Alpenwalder dialect — no doubt commanding her to force-feed me like a Michaelmas goose, I reflected darkly.

But as soon as the baroness had left, Yelena turned to me. "Do not eat if you do not wish. I will eat your share."

"Yelena!" I exclaimed in an excited whisper. "You do speak English."

"Yes," she said. She helped herself to a cheese tart.

"But why do you pretend not to?"

She shrugged. "It is not for them to know everything." She ate the cheese tart in one bite and reached for another.

"You know why I am here?" I pressed.

She rolled her eyes heavenwards at the obviousness of the question. "You take the place of the princess."

"Do you know anything about her disappearance? Where she might be?"

She hesitated, darting a glance to the door. "Perhaps. I might know something about the night she left."

"I know you made her a loan of your cloak," I said, and she gave a start before dropping her lids in a look of grudging respect.

"Perhaps you do not require what I know," she said in a demure murmur. Guimauve moved from the bed, putting out a paw in supplication. Yelena busied herself pulling a little chicken from a sandwich and feeding it to the cat.

"Do not be tiresome, Yelena," I said with governessy firmness. "Tell me!"

Yelena gave me a sly look, her expression identical to Guimauve's as he considered the spread of dishes upon the tray. "Such things are not free, *Fraulein*," she told me.

"You want me to pay you for information?"

"I am not a rich girl," she said, her lips twisting bitterly. "But I want to marry. If I have money, it will be easier." She flicked another look at the closed door, and I recalled what the baroness had told me about Yelena's romantic inclinations.

"You wish to marry Captain Durand," I said.

"His family are very proud. They think I am a peasant because I am Russian, but I am no peasant," she told me, her eyes bright with pride or hostility, I could not tell. "My father was put into prison after the attack upon the tsar."

I blinked at her. "The attack upon the tsar? You mean the bomb that killed Tsar Alexander?"

She pressed her lips together and nodded. "My father had nothing to do with this, you understand. He knew those involved, he went to a meeting or two, but nothing more. He did not know of the plot. He did not act," she insisted. It sounded to me as if he had had rather more than nothing to do with the conspiracy to assassinate the tsar, and my blood ran a little cold at the idea of an anarchist's daughter in the employ of the princess.

"How did you come to work for the princess?" I asked.

"My mother had a sister who married an Alpenwalder and I was sent to my aunt so that I would be safe. My aunt married beneath her, an innkeeper," she said, fairly spitting the word. "He expected me to make beds and empty chamber pots, and one day I said, 'If I am to do such things, I might as well do them in a palace!' And I went into the princess's household as a chambermaid. She noticed me and the way I dressed my hair," she said, touching a hand to her neatly plaited locks. "When her maid was ill, she sent for me to dress her hair. She liked my way of talking, and from then on, she sent for me often. When her maid left her post to marry, the princess offered me the post. I do good work for her," she added with pride.

"But why hide the fact that you speak English?"

She reddened. "They talk about me when they think I cannot understand. The nobles and the high servants, they all speak English. If I keep my mouth closed, they say things in front of me they think I cannot understand."

"And you blackmail them for it?" I hazarded.

"It did not begin that way," she said, her mouth thinning unpleasantly. "But often they let slip little things they do not want other people to know. I ask only for small sums and that they keep my secret. I have put aside ten pounds," she said, bringing out a small bundle from her pocket. I recognized one of the princess's handkerchiefs knotted into a pouch. She opened it to show me the assortment of coins and notes, some German, some French, even a Swedish krona or two.

"Very resourceful," I told her. The knowledge that Yelena was little better than a common blackmailer was distasteful; however, I had no wish to stem the tide of revelations.

But Yelena had said all she came to say. She knotted the handkerchief closed again and tucked it back into her pocket. "If you want me to keep your secret, you will pay me a little. And if you want to know where the princess was going, you will pay more, I think."

"I suppose I would," I said politely. "How much will you require?"

"Ten pounds," she told me in a tone that would brook no negotiating.

I suppressed a sigh. I never carried so much money upon me; it was a month's wages. Stoker, who was reckless with banknotes, his own or anyone else's, might well have tucked four times as much idly into a boot, but he was not at hand.

"My associate will pay you," I assured her.

She gave a laugh, a merry little trill that might have been pleasant under other circumstances. "I do not give credit. You will pay me," she repeated. "And then I will talk."

Yelena wrapped up four more of the cheese tarts in a handkerchief and slipped them into her pocket. She left me then, and I was glad of it. She was a distinctly unlikeable young woman, although I was not entirely unsympathetic to her plight. Still, a gift for extortion was unattractive in a lady, I thought, deciding it best not to dwell upon my own particular talents in that regard.

Whilst I waited for the baroness, I made a hasty search of the room in hopes of discovering some clue to Gisela's whereabouts or her state of mind when she left. Guimauve was underfoot, nudging my hand and making a silken nuisance of himself until I settled him on the bed with one of the chicken sandwiches.

"Do behave," I ordered. "I am trying to find your mistress." He gave me a long, cool look and then attended to the base of his tail, as if to indicate his complete indifference to the princess's whereabouts. I pulled a face and made a quick survey of the room's contents. There were no enticingly locked doors or diaries written in undecipherable code. The chancellor and baroness managed her state papers and schedule, and any private correspondence she might have kept was nowhere in evidence.

The only truly personal effects in the room were the stack of books upon the night table. There was a selection of political volumes — one on constitutional monarchies of the world, another on English history viewed through the lens of Continental perspective — and the memoirs of Benjamin Disraeli. A few books on alpinism and a selection of travel guides to mountainous regions (Baedeker's, of course) were stacked with a slender collection of poetry and *Le Livre de la Cité des Dames* by Christine de Pizan. There was also a weighty biography of Queen Christina, the sixteenth-century monarch who had traveled the Continent dressed as a man and abandoned her Swedish throne after embracing Catholicism. I thumbed through it at random, noting the passages highlighted in pencil. There were notes in the margin, little drawings and the odd exclamation mark or notation about a point of law. The princess had been particularly effusive in the chapter regarding Christina's incognita adventures, and I was not surprised. There was a stifling element to court etiquette, to the endless round of formal engagements and appearances, the restrictive clothing, the requirements of behavior and expression of opinions. I had spent only one evening in harness and found it exhausting; I could not imagine how weighty the burden of state must be when it must be endured for a lifetime. I flipped through the rest of the book, my attention drifting during a heavily annotated section on Christina's abdication.

I replaced it in the stack of books, surveying the various volumes of policy and history and political biography. Together they suggested a woman deeply conscious of her place in history and who must have felt the pressures of her position to be at times insupportable. I had theorized to Stoker that Gisela might have removed Alice as a threat to her future as a monarch, but my eyes fell again upon the assorted Baedeker's and the biography of a queen who gave up her throne. It was possible that Gisela had had a hand in Alice's murder, but it was just as possible that she had considered abdicating to begin a new life with the woman she loved.

I considered this as I thumbed through the Baedeker devoted to the Alpenwald. It was a slender volume, and I had almost reached the end when the baroness bustled in, clearly vexed. Her color was high and her monocle, screwed firmly in her eye, was fairly vibrating as she peered at me.

"Where is that dreadful girl?" she demanded.

I looked up from my reading. "What girl?"

She huffed as she plucked the book from my grasp and stacked it neatly with the others, shooing Guimauve from the bed and brushing a few stray cat hairs and crumbs from the silken coverlet.

"Yelena! She has gone out, apparently, and no one knows where — just when I actually have need of her." She huffed. She plumped a few of the pillows with a vigorous gesture, and I hastened to settle her feathers.

"Do you wish to send someone to find

her? To make inquiries?" I asked.

"Absolutely not," she told me with Teutonic firmness. "We have a timetable to meet and we will not be delayed by the likes of her." I deeply regretted the fact that Stoker and I had as yet had no chance to search the rest of the suite or hold a proper tête-à-tête after our conversation with the duke, but there would be no opportunity now. The baroness was bent upon her task and sent downstairs for one of the hotel maids to assist her. I was not at all surprised when J. J. appeared. I had learnt respect for her resourcefulness. She was quick and deft, doing exactly as the baroness instructed with a meek promptitude that seemed wholly out of character for her until she shot me a wink when the baroness's back was turned.

"How did you arrange this?" I asked J. J. hastily as the baroness left to retrieve a box of jewels. "Did you crack Yelena over the head? Is she tied up in a broom cupboard somewhere?"

J. J. pulled a face. "What on earth are you talking about?"

"Yelena. The princess's lady's maid. She disappeared this afternoon and is not to be found."

J. J. shrugged. "Nothing to do with me.

But if I were you, I would be careful."

"Why?" I demanded.

"Because if Alpenwalder women are disappearing, there is a very short list of prospective victims."

I put out my tongue at her, resuming my decorum just as the baroness returned, looking a little relieved. "At least the jewels are still here," she said grimly. Then she looked at J. J. and stiffened. It would never do to air soiled Alpenwalder laundry in front of a mere hotel maid, I realized, and I made no reply.

In the end, I was glad of J. J.'s presence, for it was absolutely a matter of all hands to the tiller. Whatever toilette I had made the previous evening was nothing compared to the effort for a formal dinner. I was washed, powdered, brushed, massaged, pinned, coiffed, dressed, bedecked, and bedizened.

"I feel like a warhorse preparing for battle," I complained at one point. "How on earth do women make a habit of dressing like this?"

The baroness managed a thin smile. "One becomes accustomed to the weight. And this is not a full state occasion," she reminded me. "Enthronings are even grander occasions with a full crown and scepter and the rod of St. Otthild as well as a mantle of state that stretches nine yards in length."

Little wonder the princess had run away, I reflected, if it meant escaping such ludicrous trappings. The baroness explained that it was only the opening of the Alpenwalder parliament and enthronings and royal weddings that called for full regalia, but an occasion as important as dinner at Windsor Castle still called for formal Alpenwalder court dress. If it had been left to the gown alone, I would have made no complaint. Borrowed from the style of the Russian imperial ladies, it had an undergown of heavy white satin thickly embroidered with Alpenwalder emblems in gold silk. The overgown was rich scarlet velvet edged in ermine, the long, slashed sleeves sweeping to the floor and lined in white satin. The deep neckline, rounded and positioned just at the edge of the shoulders, was banded in a wide swathe of more golden embroidery, which trailed down the front of the overgown and around the long train.

My hair was once again plaited and piled and pinned with an array of false pieces into an elaborate confection to hold a coronet of old rose-cut diamonds set around enormous, luscious rubies. A deep blue sash crossed from one shoulder to my waist, secured with the jeweled order of St.

Otthild, a gem-encrusted otter rampant with a sprig of St. Otthild's wort gripped in his tiny diamond teeth.

I looked to the baroness and realized she was not wearing her order. "What has become of your sash, Baroness?"

She threw up her hands in disgust. "I cannot find it. It was creased after last night and I told that wretched girl to see it pressed, but it has disappeared. No doubt she has pawned my jeweled otter as well," she added bitterly. It seemed harsh to believe so easily that Yelena might have resorted to thievery, but I remembered her resentment against the Alpenwalders and her eagerness to turn her hand to extortion. It was a small leap from there to thinking she might help herself to the odd trinket to sell, although I could hardly imagine a brisk secondary market for diplomatic honors.

While I pondered this, the baroness added the finishing touches to my ensemble. I could scarcely move for the weight of it all, but there was something about the grandeur that created within me a determination to rise to the occasion. Together the baroness and I had replicated her tricks of using cosmetics to enhance my resemblance to the princess, and J. J. had a few thoughts of her own that heightened the effect further.

She even managed to camouflage the bit of violet bruising that had risen on my chin as a result of my encounter with Douglas Norton. As I stared into the looking glass, I felt light-headed, detached suddenly from all that I had known and all that I was.

It occurred to me then that, were it not for an accident of birth, a peculiarity of the law, I might have rightfully worn such things. I was the child of a prince, the descendant of queens, and the blood in my veins was no less blue for having been mixed with an Irish actress's. If her marriage had been recognized, I would have worn such garments from my youth, enjoyed the adulation and the applause. But I would also have stifled my own spirit, I reflected. Those quirks of character that made me the woman I had become were because I had been given the freedom to do as I pleased. No royal protocol dictated my upbringing; no august personages dictated my education. I had been at liberty to study as I wished, pursuing my own interests and friendships, embarking upon travels and learning to rely upon no one but myself. I had not had the privileges of royalty, but neither had I endured the privations, and of these I could number many. Just the few days I had spent in Gisela's slippers had taught me that I could never endure the strictures of her life, the endless and tedious round of engagements and obligations. I belonged to no one, was beholden to no one. Whether I starved or whether I throve, the outcome lay firmly in my own hands. And that freedom was worth all the diamonds in the world, I decided.

"It is natural to be overwhelmed," the baroness said kindly. "But you will do this and you will do it with dignity and confidence, I have no doubt."

Her voice said she had no doubt but her eyes were not so certain. I smiled at her and squared my shoulders. "I will do my best."

I raised my chin imperiously. "Now, let us go. It will not do to be late."

CHAPTER 23

If my own metamorphosis from lepidopterist to princess had been dramatic, Stoker's was scarcely less impressive. I emerged from the bedchamber to find him standing at the hearth, posture erect, costumed in the full dress uniform of the Alpenwalder guard of honor. The livery was black, piped with brilliant alpine blue. The trousers had been changed in favor of knee breeches with white stockings, displaying the splendor of his calves as effectively as the tight coat paid compliment to the breadth of his shoulders and the slimness of his waist. The shako had been replaced by a soft cap of black velvet with a long blue plume secured with a jeweled pin. A wide riband of blue and white crossed his chest, and a black silk patch was secured over his eye. Spotless white gloves completed the ensemble.

He had been speaking to the chancellor when I entered, but when he caught sight of me, he stopped, and for a moment we were the only two people in the room, perhaps even on earth. I paused and he advanced, bowing low as he swept off the cap. I realized then that he wore a short velvet cape that swung as he moved with a sort of Elizabethan swagger.

"Most effective," I murmured.

"Dazzling," he said, brushing his mouth over my fingers.

"Yes, if you don't mind, I think we really could get on," said Maximilian, not troubling to conceal his peevishness. He was wearing a costume nearly identical to Stoker's, only trimmed with quantities of silver braid. The garments suited him, but when compared to Stoker, he seemed a penciled copy of an oil painting, and I did not begrudge him his sulkiness. He was accustomed to being accounted one of the handsomest men in the Alpenwald, and now he had competition.

I smiled at him as graciously as I could as I took his arm. In strict accordance with protocol, I was accompanied by the duke while the chancellor escorted the baroness. Stoker and J. J. — pressed into service for the evening and now changed into a stark and pristine uniform of white and black — brought up the rear. As we made our way down to the lobby, the chancellor explained the arrangements for the evening.

"We will leave from the back entrance," he said, directing Maximilian. "It is not precisely a secret where we are bound, but neither is it publicized. Discretion is key," he stressed. "Our hosts have sent a pair of private carriages and we will travel by these conveyances instead of by train."

The waiting carriages bore no crest or distinguishing marks, but it was apparent that the owner was a person of immense wealth. Every detail was of the highest quality, from the tufted silk of the squabs to the delicate Tudor rose motif on the glass panes of the lamps. The first was just large enough to admit the four of us — the baroness, chancellor, duke, and I — once my train had been folded carefully around me. The baroness and I traveled facing forward with the duke while the chancellor took the center of the opposite seat. Stoker and J. J. were relegated to the second carriage as befitted their station for the night.

The night was clear and cold and the journey took much longer than expected as we bowled briskly away, through the city and into the dark countryside of Berkshire. My aunts and I had moved often during my childhood, exchanging one country village for another very like it, all in a bid to avoid those who might seek out the Prince of Wales's semi-legitimate child. I had neither known nor appreciated their reasons for uprooting my tender self at the time. Instead, it had been an endless round of beginnings and partings. Most of the hamlets I had forgot, but one stayed fresh in my memory — a tiny settlement in the shadows of Windsor Castle, just beyond the meadows of Runnymede. I remembered the broad fields, lushly green and dotted with the fleecy clouds of sheep grazing on the spring grass. I had fallen from an apple tree there and broken my arm, I recalled. That was when I had received my first butterfly net as a gift from the aunts for my birthday. Enchanted, I had taken it on a long walk, netting my first specimen in the ring net now long replaced by a professional's. But I had loved that net, loved the feeling of the wind in my hair and the earth under my feet. It was in those meadows, chasing the lazy flap of a lepidopteron, that I had learnt my trade.

And one afternoon, late in the autumn of my twelfth year, I wandered further than usual in pursuit of *Cyaniris semiargus,* the Mazarine Blue, a pretty little Palearctic butterfly. I hopped over streams and scrambled over stiles as the afternoon drew to a close. The butterfly — a male with delectably blue coloration — eluded me, lifting itself on gossamer wings to freedom. Dejected, I stood for a long moment, collecting my whereabouts. And there it was: just ahead on the horizon. Windsor Castle. I stared up at the castle, the proud stone enormity of it rising above the landscape like something out of myth. The afternoon light lay softly upon it, gilding the cold grey battlements to a glimmering sheen that would have suited King Arthur himself. It was the most glorious thing I had ever seen, and I stood, rooted to the spot like a meadow flower, wondering about the princes and princesses who sheltered within its walls. I knew our queen was Victoria and that she lived there, wrapped in widow's weeds. Her children must have been largely grown by then, but I imagined them still in the nursery, dressed in sailor suits and lawn dresses, attending their lessons and eating milk and bread from porringers marked with a crown. Oh, how I envied them! Not their royalty, I realized with a pang. I envied them each other. I envied the sense of belonging to a family with more brothers and sisters almost than one could count, of knowing a mother's touch, of a home that stood, resolute and unchanging in the mellow autumn gold of that afternoon.

Little did I realize that I had almost as good a claim upon the place as those who dwelt within its walls, I thought as the carriages bore us out of London into the west. Such were my thoughts, and I was aware of a rising excitement, not at visiting a castle, but at setting foot in what was my family home. My ancestors had built the place, stone by stone, and had lived there, had died there, loved and hated and borne new generations within its walls. And at last, I would come home.

So lost in my own reflections was I that I did not realize we had reached Windsor until the castle loomed above us in all of its grey majesty and I felt a sudden thrust of longing for Stoker. I had told him once, as we lay curled together in the dark, of my memory of the place, of the wrench I felt that afternoon when I returned home to find the aunts had packed us up and were moving us on once more. I never saw the castle again except in memory, and each time I embellished it more, raising the towers a little higher, the battlements a little wider. I fashioned of it a faery castle, and I had confided in Stoker that the frisson of feeling that day in the water meadow had been unlike anything I had experienced before or since. Long after discovering my father's identity, I recalled that day, and I marveled at my experience, wondering if somehow the memory of my ancestors, deep in my bones and blood, had stirred at the home they had built. It was the sort of thing one could only speak of in the dark, fast in a lover's arms, safe in the shelter of his kindness. He had not ridiculed me. There had not been even a hint of a smile in his voice. Only his broad, capable hands, gently stroking my hair as I talked. He would understand what coming to Windsor meant to me.

And there it was, just as I had remembered. Only now it stood against the purple velvet of a winter sky, the windows glowing with lamplight. A river mist had risen, curling softly about the foundation stones of the castle, causing it to look as if it were floating on a cloud. *No mere mortals dwell here,* it seemed to say. *This is a place of grandeur, of royalty, of a thousand years of power, and who are you to dare to come inside?*

I shivered and the baroness gave me a concerned look. "Are you cold, my dear?"

"I am fine," I told her in a hollow voice.

I had a moment to collect myself as the carriage passed under the great gate and drew to a halt in the courtyard. The castle's footmen came forward to help us alight as the driver steadied the horses. The chancellor and Maximilian, nearest the door, made their exit first. The baroness followed, and I was surprised to find that Stoker had already alighted from his carriage and stood ready to hand me from mine. He paused, giving me just a moment to gather my courage.

"It is time," he said softly. I rested my hand in his, fixing my gaze upon him, my only anchor in an uncertain world at that moment. He squeezed my hand, so tightly I felt the bones ache, and I clasped his hand in return as I descended in lieu of the words I could not say aloud.

Behind me, the baroness and J. J. gathered my train in their arms, holding it aloft until I moved up the broad stone steps, a river of scarlet carpet flowing down the center. The footmen stood at attention, the buttons of their livery sparking in the torchlight. Maximilian stepped forward and I relinquished my hold on Stoker, leaving my hand on his as long as I dared.

"Ready, poppet?" Maximilian asked, baring his teeth in a smile. I put my hand on his arm and felt the baroness and J. J. lower the train, unfurling it behind me. The weight of it dictated that I move slowly, in a stately walk very unlike my usual energetic gait. At the top of the steps, an official of some sort in a dignified uniform waited for us, bowing respectfully.

"Your Serene Highness," he pronounced. "Welcome to Windsor Castle. This way, if you please."

I accepted his greeting with a grave inclination of the head, and Maximilian and I followed as he led the way into the castle proper. A housekeeper came forward to collect J. J., and she gave me a little nod as she followed. I had kept my part of the bargain and got her into the castle. What she did with the opportunity was up to her.

I turned my attention to the dignitary who was keeping up a courteous patter as he escorted us. "Each of our foreign guests has been assigned an English host, a way of making the visit a more cordial and personal one," he explained. "Your host is waiting here. The others have all arrived, so once you have been introduced, we will proceed directly into dinner."

We approached a door, heavy oak carved thickly with the motif of oak leaves, and the footman standing outside threw it open. The room was smaller than I expected, a sort of anteroom, I supposed, furnished in serviceable but not grand style. Across the room was a bank of windows, the curtains drawn against the chilly night. A fire burned merrily on the hearth, and in front of it, warming himself, stood a distinguished Englishman in formal evening dress. He turned, a smile of welcome on his lips.

The smile faltered only slightly as the official made the introduction. "Your Serene Highness, may I present your escort for the evening, Sir Rupert Templeton-Vane? Sir Rupert, Her Serene Highness, the Hereditary Princess of the Alpenwald."

If my heart had stilled at the sight of the castle, that was nothing compared to the reaction when I came face-to-face with Stoker's elder brother. Sir Rupert, the second of the Templeton-Vane brothers, had, upon occasion, come to our aid. He was the most conventional of the siblings, preferring a life of rectitude and regularity to the flamboyant extravagances of the eldest — Tiberius — or the cheerful mischief of the youngest, Merryweather. The fact that he and Stoker seldom saw eye to eye was no great mystery. They were as alike as chalk and cheese, they claimed. And yet. From time to time, I caught a glimpse of the daring and dash that ran like wildfire through the Templeton-Vanes behind the façade of correctness.

From behind me, I heard Stoker's muffled

curse and I went forward, extending my hand to Rupert. "How do you do, Sir Rupert?"

Rupert bowed over my hand, pressing his lips to the gloved fingers. "How do *you* do, Your Serene Highness?"

Without rising, he lifted his dark gaze to mine. I gave an imperceptible shake of the head and he straightened.

"May I present the rest of my entourage?" I said, launching into introductions. Maximilian looked bored whilst the baroness and chancellor were polite.

"How very kind of you to welcome us," I said, infusing my words with a trace of a German accent.

"Not at all, madame. There are few things in life I enjoy more than a partner at dinner whose conversation is certain to entertain," he said, his mouth twitching.

The castle usher made a discreet gesture and Rupert extended his arm. "Shall we go in?"

I accepted his arm and he covered my hand with his own, pressing tightly. "How happy I am to further the cause of Anglo-Alpenwalder relations," he said loudly. I smiled at him and he dropped his voice. "What in the name of seven hells is going on?" he asked in a harsh whisper, still smiling as we made our way into the corridor.

"You sound just like your brother," I whispered back.

"Miss Speedwell," he began.

"The last time we met, you called me Veronica. And you said I could call you Rupert," I reminded him.

"I was rather influenced by that diabolical drink you gave me," he retorted.

"Aguardiente," I said. "I regret I do not have my flask upon my person at present. This ensemble does not permit such appurtenances."

"Veronica," he said, tightening his grip, "we have perhaps thirty seconds before we reach the dining room where two dozen dignitaries and officials are waiting to eat dinner with you and then sign a peace treaty binding two countries in perpetual friendship — a treaty upon which I have labored for the better part of a year and for which I am to receive advancement. Please tell me that you are not intending to bring me to ruination by somehow contriving to destroy this."

"Certainly not," I assured him.

"Then would you please explain why else you are here if not to jettison my career?"

"I did not even know you were involved!" I protested. "Stoker never told me you had a post in the Foreign Office."

"I do not, as it happens. My role is a more personal one in Her Majesty's household," he explained. "I am a sort of liaison. It is my task to bring together those who would not ordinarily work in tandem to accomplish goals set by the queen and her closest advisers."

"Against the will of the government?" I asked.

"Of course not." He sounded appalled at the very idea. "But sometimes what the government wants is for matters to be handled discreetly. In this case, it would be far too complicated to broker this treaty publicly and offend the German Empire, and it would no doubt make the empress's position even more difficult than it already is."

"I will not fail you," I promised. "Your treaty will be signed."

"It will hardly be legal if it is signed by Veronica Speedwell, spinster, of the Marylebone parish," he muttered.

"It is not like you to be rude," I told him in a soothing tone. "I fear you are hungry and it is making you dyspeptic."

"I am not hungry. I am having an apoplexy," he said, taking out a handkerchief and dabbing at his brow. I peered at his face.

"You do look rather florid. Would you like to take a moment?" I asked kindly.

He stopped before a tall pair of double doors. "There is no time," he told me, fixing a thoroughly unconvincing smile upon his lips. "We are here."

CHAPTER 24

Much of the evening passed as if in a dream. I was seated between Sir Rupert and the French delegate, who bowed deeply and kissed both of my hands when he was presented.

"General de Letellier," Rupert murmured. "The general is the French signatory to the treaty."

The general swept me a bow, clasping my outstretched hand.

"Your Serene Highness," he murmured against my gloves, and it felt as much like a seduction as a greeting. He was at least thirty years my senior, with a tightly girdled waist and hair pomaded thickly against his head, but what he lacked in personal charms he more than compensated for in gallantry. "The English are very casual," he remarked. "We ought to have been introduced in the anteroom, but I must not care about etiquette when it means I have the company of such a lady all to myself."

He stepped sharply in front of the castle footman to push in my chair with his own hands, taking the opportunity to glance swiftly down my décolletage.

"Merveilleux," he murmured.

"I beg your pardon," I said, widening my eyes at him. I reflected then that my ordinary instincts in such situations could not be reliably called upon. I had often been complimented, inveigled, caressed, and otherwise importuned in my travels, and it was my experience that a few sharp minuten — tiny pins meant to fix a butterfly to a card — when judiciously applied to an offender's person invariably rendered him apologetic. But that would hardly do in this case. To begin with, I risked causing grave insult to the other signatory of the treaty. Beyond that, there was every possibility that he would object strenuously to being stabbed. Men, as it happens, were often not enthused about such a development, I had observed.

"I was marveling at the generosity of the good God," he told me as he took his seat. "To make a woman royal is a gift from the Almighty. To make her beautiful as well, that is an abundance of favor."

"Is there a Madame de Letellier?" I asked pointedly.

He nodded towards a lushly curvaceous brunette dressed in rose pink taffeta and leaning very close to Stoker, her mouth curved into a smile.

"That is Honorine," he said. "I will not introduce you, for you will not like her. Other women never do. But the men . . ." He raised his eyes heavenwards and made an ecstatic sound in the back of his throat. Madame de Letellier was a few decades younger than her husband, and I could well imagine how she had come to his notice.

I said nothing but inclined my head a fraction, just enough to set the jewels on my tiara trembling as I reached for my menu card. Inscribed in elegant French, it detailed the courses we were about to receive. I conversed politely with de Letellier for the first course, a clear consommé.

"Is this your first trip to England, madame?" the general inquired as we sipped.

I took a spoonful of soup to delay answering. The longer it took me to reply to his queries, the fewer of them he could pose, I reasoned. And that meant not quite as many opportunities for me to stumble in my masquerade.

I sidestepped the question and posed one of my own. "England is a charming place, I think," I said slowly. "What do you make of it?"

The general launched into a lengthy speech about his host country whilst I applied myself to my soup, occasionally offering a wide-eyed nod of agreement to encourage his monologue. Most men loved nothing better than holding forth on their opinions, and the general was no exception. He detailed his thoughts on the weather (appalling), the landscape (passably pretty), the politics (incomprehensible to outsiders), and the handsomeness of the women (lacking).

I nearly bristled at the last until I realized I was not, for the purposes of the evening, supposed to be an Englishwoman.

"But," he added as I spooned up the last of my consommé, "there is an idealism about the English which I find irresistible. We French are pragmatic. We see things as they are, but John Bull, the typical Englishman? He sees things as he wishes them to be. Like children, they play at being empire builders, wanting all the world to drink tea and keep the stiff upper lip. But it can never succeed."

I looked at him in surprise. The general was rather more perceptive than I had realized. "You do not believe in empires?"

His smile was rueful and deeply attractive. "My dear madame, one cannot build an empire without paying for it, and the cost is always too high, as France learned to her sorrow. Ask them all — Alexander, Caesar, Napoléon — they were authors of empires and what did it profit them? They died as all men must. And their empires crumbled to dust." He waved his hands. "No, madame. The game of empires is one that cannot be won. That is why I am here tonight."

"We have that in common," I told him. "I believe in self-determination, that all peoples have a right to be left to govern themselves as they see fit."

He raised an eyebrow in surprise. "Surely only if they have the education to do so under democratic principles," he stated.

"You would see the gospel of Montesquieu preached throughout the world," I teased.

"All men must be schooled to take their destiny in their hands," he said gravely. I glanced across the table and saw Stoker laughing at some witticism of Madame de Letellier.

"And what of the women?" I challenged her husband. "Should they have no role in shaping the future of their countries?"

The general took a long sip of his wine.

"Ladies do not always have the capacity for understanding matters of governance. Excepting yourself, of course," he added with a gallant little bow.

"All the more reason to educate them as well," I told him. I pointed to the centerpiece then, a lavish silver epergne stuffed with hothouse roses and lilies and St. Otthild's wort, a floral compliment to the nations represented around the table. Atop the flowers, in a display of symbolism that entirely escaped me, perched a pair of stuffed birds with bright plumage. *"Eclectus roratus cornelia,"* I told the general. "The Sumba Island eclectus parrot. You see how one is pale green and the other a brilliant scarlet?"

He nodded. "Of course, the male is so dominant and attractive."

"That is not the male," I corrected. "The male eclectus is green, the color of his surroundings, meant to blend in and go unnoticed. It is the female which boasts the glorious scarlet plumage. You, my dear general, have made the very common mistake of believing, as so many others do, that the male of the species is the default. I would like to refer you to Antoinette Brown Blackwell, whose very excellent work, *The Sexes Throughout Nature,* corrects this error on the part of Mr. Darwin —" I broke off at the expression of bemusement on his face. Too late, I realized that Gisela might converse knowledgeably about stamps or cheese, perhaps even politics, but she most assuredly would not lecture on the subject of natural history.

Luckily for me, the general was more attentive to my face than my topic of conversation.

"How stern you look!" he said. "That I have caused such a lovely face to look so forbidding, I will never forgive myself."

A sharp retort rose to my lips, but I felt a quick pinch from my other side. Rupert was still talking in a desultory fashion with an elderly Frenchwoman — something about porcelain — but his hand had slipped under the table to nip me hard upon the leg.

"Madame, you are quite well? Only you look pained," the general said, his expression one of grave concern.

"I am quite well," I assured him. "Just a passing discomfort."

He leaned near, lowering his voice conspiratorially. "It is the English food. My liver has complained since I crossed the Channel. Nothing but beefsteaks and potatoes, so many potatoes," he mourned. "I recommend a strong tisane of peppermint. It always soothes the stomach."

I thanked him politely and just then the consommé bowls were taken away and the next course laid. I turned to find Rupert staring daggers at me. "Is it absolutely necessary to spout Radical philosophy at the general?" he demanded in a whisper.

"It is hardly Radical to propose that women have a say in government," I told him.

"It is to anyone sitting at this table. And evolutionary theory? I hardly think the Princess of the Alpenwald has even heard of Mr. Darwin much less is conversant with his detractors."

"Antoinette Brown Blackwell is not precisely a detractor —" I broke off as Rupert began to glower at me.

"You are doing it again," he said tightly.

"I think my conversation amuses the general," I said, lifting my fork.

"Do not worry about amusing him," Rupert said as he stabbed his woodcock. "Your only concern is getting through this horror of an evening without anyone becoming the wiser as to who you are."

I gave him a demure look that I hoped would signal my agreeableness, but he ignored me, eating his way stolidly through the course until the plates were changed.

"You will give yourself indigestion if you carry on this way," I advised Rupert as I turned back to the general.

The Frenchman was staring at his new plate mournfully. Slices of rosy beef were arranged artfully with piped pureed potatoes. "You see? Beefsteaks and potatoes," he lamented.

I pointed to the menu. *"Rosbif et pommes dauphines."*

He shrugged. "You may call it by a pretty name, but it is still the food of the British peasant." He poked at the meat with his knife. "This steak is overcooked. It grieves upon my plate."

The slices of beef were pink and succulent-looking, but every Frenchman I had ever known preferred his beef very nearly still on the hoof. I signaled to the footman behind me, who sprang to attention.

"Your Serene Highness?"

"I am afraid the general cannot eat his steak. Kindly bring him one that is much less thoroughly cooked. And a salad, lightly dressed with oil and vinegar."

The footman whisked the offending plate away and the general gave a little crow of delight. He leaned towards me, his voice a caressing whisper. "You know, I say to myself, Achille, how can this lovely creature, so natural, so unspoilt, be a princess? I begin to doubt that you are the princess," he said, smiling broadly. "Perhaps you are the faery changeling!"

A frisson of terror surged down my spine, icy as a chilblained finger. "Oh?" I said faintly.

"But then to see you command this fellow so expertly, I know you are a woman accustomed to giving the orders." He regarded me with a practiced gleam in his eye. "Now I must mourn that you are a princess, so far out of reach," he murmured. His gaze dropped lazily to my décolletage again and then rose, unwillingly it seemed, back to my face. "I think I will write poetry to you."

"I beg you will not trouble yourself," I told him.

"What is trouble when there is such beauty in the world?" he demanded. He launched into a lengthy poem in French, only half of which I understood, larded as it was with vernacular terms and metaphors that I suspected were slightly indecent. As the footman refilled his glass, I realized he had taken a great deal of the wine and had as yet consumed very little of the food.

He raised his glass to the light, studying the color. "Do you know, madame, there are those who say you should only taste wine from a goblet made of black glass so that the eye may not be fooled by the color, that only the senses of the nose and the tongue are to be trusted. But what a loss! See this beautiful color, like the velvet of my first mistress's favorite gown. And the bouquet!" He inserted his nose deeply into the glass, sniffing hard. "Such heavy fruits! Cherries and the red currant, so subtle and ripe. This is a very good wine, a wine so good one may dine upon it."

That seemed what he was inclined to do. He finished two more glasses before his food arrived, and when it did, he stared at his fork as if slightly confused by it. I exchanged my plate with his and cut his meat swiftly into little pieces before handing it back.

"Eat," I ordered.

"I am yours to command," he said with limpid eyes. He had eaten half the steak by the time the plates were cleared and there was a brief struggle as the footman removed his. The general clung to it, grumbling as he snatched another piece of steak.

The next course after the roasts was a lovely entremets of artichoke with a parsleyed white wine sauce. The general ignored his entirely in favor of picking desultorily at a jellied orange until the pudding course was served. He brightened at the fanciful display of *pouding* Sax-Weimar, a chocolate pudding lavishly embellished with cream and butter biscuits. He took a spoonful, rolling his eyes ecstatically in pleasure and making rather unseemly noises of appreciation. The footmen had attempted to take his glass of Bordeaux and pour the dessert wine, but the general would not hear of it, holding it up protectively out of reach and snapping his teeth at the hapless servants.

"What the devil is happening over there?" Rupert demanded.

"The general is most appreciative of the vintage served with the meat," I told him.

Rupert edged back in his chair and peered around me discreetly. "He is drunk as a lord," he pronounced in obvious disgust.

"All the better," I whispered. "It means he is less likely to notice any imposture on my part."

The tablecloth moved as the general's hand crept near, landing on my thigh. Rupert glanced down, reddening. "This cannot stand," he began, half rising. "It is bad enough the man insisted on red wine being served during a course with artichokes, but this is quite too far."

I clamped my hand over Rupert's to stay him, careful to keep a smile on my lips in case we were observed. "I have the matter in hand, I assure you, Rupert. I have dealt with far more importunate men upon my travels. Leave it to me and eat your pudding."

He subsided in his chair and applied himself to the sweet. The general's hand crept higher, caressing the heavy satin draped over my thigh. Casually, I reached for my saltcellar, heaping the tiny spoon full.

"General," I said suddenly, nodding towards the wall to his right, "is that painting French? I think it must be a Delacroix." The painting in question was a long canvas, some four yards at least, featuring the allegorical figure of Time being crowned by Glory and Honor.

He turned his head, giving me just enough time to drop the salt into his wine. "A Delacroix here? It would be unthinkable," he pronounced, turning back to me in some befuddlement. "Delacroix is the greatest painter France has ever produced. It is impossible that such a vast canvas should not hang in the Louvre."

"Silly me. I am not a scholar of art," I told him with a modest air. "Now, we have a custom in the Alpenwald, that the last of the wine must be drunk very quickly," I said, raising my own glass of muscat. "It is a sort of tradition. To ensure good health," I added quickly. I quaffed the last swallow of wine in one go, then raised my glass to him.

"*À votre santé!*" He downed the rest of the wine, shuddering. "It was badly served. There was sediment," he told me seriously, smacking his lips. He paused a moment, then his expression turned to one of puzzlement, then outright concern.

"Madame," he murmured. "You must excuse me."

He thrust back his chair, knocking squarely into the footman. I applied myself calmly to my pudding. Rupert pretended to brush a crumb off of his lapel, turning his face towards me. "Did you just poison the French delegate to the Treaty of Windsor?" he demanded.

"Not in the slightest," I replied. "Salt is an emetic, not a poison."

He groaned as he turned back to his dinner partner. I continued on with my *pouding* Sax-Weimar. After several minutes, the general returned looking a little green about the face and dabbing perspiration from his temples.

"Feeling better, General?" I asked brightly.

He nodded, resuming his place. The footman presented a fresh dish of the pudding but the general waved him off hastily. "A cup of tea please," he pleaded. "Very weak. Nothing more."

The general spent the rest of the meal nursing his cup of tea and shuddering every time he looked at food. It was not the kindest method of handling the situation, I reflected, but it had always proven mightily effective. I glanced down the table to see Stoker still deeply engaged in conversation with Madame de Letellier. She laughed at something he said, exchanging his empty plate of pudding for her full one, and he attacked it with gusto. I gestured for the footman to fill my glass once more with the muscat the general had declined.

"But only halfway," I instructed. After the lavish amount of champagne I had consumed the previous night, I intended to keep a clear head about me for the signing of the treaty.

When the last of the plates had been cleared, Rupert rose from his seat. "Your Serene Highness, my lords, ladies, and gentlemen," he said. "We have been invited to take our champagne in the lantern room."

Stoker sidled up behind me. "Did you have a nice dinner with Rupert?" he asked, grinning.

"I think your brother is rather put out with us," I told him.

He shrugged. "Nothing that has not happened before."

I nodded towards his dinner companion, Madame de Letellier. "Your partner is very pretty."

His mouth twitched. "Enchantingly so. But she did not spend the meal leering into my gown. The general seems entirely taken with you."

"Oh, he is. We mean to marry in the spring. We shall name our first child after you if it is a boy. Or a girl. Revelstokia."

He gave a snort of suppressed laughter behind his gloved hand. There was something utterly delicious about sharing a jest with him, a secret laugh that no one else in that company could understand.

"Your Serene Highness," the chancellor's low voice interrupted my reverie. He gave me a tight smile. "You are doing very well," he said, lowering his voice. "Not much longer."

We entered the lantern room. Above swung the lamp for which the chamber was named, an enormous lantern that cast a warm glow over the octagonal room. Across the expanse of thick carpet, a table had been laid with a white cloth, and enormous silver champagne coolers had been filled with ice. Dark green bottles were nestled in the snowy piles, rivulets of water running down the golden labels. Behind the table, footmen were discreetly opening bottles and filling coupes.

Standing in front of the table was a diminutive figure dressed all in black. For a moment, my heart stilled in fear at the notion that it might be my grandmother. But this woman was too slender; although her figure was lushly plump, it had not yet achieved the dumpling roundness of the queen's. Her face bore traces of grief, marking a visage that had never been pretty but might once have been handsome. It was a purposeful face, full of character, with a stubborn chin and a level blue gaze. Her gown was the latest Paris fashion rendered in stark black silk and heavily embroidered in jet which clacked when she moved. Dark hair, threaded with silver, had been pinned tightly back beneath a widow's peaked cap. A long black veil hung to her ankles, and at her neck a brooch of enormous diamonds shimmered and shattered the light.

She held up her hands, more diamonds glittering as she moved. "Welcome, friends," she said in English accented by an edge of German. "Welcome to Windsor Castle, where we take our first steps towards a lasting peace."

She came towards me, hands outstretched. I recovered myself just in time to make her a low curtsy. "Your Serene Highness," she said, taking my hands in hers and lifting me.

"Your Imperial Majesty," I returned in a low voice.

She looked at me a long moment, studying me. Then her face wreathed in smiles. "We will not stand on ceremony, Gisela," she said, wrapping her arms about me. "Give me a kiss, child."

There was no response to make except to return her embrace. I had recognized her at once from her photographs, of course. This was Her Imperial Majesty, the Dowager Empress of Germany, Princess Royal of Great Britain.

And my aunt Vicky.

CHAPTER 25

The next several minutes were occupied
with the handing out of champagne glasses
and the greeting of the other dignitaries.
Toasts were proposed and drunk, and
through it all, I felt nothing but a blank calm
I could not escape. I said the proper things
and made the proper gestures, and yet I
wanted only to run.

The chancellor crept close to me at one
point. "You said she was at Sandringham,"
I hissed at him through smiling teeth.

He glanced at me in surprise. "It was
thought so, but she clearly wishes to cele-
brate her achievement in bringing this
about. Do not distress yourself, my dear.
You are doing perfectly well."

He moved away and I realized he did not
— could not possibly — understand the
true source of my distress. He did not know
of my relationship with the royal family. But
Stoker and Rupert did, and between them,

they managed to keep close to me, one or the other always near at hand should I have need of them.

The toasts were finished when the empress rang a little bell. A footman appeared with a leather folio, presenting it to her with a flourish. Another small table had been draped with a cloth and atop this were three pens, each resting in a narrow tray of mother-of-pearl.

The empress opened the portfolio and produced the copies of the treaty. It was a single page, shorter than I expected, but beautifully rendered with elegant copperplate and flourishes. At the top, it read *Treaty of Windsor Castle, January 1889.* A moment of history, I thought as I gripped the pen tightly in my gloved hand.

The general, entirely revived by the excellence of the champagne, beamed at me. He bent and scrawled his signature on the first copy as I put the pen to mine. I glanced at the chancellor, who gave an almost imperceptible nod of the head.

Gisela Frederica Victoria Helena. I had practiced the princess's signature until my fingers cramped, and the result was a triumph. There was a little stutter on the "G," a hesitation as I held the pen poised over the paper, ready to commit forgery on an international and most likely felonious scale. But then I had taken a deep breath and pressed on, gaining confidence with each letter.

As I signed, the general applied his own signature to his copy, a trifle unsteadily, shaking his head once or twice to clear the cobwebs, no doubt.

It was done. We exchanged copies and countersigned, then Rupert stepped forward to put his name as witness to the treaty. The general straightened and saluted me, wobbling only slightly. "I am your servant, Your Serene Highness. It is my ardent hope that the bonds of our friendship will never be tested by the ambitions of the kaiser, but if they are, you may rest assured that the Alpenwald will never know a truer ally than France."

He took a deep breath, summoning his composure, and bowed deeply, executing a perfect curtsy in my direction.

"Thank you, General," I said gravely. "The Alpenwald is grateful for the friendship of France."

Everyone applauded then and fresh champagne was poured. As the glasses were passed, the door opened and a plump gentleman in elegant evening dress entered. He glanced around the room.

"Have I missed the party, then?" he asked, rubbing his hands together.

I gripped the pen in my hand so tightly I heard it crack.

A footman stepped forward, blushing for his tardiness at not announcing the newcomer as soon as he arrived.

"His Royal Highness," the footman proclaimed. "The Prince of Wales."

I had seen my father only twice before and both times in passing. He advanced, smiling broadly and gesturing for a glass of champagne. I could not move or speak, but stood, staring at him in mute . . . what? Horror? Longing? Resentment? There were no words for what I felt in that moment. I was unmoored, as adrift as I had ever been in my life, and a roaring sound rose in my ears, shutting out the sudden burst of excited conversation at the prince's appearance in the room.

Suddenly, my arm was gripped hard just above the elbow. "Oh dear," said the empress coolly. "You seem to have spilt ink on your glove."

I glanced down to the ruined pen still clutched in my nerveless fingers. I opened my palm to find pieces of it sitting in a pool of ebony ink on the ruined kidskin. "Come," the empress ordered, steering me by the arm. "We must wash your hands."

She guided me to the corner behind the champagne table, in the opposite direction from the prince. The baroness started forward to help, but the empress waved her off with an imperious gesture. I attempted to give the baroness a reassuring smile, but my mouth would not curve. I forced myself to walk calmly with the empress. In the corner there was only paneled wall, but she depressed a bit of molding and a hidden door sprang open. She led me through, closing it behind us. We were in a narrow corridor, a hushed passageway, thickly carpeted and leading deeper into the castle.

She did not speak as she moved, never hurrying but somehow covering the distance swiftly as she led me down the passage and through another concealed door. We passed through a small octagonal dining room and into another corridor, up a small staircase, and finally into a lavatory tiled in plain white and green and surprisingly plain for all its modern conveniences. She closed the door firmly behind us, locking it.

She turned, folding her hands together over the key. "Now, why don't you tell me who you are and what you have done with Gisela?"

Her eyes, brightly blue and slightly protuberant, were watchful. She came only to my chin, but a royal upbringing and lifetime spent in the strictest courts of Europe had honed her imperiousness to a fine edge. I did not bother to lie. I would not have known how to begin.

"How did you know? I thought I was doing rather a good job of it."

She did not smile, but the tightness of her lips eased. "I met Gisela last year at the baths at Friedrichsbad, where we both went to take the waters. We got to know one another quite well."

"The chancellor said you had never met!"

"The chancellor knows only what Gisela wishes him to know," she said with a knowing smile. "I presume he put you up to this. He of all people would know his princess from an imposter."

"It was the chancellor's idea," I admitted.

"How much is he paying you?"

"Not a shilling," I told her.

She raised an imperial brow. "Then why are you doing this?"

"For the sake of the treaty," I said.

She regarded me a long moment, then shook her head. "You are a most remarkable person, Miss —" She gave me an expectant look.

"Speedwell," I supplied.

I had not expected her to know the name, but her eyes went wide. "Not *Veronica* Speedwell? Bertie's girl?"

"You know who I am?"

"Of course," she told me. "I was newly married when all the business with your parents happened." She waved a hand as if to brush aside the unpleasantness of my parents' marriage, my father's abandonment, and my mother's subsequent suicide. "Bertie — His Royal Highness," she corrected swiftly, "and I have always been close. He wrote to me often in Berlin. I helped him with his troubles."

I did not much care for being characterized as one of his "troubles," but there seemed little point in quibbling with her over the matter.

She tipped her head, her gaze bright as a bird's as she looked me over. "You are very like Gisela. The resemblance is remarkable, in fact. But these things happen in families and you both do share a connection some generations back. Little wonder the chancellor thought to make use of you. But how did he come to meet you?"

"I was introduced to the princess a few days ago. The Baroness von Wallenberg noted the resemblance and when the princess went missing, she suggested the impersonation to the chancellor."

Her gaze sharpened. "Gisela is *missing*?"

"Not precisely. She seems to have left of her own accord and means to return in due course. It is just that no one is certain of where she is."

"So she *is* missing," she replied tartly. "And Scotland Yard know nothing of this?"

"The chancellor thought it best not to tell them. He was afraid that the princess's absence might signal disrespect to the French and the treaty might never be signed."

She considered this a moment, then nodded. "He was right to worry. General de Letellier is a touchy sort of man. Very conscious of French dignity and easily offended. But how on earth did the chancellor think he could get away with this ridiculous charade?"

"But he has," I pointed out. "You are the only one who has detected the masquerade. The French have signed the treaty. The chancellor has a secret document giving authority to me to sign on behalf of the princess. I am dubious of the legality of the thing — no doubt I have broken a dozen international laws — but the chancellor does not seem terribly worried about the prospect."

She shrugged. "The Alpenwalders are acting in good faith inasmuch as they are committed to aiding the French against my son." Her mouth twisted a little on the last word. How thankless to be the mother of such a child! She seemed to intuit my thoughts, for she gave me a thin smile. "You have never met your cousin, the kaiser. Be grateful, child."

There was no tactful answer to this, so I did not attempt one.

"Do you mean to unmask me?" I asked with more bravado than I felt.

Her response was oblique. "Do you know why I wanted this treaty, Miss Speedwell? Not simply to thwart my son. It was my husband's great ambition to bring Germany into the modern age, no more looking fondly backwards to the military parades and battlefield glories. He was a good man, the Emperor Friedrich. His father wanted nothing to do with his liberality, with his desire to bind Germany to the rest of Europe. My Friedrich waited all of his life to ascend the throne and remake his fatherland. By the time he became emperor, he was dying."

There was no bitterness in her words, only resignation to the cruelties of fate. "My poor

Fritz was emperor for three months. For the whole of his short reign, they ignored him, those ministers and generals and *Bismarck*," she said, fairly spitting the name. "They took one look at a dying man and knew his grip was too weak to hold power. They passed him over and went directly to the son, praising him and promising to make his wildest dreams of German domination come true. This was the great mistake, you know. They think they can control him, can use him for their own ends. But no one can control my son, and they will learn this too late. My only hope is that it will not be too late for the rest of the world."

She paused, fixing me with that austere blue stare. "You are really doing this for the sake of the treaty?"

"I am."

Silence stretched between us, brittle, until she gave a sigh. "Well, I have worked a year to bring it about. I am hardly going to take a hammer to it with my own hands, am I?" she asked. Something within me, taut and painful, eased when she said those words.

She inclined her head to my stained glove. "Take that off. Carefully. You don't want to spot Gisela's gown."

I peeled away the soiled glove as well as its spotless mate. I washed my hands carefully to remove all traces of the ink, taking my time. The soap was good plain stuff, smelling faintly of lavender. There would be no cakes of finely milled French soap here, I reflected. Only good, honest English soap scented with lavender.

"The lavender is grown in the fields around Sandringham, in Norfolk," she told me as she played handmaiden, holding out a towel for me to dry my hands. "It is his favorite house. Have you met him?"

She did not say my father's name. She did not have to. "Never."

"Would you like to? Properly, I mean. And privately. It could be arranged. After all, I suppose I owe you something for what you have done tonight."

I thought of that sharp twist of longing I had felt when I looked at him. Was it the call of blood to blood? Or was it simply the childish wish to be recognized, to be owned by one's begetter? I imagined that brilliant winsome smile turned upon me as I basked in its warmth, the kindly eyes crinkling as he looked at me.

"No," I told her.

The empress gave me a long look. "Are you certain?"

I nodded, the jewels in my tiara clattering. She touched one. "I never cared for tiaras with the gems *en tremblant.* Terribly noisy, I always think."

Impulsively, I put out a hand, laying it gently on her sleeve. "Please, ma'am. I do not want to meet him at all. Not like this."

She considered me a long moment. "Very well. Give me ten minutes. I will make your excuses and say you are unwell. Your carriages and entourage will be waiting for you out front."

I thought of the suite at the Sudbury, yet to be searched. "If you please, can you keep the others here as long as possible? I need only one carriage and the black-haired gentleman with the eye patch."

Her gaze sharpened. "Is this to do with Gisela's disappearance?"

"In part. And another matter."

"As you wish. Ten minutes. Find your way to the front of the castle and I will have the fellow meet you there. I will keep the others as long as I can."

"What will you tell them?"

Her thin smile was once more in evidence. "That is the advantage of being an empress, my dear. I do not have to tell them anything at all."

She turned to the looking glass and straightened the peak of her widow's cap. "I shall never be reconciled to this," she said with a dour look at it. "Black does not suit me."

She gave me a last look over her shoulder. "Thank you, Veronica."

"You are welcome, Your Imperial Majesty."

Her smile was gentle. "My nieces and nephews all call me Aunt Vicky."

She left me then, my aunt Vicky, the Dowager Empress of Germany. I took a breath, as deep as I could with the tight lacing of the corset, steadying myself against the washbasin.

Before I could gather my thoughts, the door opened once more and J. J. Butterworth slipped inside. "You look like something the cat sicked up," she told me cheerfully.

"What an enchanting person you are," I replied.

She grinned, unrepentant. "Do not wait for me when you leave tonight," she instructed.

I blinked at her. "You mean to remain behind? At Windsor Castle?"

She shrugged. "I have a story to chase."

"This was your plan in coming all along, was it not? You used us to gain entrée to the castle because they would never permit a journalist inside if they knew who you were. What now? Rifling through the queen's wastepaper basket?"

Her smile would have suited a cream-filled cat. "Something like that. Do not spare a thought for me, Veronica. I will have what I came for. And I promise not to involve you," she added with an exasperated sigh. "I know you were about to ask."

I flapped a hand. "I do not care. Just go."

She left in a whirl of aprons and indignation, but I scarcely noticed. She was hardly likely to burn the place down around everyone's ears and I almost did not care if she did. Rage simmered within me, coupled with some other, more painful emotion that threatened to flay me alive. I was in Windsor Castle, wearing a fortune in jewels, with my father a short distance away.

The room was suddenly stifling. Gathering my skirts in my hands, I rushed out, down the tiny staircase, and past the door I had entered. I was in a different part of the castle, and I passed through rooms I had not seen. One had walls bristling with weapons of every description, pikes and swords arranged in patterns, while another sported a gallery of paintings of men who had been instrumental in Napoléon's defeat at Waterloo. No one stopped me or stood in my way as I fled. I hastened from one vast chamber to another until I came at last to the vestibule where we had entered. The guards stood at attention as I passed, fleeing down the crimson carpeted stairs like Cinderella as the clock struck midnight.

CHAPTER 26

Upon our return to the Sudbury, Stoker and I hastened to change back into our own clothing. It required the utmost ingenuity to divest myself of the jewels and hairpieces and garments without help, but I was almost frantic in my haste to rid myself of Gisela's things. I had had enough of playing at being a princess, I decided grimly.

As I dressed, the familiar tweed felt like armor, bracing me against an uncertain world. It was as much a part of me as my own skin, and I understood only then how much wearing Gisela's clothes and jewels had affected me. I had not been entirely myself dressed as I had been in the trappings of royalty. Now I was Veronica Speedwell once more, and as I finished buttoning my jacket and shot my cuffs, I felt invigorated as I had not since we had begun this endeavor.

I had related to Stoker my exchanges with

Aunt Vicky and J. J. as well as the information that Yelena was a blackmailer. We did not speak of my father; some things were too near the bone for casual discussion, and I was not ready to think about the opportunity I had let pass me by. Stoker came to collect me just as I finished, having concluded his own struggles with the false moustaches.

"I think the bloody things took off half my skin," he complained.

"Never mind that now," I told him. "We will have only a little time to search. I managed Gisela's bedchamber earlier but found nothing."

"I did the same for Durand's room just now," he said.

"Did what for Durand's room?" I could just make out the large form of the captain silhouetted in the doorway.

"May I help you, Captain?" Stoker inquired politely.

"Where are the others?" he demanded.

"Still at Windsor," I informed him. "Where you ought to be. The chancellor was most put out that you could not be found. Where is Yelena?"

Durand's eyes were limned red with the signs of unshed tears, and a small muscle jumped unsteadily at his jaw. "I do not know."

"She is not with you?" Stoker asked narrowly.

"If she were, would I ever have forsaken my duty?" He was clearly aghast at the very idea of such a thing. "I stayed behind to look for her."

"Is that not a dereliction of duty?" I inquired.

"I do not care," he said, thumping his chest with one fist. "What does it matter if my heart is gone from me?"

I sighed. Durand was clearly as big a romantic as Stoker. "You read poetry, don't you?" I asked.

He blinked at me. "Yes. I write it also."

"Of course you do," I murmured.

Stoker shot me a villainous look. "Veronica, contain your worse impulses. The captain is clearly distraught."

Durand blinked. "What is this word?"

" 'Distraught'? It means upset. Deeply upset," Stoker told him.

The captain nodded slowly. "Upset. Yes, this is true. My Yelena is gone."

His face crumpled and for one terrible moment I thought he was going to weep, and I had had quite enough of crying men for one day.

I spoke to him in a brisk tone, calculated to stiffen his mettle. "Come now, Captain. It cannot be as bad as all that."

He fixed me with an imploring look. "I know you find things," he said. "I have heard the baroness and the chancellor speak of it."

"We do have some experience," I said with a modest gesture.

"Then you will find my Yelena. Please."

I sighed and looked at the clock. Time was getting on and this might easily be our only opportunity to search for any clues to where the princess had gone or who had been responsible for Alice's murder. "The baroness said she received a note and went out, quite suddenly."

"A note from whom?" he asked, thrusting out his chest manfully. "If it was another man, I will kill him."

"There is really no call for that," I told him firmly. "It did occur to me that perhaps Yelena was summoned by the princess."

Something like hope kindled in his eyes. "You think so?"

I shrugged. "It is possible. We still do not know where the princess is. It is conceivable that she had need of Yelena and sent for her with instructions not to reveal anything of the matter to anyone."

He thought, stroking his moustaches as he pondered. "This is possible," he said. Then he shook his head, slowly and from side to side, like a buffalo. "But I think it is not true. Yelena would have told me."

I considered Yelena's mildly extortionate activities and groped for a tactful way to raise the matter with Durand. Stoker had no such scruples. "Did you know she is a blackmailer?" he asked suddenly.

Durand guffawed. "A blackmailer! That is a harsh word for a little harmless exchange of monies."

I gaped at him. "You knew?"

"Of course I knew. My family will — what is the English phrase? — cut me up when I marry her."

"Cut you off," Stoker corrected.

"Yes, thank you," Durand replied. "They will cut me off. I will have no monies of my own except what I earn as captain of the princess's guard. Yelena and I like nice things," he finished blandly.

"So you conspire *with* her to extort money from people?" I asked, still aghast.

He shrugged. "It is easy for a man in my position to see things. It is natural for me to tell them to my fiancée. But Yelena is her own woman. What she does with such knowledge is not for me to say." He turned to Stoker. "You understand, no? You cannot control your woman either."

"I am *not* anyone's woman but my own," I returned hotly. Stoker slanted me an oblique look but said nothing.

"Will you help me find her?" Durand asked piteously.

"Certainly," I told him, baring my teeth in a savage parody of a grin. "I think you quite deserve one another." More than that, I had just realized that Durand carried keys to all of the rooms. It would not be necessary to pick the lock of the lumber room, thus making up for the time we had spent listening to his romantic woes.

Either Durand's grasp of English was too poor to comprehend sarcasm or he did not care. He slapped his thighs. "Good! We will begin now, please."

"I will require your key to the lumber room," I said, putting out my hand. "Mr. Templeton-Vane and I will begin there," I added, omitting the fact that we had business of our own in that location.

Stoker spoke then. "I think Yelena's room should be searched first. If she left in anticipation of going to the princess for any length of time, she would have taken a few things with her — nightdress, money, that sort of thing."

"A perfect task for you, Captain," I agreed.

"I am not a woman," he protested. "I will not know if lady things are missing."

"Lady things?" I asked, staring hard at him.

He flushed, the most brilliant incarnadine shade, and I realized then what he was speaking of.

"Oh, for heaven's sake," I muttered. "Very well. I will look through Yelena's things. Stoker, come along, please. Captain, you can at least keep watch and make certain the others have not returned. We will rendezvous in the lumber room in a quarter of an hour."

I did not expect it would take long to search Yelena's meager possessions, but I intended to be thorough. While Stoker looked on, I examined the contents of the dresser, counting six chemises and sets of petticoats as well as underdrawers, each neatly embroidered with a day of the week in a whimsical pattern with lovers' knots and daisy chains. A full complement of menstrual rags were tied into a bundle and stowed beneath the undergarments. A small enameled watch lay on the washbasin, and her purse, fat with coins and notes, was where we had left it.

"Nothing appears to be missing," I said at

last. "There are four dresses hanging in the wardrobe and the only things gone are those she was wearing today. Her money is here, as is her watch —" I broke off suddenly as Stoker turned from where he had been making his own inventory of the wardrobe. "What is it?"

He thought a moment, then opened the wardrobe again. "Didn't Yelena give the princess her cloak to wear on the night she disappeared?"

"Yes," I said, noting the toothbrush and tin of tooth powder resting on a washing flannel on the top of the dresser. A tin contained a cake of soap, a little worn and smelling of violets.

Stoker pointed to the wardrobe. "She gave the princess her cloak, and yet here is a coat, long and warm, and a thick scarf tucked into the collar. Surely she would have worn it if she went out today. And look." He reached down and lifted out a pair of stout overshoes. "Her warmest things are still here. And if she did mean to go out, she would never have neglected to wear overshoes." He straightened, his expression grim. "Money and warm clothes still here? Yelena never left the hotel."

"Then where in the name of Priam's petticoat is she?" I demanded. He replaced the shoes and we left. There was no sign of Durand as we made our way to the lumber room. To my surprise, the room was unlocked, the gasolier burning.

"Durand must have already searched in here," I mused as we surveyed the room.

"Then why give us the key and not mention it?" Stoker asked in a distracted voice.

I shrugged. "It is possible he is responsible for Yelena's disappearance," I said. "He is a moustachioed man," I reminded Stoker. "Just like the fellow on the mountain when Alice died. J. J. thinks it was Douglas Norton, but what if it was Durand? He might have had a hand in Alice's death and Yelena knew too much to be trusted."

"He is going to marry her," Stoker protested.

"All the more reason to dispose of her if she proves a liability," I said. "She is a nasty little blackmailer."

"Your opinion of your sex is chilling," Stoker said.

I said nothing as I turned my attention to the various impedimenta of travel in the room. I detected the baroness's meticulous hand in the orderly piles of trunks and stacks of baggage. Everything was neatly labeled and arranged according to the importance of the owner. A single carpetbag bearing Yelena's name was perched on a shelf in the corner.

"You are quite right. She did not leave," I told Stoker. "Not without her bag."

I went and opened it, expecting to find the usual odds and ends that accumulate during travel. Instead, I reared back in horror as I saw the face of a man staring up at me.

"What is it?" Stoker hurried to my side as I reached into the bag with nerveless fingers. "What in the name of the seven devils is that?"

I lifted out what was — mercifully — not a face, but a canvas mask, fully painted with features, including a pair of dark moustaches. "It is a climbing mask," I told him in some relief. "I read about them in Alice's notes. Some alpinists wear them to protect the skin from the sun at altitude." I turned it over in my hands.

"Yelena is no climber," Stoker pointed out. "So what is she doing with that thing?"

I stared down at the monstrous thing, looking for all the world like a trophy, a visage peeled away from a defeated foe.

And suddenly I knew.

"Alice's death. That mysterious moustachioed man on the slopes of the Teufelstreppe," I began.

I did not have to finish. "My God," Stoker breathed. "The murderer used it to conceal his features. He must have been known — too well-known to risk anyone recognizing him."

"Most likely not Durand, then. This points to the duke," I reasoned.

"What if Gisela found this?" he asked. "Max already had a worthy motive to put Gisela out of the way to gain a throne for himself. If he murdered Alice and the princess discovered his guilt, then he would be stupid not to remove her."

"Or he might have done it at her behest," I pointed out. "Without Gisela here to answer for herself, there is no way to know if she is author of a plot or its victim."

"And if Yelena discovered it among his things, she would recognize a tidy opportunity to blackmail him for money to keep quiet. Yet another desperate turn of the rack screw on a man already pushed to his limits."

He folded the mask and tucked it into his shirt for safekeeping before moving on to Max's trunks. He poked idly through the silk linings and boot compartments. "Nothing here," he said in a tone of marked disappointment.

I passed to the chancellor's boxes. Some

451

were locked and marked with his cipher — no doubt for the storage of confidential papers and valuables, although the costliest items, the parures of the princess's jewels, were secured in the locked strongbox in the princess's bedchamber. I carried on, opening the baroness's bags. There was precious little inside them, I realized as I searched. A bit of spilt face powder, a lace shoe with a broken heel and its mate, tied together with a bit of ribbon. No doubt they were favorites and meant for the cobbler to be mended.

I closed her boxes with a huff of annoyance. I had been so certain we would find something of note, I reflected peevishly.

"Veronica," Stoker said in a slightly strangled voice.

"What is it?" I asked as I opened a hamper of tinned Alpenwalder delicacies. I pulled a face at the pickled cabbage and pungently aged cheese.

"Come and see this," he said.

"I am rather busy," I told him as I opened a box of cheese experimentally and gave it a sniff. I reared back as if I had been struck. It was utterly vile. Little wonder Julien d'Orlande did not like it in his kitchens.

"Veronica, *now*," Stoker ordered.

I turned, prepared to give him a piece of my mind for his peremptory tone when I saw his face. It was set in a grim expression as he stared down into a trunk marked *BOOKS*. I went to him, but I knew. Of course I knew. Before I looked down into the open trunk and saw her, nestled there amidst the magazines and books that had been tucked neatly around her, I smelled her — the faint, unmistakable fragrance of death.

Yelena.

"Of course she is dead," I said, striving for calm. "I mean, we knew it, did we not?"

Stoker did not reply. With a surgeon's practiced eye, he was surveying the body.

"How?" I asked.

He shook his head. "Poison? There are no visible marks of a weapon. Ah," he said, bending swiftly. He tugged aside the collar of her dress to reveal a livid line of dark violet. "Strangulation, I would guess from the bruises," he said, bending to examine her hands. "No indication that she struggled, so whoever attacked her did it swiftly and with strength. She had no chance, poor girl."

I had not liked Yelena, but the thought of her, caught unawares by someone, struggling for breath, vision narrowing to a pinprick of light in the darkness and

453

then . . . nothing. It was ghastly.

Stoker lifted her gently, and as he did so, a length of white silk was revealed. I slid my hand under her body to pull it free. It was heavily creased, and Stoker regarded it with a practiced eye. "Possibly the murder weapon," he said grimly. "The width fits the bruising around her throat."

I held the silk in my hands. It ought to have been cool from lying under Yelena's dead body, but I fancied it was still warm, warm from strangling the life out of her.

"I know who did this," I told him.

He glanced at the label on the trunk. "It is Maximilian's case."

"This is the riband of St. Otthild. And Maximilian was wearing his tonight. As was the chancellor. And who would need a mask with painted moustaches to masquerade as a man?"

He blinked at me. "But surely the baroness of all people would not —" Stoker began.

"Oh, but she did," said a voice from the doorway. The baroness stood there, a small pistol in her hand, leveled at Stoker's heart.

"Not again," I muttered.

She smiled a mirthless smile. "You are rather prone to being the victims of homicidal attacks, are you not? You do have a penchant for putting yourself into dangerous situations. You see, you are not the only one capable of scientific inquiry, Miss Speedwell. I have made it my business to discover a few things about you."

"Things that are supposed to be confidential," I told her.

She shrugged. "Intelligence matters are often shared between allies."

I glanced at Stoker. "I thought our activities were not a part of the official record."

"They are not. But there will always be those who gossip, no matter how discreetly, and your activities have given you a reputation for fecklessness," the baroness affirmed.

"Fecklessness! We are never feckless," I told her coldly. "We are full to the *brim* with feck. Now, kindly put down your weapon and let us discuss this like rational people. It is obvious that you strangled Yelena after murdering Alice Baker-Greene. You might yet redeem yourself if you reveal what you have done with the princess."

"I have no idea where the princess is," she returned. "If I did, I would be infinitely happier." She cocked her head like a bright little bird, the light glinting on her monocle, and gave a brisk twitch of the weapon. "Now, I have the gun, which means I am in command here. Miss Speedwell, you will remove your clothing, down to your chemise. I apologize for the indelicacy, but it is the only way to be certain that you are not armed. You will be quick about it." I glanced at the door, wondering what had become of Durand.

"The captain," I began, but she jerked her head to the side and I saw, just peeping out from behind one of the trunks, a pair of booted legs.

"Have you killed him?" I asked.

"Not yet. He is merely unconscious. He bled a lot," she added ruefully. "I hit him in the head and it has made a mess. I will have to clean that up and I do not like a mess."

I opened my mouth and the gun in her hand twitched towards Stoker. "Miss Speedwell, I told you not to attempt it. I will not shoot you. I will shoot Mr. Templeton-Vane instead."

She had, unerringly, found my Achilles' heel. The fact that Stoker had very recently been shot weighed on my conscience. It was the latest in a long line of such misadventures, but it had been the most serious — far too serious to permit a repeat performance. I would take chances with my life, but not his. I undressed swiftly, removing the corset with its slender blade and the knife from my boot as well as the minuten

456

neatly embedded in my cuffs. When I had finished, I stood, shivering in my chemise and underdrawers.

"Now you," she told Stoker.

"I would rather not," he said, flushing to the tips of his ears.

"I will not be delayed," the baroness told him, gesturing with the revolver. "Do as you are told."

Still he hesitated, and suddenly I understood the reason for his reluctance. "Oh, Stoker," I murmured. "How could you?"

"I was in a hurry," he muttered. "I wanted to get to my spoonbill."

His blush deepened as he looked to our captor. "You see, Baroness, I received a rather important trophy — a roseate spoonbill, *Platalea ajaja* —"

"The baroness does not care about the Latin," I interrupted.

He carried on as if I had not spoken. "And in my eagerness to examine the bird, I am afraid I dressed in haste this morning and am only wearing trousers."

"Then you are going to be very cold," she said. The revolver jerked again. "Disrobe."

He did as she said, pulling off his coat and shirt and dropping them on top of his boots. He hesitated at the buttons of his trousers, then unfastened them, stepping out of the

457

garment and standing mother naked before her.

"Thank you both for being so obliging," she said. "Now, open that trunk," she instructed, pointing with the barrel of her pistol to an enormous iron-banded affair. Stoker threw back the lid. "You will find rope inside. Tie your companion," she instructed. He did so, knotting the ropes as loosely as he dared around my wrists. "Put your arms about his neck," she told me. I obliged her, looping my bound arms over his head in a parody of an embrace.

"Good," she pronounced. "Get into the trunk."

It seemed a rather snug fit and was awkward to maneuver, arranged as we were with my arms around Stoker.

"Mr. Templeton-Vane on the bottom," she said. Stoker settled himself, drawing me down on top of him. He settled me as gently as he could, curving his body around mine with such innate sweetness, I might have wept under other circumstances.

It was a tidy little conundrum, I reflected. And the baroness had done an admirable job of rendering it just difficult enough for us to maneuver. But she would have to put the revolver down in order to strap the trunk closed, I decided, and that was when

I would strike, levering my legs up and smashing them into the lid, forcing it backwards and into her.

But the baroness anticipated this. She gave me a thin smile as she came near, bending over us. "Good night, children." She raised her hand, the butt of the pistol gripped tightly in her palm. She brought it down swiftly against Stoker's temple. He gave a single sigh as he slid into unconsciousness, and I heard a roar of outrage — my own, I realized — just as her hand rose for the second blow.

And then a black curtain descended, blotting out the light.

CHAPTER 27

I struggled awake slowly, so slowly, as if I were swimming through treacle. Every bit of progress towards consciousness was a battle, and my senses returned not all together but one at a time. First was smell. Blood and salt and oil, I thought as my awareness was revived. There was a sense of cold, such perishing cold that I thought I would never be warm again, and the air in the trunk, close and damp, smelt of the sea.

I could hear the steady beating of waves, the rhythmic slap of water against an iron hull. We were seaborne, then, I realized dazedly. Somehow the baroness had contrived to have our trunk conveyed onto a boat of some sort. But where were we bound? And what did she mean to do with us when we arrived?

I had no sense of the passage of time, no way to judge how long we had been held in our makeshift prison. She had taken the precaution of tying a piece of fabric over my mouth, and Stoker's as well, I had no doubt. It was an easy enough matter to scrape it loose by means of twisting my head. (In my experience, abductors never will tie gags tightly enough. It is a skill more of them ought to practice.) It hung loose around my neck, unpleasantly damp from having been in my mouth for some time.

There was no light, no indication of day or night, so I assessed my own condition for clues. I was mildly hungry and experiencing only a faint inclination to attend to the needs of Nature, so we could not have been aboard for too long, I decided. My hands were still bound, which I did not like at all, but I found this much more tolerable than the gag had been.

I flexed my feet and immediately rammed my toes against Stoker's legs, causing him to groan. "Stoker, are you awake?"

For a long, terrible moment, there was no reply save silence. Then, like a bear rousing itself from hibernation, came a series of snuffles and grunts and I realized he was freeing himself of his gag.

"Where in the name of seven hells are we?" he demanded.

"At sea," I told him.

"I deduced that," he replied with considerable *froideur.* I decided to overlook his sulkiness.

"There is no call to be in a temper," I said. "Just because we have been abducted. Again."

"I think there is every call to be in a temper," he returned. "This is precisely the sort of predicament I was trying to avoid."

"I certainly hope you do not mean to suggest this is *my* fault," I began.

"Suggest? No, I am stating it outright," he told me. "I am saying it plainly. If you like, I will have it printed on the front page of the *Daily Harbinger* or spelt out in electric lights in Piccadilly Circus or tattooed on my backside — which, I would like to remind you, is in fact naked at this moment."

"I think that is a trifle unfair," I said, attempting to conceal my sense of injury.

"Unfair? Veronica, what is unfair is that *yet again* an attempt has been made upon our lives, one that may yet succeed," he said in real bitterness.

"Do not be so melodramatic. This is hardly an attempt on our lives. We were merely rendered hors de combat, put into a trunk, and loaded onto a boat."

"A boat that is at sea and from which we will most likely be flung into the ocean," he said. This would never do. He was distinctly in the grip of "the morbs" and I would not stand for it. We were companions in adventure, and it was my duty to buck his spirits.

"That is a decidedly pessimistic way to view the current situation," I said a trifle more cheerfully than I felt. "I prefer to believe we will prevail. But I am the rara avis, a true optimist."

"You are not an optimist. You are a fantasist. You cannot really believe that just because we have eluded a fatal conclusion to every previous unexpected peril that we must do so again. Sooner or later, our luck will run out, Veronica. And that day may very well be today. How can you accept this with such blind and reckless equanimity?"

This was no mere momentary gloom, I realized. He was, for perhaps the first time in our acquaintance, well and truly in despair. I was silent a long moment. He had been angry with me before. When his dark moods were upon him, anger was his frequent companion. I bore the vagaries of his temper with composure. His flashes of irritation were no source of bother to me; in fact, if I am honest — as I have sworn within these pages to be — I will admit that when his ire rose, it more often than not roused some rather different emotion in me. Because I knew his rage, even in a burst of white-hot passion, would never cause him to inflict harm, I could view it from a position of detachment, appreciation even. It would have been a rare woman not to enjoy the sight of his muscles taut with emotion, his eyes flashing sapphirine fury, his hair tumbled as he thrust his hands through it. I had even, upon occasion, deliberately prodded his patience to the snapping point in order to turn that hectic emotion to some more personally enjoyable activity.

But this reaction was calculated in its coldness. This was no sound and fury that signified nothing. This was a withdrawal, a pulling back within himself like a wounded thing, guarding and protecting himself. From me.

I rested my head on his shoulder. There was nowhere for him to move, but I felt his muscle flinch in protest. He would offer me no willing succor.

"I am sorry," I said softly. "You are quite right. I did fling myself headlong into this endeavor without ever believing the consequences would come to this. And I did so knowing that you would follow. As you always do."

"More fool me," he said into the darkness.

"I only wanted —"

"I know what you wanted."

"To find justice for Alice Baker-Greene. And then to help the Alpenwalders," I finished. "It seemed a noble pursuit."

"To find justice? To help the Alpenwalders?" His voice was frankly incredulous. "Just now, when we are facing death yet again, I would very much appreciate it if you could be bothered, just this once, to tell the truth."

I reared back in shock, slamming my head into the side of the trunk. "I *beg* your pardon? Are you calling me a liar?"

He took a deep breath, as deep as the confines of the trunk would permit, and exhaled slowly, ruffling my hair. "Not intentionally," he said. "You are as dishonest with yourself as you are with me."

"Dishonest! If we were not locked in a trunk and possibly destined for a watery grave, I would demand satisfaction."

"Demand all you like. What you will get is the truth. You are in the grip of a very strong delusion if you think you did all of this in order to help Alice Baker-Greene or the Alpenwalders."

"To what other motive would you impute my actions?" I asked icily. "I could hardly be driven by remuneration considering we

465

will not be paid for our efforts. It is not public adulation since our actions must remain private. So, fame and fortune are not my aims. What drives me then?"

"Ennui."

"Ennui?" I laughed aloud. "You think I am bored?"

"I think you are *afraid* of becoming so," he corrected. "You have your work, which you enjoy but which offers no real sport now that you have curtailed your field expeditions. You no longer travel the globe in search of specimens, meeting new acquaintances and testing yourself against the most demanding of circumstances. Those are confining conditions to one who has been accustomed to the most liberal of freedoms."

Confusion settled over me, and I could not reply as he went on.

"But most of all, I think you are afraid of becoming bored with me."

"With you?" My laugh emerged on a sob. "How, I implore you, could any woman be bored with you? You are changeable as the weather, Revelstoke Templeton-Vane. I could no more predict your moods than I could those of a volcano. I wake each day never knowing if I will find you wreathed in smiles or taking out your grievances on a stuffed walrus. You are the least boring man ever fashioned by Nature."

"Perhaps you will not become bored with me," he amended. "But you could well become bored of who you are when you are with me."

"Who am I when I am with you?" I whispered into his shoulder.

"A domesticated creature," he replied. "One who fears her wings have been clipped. You've no liking for cages, Veronica. And I think you fear that in allowing yourself to love freely, you will find one of your own making."

"That is ludicrous —" I began.

"You needn't persuade me," he cut in. "It is yourself you have to convince. Do you really mean to tell me you have never lain awake at night, worrying at what you have become? That a settled, domestic life has become your destiny? That we will trudge on from year to year with the only variation being whether Cook sends up treacle tart or Eton mess on a Sunday for pudding?"

"Only you would think to bring up the subject of food at a time like this," I chided. "I can hear your stomach growling from here."

"And I can see you, fleeing the scene of a conversation we ought to have had weeks ago," he said, refusing to rise to the bait.

I remained silent, stubbornly so. It was my only defense. I could not remove myself, but I could remove my response, I decided as he went on.

"Veronica, I know you said you would never marry, but —"

"Do not dare," I hissed, thrusting a pointed finger between his ribs. "Do not even *think* of proposing marriage to me under these circumstances."

"Then under which?" he asked, his voice lit with sudden hopefulness.

"None! I thought you understood me," I blazed back at him. "Did you think I spoke in jest when I said I would never marry you?"

"No, but I thought —"

"You thought I would change my mind," I jibed, thoroughly enraged. "You thought I was a woman, inconstant as the moon, and I would be persuaded by pretty speeches or spirited lovemaking or some other romantic nonsense. But I will not be swayed," I warned him, poking again hard. "I will not be swayed."

"Very well," he said. "But it does not always have to be settled domesticity or murderous pursuits. We might travel a little, you know. Find a meeting place in between dull routine and homicidal peril."

"I suppose," I said.

"Then when we emerge from this — if we do emerge — we might plan a voyage," he suggested.

The lid of the trunk was flung back at that moment. A lantern bobbed above us, the sudden gleam blinding us after the impenetrable blackness of the trunk. I moved to shield my eyes against it, but my wrists were grasped firmly and I was hauled to my feet, disentangled from my awkward embrace with Stoker, and set unceremoniously on the deck. Stoker followed, ungently handled by a few roughly clad sailors who grinned at his state of dishabille.

The baroness held the lantern aloft, bracing herself on the shifting deck. "So, you are awake. That complicates matters, but nothing we cannot manage."

She signaled to the sailor holding my arms, who shoved me towards the railing. Just beyond, the icy grey water rolled and heaved, peaking in foaming white ridges. It looked absolutely frigid, and I had little doubt Stoker and I would perish within a very few minutes of being flung overboard. The idea that he had been correct about our imminent demise would be of little consolation, I reflected. And I had spent our last conversation quarreling with him. It was not a memory to treasure. The least I could do was give us a chance at survival, and the first step towards that end was the purchase of time.

I dug in my heels and faced the baroness. "I want to know why," I said, counting on the imperiousness of my tone to bring her to heel. She might be an aristocrat, but she had lived her life at the beck and call of her royal mistress, and my resemblance to that august lady seemed to play in my favor as she responded automatically. A wiser woman would have simply hurled us overboard without delay, but few people can be quite so cold-blooded, I had observed. Most folk, even those experienced in murder, required a moment to steel themselves against taking a life.

"I had no choice," she said.

"Of course you did. One always has a choice." My words were chosen deliberately. It has been my experience that few people care to be directly contradicted and will almost always rise to the bait when it is dangled. Give them a chance to justify their actions and you might as well settle in for a nice long chat. No one ever likes to think of themselves as the villain, so any opportunity to cast themselves as hero will be seized like a greedy child after a chocolate.

"I had no choice," she repeated, coming closer, her breast rising and falling heavily. "The very future of my country was at stake."

"I hardly think so," I told her in a deliberately bored voice. "Surely you exaggerate."

"I do not!" She stepped nearer still. "You know nothing of my troubles."

"Because you do not really have troubles," I told her patiently. "You merely invented some in order to justify murdering your princess."

"How dare you! I would not harm a hair upon her head!"

"You *say* that, but here we are. The princess is missing, her maid has been strangled, and now you are attempting to murder two more people. How do we know you have not actually killed your princess? That is regicide, you know." I wrinkled my nose. "Or is there another term for it when you kill a princess and not a king?"

The sailors began to shift uneasily. "You killed a princess? That is not on. You said you had to toss these two overboard because he" — the sailor holding my arms jerked his head towards Stoker — "inflicted himself barbarously upon your daughter. But she don't seem too ill-used to me."

"I am not," I told him kindly. "Besides, if that story were true, why would she wish to kill me? Wouldn't I be her beloved and greatly wronged daughter?"

The sailor next to him gave him an ungentle shove. "I told you it was a Banbury tale!"

"Also, I should like to point out, I am not a rapist," Stoker said in tones of hectic outrage.

"That is true," I agreed. "I can vouch for his character."

The men looked doubtful, but one pointed to the elaborate dragon tattooed on Stoker's pectoral muscle. "A fellow navy man," he said, rubbing his bewhiskered chin. "Where did you get that, now?"

"After the Siege of Alexandria," Stoker told him.

"You were there! Bill, this lad were at Alexandria, same as us," the sailor crowed in delight. His companion gave a short nod of recognition. "What ship?"

"HMS *Luna*," Stoker said.

"A fine ship she is," the sailor told him proudly. "Thomas Corrigan, HMS *Orkney*. This is my mate, Billy Weaver, of the same. Munitions men, we were. And you?"

"Surgeon's mate," Stoker said.

Thomas Corrigan gave a soundless whistle. "Well, if that don't beat all. A surgeon's mate!" He narrowed his gaze at the baroness. "Ye've lied to us and tried to set us against this fellow and his lady. We'll not harm a hair on his head, no matter how much you pay. He is one of our own."

The baroness burst into a torrent of infuriated German, but the sailor merely held up his hand. "Screech like a parrot, but you'll not change our minds."

The baroness started forward, hands upraised, but Weaver leapt into the fray, seizing her firmly about the waist with one broadly muscled arm and pinning her arms tightly with the other.

"How dare you lay hands upon me! I will report you to the authorities," she shrieked.

Thomas Corrigan darted a look at Stoker. "What sort of trouble can she make for us?"

"The kind you do not want," Stoker told him. "But my associate and I will intercede for you if she tries."

"That's mighty decent of you considering," he replied. His expression was sheepish, and he ducked his head towards me. "Sorry about the trouble, miss. We meant no harm."

"Not at all," I assured him in my most gracious manner. "But we would very much like to return to the shore now."

"We will have you there in a trice," he

promised. He raised his voice to the wheel-house. "Ned, come about! Back to Green-wich," he instructed. He looked at the baroness. "What should we do with her?"

"For now, I would bind her hand and foot," Stoker told him. "We will think of a plan of action by the time we reach Green-wich. How far out to sea are we?"

Corrigan shrugged. "No more than an hour, but we were running against the tide. 'Twill be faster on the return." He signaled to his mate and the fellow began to tie the baroness with a bit of stout rope. The fight seemed to have gone out of her, and she submitted to the indignity without a protest. While he worked, Corrigan hunted down a coat for me and an extra pair of trousers and a fisherman's jersey for Stoker. The trousers came only halfway down Stoker's calves and the jersey looked as if it had been knitted for his younger brother. But we were somewhat warmer at least. He heated drinks for us, tea with hefty measures of rum added in, and thrust the steaming cups into our hands as we returned to the deck.

"Rather surprised at that," Corrigan said, jerking his chin to where the baroness sat, mute and miserable at the railing. Weaver stood next to her, keeping careful watch upon his prisoner.

"Thought she would have put up more of a fight."

"She knows she is done for," Stoker said. "There is no escaping the trouble she has crafted for herself."

The baroness set her face to the wind, not deigning to look at us. I left Stoker and the sailors exchanging navy stories and went to sit next to her. She did not look at me, but sat, face to the wind.

"I do not bear a grudge over these kinds of things," I told her. "I have nearly been murdered too many times to take it personally. But you might do me the courtesy of answering a question or two."

"What do you want to know?" she asked in a dull voice. She stared ahead into the darkness. Somewhere in the night lay the wide green expanse of the Thames. Her shoulders were erect. Even in defeat, she would not relax her posture.

"I presume you were the one who cut Alice's climbing ropes," I began.

She nodded but said nothing.

"It would take a cool nerve to do that," I observed. "I did not realize you were a climber."

She curled a lip. "I was the most accomplished lady climber in the Alpenwald in my youth — the first woman to summit the Teufelstreppe. There is a paragraph about my accomplishment in that little guide you were reading," she said with a sly smile.

"The Baedeker? Is that why you snatched it out of my hands? I thought you were irritated about Yelena and simply wanted to tidy up." I was a little put out with myself for never suspecting her real intention had been to keep me from reading the Baedeker. Now that I knew the baroness had been an alpinist, it all seemed perfectly clear. "I imagine you waited until Alice was at the most treacherous part of the climb."

She did not respond for a long moment, then sighed. "Climbing skills, once learnt, are forever. It was many years since I was on the mountain, so I knew no one would suspect that I had made my way up to find Alice, but it was simple enough. I had only to set out earlier than she did. I hid around the side of a boulder, and when she reached the first step of the middle of the Teufelstreppe, I emerged and sliced cleanly through the rope. Only I left it almost too late. It took longer to make the cut, even with a sharp blade, and she almost got a foothold on the step before she fell. She stretched out her hand to me as she went."

The baroness turned to me, and I saw

there were tears in her eyes, whether from the brisk wind whipping off the river or any excess of emotion, I could not say.

"She grasped my coat as she fell. I did not realize at the time that she had taken hold of my summit badge. Only later did I notice it was missing, and there was no way to know where it had fallen. I thought someone might eventually find it and I would simply say I had lost it on a previous climb."

"But no one did find it," I said, working it out as we spoke. "Because it was still clutched in Alice Baker-Greene's hand when she died. And because it was found in her hand, it was mistaken for her own badge and buried with her. She took the proof of your guilt with her to the grave."

She shook her head. "You cannot imagine my horror when I realized what must have happened."

"And no one was the wiser until the princess arrived at the club and noticed the photograph of Alice in her coffin — wearing a badge for her burial. But the badge at the exhibition was Alice's, marked with a nick that the princess knew about and recognized immediately. And this immediately raised the question, 'Whose badge had Alice been buried with?' Coming hard upon Stoker finding the cut rope, Gisela must have realized instantly that if Alice had not worn her own badge that day, she could only have been buried with her murderer's badge."

She clutched her hands together, the knuckles whitening.

"Is that why you harmed your princess?" I asked.

She rounded on me, her expression fierce. "How many times do I have to say it? I would never harm my princess!"

"Then where is she, Baroness?"

"I do not know," she told me, her voice small and defeated. "She has run away before, but never for so long."

"When she left before, it was to be with Alice, wasn't it?" I ventured. She did not respond, but the stubborn set of her chin told me I was right. "We compared the dates of her absences from the Alpenwald with the times Alice was climbing in remote areas with a companion she referred to in her journal by the letter 'D.' Dolcezza."

"The sweet one," the baroness said, the words bursting forth in a torrent of rage. "It was wrong, her association with that woman. It brought out all of her worst instincts, her inclination to liberality, to modernization. It taught her to neglect her duties and to scorn our traditions."

"Alice Baker-Greene was a suffragist," I recalled. "She demonstrated for all sorts of causes, education for all, Irish Home Rule, the rights of workers, and open immigration. All the things in which Princess Gisela was interested. I have seen her books, remember?"

"Books given her by that woman," she spat. "They sat up for hours, far into the night, talking of such things, making plans to change our country, to strip away all that we hold dear. And Gisela neglected her duties to be with this foreigner who had befriended her. It was a kind of madness. I tried to speak with her so many times about her responsibilities, about her duty to marry and secure the succession, but she would argue with me, trying to explain about education and votes for women and the rights of animals," she said, her mouth twisting bitterly. "Animals! She was no longer the Gisela I knew, but I believed she would return to us. She was too proud, too much of an Alpenwalder, to neglect her people."

"Then why eliminate Alice?" I asked. "If you were so certain that Gisela would overcome her feelings and do her duty, why act at all?"

"Because she was blinded by her idealism

— idealism instilled in her by that creature! Every day our Gisela became more radical in her opinions, wanting to change things, to make it all different and modern," she said, her mouth twisting bitterly. "Every day she moved further away from us."

"And you realized Gisela was thinking of renouncing her throne," I said suddenly. "I saw the passages she had highlighted in the biography of Queen Christina about abdication. Your princess was considering the unimaginable — giving up her royal destiny. You could not have that, could you? You could not take the risk that Alice would take her away from the Alpenwald forever."

"Gisela belongs to her people," she said. "The crown is her right but also her responsibility. She has a duty to perform."

"And you were going to see that she did it, no matter what. So Alice had to die, to remove the distraction she had become, the dangerous ideas she had instilled in your princess. Her influence over Gisela threatened your own."

Something flickered in her expression and I seized upon the hunch. "Because that was the real problem, wasn't it? You couch your confession in terms of destiny and service to the people of the Alpenwald, but it is much simpler and dirtier than that, is it not?

If Gisela abdicated, your post as lady-in-waiting would be at an end. All the opportunities to profit from your court appointment, the lavish lifestyle you enjoyed in the castle, the influence — all of it would vanish in the snap of the fingers."

"I will not dignify such an accusation," she said loftily.

"You do not have to," I said. "I am convinced of it. You murdered Yelena as well. As close as she was to the princess, she must have guessed something of her feelings for Alice and your resentment as well. Or did she find the mask and put the pieces together herself? I imagine she was blackmailing you. Poor stupid Yelena! All she wanted was a little money so she and her captain could marry. And she was mercenary enough to think she could risk making an enemy of you, not realizing that you are every bit as calculating. It was not sentiment or loyalty to your country that drove you to murder Alice Baker-Greene. You meant to keep Gisela under your guidance. With Alice gone, she would have turned back to you, leant upon you for support — and of course she would have rewarded that support, would she not? You intended that your princess should never leave the Alpenwald so that you could continue to feather your nest as you have for all these years. So simple a motive and so venal."

She turned her shoulder towards me and faced into the wind once more. "You understand nothing," she told me.

"On the contrary," I said. "I understand everything."

CHAPTER 28

At last, just as dawn was breaking over the horizon, we reached the docks at Greenwich. Stoker and I had, after a spirited exchange of views, decided to hand the baroness over to the authorities.

"You've no call to summon the police, do you?" Corrigan asked nervously.

"It would be no more than you deserve," Stoker replied with a narrow look.

Corrigan ducked his head. "C'mon, guv. You know what it's like for a sailor, trying to make an honest shilling. Sometimes the work just isn't there, and I've seven mouths to feed at home, I do. And Weaver there has nine."

"Remind me to have an instructive discussion with your wives on the precautionary arts," I told them.

"Come again?"

"Family planning," Stoker explained dryly. "It would keep your wives from being subjected to more expectations and you lot from having more children than you can reasonably support."

"That's not natural, that isn't," Corrigan protested.

"And starvation is?" I put in tartly. "I shall send along pamphlets. Promise to read them and we will not refer this matter to the police."

Corrigan relaxed visibly. "That's mighty kind of you, miss."

He gave me an address to direct the pamphlets to as Weaver took up the bound form of the baroness and set her onto the dock. Her hair had been whipped free of its plaits, and it hung in great silvering hanks about her face. She looked older, but there was still a trace of defiance in her eye.

"You cannot possibly think that you will get away with handling the lady-in-waiting to the Hereditary Princess of the Alpenwald in such a fashion," she said, lifting her chin to an imperious angle. "I demand that you release me."

"Oh, we will," Stoker assured her. He pointed behind her. "Into their care."

Coming down the dock were a number of figures, cloaked and hooded against the chill, but each wearing the distinctive dark blue of the Alpenwalder wool — Captain

Durand, his head wrapped in a considerable bandage, flanked by the chancellor and the duke, their expressions grim with purpose. And leading them all, Her Serene Highness, Princess Gisela.

The princess spoke in a low voice that commanded attention. "Baroness von Wallenberg, according to the authority of the laws of the Alpenwald, you are to be taken into custody by the chancellor's men and transported back to our country, where you will stand trial for the murder of Alice Baker-Greene."

The baroness gambled all in one last throw of the dice. "You will never find me guilty! You cannot. You have no proof."

"No, they do not," said a new voice. From behind the chancellor came a creaking noise, and he stepped aside to permit an elderly woman in a Bath chair to propel herself forward. "But I do," she said.

"Pompeia Baker-Greene!" I exclaimed softly to Stoker.

She held up a small, familiar medal. " 'Alpenwalder Kletterverein Gipfelabzeichen,' " she read in halting German. "Your summit badge, Baroness. Buried with my granddaughter. And the climbing rope cut by your hand."

The baroness looked around wildly, but

485

there was no mercy to be found.

"There is also the body of Yelena and a mask that matches the description of the figure seen on the Teufelstreppe the day Alice died," the chancellor said. "You cannot escape this," he added sternly. "You will answer for what you have done."

At this, the baroness gave a deep groan and seemed to fold in on herself. The chancellor signaled and Captain Durand came forward slowly to take her in hand. As he led her away, the figure in the Bath chair pushed herself towards us.

"Mrs. Baker-Greene," Stoker said, inclining his head.

"One and the same. Mr. Templeton-Vane, I presume? Miss Speedwell, it is good to see you again," she said, giving me her hand. It was cold and rough, the flesh tempered by decades of pitting herself against the unforgiving granite of the world's most demanding mountains.

"It is an honor," I told her.

Princess Gisela came to stand behind her. She glanced at Stoker's unorthodox garments and the coat flapping about my calves.

"Come. The pair of you must be half-perished from the cold. Let us return to the Sudbury. There are many things to say."

As we walked away, Stoker put his arm through mine as Tommy and Billy waved an obviously relieved farewell. "It would serve them right if we handed them over to Mornaday," he mused. "After all, they did conspire to abduct us."

"An abduction they ultimately abandoned," I reminded him. "Besides, we now know two men in possession of a boat and flexible morals who feel they owe us a favor. That, I have no doubt, will someday come in handy."

Stoker groaned by way of reply, but I stoppered his protest with a kiss, short and hard.

"You owe me a pound."

"Why in the name of seven hells do I owe you a pound?"

"Because an Alpenwalder has indeed proven our villain," I said with deep satisfaction.

He reached into his borrowed pocket, but I stilled his hand with my own, clasping it warmly.

"Keep your money this time. Come along, Stoker. The sun is rising, and we have lived to see another day!"

A few hours later, we were bathed and dressed and comfortably ensconced in the drawing room of the princess's suite, devouring plate after plate of Julien d'Orlande's best efforts.

"Try the miniature pork pasty," I urged Stoker as I passed him a tiny pie capped with a caramelized shallot. "He has done something quite wonderful with apple and sage."

He took one, passing me the tray of petite éclairs stuffed with violet crème. The princess watched us in bemusement.

"Do you always take your own attempted murder in your stride?"

I considered this. "The first time is unnerving," I admitted.

"But when it gets to be habit," Stoker added, "one must adapt a rational attitude and make certain to eat to keep up one's strength."

I resisted the urge to pull a face. For a person who had spent the greater part of our confinement complaining bitterly about the predicament, he was quite sanguine now that he was warm and fed.

"You must forgive me," Gisela said quietly. "I had no idea anyone would be in any danger at all."

"There would not have been if they hadn't meddled," Maximilian put in — reasonably, I decided.

"The duke is correct," I said, reaching for

an adorable cherry tartlet glazed with amaretto syrup. "We exposed ourselves to danger with our investigation."

"An investigation about which you neglected to inform us," the chancellor said in a tone of lofty reproach.

"As you neglected to inform us of the potential dangers to the princess," Stoker reminded him, smiling coolly over a *tarte au citron.* The chancellor had the grace to look embarrassed.

"I remain abashed at my failures," the chancellor said.

"Hardly yours," Gisela put in. She stared hard at Maximilian, and to my astonishment, he flushed deeply.

"Duke Maximilian?" I prodded.

He shifted in his seat, then burst out in a torrent of speech. "The princess and I have had a lengthy and comprehensive discussion and she has impressed upon me the fact that I have, in every possible way, let down my country, my name, and my royal blood. I extend my deepest apologies to you, Miss Speedwell, and to you, Mr. Templeton-Vane." He turned to the princess. "I apologize to you as well, Your Serene Highness. I know, too, that you cannot forgive me. I will not ask because I do not deserve it. I will resign my commissions formally and withdraw from public life in the Alpenwald. I await your further instructions."

He rose to his feet and bowed sharply from the neck. "I am, contrary to the cowardice and weakness of character I have demonstrated here, your servant, Your Serene Highness." He drew his sword from his scabbard and laid it gently at her feet. "I offer you the resignation of my commission in the Alpenwalder Guard, and I will accept whatever punishment you see fit to mete."

He bowed once more and left us, shutting the door softly behind. "Princess," the chancellor began, "do you not think you should speak with him?"

The princess shook her head. "No. I think a little time to meditate on his sins will do Maximilian a world of good. Besides, we have other matters to discuss." She turned her attention to Stoker and to me.

"I really am very sorry that you were brought into this farrago," she began. "I never meant for any of it to happen."

"I think I can piece together some of it," I told her. "It began that day in the Curiosity Club when Stoker realized that Alice's rope had been cut."

"Did it?" She sighed and gave Pompeia Baker-Greene a sad smile. "I think we both wondered. Alice was such a careful climber, so mindful of risk. It seemed impossible to us that she would have made any such elementary mistakes, especially on a climb she had done so many times before."

"I made my peace with it," Mrs. Baker-Greene said slowly. "One learns to when there have been enough of these kinds of losses. I wrote to the princess and told her that one must befriend grief. It is a companion that never leaves."

I thought of the losses I had known, my aunts, my friend the baron. And others. For some, grief was a devil, to be shut out upon the doorstep and ignored. But the notion of accepting that it would be a constant visitor in one guise or another seemed to me the beginning of wisdom.

"I tried," the princess said, a plaintive note creeping into her narrative. "But I could not dismiss the idea that something was wrong. Then when Mr. Templeton-Vane found the rope, I had the first real proof that I was not simply rejecting the banality of an accident befalling Alice. And at that moment, another proof fell into my hands."

"The summit badge," I said.

The princess nodded. "Alice was buried with a badge and I assumed it was hers. They said she had been found with a badge clutched in her hand and they pinned this to her clothing before she was laid to rest. But no one realized at the time that she had not worn her badge that day. The badge in her hand was the baroness's."

"The baroness told me that Alice tore it from her during the final struggle," I put in gently.

"I suspected something like that as soon as I saw a badge amongst her things. It was Alice's, I recognized it at once. There was a little nick on one edge, you see. She used to joke that she would make me replace it for her," she added with a smile. "And the back of each is engraved with a tiny number unique to the recipient. This is so the badge may be returned to its owner if it is mislaid. When I saw Alice's own badge with her things at the exhibition, I wondered immediately — *whose badge had Alice been clutching when she died?* Alice was climbing alone that day. It was a dangerous practice and one I discouraged, but she knew that mountain. It would have been a simple exercise for her. But if someone else was with her, why had no one come forward?"

"Unless they had something to hide," Stoker put in.

"Exactly. I could not take the risk that the rope — thus far the only piece of evidence linking her murderer to the crime — would go missing. I had to take it into my own possession for safekeeping, but without alerting the murderer, whoever that might be. And I needed Pompeia's help to secure the second and most damning piece of evidence — the murderer's badge that had been buried with Alice. But most importantly, I could not permit Pompeia to learn of Alice's murder from anyone but myself. I owed her that."

"So she borrowed a maid's cloak and put herself on a train," the elderly mountaineer said, smiling fondly at the princess.

The princess returned the smile. "It was a stroke of grave misfortune that the storm happened to blow in that night. You see, I had it all worked out on the timetable. I would go to the Midlands, speak with Pompeia, and return by the milk train and be back in my suite before anyone missed me. She would authorize an exhumation to retrieve the murderer's climbing badge from Alice's body, and by examining the badge, we would have the piece of evidence we needed to find her murderer. Once that had been arranged, Pompeia would follow a day or so later, after she had arranged to retrieve the badge whilst I followed my official program and signed the treaty."

She gave me a searching look. "You *did* sign the treaty, did you not?"

I nodded. "I have my doubts about its legality, but I signed it."

Her smile was one of satisfaction. "I will make it right. I will tell them our copy was destroyed in a clerical accident and we will execute fresh papers. The important thing was to secure the meeting with the French in person and play out the little drama of diplomacy. The rest is simply paperwork."

It was a cynical view, but perhaps that ought not to have surprised me. Rupert had said much the same.

Stoker retrieved the conversation, steering us back to the princess's narrative. "But when the storm blew in, you were stranded in the Midlands."

She nodded. "It was the worst snowstorm in a decade, so they said. We were snowbound in Pompeia's house. The good news is that it meant no one was abroad to see me away from London. But it meant Miss Speedwell was forced to take my place." She smiled. "I hear you were more than adequate. I am grateful."

"I did my best," I told her.

"But you did not undertake the masquerade to help the Alpenwald," the chancellor said, clearly sulking.

"No," I admitted. "I did it because I wanted to solve the mystery of what happened to Alice Baker-Greene."

"And in doing so, Miss Speedwell has done us a very great service," the princess insisted.

"Has she?" the chancellor queried. "You were already on the trail of the murderer."

"And everything else I was in London to accomplish would have been destroyed without her taking on my role of princess," she told him. "We will be grateful to Miss Speedwell and her companion."

This was clearly to be the official position of the Alpenwalder government, and the chancellor bowed his neck to his princess, his moustaches gleaming in the morning light.

"What will happen to the baroness?" Stoker asked.

The princess's mouth thinned. "She has been given into the custody of Captain Durand for extradition to the Alpenwald. She has decided to waive her right to a trial and acknowledged her guilt."

"So she will be sent to prison," I ventured.

She said nothing for a long moment, and when she finally did speak, it was with a chilly finality. "She murdered not only Alice Baker-Greene but Yelena Borisovna. As the

495

intended husband of the victim, Captain Durand has certain rights."

"Rights?" Stoker inquired.

The chancellor cleared his throat. "The captain has elected to sail from England to Germany and make his way down the Rhine. A sea voyage this time of year is a perilous undertaking," he said blandly.

Which meant that anything the captain cared to do to see justice served upon the baroness would be accepted with a blind eye by the princess and her chancellor. I shivered as I realized how rough that justice might be. Was she to be bundled into a sack and tossed overboard to drown as she had intended for us? Given the quick mercy of a bullet before being disposed of in the river? Or would Durand choose for her to be locked in a dark fortress for the rest of her life? The possibilities were grim.

The princess turned back to us, brisk and businesslike. "I mean to open Alice's exhibition on schedule tomorrow evening. Will you be there?"

We exchanged glances and nodded. "Of course, Your Serene Highness. It would be an honor."

CHAPTER 29

The next evening, we arrived at the Curiosity Club an hour before the exhibition opening in order to attend to the last details. Lady C. was a whirlwind of activity, supervising the polishing of the display cases and the dusting of the various displays.

"That goat is most unsettling," she remarked to me, pulling a face. "Ought we to leave it?"

"Oh yes," I told her, not relishing the battle that would ensue should we remove Stoker's pride and joy.

At last the preparations were finished. A wide velvet ribbon had been stretched across the doorway, to be cut by the princess to officially open the exhibition, and tables had been laid with vast silver coolers of iced champagne and enormous wheels of Alpenwalder cheese adorned with bunches of hothouse grapes. Trays of lobster patties and hot roast lamb pies were passed, and Julien's enormous sugar homage to the castle took pride of place. The guests circulated, taking in the maps and photographs and pausing to admire Stoker's goat as well as a rather bedraggled stuffed otter that had been sent at the last moment by a prominent Londoner of Alpenwalder descent.

I was most interested in the reaction of the princess and Pompeia Baker-Greene. They remained together, lost in contemplation whilst the other guests mingled, drinking champagne and chattering loudly about their own travels and travails. The princess was claimed by Lady C. to make the rounds of dignitaries while Stoker and I went to stand next to Pompeia. Her Bath chair had been moved in front of Alice's portrait, the photograph of her standing atop a mountain peak, a suffragist banner in hand. Pompeia Baker-Greene sat regarding it thoughtfully as she took immoderate bites of Alpenwalder cheese and sipped at her champagne.

"She was a remarkable woman," I told her. "I wish I had known her better."

"She would not have liked you much in the end," Pompeia said firmly. The corner of her mouth quirked up in a grin. "But only because she was sometimes wary of kindred spirits. And you, Miss Speedwell, are like my granddaughter — an uncommon woman."

I grinned. "I am glad you were able to come, although I wish the circumstances had been more pleasant."

Her steely brows rose. "Why? Death is part of life, child. It is not the end. It is not even the middle. It is merely a doorway. Alice is no further away from me than if she had stepped into the next room."

"You are a philosopher," Stoker told her.

"I am an old woman," she corrected. "And I have neither the time nor the patience for pretense." She looked up at him with an assessing eye. "I am also a connoisseur of good-looking men, and you, my dear boy, are an extraordinarily attractive one. Now, wheel me over to where they are pouring more of this champagne and I will teach you a thing or two about women."

He did as she told him, putting his head close to hers as he refreshed her glass. I was still watching them when the princess moved to my elbow.

"Should you stand so near me?" I asked softly. "Someone else might notice the resemblance and surmise what we have been up to this week."

She looked down the length of her regal nose. "I am taller and my jewels are much better," she said, not unkindly. "I do not think we will be found out. Tell me, did you enjoy playing at being a princess?"

I considered for a moment. "Not really. It is a great deal of work and very little freedom."

"Ah," she said, smiling gravely. "You understand me. Few people do. Alice saw the cage for what it is. Gilded and studded with diamonds, but it is still a cage. That is what made her such a good friend," she added, her gaze drifting to Alice's portrait.

"Friend?" I asked gently.

She caught her breath but did not look at me.

"I understand," I told her.

She canted her head, giving me a thoughtful smile. "I think that you do. Our relationship was not one I could ever acknowledge openly, you understand. Such a thing is not possible here in England. In the Alpenwald, it would be utterly unthinkable. But she was the love of my life."

"That is why you could not bring yourself to agree to marry Maximilian," I murmured. "Because your heart lay elsewhere."

"How did you know?"

"I found the sketch — tucked under the endpaper of Alice's ledger. The sketch was illuminating and clearly drawn by someone who loved you intimately."

She closed her eyes, briefly, and an expression of pain flickered across her face. When she opened her eyes again, she had recovered herself.

"Well, I will not be the first monarch to put aside my youthful love and marry for reasons of state," she said, turning a heavily jeweled betrothal ring around on her finger.

"Maximilian?" I was aghast, but Gisela was matter-of-fact.

"The wedding is to be in the spring. I will advance him the money he requires to pay his gambling debts and he will spend the next few months proving himself to me. Given how grateful he is for my forgiveness and his own embarrassment at his actions, he will be entirely biddable as a consort."

"But after all he has done —"

She turned to me, and there was a worldliness in her gaze that spoke to long experience of the failures and foibles of men. "Miss Speedwell, you have known Maximilian a few short days. I have known him all of his life. He is a good man. He just does not know it yet. Responsibility will be the making of him, I will see to it."

"He put a threat into a box of chocolates for a fright," I argued. "And he arranged for a bomb to be thrown at you."

"A silly note and a firecracker," she replied

with a curl of her lip. "He has told me all about his debts, and I can assure you his travels will never again take him to Deauville. I will pay what is owed, and that will be an end to the matter."

"I can only say that you are the best judge of the duke's character," I said, my voice unenthusiastic to my own ears. She smiled.

"Do not forget, Miss Speedwell, he kept my secret when I asked him to. When I had need of him, real need, he was as stalwart a champion as anyone could wish. He pretended to have a tendresse for Alice so that she could stay in the Alpenwald without anyone growing suspicious. And I turned to him again when I decided to steal the badge and the rope from here," she said softly, her eyes lighting with amusement. "He proved a rather better housebreaker than I might have expected. And then when I went to Pompeia, he told no one where I had gone."

I blinked at her. "He swore he did not know," I began.

"Oh, he knew. And he told no one, just as I asked of him. For a long while he even pretended to be courting Alice in order to throw off any possible suspicion that she came to the Alpenwald to see me. He has been a good friend, and he will make me a good husband," she said firmly.

"Will you be happy with such a choice?"

She regarded me in obvious surprise. "Happy? I am a princess. It is not my place to be happy. It is my place to govern. And I will do so as Alice and I discussed. I will bring my country into the new century with new ideas. There will be resistance to our progress, and I am prepared for that," she added, her gaze steely. "My own personal happiness matters nothing when weighed against the well-being of my people."

"Then I wish you every success, Your Serene Highness," I told her.

I moved to curtsy, but she put out her hand to shake mine instead. "Thank you, Veronica Speedwell."

CHAPTER 30

At the princess's invitation, Stoker and I traveled to the Alpenwald as guests of the royal family and were accorded far more prominence than we might have expected. I amused myself en route by reading the *Daily Harbinger,* which devoted several issues to the upcoming nuptials complete with sketches of the princess's trousseau. There were no articles written by J. J. Butterworth, a notable omission, and one that told me she had not yet succeeded in breaking the story she had followed into Windsor Castle. Whatever game was afoot, I had no doubt she would, in the end, prove an able hunter. I was pleased to find a small article near the back of the newspaper that made mention of an expedition embarking upon the Canadian Rockies — an expedition that included Douglas Norton. He had, it was noted, left London in some haste in January and had decided to set out at once for the wilds of

Alberta.

Stoker was occupied with his book — a saucy French novel that had been banned in seventeen countries — and with a hamper packed to the brim with various delights from the kitchen of Julien d'Orlande, the journey passed pleasurably for both. The night before the wedding, we were summoned to the princess's audience chamber. We had been lodged in Hochstadt's best hostelry, a timber-framed inn that looked like something conjured by the Brothers Grimm. Every part of the small city had been bedecked with flower garlands in honor of the nuptials, and the air was heavy with the scent of the blossoms of St. Otthild's wort. We arrived promptly, just as the clock tower in the town hall chimed the hour, sending forth an enormous mountain goat to bleat the time.

The princess received us in her throne room, sitting upon a carved and gilded chair hung with azure blue silk. She rose as we approached, smiling broadly. She beckoned to the chancellor, who came forward carrying a small cushion. Atop it rested two medals, each struck with an otter blazoned in tiny sapphires.

"The Order of St. Otthild, First Class," she told us as she gestured to the floor. Two blue velvet cushions had been laid for us, and we knelt as she presented us with our honors. It was the first of such dignities that either of us had been accorded, and I was conscious of a rush of pride that we had been of use in the princess's time of need. And as I noted the emerald-eyed stare of the lofty Guimauve, tucked behind his mistress's skirts, I was grateful that this time at least, we had neither of us acquired a new pet as a souvenir of our investigations. A flurry of journalists attempted to question us as we left the palace, for we were a story in our own right, and I laughed much later to find our photograph, blurry and indistinct, featured in a column in the *Daily Harbinger* with J. J. Butterworth's byline, explaining that we had received our honors for "undisclosed services to the Alpenwalder Crown."

True to his word, the chancellor presented us with a clock, enormous and brightly painted and featuring a sinister-looking goat which bleated the hour and which I insisted Stoker keep to adorn his folly.

The next day we stood proudly in the cathedral as the princess walked down the aisle to take Duke Maximilian as her husband. We watched them exchange solemn vows, pledging themselves to one another for eternity, and I fancied I detected a new seriousness about the duke. I could only hope that purpose and responsibility would settle him. For her part, the princess seemed happy enough, satisfied that she had done her duty by her country. And as she passed us, I saw a glint from within her bouquet of flowers, roses and St. Otthild's wort and cascades of ivy. It was only a moment, but I recognized the glimmer of an Alpenwalder summit medal, and I guessed whose badge the princess had chosen to carry with her on her wedding day. Alice Baker-Greene would never be far from her thoughts, I knew.

When they had signed the register and the procession had made its way out of the cathedral, we emerged into the sunlight to find the square thronged with Alpenwalders, flinging petals of St. Otthild's wort into the air in celebration. The bells rang out and trumpets sounded and beer ran from the fountains. Stoker turned to me, the sunshine brilliant as it gleamed upon his hair. In spite of the crowds, he wrapped one strong arm about my waist and kissed me, a thorough and expert effort that left me breathless.

"You are grown sentimental," I said lightly. "It must be the romantic in you. Next minute you will be quoting Keats at me."

His mouth, warm and supple and infinitely skilled, curved into a smile. " 'You are always new; The last of your kisses was ever the sweetest.' "

The prick of sudden tears stung my eyes and I brushed aside a petal of St. Otthild's wort. I put out my hands, taking his lapels in my grip. "I am sorry, Stoker."

"For what?" His gaze searched my face.

"That I cannot give you this — what Gisela and Maximilian have done today. If you need this, this proper and legal thing in the eyes of the world, I understand. I will release you," I told him even as I clutched him fiercely.

He covered my hands with his own. "Will you change your mind about marriage?"

"Never," I told him. I paused, wondering if I would have to give voice to my feelings, if I *could* give voice to them. But it seemed he understood much of what was in my heart.

"Neither will I," he replied. "And even if I did, I would not do that to you. Veronica, I have no need to pin those wings of yours to a card and put a label to you — *Mrs. Revelstoke Templeton-Vane.* You are, and always will be, Veronica Speedwell. And I could never wish you different than you are. Now, let us go back to London where we belong."

I thought of the letter nestling in my pocket which beckoned us on to a new adventure. "With perhaps just a little detour on our journey," I said, linking my arm with his.

"What detour?" he asked, narrowing his eyes.

"That," I told him, "is for me to know and you to discover."

His eyes lit with amusement. "Very well. But I may also know a thing or two that you do not."

"Oh, really? Tell me," I urged.

"Better yet. I will show you." He leant near to my ear, his lips brushing my lobe. " 'I will imagine you Venus tonight and pray, pray, pray to your star like a heathen,' " he murmured.

"God bless John Keats," I replied fervently.

He escorted me back to our lodgings and proceeded to demonstrate for me the wisdom that Pompeia Baker-Greene had imparted during their private conversation. The next morning, utterly sated and rather tired after a vigorously sleepless night, I rose early and dressed, careful to ease out of the room quietly so as not to waken Stoker, who was, poor fellow, utterly demolished with fatigue.

Making my way to the cheesemonger, I selected the largest, most delectably fragrant cheese I could find and ordered it sent to England to Pompeia Baker-Greene.

"Would you care to include a message, *Fraulein?*" the cheese maker inquired.

"Not at all," I told him with a smile. "She will know what it is for."

I stepped out of the shop and into the cobbled street just as the sun topped the flank of the devil's staircase, warming the side of the mountain with its golden light. The sky was a brilliant blue, and the hillsides of the lower slopes, bright green with spring grass, were dotted lushly with the first buds of St. Otthild's wort. A passing breeze caught the top of the Teufelstreppe, blowing snow off the peak in a long, lazy trail of powdery white, like the last feather from an angel's wing as it ascended to the heavens.

I drew in a deep breath of cool mountain air and turned my face to the rising sun for just a moment. I thought of the discoveries we had made in the course of this adventure, the secrets left unspoken. And a whisper of a chill breeze brushed across my face, like the passing of a shadow over the moon.

Just then, a familiar voice called my name from above, and I looked up to see Stoker, sleep tousled and smiling down at me from the open casement.

I pushed aside all thoughts of peril and secrets and raised my face once more to the sun. Whatever lay in our future, whatever our destiny, we would face it together, stalwart and devoted, I vowed. Excelsior!

AUTHOR'S NOTE

The Alpenwald, with its customs, language, folklore, inhabitants, flora, fauna, and history, is entirely fictitious, as is its capital of Hochstadt and the Teufelstreppe. While many British princesses married into German principalities and duchies, George III's only sister to do so was Princess Augusta, the Hereditary Princess of Brunswick-Wolfenbuttel. Although Empress Frederick (Queen Victoria's eldest daughter, the Princess Royal) was in England during January 1889, she did not broker a secret peace treaty in opposition to her son the kaiser.

Alice Baker-Greene and her family are also fictitious, although many female mountaineers were making audacious climbs during the nineteenth century, and two in particular — Annie Smith Peck and Fanny Bullock Workman — did indeed hold up suffragist banners in their photographs. The climbing rivalry between these two mountaineers was legendary and both have provided inspiration for the character of Alice Baker-Greene.

Many operas have been written with Atalanta as their subject, most notably by Handel, but the particular work referenced in this book does not exist.

St. Otthild is also a figment of the author's imagination, as are her otters rampant.

ACKNOWLEDGMENTS

As ever, tremendous gratitude to the team at Berkley/Penguin, Veronica's champions and my collaborators. Particular thanks to Craig Burke, Loren Jaggers, Claire Zion, Jeanne-Marie Hudson, Jin Yu, Jessica Mangicaro, Jenn Snyder, Ivan Held, and Tara O'Connor. The marketing, sales, publicity, and editorial departments are full of dedicated and talented people who give their all to Veronica and I am hugely grateful for their generosity. The art department has created exquisite covers for every novel, but this one goes above and beyond.

For more than twenty years I've had the privilege and joy of working with my agent, Pam Hopkins, and this is my sixth adventure with my editor, Danielle Perez. They are gifted, kind, and insightful women who have given me advice as well as friendship, and I am a better writer for knowing them.

Many thanks to Ellen Edwards, the acquiring editor who gave Veronica a home, and Eileen Chetti, my copyeditor who keeps Veronica tidy with eagle-eyed precision.

Much love to those who offer practical support, sympathetic ears, kindly advice, and safe spaces: Jomie Wilding, the Writerspace team, Blake Leyers, Ali Trotta, Delilah Dawson, Ariel Lawhon, Joshilyn Jackson, Lauren Willig, Susan Elia MacNeal, Robin Carr, Alan Bradley, David Bell, Rhys Bowen, and the Blanket Fort.

For Mom, Dad, and Caitlin — you are my everything.

For Phil. Forever. For always.

ABOUT THE AUTHOR

Deanna Raybourn is the author of the award-winning, *New York Times* bestselling Lady Julia Grey series as well as the *USA Today* bestselling and Edgar Award nominated Veronica Speedwell Mysteries and several stand-alone works.